MT. PLEASA[illegible]
PLEASANTV[illegible]
W9-AQD-950

BEWARE THE MERMAIDS

BEWARE THE MERMAIDS

A Novel

CARRIE TALICK

alcove press

This is a work of fiction. All of the names, characters, organizations, places and events portrayed in this novel are either products of the author's imagination or are used fictitiously. Any resemblance to real or actual events, locales, or persons, living or dead, is entirely coincidental.

Copyright © 2021 by Carrie Talick

All rights reserved.

Published in the United States by Alcove Press, an imprint of The Quick Brown Fox & Company LLC.

Alcove Press and its logo are trademarks of The Quick Brown Fox & Company LLC.

Library of Congress Catalog-in-Publication data available upon request.

ISBN (hardcover): 978-1-64385-824-1
ISBN (ebook): 978-1-64385-825-8

Cover design by Lynn Andreozzi

Printed in the United States.

www.alcovepress.com

Alcove Press
34 West 27th St., 10th Floor
New York, NY 10001

First Edition: August 2021

10 9 8 7 6 5 4 3 2 1

For my mom, Nancy, who deserved a better ending.

Live now, baby, don't wait. Waiting only makes you want more and experience less.

—Nancy Niemi

PROLOGUE

For the first time in twenty-seven years, a warm and ancient Mayan wind blew up from the Southern Hemisphere in the wee morning hours. It whipped itself across the plains of Central America, kissed the beaches of western Mexico, until it finally whooshed into the quiet little town of Hermosa Beach in Southern California. Almost no one noticed except a couple who were skinny-dipping in the ocean—and every single dog in the neighborhood. The uneven chorus of barking came from the designer French bulldogs and Labradoodles who populated the upscale beach town and collectively succeeded in waking up most of the local citizenry. Shoes were hurled, curse words were hissed, and Ambien was taken, as the dogs, who were just doing their jobs, quieted down and whimpered their warnings instead.

One Hermosa Beach resident woke when she heard the breeze rattle her bamboo wind chimes. She sat up, and although it was barely three AM, she felt more awake than she had in years. Awash in a calm energy, she wrapped herself in a light-gray sweater and stepped out onto the balcony, careful not to disturb her snoring husband. Under a full moon, the soothing chimes gently clunked together in the wind, which to her surprise was warm, almost balmy, with a hint of salt and spice in it, unlike any other wind she had felt off the coast—even those wildly fun and unpredictable breezes she enjoyed while sailing around the cliffs of Palos Verdes, her favorite pastime.

She let this strange wind embrace her. But the wind did much more than that. It was a spirit wind with a mystical power that carried a trace of defiance, a rebellious insistency, a discordant stream that sought out certain unsuspecting souls whose lives perhaps needed a little stirring. That one such soul belonged to Nancy Hadley.

CHAPTER ONE
TROUBLE BREWING

Nestled between the enormous San Pedro shipping harbor to the south and the upscale nouveau riche, yacht-infested Marina del Rey harbor to the north, tiny King Harbor Marina in Redondo Beach was awash in golden California sunshine as Nancy Hadley approached the yacht club from the long stretch of Ocean Drive.

Only twenty fast-ticking minutes ago, Nancy had sat up in a panic, coffee in hand, when she realized she was supposed to meet the King Harbor Yacht Club Charitable Committee at the marina. She had been staring at her cat, Suzanne, who was curled up on an empty dry-cleaner bag on the floor, as she recalled that her husband, Roger, was golfing this morning with Cliff Dunhill. She could still hear him bellowing as he blamed the housekeeper for losing his golf pants, which he apparently eventually found in said bag. A small ding of a text came in and launched her into action.

Good morning, Nancy. My ladies and I will meet you at the Bucephalus at 11am sharp for the inspection. Best, Faye Woodhall.

Nancy quickly showered, pulled on a pair of white jeans and a navy tank top, strapped on her sandals, and raced to her Volvo with wet hair and a tube of half-open mascara. She proceeded down Harbor Boulevard toward the ocean, careful not to mow down skateboarders, beach cruisers, and pedestrians with dogs in baby strollers.

Her window down, she started to relax and settle into her short drive as that same salty wind that had washed over her the night before breezed into her car window. It felt so good that she slowed for a moment and enjoyed the balmy gust as it mussed her hair. She spotted a pelican drafting on it over the marina and smiled.

Nancy parked, pinched her cheeks to get a little color in them, then walked over to the entrance to G dock and looked over at her sailboat *Bucephalus* as it lazed in its slip. She pulled her hair back in a bun just as an ancient, stately, gleaming black Mercedes S-Class Pullman rolled up. The driver stopped the enormous car, got out, and opened the back-seat door.

Faye Woodhall materialized from the car in one motion, like Nosferatu emerging from his coffin. She was impeccably dressed in a yellow silk jumpsuit, a wide-brimmed black hat, and a lavender Birkin bag. Faye was tall and thin with high cheekbones and a sharp jawline that gave her an overall air of stoicism reserved for high society. Behind her, two ladies followed, each possessing the same stiffness but with less authority.

Only the day before as Nancy was washing her hands in the marina club bathroom, Faye Woodhall had emerged in the same way from the handicap stall and sneaked up next to her with the stealth of a silver-haired vampire to inquire about auctioning off a sunset cruise on their sailboat *Bucephalus*—of all things—to support the Institute for the Noetic Sciences, a society devoted to the "metaphysical study of higher consciousness." Faye had said this with a note of condescension as if this were common knowledge.

"Like meditation?" Nancy asked.

"It's been known to help those afflicted with ulcerative colitis," Faye had coolly replied.

"Colitis." It was all Nancy could say in return.

Every year the charities were more obscure. Faye had come from old money up in San Francisco. Either lumber or railroad, Nancy couldn't remember which. But her family had been disgraced by her Ponzi-scheme-running father, who had been tried and convicted of fleecing some of the wealthiest families in the city. Faye was forced to abscond with the few shreds of dignity she still had, along with what remained of her trust fund, and had landed in Southern California to start anew. Nancy supposed Faye was allowed her peculiarities.

One of the formerly disgraced heiress's companions held out a white-gloved hand. Faye did the introductions in her low-pitched tone. "This is Madeleine Schnell, of the Modesto Schnells, and Lucinda Lassy; her family is in real estate. They own half of the Palos Verdes peninsula. Thank you for allowing us to see *Bucephalus*."

Nancy greeted them and nearly curtsied but then stopped herself. "My pleasure." A tiny smile lit her lips. "Right this way, ladies." Nancy led them to her beloved sailboat, which she and her husband Roger owned together.

Faye began to impart her knowledge of *Bucephalus* with the same flair Robin Leach had used while hosting *Lifestyles of the Rich and Famous*. She might as well have had a microphone and a glass of champagne in her hand. As they approached the slip, even Nancy was captivated.

"*Bucephalus* is a thirty-eight-foot Beneteau, an impressive sailing yacht from a family-owned company in Northern California. It was named after Alexander the Great's horse. As I understand it, the Hadleys have added extensive creature comforts, such as a Bose sound system and a flat-screen TV. The original interior wood was replaced with imported Norwegian teak," Faye explained.

The other two ladies murmured their approval of the boat's heritage and improvements, especially anything remotely related to Scandinavia, an area considered desirable to rich people for reasons unknown.

"It's built and equipped for racing and considered one of the finest vessels on the sea, having won the Border Dash four times in the recent past. It has a spinnaker and a full set of Kevlar racing sails, but it's also a wonderful option for an afternoon sail. I'm sure a sunset cruise experience will be an excellent auction item for our distinguished patrons."

As Faye spoke, Nancy led them down to the end of the dock where her boat was moored. "Here she is . . ."

The women beheld the vessel as it gleamed in the morning sun. Nancy's pride swelled, and she held out her arms to present *Bucephalus*. Her sailboat was impressive and in perfect condition, the teak well oiled, the cockpit clean, the cushions bright and perfectly positioned.

Nancy's beaming smile also came from the fact that she could sail it. She'd learned how to sail from her Finnish grandfather, Oskar, on a handful of summer trips up to the delta outside Stockton, where he would take her out on his modest boat. She'd learned about knots and mooring balls, when to tack the boat to turn it, and how to navigate. But mostly Nancy's grandfather had taught her how to sail on instinct—how to read the wind like it was one of her favorite books. She'd learned to pay attention to its subtleties. She loved how her eyes grew brighter and more focused, how sailing cleared her mind and relaxed her at the same time.

Her intuition also made her a better sailor than most, including her husband, Roger, who openly resented it. In fact, her last-minute tack after reading a shift in the wind in yesterday evening's beer can races had garnered another win for *Bucephalus* and her crew, much to the dismay of "Captain" Roger, who considered an order contradictory to his direction an act of mutiny.

"You know the British navy hanged people for less," Roger chided as he gripped his navy grog post-race at their table overlooking King Harbor Marina. Outside, seals barked loudly and jockeyed for space on the dock below, while Nancy enjoyed a small smile.

"Rog," Nancy said, "victory cocktails are much better when there's an actual victory." She tipped her gin and tonic in his general direction, which, given his constipated expression, only served to infuriate him further.

"Cheers to that," one of their racing partners, Mac, said as he downed his beer.

"She's right, Rog. That outside line caught more wind right when we needed it," Tony piped up.

"Outside line, my keister. You are traitors all," Roger grumbled as he sat back and looked around the room. Nancy was just starting to relax when Claire Sanford came up, leaned over Roger, placed a lacquered red fingernail on the dimple of his chin, and said in a sultry tone, "Winner, winner, chicken dinner!" And then Claire let out a loud Jersey cackle as Roger kissed her hand. The audacity of the move silenced Nancy.

Nancy frowned at the recollection, resolving to take the issue up with Roger later tonight, just as Faye Woodhall said, "May we board?"

"Of course!" Nancy said as she came off the memory. "Watch your step." She was leading the ladies down to the steps to board the boat when the yacht club women froze at a strange noise. Nancy heard it too. She turned her head toward the boat. The noise seemed to be coming from inside the salon. A rumbling followed by a squeaking noise.

"Perhaps your cleaning crew finishing up?" Madeleine Schnell suggested. Nancy had turned down Faye's offer to have her cleaners come yesterday and instead had called her own.

She half nodded, considering this possibility. But she was sure they had finished by now.

Faye squinted in the direction of the boat, as if she recognized the sound, but she remained quiet.

Nancy quickly hopped up the steps and onto the stern deck. The three women followed until all of them were stacked one upon another in the cockpit peering down into the salon.

A long, tanned leg appeared, seeming to float in midair. Nancy stared at it, not comprehending what she was seeing. Then a giggle rose from the interior of the boat. But that was no giggle. It was a cackle. A cackle Nancy knew well. Nancy threw back the door to the salon and was met with a shocking view—the white, fuzzy ass of her husband, wrapped between the naked legs of a woman. The serenity of her Sunday morning was broken by the squeak of Roger's boat shoes against the teak floor of the galley as he vigorously humped Claire Sanford on the salon table of her beloved *Bucephalus*.

Roger turned fast, his face, red with desire, now turning ghostly white.

Nancy stood there, frozen, processing.

"Oh shit," was all Roger could muster. He backed away from Claire, who crossed her legs in a fluid motion and began to do up her unbuttoned silk shirt, an ostentatious purple bra peeking out from underneath. Her movements were impossibly graceful. Roger, trapped by his green golf pants at his ankles, stumbled backward, sending two plastic wineglasses flying. The opposite of graceful.

Nancy came to and took one long look at her husband, who began to bluster about how she shouldn't be there as he fumbled with his god-awful golf pants. Then she looked over at Claire, who shrugged. The hot burn of embarrassment started in Nancy's chest and ran all the way up to her cheeks. She turned to see the yacht club ladies standing right behind her, staring wide-eyed, stunned into silence. Except Faye Woodhall, who only looked at Nancy and then looked away.

Nancy could have said a thousand things. She could have screamed. Cried. She could have knocked Roger out cold with a winch handle and no one would have blamed her. But she turned to Faye and said, "You said you had a good cleaning crew? Looks like you'll need it."

Nancy turned on her heel, hopped off the boat, and walked away from the charity ladies, away from Roger, who was now yelling at her to come back, away from the vision of Claire's tanned naked legs and heaving breasts, and away from her *Bucephalus*. She didn't heed his calls. She didn't stay to be polite to Faye Woodhall et al. She didn't look back. She hurried to her car, turned the key, and drove, not knowing where she was going, but direction didn't matter. She rolled the windows down and let the warm wind envelop her as the afternoon sun grew hot and the panic inside her grew cold.

If Nancy had a nemesis in the world, it was Claire Sanford.

Claire hailed from the East Coast. Not Manhattan, like she led so many to believe, but Hoboken. Across the river but worlds apart. Cunning and smart, Claire had clawed her way out of Hoboken and all the way into the upper echelons of society. Beautiful in a sharp, angular sort of way, she wore her short, sleek, red hair parted on one side, which allowed her piercing blue eyes to notice details about people that she'd toss out like emotional hand grenades: "Didn't I see that dress at our last Yacht Club dinner? Is that Valentino? Chanel?"

Claire had chuckled after she made this last snide comment to Nancy's best friend, Ruthie, a devoted TJ Maxx shopper who prided herself on stretching her budget. Ruthie smirked and blew Claire off as a snob, but Nancy was furious.

After all, Claire had a proven reputation as a gold digger who had acquired her wealth through a string of advantageous yet short-lived marriages. Suspicions had swirled when more than one of her husbands had dropped dead within two years of matrimony. Then again, she did go for those types who teetered on the edge of the grave. She openly flirted with eligible bachelors and married men alike, testing boundaries for weak spots in marital unions. If she found them, she'd exploit them. As a result, she had no female friends at the club. She didn't care. Women were of no interest to her. She had bigger fish to fry, richer men to marry, fortunes to fortify.

The fact was, when Claire decided she wanted something, she found a way to get it.

Nancy should have known.

CHAPTER TWO
ALL NAVIGATION LOST

Nancy had once read that rapidly collapsing stars could emit an enormous amount of energy, resulting in an explosion that retracted and then turned into a black hole. This was how she felt after seeing Roger entangled in Claire's naked legs with the charity league as a captive, horrified audience. She felt as if someone had hit her squarely in the chest with a sledgehammer. She was unable to take a deep breath. A series of tiny panic attacks kept overtaking her mind and body, making it hard to concentrate. But under the shock of infidelity and the anger of humiliation, there was dread, too. Old damage had crept in like an out-of-control virus. Upheaval was at her doorstep, and it was paralyzing.

Nancy Niemi Hadley wasn't born a fussy baby, nor had she been a child prone to anxiety or panic. She had been a happy and confident girl growing up in a small suburb of sunny Ventura, California, in the late 1970s. At the tender age of twelve, not fully understanding that women were limited to professions like teacher, nurse, and secretary in those days, Nancy dreamed a little bigger and thought of being a travel correspondent like Martha Gellhorn, globe-trotting around the world, writing about war, and challenging the likes of Hemingway. Her days were filled with ideas and dreams that she would sketch out while she munched on Doritos and read Nancy Drew mysteries.

Then a sudden disturbance came slithering in to destroy her idyllic childhood. Just like all trauma, she didn't see it coming.

She was the only child of blue-collar parents of Finnish descent, who were steeped in the belief that hard work cleansed the soul and that being a good Lutheran would absolve all sins, no matter how grave the transgression. Nancy's mother, Grace, was a petite spitfire of a woman, with flaxen hair and lilting eyes, which always gave the impression that she was in a state of understanding or mild sympathy. She never wore lipstick, but her full lips were a pale pink that played against her luminous peaches-and-cream skin. Naturally buoyant, Grace either hummed or whistled throughout the day as she moved around the house. When she breezed by Nancy, she smelled like a mixture of lavender, lemons, and Ivory soap. Grace taught Nancy how to cook, how to read, and how to iron pillowcases, a skill Nancy deemed entirely useless.

"Why am I ironing pillowcases?" Nancy protested.

"How do you expect to take care of a husband and a household if you don't learn the basics?"

"I plan on having staff for this." Nancy slaved on dramatically.

"Until then, soldier on, Cinderella." Grace's hands were the only thing that betrayed her age, bearing wrinkles, cuts, and scars from her daily chores and cooking. But in every other way, Nancy's mom seemed young, vibrant, and happy.

Her father, Karl, was blessed with a head of blond curls, piercing blue eyes, and a dimpled smile that her mother found irresistible. Simple transgressions that would cause Grace to raise her voice—pipe ashes carelessly dumped in a coffee cup, crumpled underwear in the bathroom—were instantly forgotten when Karl flashed her that smile.

Karl adored his bright and precocious daughter, Nancy. He was the only one in the world who called her Nan, an endearment she loved. He tried to make her laugh, even in church, which got them both in trouble. He worked as an aircraft training specialist and would often go out of town for weeks at a time. He'd come back with exotic gifts for Nancy: a tiny ship in a bottle from Maine, peach-flavored jelly beans from Atlanta, sand dollars from the beaches of Sanibel, Florida. But it was the hug he gave her when he came home, the smell of his cherry tobacco, and his larger-than-life presence that Nancy really treasured. Every time he rushed through their front door, he would take her mother by the hand, spin her around, and kiss her on the neck. Nancy was never happier than when it was the three of them together again.

That's why that day felt like a flash flood of black, icy water, rushing fast and hard to loosen her foundation. She was on her way home from seventh grade on a blustery November afternoon, the waves wild and crashing on the distant shores of Ventura beach as the sky darkened overhead. As she strolled along the sidewalk, pondering how she and her dad were going to construct a bridge out of Popsicle sticks for her school project, two black birds squawked from their positions on the fence as if sounding a warning. She looked up and saw her mother burst out of the front door and look down the street, panic in her pale-blue eyes, cheeks stained with tears. When she saw Nancy, Grace tried to compose herself. But it was hard to hide raw emotion. Nancy took one wary step up to the porch, not knowing what was going on. She peered into the house and saw shards of broken glass, a coffee table overturned, a lamp broken.

"Mom, what's going on? Where's Dad?"

Her mother grabbed her and averted her view into the house. She said, "Honey, I need you to go over to the Largents' house until I come to get you, okay?"

Nancy detected a wild fear in her mother's voice, and it unnerved her. Her heart fluttered and a shiver ran up her back. "Mom, what's happened? Is Dad okay?"

Her mother knelt down, looked her in the eyes, and forcefully said, "Go to the Largents'. I'll come over there later." Nancy's stomach churned; the world in front of her tilted.

It wasn't long before she knew the truth. Her father had arrived home drunk and announced he was leaving them. He raged inside the house, blaming Grace for his own betrayal, his fury—thinly masking his shame—eventually turning physical. Thankfully, he hadn't raised his hand to Grace but rather the lamp and coffee table, which took the full brunt of his anger before he stormed out and threw her the keys to their only car. Karl, Nancy's father, in the grips of what she learned later was a full-blown midlife crisis, had abandoned her beautiful mother for a seventeen-year-old girl who worked at the Camarillo train station. They were moving to Miami, he said. The girl was pregnant, he said. Don't contact him, he said.

"He means you, right? He's just leaving you. He didn't mean me. We're supposed to build our bridge tonight, and he . . ." Nancy, for the first time in her life, felt the unfamiliar shifting sands of dread deep within her. She looked up at Grace's anguished expression.

"Mom? He'll come back for me, won't he? He won't leave me. He loves me. Even if he doesn't love you!" She needed to separate the two ideas. She couldn't be left by her dad, the one who called her Nan and made her laugh and had taught her how to throw a softball. Daughters weren't the same as wives.

She felt her mom's arms gently cradle her.

"No!" Nancy broke away from her. "I'm not going to let you do this!" Nancy took off running in the direction she thought her dad would go, to the train station, and she heard her mother calling after her. Her heart was beating out of her chest as she sprinted, tears streaming back into her hair. She got to the fence where she could see the train platform, but it was empty.

The dark clouds opened, and it began to rain. Nancy collapsed against the fence and sank down in the long grass and felt the cold drops of water mix with her hot tears. As the rain came down, she started to pray, not to God, but to her dad. "Please, Daddy, come back. Please don't leave me."

Nancy heard the voice of her father calling her name. She turned with a start from her position in the long grass. The rain had subsided, and it had gotten dark while she sat against the fence. A beam of light blinded her at first, and she called out, "Dad?"

"Nancy, thank god." It wasn't her dad but Hank Gentry, a local police officer living in the neighborhood, who approached her. He helped her up, but she was still disoriented. "Dad? Is my dad with you, Mr. Gentry?"

At first Gentry didn't say anything, and then he finally uttered, "Let's get you home, girl."

As the months went by, Nancy remained certain that her dad would contact her. She checked the mailbox every day in case he sent a letter, and some evenings she would sit by the phone in the kitchen, waiting for it to ring, until her eyes grew heavy and her mother gently ushered her to bed. But the calls and the letters never came. Nancy's heart broke in a place that never healed.

When she finally accepted that her father was gone, when some of her own blinding pain subsided, she had room to understand her mother's pain as well. While Nancy had lost a father, her mom had lost her husband, and any security that he offered went with him. Nancy realized that Grace's heart must be broken too. That night, when her mom tucked her in bed, Nancy reached out and held her hand, the first gesture of love toward her mother since her dad had left them. Grace looked into her daughter's eyes and let Nancy cry. She fell asleep by Nancy's side, and they stayed there until morning.

As if being abandoned weren't humiliating and painful enough, her mother was unable to pay their bills, and six months later they were evicted from the only home Nancy had known.

On a blustery February morning, two apologetic police officers stood on the porch, one nervously playing with his hat while Nancy and her mother carried out their belongings in suitcases and trash bags. Grace chirped at Nancy to hurry with the rest of her things. Nancy thought her mother marched like a tiny little warrior, her head held high, past the officers. When one of them offered to help, she waved him away and lugged the large suitcase past the officer and not so accidentally hit him in the groin. He grimaced in pain as she heaved the bag out and into the trunk of her car with the strength of Thor. Grace never looked back at the officers, unwilling to entertain their sympathy. She drove away from Ventura without shedding a tear, her gaze determined and straight ahead.

"At least I got you, baby girl. And a full tank of gas. That's all I need."

Grace was giving off resilient energy, but Nancy heard the uncertainty in her voice when it cracked on the last word.

Nancy's panic rose in her chest, like the wings of a bird beating against a cage, but she didn't let it show. She wouldn't burden her mother further. "You'll always have me."

Grace just nodded and drove toward the ocean. They stopped at a vista point somewhere north of Malibu. As they stared out at the Pacific, Nancy saw her mother weaken and rest her forehead gently on the steering wheel. She had never seen her mother break down before, and it was like an emotional earthquake, a cataclysmic upheaval of everything that made her feel safe. Her family destroyed, her home gone, her mom broken. When Grace finally looked at her, she appeared wilted, her strength drained. Nancy was twelve years old and called upon to console her mother, who had just lost everything. She held her mom's hand and said, "It's going to be okay."

Nancy learned three things that day, staring out at the Pacific. *There's no guarantee that everything is going to be okay. Most things are out of your control. And safety is more important than happiness.*

Old damage had a way of flaring up when you least expected it. Like hemorrhoids or hot flashes. It could take you out at the knees.

Forty-five years later, that dread was back. And the lessons still rang true. Nancy sat in her car for a long while and stared out at the vast expanse of ocean from a cliff in Palos Verdes. The same unending, bottomless anxiety thrumming throughout her veins, she trembled as she gripped and regripped the wheel. Her breath was uneven, and she couldn't slow her reeling mind.

What now?

And then an answer came as if delivered by the grace of Grace.

She pointed the car back toward Redondo Beach and found herself on Ruthie's doorstep.

CHAPTER THREE
ME HEARTIES

Ruthie Davenport lived in a small beach bungalow with a charming front porch and a yard full of tomato plants, lavender, and milkweed. Butterflies and bumblebees floated happily around the blossoms in her small garden, which was a rather peaceful setting, given all the tumult about to happen inside. A 911 text had been sent to Nancy's posse of girlfriends, and they were all beginning to arrive.

Lois came in through the small front gate. Ruthie's candles were already lit, incense burned, and Joni Mitchell emanated from the vintage Marantz stereo, singing about the last time she'd seen Richard. Otis, Ruthie's ratty but adorable pug-terrier mix rescue dog, was wriggling around on his back, playing with his favorite stuffed dinosaur toy, when he heard the click of the gate. He instantly jumped up and got out one bark before he saw Lois. He wagged his tail in a dog-joy frenzy and rushed to greet her.

"Hiya, boy!" Lois took out a stash of turkey jerky and slipped a few pieces to the little dog. Otis scarfed it down and then began to lick Lois's face in gratitude as she bent down to pet him, her soft, permed mop of blond hair holding up her sunglasses. Lois murmured, "Who's your favorite auntie?"

"That would be Judy," said Judy, who had appeared near the front door. "I brought him bacon treats."

"Stepping it up, I see. Devious." Lois smiled at Judy.

Ruthie came out onto the porch and looked down at her dog, who was still licking his chops. "Don't feed him jerky. He'll get the shits," she scolded.

"Never," Lois said guiltily as she hid the baggie. Ruthie stood on the porch, wearing purple leggings and a black oversized flowing shirt. Her shiny auburn hair stuck out like star points from her bun, held by a hair clip, her gold bangle bracelets rattling as she dangled two clean wineglasses in front of her.

"Get in here, I'm parched! Nancy is on her way over. Apparently, there's *news*. Bad news." Ruthie looked at her girls with raised eyebrows as they entered the house.

Ruthie's cottage was one large open room with French doors that had been swept open to let in the evening breeze. The room faced west, and soft pink clouds floated by as pelicans lazed on the breeze overhead. The kitchen was the heart of the house, with an island made for entertaining. Four sea grass barstools surrounded it, and in the center three short, squat sandalwood candles glowed brightly. The house was cozy and tasteful, full of Balinese and Brazilian trinkets from Ruthie's travels, original art on canvas, and framed photos of all four of them in different stages of their lives, dating back to high school.

"What do you think is going on? Roger, maybe?" Judy asked.

"It involves Roger, of course. That cad has done something awful, I'm sure of it. It's in his genes, I swear. Men go through menopause too. But instead of hormone replacement therapy and brittle hair, they get Maseratis and mistresses," Ruthie said.

"Only sounds fair, then, that we get margaritas and manservants," Lois added. "Hey, do you have any antacids?" She got up to investigate. Otis followed the lady with the turkey jerky.

Judy, notoriously indecisive, hauled a huge grocery bag onto the kitchen counter filled with all manner of snacks.

"Judy, did you buy Trader Joe's out of cheese?" Ruthie asked.

"I just couldn't decide. Besides, I have some news of my own. But we'll wait until we see what's going on with Nancy."

Ruthie raised her eyebrows and let out a whistle. "The blender is going to be busy tonight."

The girls took up their usual tasks with an unspoken ease and efficiency. Lois opened various cheeses, Ruthie opened the tequila, Judy opened jars of pickles and olives. Otis served as a canine Swiffer lapping up any tidbits of cheese that dropped. The energy was more than friendship. It was a safe zone—unlike family, with its obligations and burdens of blood relatives. Nor was it weighed down by complications that came along with lovers or husbands. What they shared was love, in the deepest, most trusting way, because it was chosen. The blender whirred to life.

Just then, Otis let out a happy bark, which meant Nancy was at the gate. Ruthie and Judy rushed to the porch, joined almost instantly by Lois, who was munching on antacids. Before them stood Nancy, slightly shaking, eyes weary, seemingly frozen at the gate.

"Roger," was all Nancy could muster in her weakened state.

"Let's get you in the house and get some booze in you before you collapse."

Judy and Lois took Nancy by the elbows, led her into Ruthie's house, and deposited her in a deep-seated chair in the living room. Ruthie came over and was hovering over her, fighting the urge to check her vitals, when Nancy finally spoke.

"I, along with three horrified charity ladies, walked onto *Bucephalus* and caught Roger boffing Claire Sanford."

Judy gasped. "Good God!"

Ruthie smirked and said, "The snarky redhead?"

Lois produced a blended margarita with salt on the rim and handed it to Nancy just in time. Judy, Lois, and Ruthie all stood there for a moment and didn't say another word. Nancy took a good long sip of the frozen concoction and then threw her head back and groaned.

Ruthie finally broke the silence. "Putz."

Nancy nodded and let her first tear of frustration fall.

Lois went to get the pitcher of margaritas.

"Claire Sanford . . ." Ruthie pondered aloud. "I thought she had her sights set on that old fart Stanley Rosenthal and his mattress empire."

"You didn't hear? Stanley keeled over during a two-hour tennis match with Larry Valone," Judy said.

"Valone . . . is he the car dealer with the hair plugs who always wears a puka shell necklace?" Ruthie asked.

"I believe that's him," Judy confirmed.

"I went on a date with Larry once. He tried to sell me a used Mazda with low miles during the appetizer course."

"Who died?" Lois asked, as she returned with margaritas for all.

"Stanley Rosenthal."

"How did he croak?" Lois asked.

"Heart attack. Apparently, Larry and Stan got into a fight over whether a serve was in or out during a tiebreak to win their tennis match. Stan's last words were, 'As I live and breathe, that serve was out, you lying gigolo huckster!' "

"Not the noblest of last words," Lois said.

The women finally took their seats in the living room as Otis eagerly ran between everyone's legs, hoping someone would drop a cracker or some prosciutto. Lois discreetly slipped the little dog a cheese curd, which he happily gobbled up before opting to sit next to her in hopes that his good fortune of cheese curds would continue. Nancy was nearly done with her frozen margarita.

"I should have seen this coming."

"How?" Judy asked.

"The beer can race. I ignored his orders because the wind shifted, and I knew we could take advantage of it. You all know how Roger likes to punish me when my rightness causes us to win the race?"

"A topic we shall take up at another time, but yes," Ruthie said.

"Claire Sanford was at the club flaunting her augmented breasts all over Roger, and he ate it up like key lime pie. I just thought he was getting back at me for my small mutiny aboard. I didn't think . . . because he was flirting with everyone, even Rita." Nancy felt her face grow hot, embarrassed. He had made a pass at their waitress that night too. "And then we all walked on the boat and there they were, naked and humping on *Bucephalus*."

Ruthie shook her head, her anger palpable. Lois slurped down her margarita and went to make more as Judy nervously started making little cheese-and-cracker sandwiches.

Nancy slumped down into her chair, her anxiety on high alert.

"Okay, we're ordering Thai food. Get comfy. We're going to be here awhile," Ruthie announced as she headed into the kitchen.

Judy knelt down next to Nancy, took her hand, and held it to her cheek. Judy's skin was warm. "That's the saddest thing about betrayal: it never comes from your enemies."

"I'm such an idiot," Nancy said quietly.

Lois walked back in with another pitcher of margaritas and said, "How's our girl?"

"One margarita down and knee-deep in self-loathing," Judy answered.

Nancy looked up at Lois and nodded at this assessment. She held up her empty glass as Lois poured more of the tart tequila concoction into it.

Thirty minutes later, the Thai food had arrived and Nancy was camped out under a blanket in an Adirondack chair on Ruthie's back porch. The sun had begun to sink slowly into the Pacific. Otis was curled up on her lap, offering up all the emotional dog support he could muster, which consisted mostly of napping and the occasional affectionate snort.

Judy opened a bottle of white wine as Ruthie came out with two bowls of Thai food from the local place in the village, renowned for its green curry. Ruthie offered one to Nancy, but she simply took the bowl and set it down on the side table, untouched. Ruthie dug into her curry as Nancy studied the horizon as if a missing ship would appear.

"I feel like an asshole," Nancy finally said.

Ruthie nodded as she nibbled on a carrot slice and said, "You are entitled to feel like a trusting, loving fool, but you are not permitted to feel like an asshole. You did nothing wrong."

"It's true," Lois added. "He's the scumball here, not you."

Otis was awake now and torn between offering continued emotional dog support and the bits of chicken curry Ruthie kept dropping on the deck. He leaned his head over Nancy's knee so he would be in the perfect position to catch a piece if it fell.

"I should have seen this coming."

"Oh, for shit's sake, Nance. You've been a people pleaser your entire life. Of which I have been a great beneficiary, I'll admit. But I cannot allow you to sit here and stab holes into yourself with the sharp blade of hindsight, only to have you rewrite history so that somehow Roger's Viagra-fueled sexcapades with that gold-digging tramp are your fault. That man has never deserved you."

Nancy nodded. But there was something Ruthie and Judy didn't know. Roger had done this before. She hadn't been totally blindsided by his philandering behavior. She acknowledged that she'd thought his age would stop him, or at least stifle his urges.

Lois asked, "Any word from him?"

Nancy shrugged. She had turned off her phone the minute Roger called, which was approximately three minutes after she left the boat. That was roughly four hours ago. Nancy handed her phone to Lois, who turned it on.

"Whoa. You have fourteen missed calls and thirty-two text messages. All but one of them are from Roger. The other is from Stella."

"Read the one from Stella," Nancy said.

"*Hi Mom. Just heard from Dad. WTF. Call me.*"

Nancy sank deeper in her chair. She wondered how long she could stay here on Ruthie's deck, letting the weeks go by in hiding, having wine and food delivered to her chair. It wouldn't be so bad. She had Otis. She could send for Suzanne the Cat.

Lois raised her wineglass and nodded to Ruthie, who poured her some and said, "So, the charity committee saw Roger and Claire going at it like two middle-aged rabbits? Those women must have been appalled."

"I bet that's the most ass Faye Woodhall has seen since women got the right to vote," Ruthie said as she fiddled with a sugar snap pea.

Nancy couldn't stop a slow smile from appearing on her face. "You are not going to make me laugh."

Ruthie smiled and said, "Can't hurt to try."

"What was the reaction of the charitable society ladies anyway?" Lois asked.

"Well." Nancy thought about it for a second. "The two ladies that accompanied Faye were both stunned at first, and then they gasped. But Faye was silent. She didn't say a word. Didn't even raise her hand in shock or anything."

"Well, it's possible she's half-dead, being kept alive by vodka, calcium tablets, and pure, unfiltered disdain," Lois said.

"Oh, stop. You're just being mean," Nancy interrupted. "I just got the feeling that Faye felt it was beneath her to even be there, witnessing someone else's melodrama."

"I can see that. Melodrama is typically reserved for the lower classes," Ruthie said.

"Speaking of melodrama, I have some news too," Judy offered.

"Oh, thank god," Nancy said. "Please take the attention off of me. My story has grown tiresome."

Judy took a deep breath and said, "I got a call today from the park ranger's office up in Kings Canyon. They found Gordon."

The three women sat there, stunned.

Lois tentatively asked, "Is he . . . alive?"

"No." Judy had tears in her eyes. Ruth and Lois both reflexively went to Judy's side to console her. "After all this time . . ."

For two long years, Judy had sat grieving as a pseudowidow after her husband Gordon went on a hiking-and-camping trip alone in the High Sierras, a mountain range five hours' driving distance north of Los Angeles. He had never come home. He had been a man of the woods, trails, and national parks his whole life, but he was also a sixty-two-year-old hiking alone above twelve thousand feet. An unnecessary risk that Judy still hadn't quite forgiven him for.

"The rangers believe he tried to find a safe place behind some boulders to keep himself out of the wind, but it got down to eighteen degrees that night. He was wearing a cotton T-shirt and jeans." Judy shook her head. "They think he lost consciousness when his body temperature dropped. And he just fell asleep. It makes me feel better to know that he wasn't crushed by a boulder or mauled by a bear."

Nancy had a lump in her throat but managed to say, "I'm so sorry, Judy."

"Same," Lois said.

Ruthie nodded.

Judy took a deep breath and wiped her face. The girls slowly went back to their own seats and gave Judy some room.

She regained her composure. "The other piece of news is that I can claim his life insurance. Without a body, life insurance is void. My agent put in the claim right after he heard."

Considering Judy was still working two part-time jobs to make ends meet at the ripe old age of fifty-seven, Nancy hoped the sum was enough to help her.

"He left our boys a nice sum. And I will get a check for five hundred thousand."

"Whoa." Lois muttered.

"Holy Moses," Ruthie added.

"Thank god, Gordon," Nancy whispered.

Judy said, "There is a certain amount of relief, I suppose. When we had his celebration-of-life ceremony, I knew he was gone. I could feel it. This brings the last bit of closure, I guess. And now this money." She sighed. "I'd give it all back to spend another day with him. It's more than I know what to do with. I don't even know where to start."

In light of Judy's chronically indecisive nature, Nancy and Ruthie gave each other a knowing look. "Champagne is always a good start."

Judy nodded.

"Great idea." Lois headed to the kitchen.

Judy piped up, "I brought three kinds."

The girls talked about their favorite memories of Gordon over the years and toasted to his memory. As the night passed like a warm ocean breeze, Judy shed a few more tears, some from relief, some from sadness, but enough to begin to wash away the pain and gently usher in a kind of peace. Nancy, in a flash of wistfulness, wondered if she would have felt that way about Roger if he had unexpectedly died in the wilderness. Then it occurred to her that the only way Roger would be caught dead on a mountain was if an avalanche plowed through the cocktail lounge at the Deer Valley Lodge.

* * *

It was a little after nine PM when Nancy finally put her blanket aside and sat up in her Adirondack chair. Margaritas, Thai food, news of Gordon, and time spent with her best friends had done its job, at least for now.

"Well," Nancy said slowly, "I have to go home." The statement pained her. She didn't want to be anywhere near Roger. Didn't want his hands pawing at her to get her to listen to his excuses, and boy, she couldn't wait to hear this excuse. She didn't want to fight against his demands that she forgive him. Didn't want to face the untouchable truth.

"Why do you have to go home? I have plenty of room here."

"The cat will die."

"Bring the cat."

"Otis hates cats. Plus, Suzanne would kill Otis with one swipe of her agile, lethal paw if given the chance."

"Hey, Otis can handle his own."

Otis looked up at Nancy from his prostrate position and snorted softly, as if knowing he had no chance in hell against that cat.

Lois offered, "Come stay with me and Chris. The kids are long gone, and it'll give me a reason to sell Chris's hideous beer stein collection on Facebook Marketplace."

"I have my guest suite perpetually made up. With the good sheets," Judy said.

"Thank you. All of you. But you know I have to go home."

Ruthie put down her wineglass and sighed. Judy took her last sip. Lois shook her head.

When Nancy emerged from the chair, she felt like she was climbing out of a mud bog. Her body felt heavy, as if actively fighting against her intention to go home. The girls helped her gather her things, looks of deep concern etched on their faces. Nancy knew what she was facing there. The girls did too.

She took a last swig of chardonnay for courage, wiped her mouth, and headed back to Hermosa Beach and her cheating shit-head of a husband.

CHAPTER FOUR

THE THING ABOUT ROGER

Roger was accidentally conceived on the bucket seat of a Buick Skylark after a prime rib dinner at the Red Fox Bar & Grill in Bloomfield Hills, Michigan, in 1961. Unbeknownst to his soon-to-be mother, Abigail, he grew in her womb for two weeks while she and her ambitious boyfriend, Wayne, took off in that same Buick for California with dreams of a future as aeronautical engineers living in a coastal cottage by the beach.

So, when Abigail missed her first period and the knowledge of Roger's existence became clear to her, she told Wayne, who sat dismally drinking whiskey in their beach house full of moving boxes. They came to a quick and united decision. There was no room in their plan for a baby. Roger was unplanned and unwanted and regretfully had to be dealt with. After all, Abigail wasn't just a farm girl anymore. She hadn't become the first female engineering graduate of Michigan State University just to get pregnant and become a housewife. Hell no. Her ambitions far outweighed her humble beginnings and meager circumstances. She had dreams of designing jets and propulsion systems. She was born to exceed every expectation anyone had for her. She was driven and smarter than most men, with the ability to keep her emotions in check. Even as a child, Abigail had exhibited little to no emotion at coming-of-age traumatic events, including the death of her favorite chicken, Chuckles, to a hungry weasel. Her stoic father told her he saw it as her strength, which only served to further tamp down any emotions that might crop up. Sensitivity and empathy were simply not part of her makeup. This helped immensely in the male-dominated world of engineering, where, just as there was no crying in baseball, there was no place for feminine qualities such as, say, feelings. She understood data, numbers, physics, and cold, hard facts. Motherhood, especially the loving and nurturing aspects of this particular endeavor, were far too messy and not at all part of her plan.

As for Wayne's feelings on the matter, Roger's existence was a cataclysmic monkey wrench in his plan for world domination. He and Abigail had a shared dream and a solid plan for becoming fabulously wealthy, traveling the world, and perhaps even sailing around it. Wayne's way of dealing with the matter of Roger was to simply act as if he didn't exist. So, with a simple nod to Abigail when she talked about ending her pregnancy, he eliminated Roger from his consciousness.

On a Saturday morning in June 1961, Abigail found herself driving to a private clinic in Beverly Hills known for certain procedures and absolute discretion. She sat in the waiting room with three other women, each seemingly bowing her head in quiet shame, which she couldn't understand. She filled out the paperwork, used a false name, and had cash on hand for the procedure. She wanted no paper trail, no record of the event. When her fake name was called, she walked back into the sparsely furnished room that held a single gynecological table with stirrups. The nurse instructed her that the doctor would be in soon. She sat down and waited for the attending doctor to come in. At least, she hoped it was a doctor. She really didn't have any idea. As she sat there, she stared at the gestation photos on the wall. How big a baby was in the womb at six, ten, and twelve weeks. She studied the posters with an engineer's brain, noticing the changes in the fetus over time, but she applied no emotion to the observation. Instead, she looked at her watch and wondered if she'd be able to meet Wayne for dinner.

The door opened, and a middle-aged man walked in. Abigail noticed he had a warm handshake and kind eyes. He looked at her with a sad smile.

"Jane, is it?"

Abigail nodded at the use of her fake name.

"Tell me about your situation," the doctor said.

"Well, I want to end my pregnancy."

"I see, of course. You're on your own?"

"No."

"So, you know the father?"

"Of course I know the father; I'm with the father. What kind of loose woman do you think I am?"

"I'm sorry, it's just that many women who come here are under rather difficult circumstances. So, I take it that it's a financial decision?"

"No, we're both engineers. We live in a lovely cottage by the beach," Abigail answered confidently.

"I see. So, if you don't mind my asking—and by all means, you can tell me to mind my own business—but why is a perfectly healthy young woman in a happily committed relationship with the father of her child, who is also financially able to raise a child, choosing to end a pregnancy? The only reason I ask is that sometimes it's not as easy as it seems to do something like this."

Abigail sat there for a second. Something inside her stirred. It wasn't an altogether foreign feeling, but it wasn't common either. Doubt crept into her consciousness as she struggled to find an answer the doctor could accept. Or perhaps she was trying to find an answer she could accept. Wayne certainly didn't want to father a child. And he would be severely disappointed if she came home pregnant and, worst of all, with the intention of becoming a mother. She wondered if her dreams of achievement would have to suffer for her to have a child. Motherhood was just not part of her mission. But she looked up at the poster of the six-week-old fetus, and for the first time she felt connected to the growing baby inside her. She looked at the doctor, then down at her belly, and sighed. "I don't think I'll be needing your services after all."

The kindly doctor helped her up and rested his warm hand on her arm. "Good luck, Jane."

Abigail bid him farewell and drove home to Manhattan Beach.

Seven months later, Abigail and Wayne were married three short days before Roger was born. He was a bubbly, healthy baby boy clocking in at a little over eight pounds, with a hearty appetite and an ability to cry so loud dolphins could hear it from a mile offshore.

Roger's mother and father engineered ways around the hardest parts of parenting. Abigail found a family in the neighborhood who could watch Roger while she worked full-time. Wayne also worked full-time and was quickly promoted year after year, a direct consequence of becoming a "family man," as his supervisor put it. Abigail was certain this was the chief reason Wayne liked being a father.

Their small family prospered, and as soon as Abigail could have it done, she got her tubes tied to prevent any more children from cramping her promising career and social lifestyle. Roger grew up in a stable if not exactly loving home, and he flourished in school. He clearly had inherited the brains of his mother and father. But he had also inherited something else from them. Something he would find out about years later, quite by accident.

* * *

Back in the late eighties, brain mapping, genomes, and gene therapy were little-known theories shrouded in mystery and confusion. If discussed at all, these topics were relegated to the likes of science fiction authors. Or quacks. But there was a small malfunction in Roger's DNA. The combination of Abigail and Wayne's DNA had come together to make a perfect physically healthy baby boy but with a slightly mutated gene affecting the middle of his brain.

Roger stumbled upon this biological detail when he was two weeks shy of his fortieth birthday. He had gone in to the UCLA medical center at the urging of Nancy to, as she had put it, have his head examined—stress headaches had been recurring. While there, he saw his physician talking to a man he recognized, Dr. William Holm, a professor at the university and an old college fraternity brother. They got to talking, and Dr. Holm asked Roger if he could take his brain scan, as he was putting together a study on brain functionality. He explained that Roger and a few others would be the baseline for his working hypothesis. Roger obliged, took his fifty bucks, and fell asleep in the MRI machine.

After a week, Dr. Holm called Roger into his office at the university. Roger showed up at two thirty PM the following Tuesday and pawed through *Rolling Stone* with sweaty palms, certain he had a tumor on his brain stem. Dr. Holm came in holding an ominous manila folder. Roger audibly gulped.

"Hey, Roger," the doctor said, but he must have read the pall of dread on Roger's face. "Oh, my. I didn't mean to scare you—you're not dying."

Roger exhaled, having held his breath so long he felt dizzy.

"No, no, you're fine! In fact, you're rare!" Dr. Holm said. "Get this. Roger, it turns out you're a psychopath." He smiled cheerfully.

Roger sat there dumbstruck, staring at the MRI charts Holm had laid out for him.

"Hey, I know I'm not the nicest guy around, but it's not like I would take a chain saw to some coeds," Roger said, sounding more alarmed than he was.

"No, no, Roger, I'm not saying you're a psychopathic murderer; I'm saying your brain has the same patterns as a psychopathic brain. It's fascinating. This may prove my hypothesis that psychopathy is a genetic mutation."

"This makes no sense. I'm not psycho. Hell, I don't even cheat on my taxes. Much."

"Well, you should. But that's a different matter." Dr. Holm sipped his coffee. "Having a psychopathic brain doesn't mean you're going to be a serial killer. There are other very traumatic factors that have to happen to turn a psychopathic brain into a murderous one."

"Like?"

"Well, in studying other cases where men had the same brain makeup as you, certain people did turn violent, but it was a nurture problem, not a nature problem. As an infant, one subject was violently abused and neglected by his mother to the point of hospitalization. Soon after, his violent tendencies began. I think he tortured squirrels." Dr. Holm looked out the window, as if trying to recall what hapless critter had died at the hands of a psychopathic kid.

"And where is he now?"

"San Quentin, doing twenty-five to life."

"Doc!" Roger's alarm rose.

"There's nothing to worry about, Roger. You grew up in a supportive, caring environment, surrounded by encouragement, friends, and family. It was simply a roll of the dice. Either one—or, I would say, both—of your parents were born with this genetic mutation, so when they coupled, they produced you and your particularly rare and psychopathic brain."

"So, both of my parents had some mild form of socio or psychopathic brain mutation?"

"Yep."

"That explains a lot," Roger said, as he thought back to certain momentous occasions in his life, like graduating summa cum laude, getting married, and the birth of his daughter, where his parents had remained emotionless, generally happy but wildly aloof. He'd always thought it was their way of teaching him a lesson in how to be reserved, a nonshowy characteristic of their fellow engineers. Now it seemed they literally hadn't felt anything. If they hadn't both been dead, Roger would have given them hell.

"But while you may have a brain that is predisposed to having less empathy for other human beings, you have no urge to be violent because you were never exposed to violence. If you were, we'd be having a different conversation."

"Should I be . . . I don't know . . . afraid of what I'll do?"

"It doesn't work like that. There is no trigger in your brain that will suddenly switch and turn you into Ted Bundy. It's on a more basic level, more simple than that. Let me ask you a question. When someone does something to you that is wrong—say, gets one over on you, screws you; for instance, a bad business deal where you felt intentionally cheated—how do you handle that situation?"

Roger thought back to a real estate deal gone bad. His former business partner, Rick Keller, had explained it was a mistake in the negotiations that had shorted them both on the investment. Roger later found out that he'd been the only one shorted; Keller had taken his share and bought a condo in Siesta Key. Roger frowned and felt an oily heat rise up in him.

Roger brought his fingertips together and said, "Business is personal. I would find a way to have my revenge."

"How?"

"Well, it's not like I'd hire a couple of thugs out of Compton, but I get my revenge in the end, and it's usually when they least expect it."

"So you lie in wait? For how long? What's the longest amount of time you've waited to exact revenge?"

"Fourteen years."

"That's what makes you a psychopath!" Holm said merrily. He sat back with a satisfied smile. Roger found it, and him, unnerving.

"But I live a totally normal life," Roger protested.

"Yes, as a nonviolent, well-socialized psychopath. Look, it's not normal to hold on to a grudge that long. In the brain of a psychopath, exceptionalism is the name of the game. So, if a psychopath is ever outsmarted or wronged, it's simply something he or she cannot live with until it's avenged. You like to get even. I can relate."

"What are you saying?"

"Our brain maps match. I'm a psychopath too!" Dr. Holm lifted his coffee cup for a toast. Roger obliged and then thanked him for his analysis.

As he pulled away from Dr. Holm's office, Roger turned the psychopathic-brain news over in his head before ultimately coming to the conclusion that it wasn't such a bad thing. If anything, it was a differentiating factor, one that might give him an added edge in business dealings. By the time he arrived home, Roger had taken his diagnosis in stride, as if it were a tattoo no one could see but him. It was also a secret he'd decided not to share with his wife, Nancy.

That had been seventeen years ago.

Now, as Roger waited for Nancy to get home from one of the hens' houses, he stood out on the balcony of his Hermosa Beach home, puffed on a cigar (Nancy had banned him from doing it in the house), and thought about how was he going to get himself out of this one. A marriage was a contract like any other. His little indiscretion shouldn't void the contract. It was just a matter of negotiation, and he was a master negotiator. He knew he would have to recalibrate his tactics—Nancy would naturally be very hurt and very disinclined to forgive him. But he had a plan. He'd take her to Kauai, her favorite place, for a week. Smother her in coconut oil massages, tropical mai tais, and declarations of love. They'd be back on track in no time. It would cost a pretty penny, but all business deals did. If luck tipped in his favor, this whole mess would be over by the plane ride home—business class, if necessary.

Roger's phone began chirping with the distinctive bluebird ring tone that belonged only to his daughter, Stella—one of the few rings he answered rather than allowing the message to go to voice mail.

"How's my little girl?" Stella would always be a little girl to him, even though she was thirty-six now.

"Well, the kitchen is filled with smoke after one of Sam's failed cooking experiments, but no permanent damage done. Let me step outside."

Roger could hear Sam in the background, swearing loudly at his oven.

"Okay, that's better," Stella said. "So, what's going on with you and Mom?"

"Oh, nothing to worry about. We had a—misunderstanding. Sorry to have worried you earlier. She's got the wrong idea in her head."

There was a pause, and Roger actually held his breath. Even with his diagnosed psychopathy, the one opinion that mattered to him was that of his only daughter.

"Oh, okay. So, it's just Mom being *Mom*, then? Having her annual freak-out? *Pack your bags, we're going on a guilt trip* kind of thing?" Stella joked.

"Sure," Roger said. "Something like that."

"I'm beginning to think Mom just needs a purpose. She needs something to focus on besides her husband and daughter so she can give us a break."

"We'll work it out. I'm waiting for her to get home so we can talk it out. We might head to Kauai next week."

"Oh, good work, Pops. She loves Kauai. She gets crazy sometimes. Jesus, when I met her for breakfast Saturday, she was moaning about how she thought Charlotte was in trouble and that my marriage was on the rocks, all because I said Charlotte dyed her hair purple. She's so melodramatic, it drives me nuts. I can't imagine what you go through."

Roger smiled to himself. On his side as usual. Stella had always been Daddy's girl. When she was young, she was more like a tomboy. Much to Roger's delight, she was interested in sports and she had natural athletic ability. He spent countless hours playing catch, teaching her how to throw a football and how to play golf. Nowadays, her golf handicap was lower than his and he beamed with pride as he bragged about her to his golf buddies. Her golf talents were eclipsed only by her business talents. After flying through college with honors, Stella went into advertising and became a brand director before the unexpected arrival of his granddaughter when she was only twenty-two. For a moment, Roger wondered if Stella was like her mother. But instead of pausing her career upon the arrival of daughter Charlotte, Stella proved her ambition to be as sharp as or sharper than even Roger's. She helped her colleagues win a huge automotive account and fielded competitive offers while pumping milk in the executive washroom. The president of the agency was impressed. Stella would often call her dad for advice on how to deal with certain personalities, and they would generally bond over the deals she made. Roger wondered what great cosmic good deed he had done to deserve the bright and shining light that was his daughter.

Now she was the acting CEO of a highly successful advertising agency in Los Angeles, a cash cow within a larger conglomerate. She was shrewd, smart, analytical, and cold as ice. She reminded him of, well, him. They were kindred spirits in many ways, and Roger knew he and Stella talked about things that really mattered. It kept them close.

Roger momentarily wondered if anything could shake that bond, even something as grave as his latest misdeed. He shook it off and took a sip of his bourbon, confident in the knowledge that Nancy would never disclose the ugly truth about his affair to Stella. He knew Nancy couldn't bring herself to damage Stella's relationship with her father. It would be beyond her decency threshold, a weak personality trait he would obviously exploit. So, he was safe. For this, and for many other reasons, Roger was elated that he didn't have the emotional sensitivity of the rest of the saps in the world. It was, he surmised as he looked out at the gorgeous sunset, the reason he always won.

CHAPTER FIVE
THAR SHE BLOWS

Nancy sat in her car in the driveway of her beach house with the windows rolled down, a sad Jim Croce tune playing on her car stereo. The sun had set twenty minutes ago, and as the winds died down, she could smell cigar smoke that had wafted down from the balcony. Roger must be nervous. He smoked cigars only when he was nervous or celebrating. Since this wasn't exactly a bottle-popping moment, Nancy figured he was as uneasy to face this situation as she was.

She felt exhausted even though the shouting had not yet begun. Oh, and there would be shouting. Roger would bellow. And she would yell. Nancy had never known how to hide her emotions. She had been sensitive since she was a child. She would cry when sad, laugh her head off when happy, and yell when angry, even though her mother told her it wasn't ladylike. As she grew up, she saw how some women were much cagier with their emotions, using them as weapons in relationships, eventually becoming masters at passive-aggressive behavior. Nancy's brand of sensitivity wasn't meant for the world at large, and she eventually learned how to share less and rein in her feelings more. This allowed her to protect herself from toxic friends, fake neighbors, and venomous Tupperware party hosts who would float in and then mercifully out of her life. The beautiful thing about aging was that the older she got, the less she cared. But Nancy still gave a shit about Roger. That was the problem.

She folded down the visor and inspected her face. The lines around her eyes seemed deeper, and she reflected on the fact that it might be time for a few highlights. She looked tired.

She grabbed her purse, put on a little lip tint, and pinched her cheeks to give them some color. She'd be damned if she was going to let Roger see her looking like hell, even if she felt that way.

Ruthie's last comment to her before she left that evening kept ringing through her head. "It's called a doormat, Nance. Don't be one. Not anymore." Nancy cringed as she realized Ruthie knew how much she had given Roger and this marriage. So much that she had made herself invisible and irrelevant. But how could you go from being a doormat to breaking down the door?

Nancy exited the car and shut the door. She heard the scrape of the heavy metal ashtray that Roger used for his cigars being dragged off the ledge. She knew he was stowing it away so she wouldn't see it. Another lie. She climbed the stairs like she was climbing up to the gallows, every footfall heavier than the last. The dark questions loomed. Would an apology be enough? Would a promise of change mean anything? Could she forgive him?

As Nancy was about to turn the handle, the door swung open and Roger stood there, his face tainted with sadness and an expression of possible remorse.

"There's my girl." Roger moved in to give her an awkward hug. Nancy's arms remained at her sides until he released her, and then with the wave of an arm, he ushered her into her own house.

Nancy sat at one of the barstools at the kitchen counter. She turned to look out toward the rest of the room and took in the stunning view. She loved this house. From the French blue cabinets in her kitchen to the wood beams of the vaulted ceiling, right down to the wide plank wood floor, she had loved this house from the moment they first walked into it twenty-five years ago.

Roger quickly prepared a couple of old-fashioneds for them. He set her favorite crystal tumbler in front of her full of bourbon and an amarena cherry.

Nancy took a sip and let the bourbon sting her lips as the drink allayed her nerves, like an emery board taking off the rougher edges of her emotions.

Roger was nervous too, a rare state for him. He paced across the living room floor and rambled on about inconsequential things. Something about getting the garage door repaired because it had a squeaking noise.

"Squeaking noise" brought it all back. Claire's long tanned legs, Roger's bare white ass, and the squeak of his boat shoes in the galley of their boat.

"Can we cut the shit, Roger?"

Silence. Roger stopped pacing and set down his drink in a way that made it seem like he was ready for his punishment.

"How could you do that to me?" She kept her gaze even.

Roger didn't look at her. Instead he turned back toward the kitchen and took a deep breath. As he exhaled, his shoulders slumped and he gave a shrug. "It's not that simple, Nance."

"You mean there's more than one reason you were giving Claire Sanford the high hard one on our boat?"

"It doesn't come down to reasons." Roger looked into his drink. Then he looked at Nancy. "Is there a reason that would work?"

Nancy remained silent, searching for a way forward. She knew there wasn't one. Then she asked what she really wanted to know. "Why would you put everything at risk like this? Our family, the life we've built?"

Roger stood stock-still, and she could sense his anger at being trapped. "What were you doing there anyway?" he yelled. "Especially with that pack of old crones!"

"I was there to show them *Bucephalus* to see if we could auction off a sunset cruise for charity. Further proving that no good deed goes unpunished."

Roger picked up his old-fashioned and downed it in one gulp. He set the glass down and instantly looked for the bottle of bourbon.

"Were there others?"

"On the boat?"

"No, I mean others. Over the years?" Nancy looked at him, waiting for his answer. Knowing he would lie. Two years after they were married, when Nancy was nursing Stella and too exhausted to take care of her husband's needs, she'd found a distinctive silver earring in the pants pocket of his suit. She remembered seeing the same cheap bauble on the earlobe of his secretary, Crystal, also a cheap bauble. Then, a few years later, a woman from hotel room service in Santa Cruz mistakenly called Nancy's number—because it was on the credit card file—to confirm that a bottle of champagne for two was to be delivered to Room 203, even though Roger was supposed to be in San Francisco on a business trip. Nancy had chosen to preserve her family at the time. To preserve her sense of safety, her way of life, even if it was a lie.

But that was a long time ago. And things had changed. Stella was a grown woman, and there was little holding Nancy and Roger together beyond the yacht club. Plus, it had been Claire. On their boat. With witnesses. It was too much to look away from. Like a cruise ship ruining the view of a pristine coastline, it was impossible to ignore.

Roger didn't answer immediately. Instead, he went on the attack. "Nance, do you know what it takes to be successful in this life?"

"A conscience?" Nancy interjected. She got up from the barstool and headed toward the balcony of the house. Roger mechanically followed.

Roger continued as if he hadn't heard her. "It takes balls and brains. And only certain men have the luck to have both, and I am one of those men. I can take a failing company and turn it around in eighteen months. Are there hard decisions to be made? Always. And who's going to make them? A man with brains and balls, that's who."

"What's your point, Balls for Brains?"

"Balls *and* brains! The point is, you don't have the capacity to understand me."

"Let me see if I can parse this out. You, your balls, and your brains are having a tough time being understood, and apparently the answers are between the legs of Claire Sanford?"

"What can I say? What would work? She's . . . exciting," he said. He paused a minute, then implored, "Do you understand the patience it takes to be with the same person for decades? The same warmed-over conversations, the same fights, the same sex, the same sameness!"

Good god, the gall. "Your sad plight is called marriage, you shithead."

There was a long silence.

Nancy shook her head slowly and said sadly, "She's exciting."

"She's different, that's all!" Roger replied sharply. Then he added, "Come on, Nance, let's go to Kauai. We can smooth over this rough patch poolside with some mai tais. You know how much you love mai tais. Let me make it up to you."

Nancy thought for a moment, then squinted at Roger. "Wait a minute. Is Kauai a makeup trip for your transgressions?"

Roger sputtered, "What do you mean?"

"You surprised me in '92. I thought it was for my birthday, which you forgot that year. But it was also right after your floozy secretary, Crystal, left the firm." Nancy was putting it all together and picking up steam. "And then you took me again three years later after an unnamed woman kept calling the house. You've taken me to Kauai six times over the last thirty years. So, by my count, that's six women. Am I right, Roger?"

Caught off guard, Roger stammered, "No, that was, uh . . . you've got it all wrong."

Nancy turned toward him. "Yeah, I've got it all wrong. You count on making me believe that, don't you?" She could feel something rising in her she hadn't felt in decades. The pilot light of her strength, which she'd thought had been snuffed out long ago, was relit, ever so faintly, and the trapped fury was beginning to build.

"Goddamn it, you silly hen!" Roger bellowed, his face red, his eyes bulging.

Nancy stood there in the wake of his tirade, the word *hen* still hanging in the air like a stale fart in a windowless room, thinking about how stupid she'd been. Just then that same warm breeze she'd felt at the Yacht Club came over her again, a window left open somewhere inviting it in. She took a deep breath as if she were about to yell something in return. Then she started to laugh.

"Why are you laughing?" Roger said, irritation in his tone.

But Nancy just couldn't help herself. She giggled and held her stomach and bent over and laughed until she had tears in her eyes.

Roger slugged some of her bourbon, and while Nancy laughed, he muttered, "You're crazy."

And then Nancy gathered her composure and stopped. She wiped a tear away, stared at her husband, and said calmly, "I'm leaving you, Roger."

Roger stared back with an amused expression. He huffed. "You're what?"

"Leaving you." Nancy took one last look at the expansive view of beautiful Hermosa Beach, went back in, and headed downstairs to pack a bag. Roger sat dazed in the kitchen for a moment, and then she could hear his quick, angry steps coming toward her.

"You think you can just leave me?" Roger said, standing in the doorway of the bedroom as Nancy stuffed underwear, socks, and random clothes into a royal-blue Tumi duffel bag.

"Well, if I am the silly boner-killer hen you say I am, then by all means, we have run our course. Our happiness tank is on empty, and you and Claire deserve each other," Nancy declared as she stuffed a swimsuit in her bag.

Roger sputtered for a minute, then said, "I hope you're not suggesting we get divorced."

"I'm sure that'll be part of the plan, Rog. That's what *leaving you* means. We can split what we've got right down the middle and go our separate ways. Or I'll make you a deal—you can have the house if I can have *Bucephalus* and a fair share of our investments to make it even."

This time when he addressed her, Nancy noted his change in tone. It was cold and hard. It was how she had heard him deal with Rick Keller, who'd swindled him years ago. She felt a chill run down her back.

"Oh, sweetheart," Roger chuckled. "There is no way I'm giving you a divorce. There is no way in living hell that I will let you sully the Hadley name with divorce. Not without the dirtiest fight in the history of divorces."

She shook her head slowly and said, "You should have thought about the hallowed Hadley name before you were balls-deep in Claire Sanford."

Nancy took one last look at Roger. He was glaring at her, his face red, eyes cold and hard. She knew Roger shielded her from his baser instincts. She knew he could be cruel. And now that she had crossed his invisible boundary, she could feel the gale-force winds of his fury. Best to leave and let him calm down. She grabbed her duffel bag, put Suzanne in her cat carrier, and headed toward the car. Filled with the momentary strength of being right, Nancy threw her bag in the back seat, gently set Suzanne down in the front, and started the car.

Just as she was beginning to back out, Roger came out and stood in front of the car. The headlights shone on his red face, his icy stare. He stuck his chin out and made a damning declaration.

"This isn't going to go the way you think it will, Nancy. I will cripple you. And you will never get that boat." Roger stood there with his arms crossed over his chest.

Nancy backed out of the driveway, narrowly missing Roger's golf clubs, which were resting on a stand off to the right.

"You will be back. And you will be groveling," he stated firmly.

Nancy stopped the car and stared at her arrogant, cheating husband. In one swift move, she put the car in drive, turned the wheel slightly to the right, hit the gas, and mowed down Roger's golf clubs.

Roger roared, "*No!*" He ran over to the wreckage of his clubs. "Goddamn it, woman!" He came running at the car, but she was already backing up.

This time she turned her car toward the marina, and right before she pulled away, she flipped Roger the bird.

CHAPTER SIX
CHANGES IN LATITUDE

When Nancy put her bird-flipping fingers back on the steering wheel, they were trembling. Anxiety and fear coursed through her as she took a couple of deep breaths to calm down. She headed south on PCH—the Pacific Coast Highway—driving along the coast until she started heading up into the hills of Palos Verdes. She turned right toward Malaga Cove, and a grand view of the Pacific appeared. The sun was setting behind a wall of fog, creating an eerie twilight. A bright-orange afterglow peeked out under the murky, dark fog just above the water, and the same warm breeze that had been present over the last few days gently swept the scent of lilacs into her driver's side window.

Lilacs. Their heady, sweet scent brought back memories of her mom and the last day she'd seen her alive. She'd been eighteen years old, her mother Grace only forty-three. Nancy had stopped on the side of the road on that warm July day and, using a pocketknife attached to her key chain, cut off a few of the branches in bloom, then tied them together with the elastic that had been holding her ponytail in place. She cruised to Mount Carmel Hospital in her rusted Chevy Nova and parked in the same lot she'd been using for six weeks. As she walked down the corridors, she greeted the familiar nurses, Lorraine and Elsa, and braced herself for the antiseptic smell.

As she headed down the hallway, she heard the relentless whir of the machines in every room until she reached Room 21A and caught sight of her ever-disappearing mother attached to tubes and wires. But today the lilacs fought those acrid smells, and for the briefest of moments, her mom sat up with a light in her eyes and smiled. Lilacs were her favorite.

"Oh, honey, how beautiful." Her mom smiled, albeit weakly, her glassy eyes looking Nancy over, flooded with love and pride. Nancy's heart palpitated, beating three or four times in quick succession, making her dizzy, as if it knew what was happening before her mind did.

Nancy took her mom's hand and said, "I ripped them off from Old Man Bergman's yard. I could hear his stupid dog barking his face off the whole time."

Her mom gently laughed.

"They're lovely. I apologize if I'm a little tired today."

"It's okay, Mom. We'll get you some Jell-O, and then you can rest. I'm here for the next couple hours."

"Not the lime Jell-O. I hate that shit."

"Got it, the red. I'll get Nurse Lorraine to rustle us up some red Jell-O. When you come home, I'll have it stocked in the fridge."

Her mom turned her head and looked at her, a single tear falling from her eye. "Sounds good. It's the snack of champions. How are the girls?"

"Everyone's fine. Judy can't decide on what dress to wear on her second date with Gordon. Lois and Chris are headed up to Cambria for the weekend."

Grace's eyebrows rose. "Their first time away, together? Scandalous."

Nancy laughed. "Yes, I think they both lied to their parents. But they're so great together, they'll wind up married, so what's the harm?"

"And how about Ruthie?"

"Ruthie's failing chemistry but dating some cute guy on the water polo team."

Grace smiled, then winced as she tried to move. One of the machines that was hooked to her started to beep loudly. It had happened before. Nancy waited for Nurse Lorraine, the Wednesday and Thursday evening nurse and her favorite, to come in and adjust the machines so all alarm would be quelled for a time.

Like clockwork, Lorraine arrived seven seconds later. She efficiently walked over to the machines and turned off the beeping. Her sleek black hair was tucked under her nurse's hat with bobby pins, and her bright-red lipstick amplified her beautiful dark-brown skin. She adjusted her bifocals and said, "Hi, kiddo. How was the softball game?"

"It was good. We won twelve to nine, and I hit a double over the head of a short third baseman. You think we could get some red Jell-O? Not the lime, she—"

"—hates that shit," Lorraine interrupted. "Yeah, I know. Your mom's picky about her Jell-O." She looked at Grace lovingly, then back to Nancy. "Good for you on the game. Hey, can you meet me in the hallway for a sec?"

Lorraine, always optimistic in Grace's presence, met Nancy in the hallway to tell her the things the doctors couldn't or wouldn't discuss. Lorraine had a way of delivering news in a no-bullshit manner that still had a tinge of love in it. Nancy followed her out. When Lorraine turned, her cheerful disposition had disappeared.

"Nancy, listen . . . your mom . . . she's not healing from the surgery. I think you have to . . . prepare."

Nancy blinked once and said, "Nah, she'll recover." She had rejected the doomsday predictions before. Every time they'd told her Grace might not live through the night, her mom had defied every goddamn doctor who told Nancy to "prepare." Six separate times and three different doctors. And today, on the day the lilacs were in bloom and her mom had smiled, it was a day of hope, not doom. "She's had bad days before. She'll come out of it. She's strong."

Lorraine stared at her with an expression Nancy read as concern, maybe even pity.

"Honey, it's different today," Lorraine said, and then, out of the blue, she hugged her. And that's when the long slimy tentacle of dread took hold of Nancy's heart again.

Nancy walked back in and took her usual position on the chair next to her mom's bed. Grace had dozed off. Nancy held her mom's hand and inspected her thin, cracked nails. She discreetly checked her mom's pulse and felt a faint but steady beat. She put her head on her chest and listened to her breathing. She inspected her face, so closely she could smell the sweat from her brow. Perhaps if she got close enough, she could transfer some of her strength, some of her healthy energy into her mom. She sat back and looked out the window, where a breeze was rustling the leaves on the maple tree outside. She looked over at the lilacs and thought about how brief their season was. Those fragrant, delicate blossoms appeared for only a fortnight. Maybe that was true of all beautiful things. Maybe nothing lasted. Maybe it all went away too soon.

About an hour later, when the daylight began to wane, Grace began to breathe irregularly, her breath coming in gasps, then stopping for a few seconds. The machines went off again, and this time they sounded like sirens blaring a dark warning.

Lorraine arrived within seconds and turned the machines off. She leveled her eyes at Nancy. Putting her hand on the machine that delivered morphine to her mom, she tapped it twice, delivering a double dose to obliterate any pain. Lorraine took Nancy's hand and held it, her soulful eyes full of pain. Then she left Nancy alone with her mom.

Nancy got close to Grace, whispering in desperation. The moments between her mom's fragile, ragged breaths felt agonizing.

Blind panic set her mind racing. This couldn't be the end. She wasn't ready.

"Breathe, Mom. Please. Breathe!" Nancy sobbed.

But the silence between breaths grew longer and longer. Nancy counted seconds, and when she reached thirty-one, there was one last breath that came from her tiny body as it shuddered, releasing her downy spirit so it could drift skyward. Nancy sat alone, feeling the warmth leave her mother's delicate hand, and then the coldness of the room encroached. She searched her mother's face for details to remember so that she wouldn't forget how beautiful she was, trying to hold on to her, trying to let go, trying to see through the tears, trying to unclench her stomach. Trying to say good-bye in any way that made sense.

But after a few minutes, Nancy knew her mom wasn't in the room anymore. She could feel it. She tried to stand but nearly fell over. Lorraine came back in. She came over to hug her, and then she let go and just sat with Nancy until the room grew dark. At some point, Lorraine helped her up, and Nancy was able to leave. She walked away in a deep and confusing numbness.

In the weeks after her mom died, Nancy walked through life in a hopeless fog. She went through the motions while her best friends helped her make the funeral arrangements, order flowers, and fill out insurance forms. She tried to put a face of strength out to the world. But the little girl inside her crawled into a closet in her mind and shut the door. This dark solitary place inside her was the only place she felt she could survive. Her mom, her home, her life was lost. The path back to where she had been before had disappeared. There was no safe place in the world to hide from this kind of pain, and confusion set in. She had nowhere to go and no idea how to make it to tomorrow. Everything had come crashing down in the space of a few short months. Panic and dread rose like thunder in her chest as she came to the chilling truth that she was alone. Her mother was like the lilacs. Brief, beautiful, and destined to die too soon.

* * *

Now, years later, that same crippling panic tightened its grip as she drove along the cliffs of Palos Verdes. For the third time in her life, Nancy felt lost from circumstances beyond her control. She felt the sweat on her brow, her mind reeling, not able to decide where to go, what to do, and in some ways, Nancy realized, she was the same terrified, motherless eighteen-year-old girl who'd sat in the dark in a Mount Carmel hospital room.

Her phone rang. It was Ruthie. Nancy answered but didn't say anything, as she had a lump in her throat and tears in her eyes.

"Nance, are you okay?"

Nancy shook her head. Still didn't say a word.

"Tell me where you are."

Nancy let out a sob and then sputtered into the phone, "I'm going to Terranea for the night."

"I'll be there in twenty minutes. Get a dog-friendly room. Otis can hear you crying, and he's not taking 'no dogs allowed' for an answer."

CHAPTER SEVEN
A STORM ON THE HORIZON

"Somehow drowning your sorrows is much easier when you have Mitch, the hot waiter, delivering frosty Moscow mules and fully loaded nachos poolside. Go figure," Ruthie said as she let Otis lick nacho cheese sauce off her thumb.

Such was the situation Nancy and Ruthie found themselves in for the next two days at Terranea, a swanky resort beautifully situated on the cliffs of Palos Verdes with a view across the Pacific to Catalina Island. Nancy had plunked down her and Roger's joint credit card and grief-splurged on a premium villa. The chief advantage of the villa, which cost more for a night than the average monthly mortgage payment on a modest house in Cleveland, was that Otis the dog was readily allowed. Ruthie applauded Nancy for her audacity in springing for such expensive digs, especially since Nancy had historically been thrifty. Not cheap, mind you, just value conscious.

Nancy sat mute in her beach chair, ice melting in her copper cup, staring gloomily out at the sea.

Ruthie cracked open a bottle of hyperexpensive bottled water and poured it into a doggy bowl for Otis, who gleefully lapped it up.

"Don't get too used to this fancy Fiji water, Otis. Back home you're going back to good ole Redondo tap." Ruthie took a sip of her Moscow mule. "That brings up a great question, Nancy. What are your plans after this rue-filled resort stay? Should I make up the spare for you?"

Nancy sighed heavily and watched a pod of dolphins lazily swim by. "Roger said, 'You'll never get that boat.' So full of venom. He knows I can sail that boat better than he can. He just can't stomach the thought of me having it. And truth be told, I probably couldn't set foot on it without suffering flashbacks to Claire Sanford's naked heinie all over the polished burl wood table." Nancy involuntarily winced, as if she'd taken a bullet, at the hideous vision. She sipped on her watered-down drink and slumped lower in her chair.

Ruthie deftly ordered another drink with a small *bring it on* flick of her wrist to Mitch, the pool boy. Mitch winked at her and jogged off to the bar.

"What about Stella? Could you stay with her for a while?" Ruthie asked.

"I suppose I could. But what do I tell her?" Nancy asked.

"Tell her the truth," Ruthie implored. "Her father was playing a lively game of slap and tickle with another woman. Surely she'll understand."

"No, I can't do that. I'm not putting Stella in the middle."

"She's thirty-six! She can handle it!". Ruthie said, exasperated. "Your principled ways really make it difficult for my devious, scheming brain to help you."

Nancy understood that Ruthie was only trying to help. But she wasn't going to be the one to tell Stella about her father. It would make her seem vindictive, and she couldn't be the reason Stella's relationship with her father was damaged. No, she would take the high road. But taking the high road meant she couldn't stay with her daughter. There would be too many questions. She stared out at the ocean and realized she had no good options. "Shit, that reminds me. My granddaughter is supposed to stay with me in about a week."

"I know of this great beach cottage in Redondo. Comes with free margaritas and a dog named Otis," Ruthie said.

"Okay, maybe I can stay at your house for a bit. But I promise to be out as soon as I can," Nancy said.

"Excellent. I'll make up the spare room for you and the study for Charlotte. We'll have a blast!"

Nancy grew quiet and contemplated her near future. "Thank you. You know I need a long-term plan though, Ruthie."

Ruthie softened and gave her a look of understanding. "Look—you taking this step? This is huge for you. I thought we would howl at the moon after too many cocktails, wake up with a wicked hang-over, with your resolve to leave Roger in shambles. But this . . . this is an unexpected plot twist."

Ruthie knew her too well. Nancy said, "Truth be told, that's what I thought was going to happen too. It would be easy to go back to him. He wants me back. Not because he adores me, mind you, but because I make him look good for all of his boards and country club memberships. It'd be easy to walk back into the life we built—my house, my comfortable lifestyle, my safety, my boat." Nancy bowed her head in frustration and continued, "But it's all bullshit. Maybe it has been for a while. Maybe it's the booze giving me courage, but I don't think my self-respect will let me go back."

Ruthie nodded and said, "Yes, self-respect often leads us down difficult paths."

"I'm facing divorce. I can't believe I'm going to be divorced. I have grandchildren, for Christ's sake. I'm on the cusp of that age where most people throw in the towel. I mean, sixty is looming like a damn wrecking ball, and I'm going to be single? On my own? Doesn't that sound just a little bit crazy?"

Ruthie took a moment before she answered. "No. You're not crazy to want a loving, happy marriage. But that's not what you got, kid." Ruthie lifted her floppy hat and grew serious for a moment. "Nance, Roger likes to win. He *has* to win. It's part of his nature. That's what worries me about this situation. If he won't grant you a divorce easily, it means he'll fight you with a horde of lawyers who could tie this up for years. Which means all of your marital assets will be frozen until it resolves. You'll be forced to live like a pauper."

At that moment, a balmy breeze kicked up off the cliffs and swept over into the pool area, where it blew Nancy's umbrella out of her drink and Ruthie's hat off her head. And despite the warmth of the wind, Nancy got the chills.

* * *

The next morning, Nancy and Ruthie stood in the opulent marbled lobby listening to a cellist play a soothing version of Bob Marley's "Is This Love" while they waited to pay the bill. A stunningly pretty hotel clerk named Brittany, with sun-kissed skin and a sparkling smile, had just taken Nancy's Platinum American Express card and handed each of them a complimentary cucumber water while they waited.

"Way to wallow, girl," Ruthie said as she nodded to Nancy and petted Otis, who had comfortably snuggled into her oversized purse. "I'll miss those fluffy bathrobes."

"Best to go out in an extravagant financial blaze of glory, I think," Nancy replied.

"Nancy? Nancy Hadley?" A familiar nasal voice rang out above the cellist, and Nancy cringed and turned. Standing right behind her was Joanne Rumpel, perfectly coifed and dressed in expensive resort wear that included white capri pants, a pink polo shirt, and a giant matching pink visor. Nancy could smell Joanne's perfume, a combination of gardenia and money, as she drew closer. Joanne and her husband, Earl, lived two houses down from her and Roger. They had come from Santa Monica four years ago. Rumor had it that they had bought a newly finished beach house only to immediately remodel everything in it because Joanne needed heated floors in the kitchen and an elevator to the wine cellar. They were that kind of insufferably rich. They were also shameless gossips.

"Oh, hello, Joanne," Nancy said, as she willed herself to air-kiss Joanne's cheek.

"Where is Roger? We must have champagne by the pool!" Joanne exclaimed, but then gave a confused expression as she looked over to Ruthie and Otis.

"No, I'm here with my best friend Ruthie. We were, uh . . . we were . . ."

Ruthie interjected and said, "We're celebrating."

Nancy pinched Ruthie's elbow; she didn't want this rich shrew knowing her business.

"Oh, what's the occasion? Don't tell me you got a new boat!"

Ruthie stammered for a second and then replied, "Uh, we were celebrating my divorce."

"Oh!" Joanne said with an uncomfortable laugh. "A little dark, but lord knows I've celebrated a divorce. Or three!" She pointed over at Earl, who was looking at golf literature. "Fourth time's the charm, right?"

"Well, I hope you guys enjoy your stay. We're just checking out."

"Of course, another time. In fact, we were hoping you and Roger could join us for our annual summer solstice party. It's the weekend after next."

Nancy blinked for a moment, reorganizing her thoughts to come up with a plausible excuse. "Oh, I'm not quite sure. We might be heading to the desert that weekend."

Effervescent Brittany returned to the counter. "Um, I'm sorry, Mrs. Hadley, but there seems to be something wrong with your card. It isn't going through. Do you have another one?" Her smile was blinding.

Nancy looked at Brittany for a second. And then at her card. "You ran it through and it didn't work?"

"Yes, ma'am. Twice declined. No biggie. Sometimes there's a glitch with the new embedded cards." Brittany cleared her perfect little throat.

Nancy squinted at her credit card as if betrayal were hidden somewhere in the metallic strip. She glanced over at Joanne, who quickly looked down at the marble floor. "No problem. Use this one." She handed the clerk a Mastercard, her stomach involuntarily clenching.

"Thanks! Back in a jiffy!" Brittany said with an overly enthusiastic smile as she walked to the back counter to run the card.

Joanne said, "The desert! How lovely!"

"Yes, so can I let you know about the summer solstice party?" Nancy asked.

"Of course!"

"Great," Nancy said as she waved her off. She didn't owe Joanne Rumpel an explanation of her future plans. She turned back to Ruthie, who was acting as a safe cove amid the well-dressed sharks in her social strata.

"She's like a walking, talking Bitmoji," Ruthie said as she observed Brittany, the hotel clerk.

"What's a Bitmoji?" Nancy asked, happy for Ruthie's interruption. Anything to get away from conversation with the Rumpels.

"It's like a cartoon version of yourself that you use in text messages. See? I have one."

Nancy looked at Ruthie's phone and saw a cartoon that looked like Ruthie, only cuter and younger. Cartoon Ruthie was holding a glass and had a caption that read *It's Wine Time!*

"I need a Bitmoji."

"I'll make you one." Ruthie grabbed Nancy's phone and got busy.

Brittany came back from the counter, smile gone. "I'm so sorry, Mrs. Hadley, but this one doesn't work either. *Sad face*," she said, matching her words with a frown.

Nancy felt the hair on the back of her neck begin to tingle. Without even looking in the Rumpels' general direction, she felt their eyebrows rise. How could her credit cards be declined? "Here, try this one, and if it doesn't work, do you take debit cards?"

Brittany said, "Yes, ma'am." She took the other credit card and turned back toward the counter, all previous charm gone.

Ruthie handed Nancy her phone back and gave her a skeptical look. "You don't think this is Roger's doing, do you?"

"He wouldn't cut off my credit cards," Nancy said uncertainly, then muttered, more to herself, "He better not have cut off my credit cards." She looked at her newly created Bitmoji. It had long blondish-silver hair, bright-blue eyes, a great smile, and perky boobs. It was an adorable version of her. "I love her. Besides, isn't that illegal?"

"Enhanced Bitmoji boob size? Totally legal. And so is cutting off your credit card access if he's the primary cardholder and you're just an added cardholder. Tell me you have at least one card where you're the primary," Ruthie said.

Nancy stood there, thinking hard. Were any of the cards hers?

Brittany returned with her blinding smile, sunshiny charm back intact. "Good news, Mrs. Hadley! Your third credit card did *not* go through, but I asked my manager, and she said we could just charge it to the credit card you and your husband used last month!"

Ruthie looked at Nancy.

Nancy looked at Brittany as if she were speaking some foreign language. "Of course." She had been nowhere near Terranea last month. "Refresh my memory, Brittany; what were the dates of that stay? It's for tax purposes."

"Um, let's see, you and Mr. Hadley stayed two nights. The fifteenth and the sixteenth."

Nancy quickly opened the calendar on her phone. She had Roger down for a business golf outing in Carlsbad. Not Terranea.

The gall. Roger had been here, a mere twelve miles away from their home, with someone else.

Ruthie instantly understood and muttered, "The balls."

"Yep, but not the brains," Nancy said, flustered by this revelation. She turned to answer Brittany. "Yes, thank you. Charge that card. That'll be fine."

She turned to the Rumpels, who had obviously witnessed the awkward exchange.

"So, we'll put you and Roger down as a maybe to the summer solstice party! Ta-ta!" Joanne and Earl moved away to the other side of the counter.

"Ta," Nancy said, as she gave a dismissive wave. Then she turned back to the hotel clerk. "Excuse me, Brittany. Before you run that card, how much are those luxurious fluffy Terranea bathrobes?"

"They're four hundred dollars each, Mrs. Hadley."

"Great," Nancy said. "We'll take two."

Brittany brought over the bill, and Nancy signed it. Two beautifully boxed Terranea bathrobes were delivered to Nancy and Ruthie right before they left the lobby.

"Right on! Divorce looks good on you, Nance," Ruthie said as she hugged her robe.

But Nancy's brain was spinning. None of her credit cards worked. She was a joint tenant on the bank accounts, which meant Roger couldn't cut her off without the bank contacting her first. But on all the credit accounts, she was merely a cardholder, not a primary. She couldn't even get a gallon of gas if that was the case. But would Roger really do that? Could he? If he had the stainless-steel balls to cut her off, payback was in order. But first, she had to make some calls.

* * *

After dropping Ruthie off, Nancy drove to the Yellow Vase, one of her favorite cafés in Redondo Beach, ordered a latte, and sat down at a picnic table outside. She called the number on each credit card in her wallet to find out that Roger had indeed taken her off every account. She could feel the heat rising in her face and chest like a hot flash from hell. After ruthlessly berating several overly polite call center operators, she finally spoke to a supervisor.

"How is this possible? I mean, I've had this credit card for fifteen years, never late on a payment, and you didn't think to notify me when my husband suddenly blocked my access?"

"Sadly, it happens a lot," said Shreya Shimani, the call center supervisor. "The primary cardholder has the control. But, if you ask me, you should simply apply for a new credit card with us right now. I can help you."

"How, though? I have no credit of my own."

"You share bank accounts with your husband? And you were a joint cardholder on other credit cards?"

"Yes, and I'm still a joint tenant on the bank accounts."

"So, it's still your money, still your balance," Ms. Shimani said. "You likely have excellent credit, and it's the joint account that sustains that credit rating. Let's see what we can get you."

After about five minutes of being placed on hold, during which Nancy daydreamed about how to get back at Roger, Shreya came back on the line.

"Good news. Not only did you qualify for one of our most generous credit cards, which gives you airline miles with every purchase, but your credit rating allowed for a thirty-five-thousand-dollar credit line. I've taken the liberty of approving your new card, to be sent via FedEx overnight at no charge. You should have it delivered to one fourteen Avenue J, Redondo Beach, California, nine-oh-two-seven-seven, no later than noon tomorrow."

Ruthie's address and Nancy's temporary home. Nancy smiled. She was pretty sure Ms. Shimani was smiling on the other end as well. "Shreya, thank you so much for helping me with this issue. Without getting too deep into my dirty laundry, you've literally saved the day."

There was a pause, and then Ms. Shimani said, "Mrs. Hadley, let me just say that I've had my own burdens to bear. If ever I can help out a customer who has run aground because of an incorrigible spouse, I will do so. And I don't care if this call is recorded. I've sent an email confirmation; within it is my direct line if you need anything else. Good luck."

Girl code.

Nancy smiled again. "Thank you. For everything," she said, and hung up.

It was three o'clock in the afternoon when Nancy finally got everything sorted out with the credit cards. She had to make one more stop and then head to Ruthie's. She picked up her phone and sent a group text to her girls. It simply read:

5pm at Ruthie's. Code Blue. Tacos will be served.

* * *

Across town, in a ranch-style home nestled in the tree section of Manhattan Beach, Lois was plucking dead leaves from a fern hanging in a seventies macrame plant holder on the back porch when Nancy's text came in on her phone. She called out to Chris, her darling husband of thirty-five years, "Babe, I'm going to Ruthie's tonight! Code blue."

"Blue. Is that celebratory or plotting revenge?" Chris answered from the garage, where he was building a tube amp stereo.

"Revenge!"

"All righty then. I'll see if any of the boys want to go to Ercoles for a burger. Try not to get arrested."

Lois changed into her workout pants, threw on an old UCLA sweatshirt, and headed out the door with a bottle of wine in her purse.

* * *

Over in a quiet neighborhood in Torrance, Judy sat on her sofa with a cup of tea, her finger hovering over the *Add to Cart* button on her iPad, unsure whether or not to buy a book on Amazon. Flush with the insurance money, Judy was hopelessly unable to decide how to spend it, even in the most miniscule amounts. The text from Nancy came in.

"Oh my," she said to herself, her excitement rising. Her otherwise quiet life was about to see some action.

Judy canceled her transaction, finished her tea, and went into the bedroom to put on a fresh pair of linen pants.

* * *

Back in Redondo, Ruthie came in through the front doors of her beach cottage armed with two Trader Joe's bags filled with cheese, crackers, wine, and tequila. Otis followed along, carrying his own bag of unopened dog treats.

"Otis, Nancy is bringing Suzanne the Cat over. Please try to get along."

Otis let out a whimpering *arf* of surrender.

CHAPTER EIGHT

SETTING A COURSE FOR ADVENTURE

In the days since Nancy had flipped Roger the bird in his own driveway, with the threat of divorce hanging in the air, Roger had used his time wisely. He'd reflected on the events that had transpired, smoked many cigars on the balcony, tried to feel remorse and/or culpability for the unfortunate incident with Claire Sanford, failed miserably at feeling miserable, and then proceeded to do what he did best—put the screws to Nancy in an effort to get her back under his control.

He knew that the quickest way to get her attention would be to render her helpless, and by helpless he meant moneyless. Just briefly, of course. He had promptly canceled her access to all their credit cards and waited for her to contact him—like shutting off the Wi-Fi in a roomful of phone-obsessed teenagers. It was only a matter of time before she came crawling back. Any minute now she would call him, outraged, and this would afford Roger another opportunity to lay out all the reasons it made sense for Nancy to come home and stay home. After all, he was on the verge of securing the most lucrative land development deal in the history of his highly successful—albeit ruthless—development company, and he wasn't going to let anything screw it up. Especially something within his full control, like his wife. He had to get his house in order before any real or lasting damage could be done.

* * *

Nancy shoved the cashier's check from First Bank of Manhattan Beach into her purse and put it safely next to the other two checks from Fidelity Bank and Great Western Bank. She was surprised at how easy it had been. She had walked in, filled out a form, signed her name, and in turn received exactly half the money, plus one penny, from each of the three bank accounts she and Roger shared. Half was her rightful portion. The penny was for pain and suffering. A small but significant majority, a symbolic thumb of her nose to Roger "Balls and Brains" Hadley. She had visited the banks after the Terranea episode and secured the checks right before the banks closed. Roger wouldn't know until the next morning that she had legally withdrawn half their liquid cash.

As afternoon turned to twilight, Nancy's last move was to go to the house. She filled two suitcases with her favorite things, including her French pepper grinder, a turquoise Dutch oven, a few framed pictures (none included Roger), and her Tempur-Pedic pillow, and loaded everything into the car.

On her way out the front door, Nancy looked at the Nest, a fancy thermostat mounted on the wall that could be controlled from a smartphone. Roger had bought it last year over Nancy's firm objection. She had hated the new device, mostly because she preferred the familiar, reliable old thermostat, which she knew how to use and which had never let them down. She hadn't understood why it should be discarded for this new, trendy model. It had taken her more than three months to learn how to operate the damn thing.

She frowned at the round, shiny face of the Nest and realized how much she had in common with the old thermostat. Disposed of for no good reason other than its age. Nancy tapped the Nest app on her smartphone; it opened with a swirly flair as an animated thermostat popped up right there on her screen. She turned on the AC and set it to a chilly fifty-two degrees. Then she changed the password on the high-tech instrument, closed the app, and walked out of the house she had lived in for more than twenty-five years.

CHAPTER NINE
UNCHARTED TERRITORY

Halfway through a carne asada taco, Nancy found her initial anger waning and giving way to helplessness and anxiety. The girls had listened, appalled at Roger's threats, as she relayed the story from their confrontation, then the credit card incident at Terranea. The girls' plans for payback were in full swing, while Otis had his own problems to contend with, as Suzanne the Cat had smugly taken over his dog bed. Revenge was not a normal affair for Nancy, so she struggled with it.

"How about we hire a couple of thugs to go over and beat some sense into him?" Lois offered.

"No, Roger would just offer them triple the money or worse, put them on staff as security. Plus, I don't want to *actually* cripple the man."

"Public embarrassment? Get on social media and talk about the incident with Claire?" Judy said.

Nancy thought for a few seconds and then shook her head. "No one over fifty uses social media. Besides, Stella could find out that way."

"What about a scandal?" Ruthie offered. "Roger Hadley 'and his good name' cannot afford a scandal."

"Hmmm. Could I dangle the prospect of a scandal over him to force the divorce?" Nancy mused as she finished her margarita. "Back in the day, cheating was scandal enough, but men barely get a slap on the hand for that nowadays. We'd need some type of business scandal, but I don't have any proof of that. Besides, I have to start thinking about my next steps. I only have what I took from the bank accounts. Enough to live on for now but not enough for more than a year."

"You can stay here as long as you like," Ruthie said as she fed some salami to poor, bedless Otis, who sat uncomfortably on the hard tile floor, far from the razor-sharp claws of Suzanne the Cat.

"I know, Ruthie. But I can't stay here forever. We're not Laverne and Shirley."

"I loved Laverne and Shirley," Ruthie protested.

"Plus," Nancy continued, "I have to figure out my options if Roger does tie up the divorce. I mean, am I going to end up in some bougie apartment complex like Bali Hai Gardens? They're the only places with rent control, right?"

"My flight attendant friend Holly lived in one of those for a few years," Lois said. "Constantly got hit on by other tenants. I think even the pool repairman took a shot. She said she could never relax. And they kept hosting tiki-themed potluck dinners in the courtyard. Lots of seven-layer dip, I recall. Very depressing."

"Oh god," Nancy whined. "I hate seven-layer dip."

"You will not wind up in Bali Hai Gardens, for Christ's sakes. We can think of better options," said Judy.

Nancy shrugged. "Real estate in Hermosa is out of control. Even a two-bedroom hovel on the east side of PCH is running around a million and a half dollars. It's insane." She sighed. "I'd be happy if the old bastard just left me the boat. I'd live on that."

"That seems reasonable. Why not ask him for it?" Lois asked.

"I did. In so many words, he said he'd sooner chew off his own foot than give *Bucephalus* to me. Not because he loves the boat but because he knows how much I love it. Spiteful shithead," she muttered.

There was a momentary pause in the brainstorming session as all four women thought about and dismissed one option after another. Judy popped an olive into her mouth, then sat up suddenly and said, "Hey, why don't you buy your own damn boat?"

All three of them stopped for a minute and considered it. Nancy said, "You know, that's not half bad. I could find a good used boat and get a loan. I mean, it might require some major repairs, but I know a lot about boats. Living on my own, with a slip in King Harbor, would cost a fraction of what it would cost to buy a house in Hermosa or Redondo. It would also be more affordable than renting here. That would mean I could have my own space." Nancy was becoming more hopeful with every sentence. "Plus, it has the added benefit of driving Roger crazy."

"I love this idea," Judy said, excitement growing in her voice.

"Could you teach us to sail?" Lois asked. "I've always wanted to learn how to sail."

"Oh, me too," Judy added.

"I know I could." Nancy studied the carpet, thinking about the prospect of living on a boat. It was a latent dream from a long time ago. But to actually be able to do it . . .

"How much would you need to buy a decent boat?" Judy asked.

"I imagine, depending on the year, it would cost upwards of sixty or seventy thousand."

Judy poured another margarita, took a quality-control sip, nodded, and motioned to Nancy to bring her glass over too.

"Then I have a better idea," Judy said. "Why don't I use part of Gordon's life insurance money to buy us a boat? And, Nancy, you can live on it."

Nancy, Ruthie, and Lois all stopped middrink. Their notoriously indecisive Judy had just announced a pretty solid financial decision.

"Jude, that's the tequila talking," Nancy said, as she dismissed her offer.

"No. It isn't. I was at the Back Burner this morning for breakfast, and as I sat there munching on my hash browns, I overheard Evelyn Cooper and her brood. They're what, ten years older than us? I listened to them talk for two solid hours about their hiatal hernias, incontinence pants, and colonoscopies."

"Those old crones are only ten years older than us?" Lois looked appalled.

"The point is, ever since I got this life insurance money, I've been completely paralyzed. I don't know what to do with it—so I don't do anything with it. I feel like I'm frozen, afraid to move on, afraid to hit the *Add to Cart* button for even so much as a book on Amazon. I'm tired of being afraid and unsure."

"I'm impressed you buy books on the internet," Ruthie said. "I don't trust the interwebs."

"Showing your age," Lois muttered in Ruthie's direction. Ruthie swatted her.

Judy continued, "But as we're sitting here, it occurred to me that this is how I want to spend my money. It's effortless to say yes. That's how I know it's right. Not only do I get to help one of my best friends when she needs it most, but this decision has the added benefit of getting our butts on a sailboat instead of sitting at the Back Burner talking about our impending death or, worse, incontinence pants. Horrible things happen to the asses of old people who sit too long."

Judy seemed invigorated, almost bouncing with enthusiasm. She hadn't been like that since before Gordon went missing.

Lois nodded along with Judy and said, "You know, Chris has all this cool stuff he does with his friends. Ski trips, tennis tourneys, golf outings. I don't have anything like that. I just run on a treadmill in our garage. Alone. It's depressing. Maybe sailing could be my thing."

"You could all learn the basics inside of a long weekend," Nancy said with confidence.

"Well, Nance, you do love the water, I'll give you that," Ruthie said, with a little more reluctance in her voice than the others. "But living in a marina? It's like the last bastion of aging divorcees who drink, party, and carouse." She thought for a second and then added, "I'm beginning to see the brilliance of your plan."

"Judy, are you sure?" Nancy asked. "I mean, is this how you want to spend your money? It's a lot of money."

Judy sat in her armchair and looked out into space. "When I was a girl, I went to Copenhagen with my parents. We went to that bay where we saw the statue of the Little Mermaid, her forlorn expression encased in marble forever. Maybe it was the rain or the fact my parents were fighting over something, but I found her so sad. Sitting there, waiting throughout eternity for her love to come back."

"Your grim story has a point, I hope," Lois said.

Judy shot her a look and continued. "I kept thinking about all the other mermaids below the surface, frolicking around, not caring about some two-legged, clueless man on land. Granted, I was a kid. But what I figured was that kind of blind devotion can be a trap. Sometimes love can do the same. When it's real, it can be a wonderful trap. One that wraps you up in love and support and togetherness, kids and dogs and safety. There might be other things out there, but you don't care, because you appreciate and nurture what you've got. That's what I feel Gordon and I had. We had big dreams when we were younger; then life and family changed the dreams. We were happy. But to take the safe route, to stay with someone who doesn't treat you properly or to hope for someone to change when all evidence points to more of the same, to wonder what could have been—that's the real trap, the painful one. I guess that's what I saw when I looked out at that little mermaid."

"She is a sad little thing," Ruthie acknowledged.

"So, I guess my point is, let's be the other mermaids," Judy said.

"Yes," Ruthie said slowly, and then she started to gain steam. "The other mermaids. The fun ones. The sultry sirens of the sea!"

"Exactly," Judy said. "The ones who have fun and frolic."

"I'm overdue for some frolicking," Nancy said.

"Ditto," Lois added.

"Maybe this is our adventure. We haven't done something crazy together since we went to Tahiti in the eighties. And when you don't do things, you get old, like Evelyn Cooper old. Judy's right. Maybe this is our time," Ruthie said, plucking the lime from her margarita. "We can frolic in a marina whenever and wherever the hell we want."

"Bring it on," Judy said.

"Gordon would fall out of his chair," Lois said as she looked at Judy, impressed.

"Even an ole biddy like me is allowed to have a wild side!" Judy whipped her silk scarf around her neck and adjusted her glasses. Then she added more quietly, "We're going to get insurance, right?"

"Good lord. The marina will never know what hit them!" Ruthie laughed.

Judy stretched out her hand in the center of the girls. Lois followed and put her hand over Judy's. Ruthie joined in, and the only hand left to be put down was Nancy's. They waited for her. Nancy finally put her hand on top of the three hands of her best friends, and the solidarity felt like a bolt of electricity as they all grasped hands.

Lois said, "To the boat."

Judy responded, "To the adventure."

Ruthie added, "To ruling the marina."

And finally, Nancy added, "To the Mermaids."

They all paused, looked at each other, grinning like pirates. "To the Mermaids!"

Two days ago Nancy had been in a full-blown depression, awash in self-loathing, feeling lost and unmoored. Now she felt a sense of renewal. An unexpected force buoyed her, a sense of hope, togetherness, and a call to adventure that kept the sadness at bay, like a strong, stiff wind stifling a cold, damp fog. This idea of a boat with her best friends had an energy to it, and inside her something bubbled to the surface, like little butterflies in a glass jar finally freed. Or perhaps like the mermaid who finally picked herself up, left that cold rock, and swam back into the sea.

* * *

That night Roger arrived home after spending two agonizing hours schmoozing Calvin Eldridge, one of nine members on the powerful California Coastal Commission, at Arthur J's, a swanky steak house in Manhattan Beach. He came home with a bad case of indigestion, a receipt for several hundred dollars' worth of chilled jumbo shrimp, and a dry-aged $180 tomahawk steak. Back in the day, you could buy a whole side of beef for that. Yet, after all that, he still hadn't been able to get a clear read on whether he could count on Eldridge to support his development deal for the Redondo Beach pier. Roger needed the support of Eldridge for his larger, more devious plan to work. Eldridge was solidly conservative, in the old-school Reagan kind of way. While he thought Eldridge would vote with the four other pro-development-at-any-cost bloc on the California Coastal Commission, he needed to be certain. Roger had those three votes locked up, but he was still two short of his magic number of five. But Eldridge was so goddamned straight, Roger had trouble coming up with acceptable topics of conversation.

Worse, the stiff did not drink (club soda, no ice, please) as he explained, because of his colitis. There was no cajoling him with bawdy stories from college or Vegas, there was no sly insider talk of undervalued stocks that the SEC might frown upon, and there were no rounds of three-olive martinis, those great lubricators that made big business deals happen. Instead, they'd ended up talking about

Eldridge's rare stamp and coin collection. At one point, Roger had considered stabbing himself with his fork just to stay awake.

Also, he still hadn't heard from Nancy. Perplexed by her silence, especially after he'd cut her off from any conceivable way to buy wine and cat food, Roger checked his phone one last time to see if there was any message from her. No luck. After he left the boring Eldridge dinner, he'd returned home to find all the lights off and the AC running full bore. It was freezing. California nights could dip below the low sixties, so the air running made no sense.

He checked his fancy Nest thermostat and saw that it was set to fifty-two, with frigid air blowing from the vents above. He moved the thermostat manually by turning the knob until the digital numbers read seventy-two. After drinking two double Scotches while watching a SportsCenter recap, Roger stumbled up to his bedroom, plopped two Alka-Seltzers in a glass of water (which he always drank before they totally dissolved), took off his tie, and promptly fell into a fitful sleep filled with lurid visions of Claire Sanford naked and laughing like a deranged, wanton hyena.

Two hours later, Roger woke in what he thought was a cold sweat. But when his senses returned, he stripped off his clothes, got into bed, and realized it was a hot sweat. It was as hot as the tropics in August in the bedroom. He stalked over to the Nest, which somehow was now set at ninety-two degrees, radiant heat blasting from above. He turned the thermostat back to a civilized seventy-two degrees and stood there for a second, wiping beads of sweat from his brow, making sure the thermostat wasn't going to move. After it seemed to be working, he headed back to bed and landed facedown on the sheets.

* * *

Over in Redondo Beach, as Nancy tucked herself into Ruthie's guest bed, she heard a small ding on her phone. It was an alert from the Nest that the temperature had been manually changed. She opened her Nest app and quietly tapped the numbers to set the thermostat back up to a balmy ninety-two degrees. Just the right temperature for Hell, Nancy thought. She went to sleep with a smile.

CHAPTER TEN

HER SHIP COMES IN

Two days later, Nancy and Brad Warren, the most beloved local yacht rep in all of Southern California, had agreed to meet at the Rusty Pelican, a classic sailor's hangout in Long Beach. It was the very same place where Brad had sold *Bucephalus* to Roger and Nancy nearly twenty years ago. The place had an anchor over the door, brass portholes for windows, and a beautiful polished cherrywood bar.

Nancy arrived early and walked in through the teakwood door. A strong smell of stale rum hit her first, and it took her a moment to focus in the dimly lit establishment, but she could tell she was in a world-class dive bar. Her sandals were sticking ever so slightly to the floor near the barstools. Beer steins with loyal customers' names like Fat Paul and Iron Horse hung on hooks from the ceiling next to the obligatory dusty double-D bras. Little had changed, including Doris the bartender, who came waddling out of the kitchen.

Doris's faculties and feistiness were still intact, even though nearly everything else on her had been replaced. Knees, hips, and a part of her spine were now fortified with the finest titanium and cobalt money could buy. She had one glass eye and two hearing aids turned up to full volume, so she could hear any whisper of conspiracy or discontent from across the room. Her hair was sparse, bright white, and teased to heaven, like a glorious bundle of cotton candy for the angels.

To Nancy's great surprise, Doris remembered her.

"Hi, Tootsie, it's been a while," Doris said, her good eye sharp and clear. "You up for your usual?"

"Oh," Nancy said, "I'm not sure what my usual was back in the day."

"Captain Morgan and OJ with a splash of coconut liqueur."

Nancy stared for a second, bewildered that Doris remembered, and then shrugged. "That sounds like a winner to me."

"I never forget a drink or a deadbeat. It's the motto I live by."

Doris turned her back on Nancy and began making her cocktail. It was only eleven AM, but Nancy remembered that when you walked through the doors of a sailors' bar, somehow time lost all meaning.

Just then the door swung open, and Nancy squinted at the bright light, which cast the long shadow of Brad Warren. Brad stood there in his Hawaiian shirt, his long, skinny, tanned arms outstretched to greet her, his friendly, crooked smile slowly coming into focus under his aviator sunglasses.

"Nancy Hadley. The last time I saw you, I only had two ex-wives and three kids! Ah, the good ole days."

Brad was the quintessential California beach boy all grown up. He had an easy, laid-back vibe about him, a natural charm that made women feel comfortable and men unthreatened. His blond hair was permanently tousled, as if he had just stepped off a yacht, and his skin was perpetually tanned. He also had an encyclopedic knowledge of boats. Sail, motor, historic vessels, aft cabins, racers—he knew who'd built them, who'd designed them, who sailed them, even the best years to purchase or sell them. Learning about yachts had been his love from boyhood, and now buying and selling them had cemented his stellar reputation in Southern California—not to mention it had secured him a very handsome living.

"I'll take a Cazadores with two limes, Doris," Brad said to the bartender, who nodded rather affectionately at him. "Where's Rog?" he asked Nancy.

She vaguely remembered his love of tequila. "Well, you'll be the first person I tell outside my best friends, but Roger and I are separated."

"Whoa." Brad looked at her a minute, then did his shot of tequila, squeezed both limes into his mouth, and shook his head. "I did not see that coming."

"You're not alone there."

"So, I take it this wasn't some slow decline from lovers to roommates to strangers but a rather more dramatic ending?"

"Yes, something like that."

"Dirtbag," Doris muttered from the other end of the bar, where she was cleaning dirty bar glasses.

"I'm sorry, Nance. It's gotta be tough. You guys have spent most of your lives together, right?"

"Thirty-six years," Nancy said, then downed her entire drink. "One more, please, Doris."

"So, I take it you're looking to sell *Bucephalus*? Because I can have three buyers lined up tomorrow."

Doris delivered Nancy's drink in record time and added, "On the house." Nancy took it as an empathy drink, on the sisterhood.

"Actually, I'm here because I want to buy a boat. Something I can live on—and race on."

"Oh, I see," Brad said, as he accidentally knocked his tequila glass over. He took a minute and looked at the bar. Then he asked, "Are you sure you want to live in a marina? Most marinas are filled with nothing but men. Crabby old men to boot. Old salts, divorcees, and loners. Some pervs, even. A woman living on a boat in a marina is a truly rare thing."

Doris delivered another shot of tequila for Brad and said, "Goddamn refreshing, if you ask me." She went back to cleaning her bar glasses.

"I know it's unusual. But my best friends and I are going in on this plan together. Granted, I'll be living on it by myself, but I have a pretty ferocious cat."

Brad just looked at her.

"And I'll buy a Taser. For the pervs."

Brad took a swig of his tequila but didn't say anything.

Nancy suddenly seemed unsure, as if the whole notion was batshit crazy. Maybe this wasn't smart; maybe it was foolhardy and steeped in revenge instead of reason. Maybe she should stay at Ruthie's until she could move into Bali Hai Gardens, where potluck dinners served as hunting grounds for lonely tenants.

Brad must have read her uncertain expression, because he interrupted her momentary anxiety spasm. Finally smiling, he said, "I think it's brilliant." Nancy looked up at him and held her breath. He continued, "I was just thinking about who I know in King Harbor marina that lives aboard. Someone who I trust that could look out for you. But honestly, I think you'll be fine, Nancy. You're one of the best sailors I've ever had the pleasure to crew with. If anyone can do this, you can. Plus, you have your friends. But buy that Taser, just in case."

"It's about time those boys in the marina had a woman in their midst," Doris piped up. "If you need advice on Tasers, I know a guy. Also, good to have one of these." Doris produced an aluminum baseball bat from somewhere behind the bar and gripped it with two hands.

"Thank you, Doris. Good tip." Nancy smiled at her.

"You got it, Tootsie."

Nancy looked at Brad and raised her glass. Brad toasted. "To your great new adventure."

With that, Nancy and Brad got down to brass tacks. They talked budget, appropriate beam width, which boats had the least displacement so they'd run fast, and which boats had the highest livability factor. Brad took quick notes on his iPhone.

Finally, he put his phone down. "Okay! I think I've got all I need. I'll have several boats for you to see in two days. Either here or in Long Beach, or possibly up in the South Bay."

"Whoa, that seems fast," Nancy said, a hint of uncertainty in her voice. But then she swallowed hard, tightened her grip on her glass, and said with a bit more confidence than she felt, "Perfect."

* * *

Two days later, Nancy waited on the landing that led down to the docks in Port Royal Marina. She instinctively gripped her purse tightly to her body to protect the enormous check inside. She was meeting Brad at the Port Royal Yacht Club, just south of the King

Harbor Yacht Club where *Bucephalus* was moored. But as close as the two neighboring yacht clubs were in geographical terms, Port Royal was light-years away in status. Though its charter didn't exactly state so, it was widely known as the "new money" marina. Instead of the old salts and colorful characters who haunted the King Harbor side, Port Royal's slips were filled with gleaming, ultraexpensive yachts owned by tech millionaires from Silicon Beach a mere eight miles north. They were young, slick, and shiny. And so were their boats.

So, when Brad led her down to a rather shoddy thirty-four-foot Catalina, Nancy was surprised to see such a humble boat in the nouveau riche marina. The vessel was structurally in good shape, but the paint was fading and chipped in places. Her sails were old and yellowed. This boat stuck out like a cotton-topped grandmother at a rave. On the transom, she could see the faded named. It read *Gypsea*.

"What gives?" Nancy asked.

"The owner of the *Gypsea* is the last holdout in Port Royal. He tried to fight the good fight against the tech-startup crowd, but I think he's just had enough. Between the ever-present smell of avocado toast and the reckless disregard for basic sailing etiquette by the entitled Millennials, he's opting out. He bought a one-way ticket to Florida, where he put in an offer on a fishing boat in the Keys. It's a contingency buy, which means he can't close on his new boat until he sells this one. So, he's motivated."

Nancy stepped up onto the deck of the *Gypsea* and made her way to the cockpit. The cushions were cracked and old, but the navigation equipment was newer and well maintained.

"Everything that matters has been updated," Brad told her. "The Yanmar diesel engine has just been rebuilt, there's new navigation tech up front and down below, and all eleven batteries were replaced last month. You could probably use a new cooktop, because I doubt it's been used since the early nineties."

Nancy headed below to inspect the galley, salon, and other living quarters. To her right was an L-shaped galley with a sink, a rusty cooktop, and a refrigerator. She checked to make sure the fridge worked. It was cool and clean inside. Then she made her way to the head and pumped the toilet twice to make sure the nauseating smell of septic flowback didn't permeate the boat. Smelled fresh. She turned on the shower to check water pressure, opened and closed every single hatch and window on the boat to make sure they sealed properly. The cabinets all looked to be in workable shape, nothing a little paint couldn't spiff up. The aft cabin was serviceable, although the cushions needed replacing. The only real concerns she had were the quality of the aging sails, the paint job, and the cooktop, of course. But in the big scheme of things, those were small details. She liked it. When she opened the starboard cabinet in the main berth, hanging inside, nailed to the door, was a brass sign that read *Warning: Mermaids.* Nancy smiled and took it as a good omen.

When she came up from the salon, Brad was waiting for her, seated in one of the captain's chairs at the stern of the boat, his blond hair tousling easily in the breeze.

"What do you think?"

"Well, if he could come down about five grand in price, that would leave me enough money to replace the sails, the cushions, and even put a spinnaker on."

Brad nodded. "Seems reasonable. I'll see what I can do." He hopped off the captain's chair and clapped his hands once. "Excellent. I'll make a call."

Nancy remained in the cockpit.

She moved behind the ship's wheel. She grabbed it with both hands and looked out over the water, as if already sailing, and took a deep breath. How long had it been since she'd made a decision completely on her own? Years? Decades? Ever? In her marriage, consultation and compromise had been a daily, unending slog, whether it was over what to have for dinner or where to go on vacation, with neither party ending up entirely happy about the result. But not today. Nancy was the sole decision-maker. It was both empowering and wildly nerve-racking. So much could go wrong. She took another deep breath, closed her eyes, and searched her gut. Not her head, where cold, hard reason reigned, nor her heart, where emotion and fear beat a steady drum, but her gut. Her gut was never wrong. She opened her eyes, and for the first time in as long as she could remember, she stood behind the wheel of her boat and everything felt right.

Brad came jogging back down the dock and jumped effortlessly onto the deck of the boat. He saw Nancy standing behind the wheel.

"You look like you belong there." He smiled, then added, "I told you he was motivated. I got it for ten grand less than what he was asking. Sixty grand. As long as we can have a check today, it's a done deal."

"I have a cashier's check for seventy in my purse."

"You're not messing around! Great. Once I get the all clear from you, I'll deposit it, pay the owner so he can catch his flight to Key West tomorrow, and transfer the extra ten grand back to you by end of business tomorrow. I'll also email you the contact info for the best sail guys on the West Coast," Brad said. He added, "Nancy, I think you've found yourself a fine boat."

* * *

It was two hours before sunset, and Nancy stood on the dock in Port Royal in front of her new boat. Brad handed her the boat keys attached to a float key chain in the shape of a seahorse.

"This is really happening," Nancy said as she took the keys.

Brad produced a bottle of unopened Veuve Clicquot champagne.

"For when you christen her." He smiled and handed the bottle to her.

She was so grateful for Brad's help in making this happen that tears sprung to her eyes, but no words came out.

Brad smiled at her and then gave her a strong, reassuring hug.

"You're going to do great, kid," he said. He was at least ten years younger than Nancy, but she took it as a term of endearment, which had the cheerful effect of making her feel giddy as a kid.

"Thank you, Brad."

"Bah, it's nothing for my new favorite client. Okay, I'm going to get outa here and let you get going. I expect an invite to sail soon!"

"You bet," she said. "One more thing, Brad, I hope you don't catch hell from Roger for helping me."

"Ah, a smart pirate never tells his secrets." He smiled and walked down the dock. She watched him jog off in the direction of his car.

It was time.

Nancy threw off the bow lines of her thirty-four-foot Catalina, raised the mainsail, eased her way out of the slip in Port Royal, and quietly motored out into the channel. All she had to do was head over to the King Harbor side of the marina, where her new slip waited. Brad had acquired it as part of the deal. She decided to take a slight detour and turned left for a short sail along the coast of Redondo

Beach to Palos Verdes. She wanted to get a feel for her new boat and how it sailed. As the *Gypsea* motored parallel to the break wall, Nancy readied the lines to unfurl the jib once she hit open water.

As she passed the harbor entrance buoy, the seals who were napping and sunning themselves barked loudly. Nancy let out the jib and killed the engine just as a warm gust of wind filled her sails. The boat heeled to one side, and she felt the *Gypsea* settle into a steady and confident course. For a brief moment, she and her boat were all there was. Just her, the wind, and the water. There was no Roger, no divorce, no pain, or grief, or fear. There was only the power within her and the power of nature. They seemed symbiotic, working and shifting together seamlessly. She felt the warmth of the fading sun on her face, the wind gliding over her deck, the tension in the lines that held the sails, and the salt water spraying her cheeks. She easily reached Point Vicente and decided to tack and head back toward her harbor, her new home. She let loose the jib against the wind, turned the wheel to come about, and tightened the jib to catch the wind back home. While it wasn't totally flawless, Nancy gave herself a B-plus for having done it alone.

On her way back, she was rewarded with some company. She looked up at the mainsail to discover a small monarch butterfly fluttering alongside her, keeping pace. The butterfly was way too far from land, and Nancy could think of no logical explanation for how this lone, fragile butterfly had found itself way out here. But she was happy for the company.

Once she neared the marina, the little butterfly, now safely near land, hovered above Nancy for another few seconds before flying toward shore. Nancy couldn't help but think about her mom as she watched it go.

Fifteen minutes later, Nancy smoothly navigated *Gypsea* into her new slip. Once she secured her lines and double-checked that the fenders were in place, she caught a glimpse of something at the end of her dock. It was a gift basket wrapped in blue cellophane. She hopped off and went to retrieve it. She picked it up and noticed a bottle of wine inside along with a variety of cheeses and crackers. She lifted it on board and then sat down and opened the card. It read:

To our Skipper on her new voyage
Love,
Judy, Lois & Ruthie (and Otis)

She felt high from her sail and from her new path on the water. She sat on the captain's chair, watched the last rays of the sun gently play on the water, and toasted to her new horizon. She looked around and took a deep breath before heading back to Ruthie's. A pelican was resting on the end of the dock, seemingly quietly observing his new neighbor.

"I hope you like cats," she said.

* * *

The next morning Nancy awoke early, brewed herself some strong black coffee in Ruthie's kitchen, and began gathering the rest of her stuff. All together, she had two rolling suitcases, a plastic bag full of new bedding, a coffeemaker, and two bottles of rum. Suzanne the Cat sat warily, watching the flurry of activity. Once the cat was safely locked inside the confines of her carrier, Otis mustered the courage to amble over to the screen window and sniff at her as a means of saying good-bye. Suzanne hissed at him, and Otis scurried back into the safety of the bedroom. Ruthie came out of her room, rubbing her eyes and yawning.

"You're up early, my newly minted captain."

"I'm just anxious to get settled."

"Totally get it. You need some help?"

Nancy smiled at her and then gave her a hug. "Nah, I got this."

"That's right," Ruthie said encouragingly. "You do."

Nancy gave her friend a big thumbs-up. "Call me later."

"Will do."

She pulled away from the curb and drove down Catalina Ave to the marina. Within five minutes she had pulled into King Harbor and was driving all the way down to M dock. All the docks were alphabetically appointed. She was in the last dock on the left side, which was shaped like a big horseshoe. The bright morning sun glinted off the water, and a warm, steady breeze kept the sea gulls aloft as they squawked their welcome. Nancy turned her face toward the wind and smelled the sea, a heady, glorious mixture of salt, bird poop, and engine oil. Bliss.

Nancy fumbled with her new key card and opened the gate to the dock ramp below. The rumbling of the suitcase wheels on the boardwalk ramp woke up two seals who were lazily sunning themselves on the dock down by her boat slip—number thirteen. They grumpily shoved off into the water after a few barks of protest as Nancy walked up to her not-so-new, somewhat banged up but lovingly purchased 1989 Catalina sailboat. She might not be the prettiest boat in the harbor, but she was home.

Nancy set Suzanne's carrier down on the dock and then put one foot on the dock platform. She found it harder than she thought to hoist her heavy suitcase onto the boat. She tried once more, but her fifty-seven-year-old biceps were no match for the thirty-five pounds of clothes and gear stuffed inside. She made a final heave, but the bag slipped and the suitcase fell back down on the dock on its wheels. She tried to jump down but stumbled and landed face first as she watched the suitcase roll inexorably toward the water.

"No!" Nancy cried.

Just then she heard footsteps running, and in a flash she saw a large, tanned hand grab her suitcase just before it skidded off the dock.

The figure that had saved it from a watery grave walked over and stood above her. All she saw was a warm smile blocking the bright sunlight.

"Whoa, there, I gotcha. Take my hand," the man said in what sounded like a faint Cuban accent. He held out a hand to help Nancy up from her fall.

She immediately found herself face-to-face with familiar sea-green eyes that sparkled under a navy-blue tam. It was Santiago.

Santiago was the talk of the entire female contingent of the King Harbor Yacht Club. They called him "The Marina Fox." Rumors swirled, but the prevailing story was that he had come to America during the sixties from Havana, or Colombia, or Key West. The details were sketchy and always changing. He had allegedly been married once, lost his wife either to tragedy or betrayal, and the rest of his history was unknown. This, of course, made him a constant topic of conversation among the women, who fantasized him as an ex-pirate, a famous bootlegger, or Cuban royalty. No one knew. When he came into the club, he always sat on the same barstool by the window, and he always sat alone.

Santiago was known as a man who could fix things. Anything mechanical or structural. Roger was known as a man who called contractors to fix things. Big difference.

Santiago kept his salt-and-pepper beard short and neatly trimmed, which set off his penetrating blue eyes. His navy tam was a constant fixture, and he carried within him an eternal spring of natural charisma.

"Santiago," Nancy said, flustered from the fall and his penetrating gaze. "Thank you for saving my bag."

"Seems this one was making a break for it," Santiago answered playfully.

Nancy wiped dock dust off of her shirt and tried to pull herself together. "It shall be banished to the locker from here on out," she said.

Santiago smiled warmly, lifted the suitcase onto the deck like it was filled with foam peanuts, and placed it in the cockpit. When he came back, Nancy offered him the bag carrying Suzanne the Cat.

"Can I trouble you for one more? She's a little nervous."

"Of course," he said. As he peeked at the little cat inside, he added, "Precious cargo." Santiago immediately took the bag and with great care brought the cat and her carrier on board. He gently set her down on the teak bench in the cockpit and touched his fingers to the screen. Suzanne nuzzled up against them as Santiago cooed words to her. "It'll be okay, little one; you'll get your footing soon enough."

Nancy hopped on board with the bag of bedding just in time to witness Santiago's simple kindness to her cat. She'd almost forgotten what it looked like coming from a man. Roger tolerated Suzanne but never *cooed* to her.

Nancy, for once, didn't know what to do. Then her brain started functioning again, though that wasn't an easy thing to do around Santiago. She was quite proud of herself.

"Can I get you a cup of coffee?" she asked.

Santiago looked around at the two suitcases and the bag of new bedding. Nancy could tell he was trying to surmise what was going on without being rude enough to ask.

"So, you see, Roger and I . . . well, we are, um . . ." Nancy sighed, unsure of how to politely issue the truth. So, she abandoned all etiquette. "He decided to bury the weasel in Claire Sanford, and I decided I couldn't live with an asshole."

Santiago squinted and massaged his jaw, considering the information. She detected a sense of knowing and the hint of a smile at her bold comment.

"So, this is my new home. And you are my first guest. It might take me a minute, but I can unpack the coffeemaker and get some brewing in no time."

"Please do not trouble yourself. I have to finish up some work on Dawson's boat across the way, so I should be heading back anyway."

"You're right; at the moment, coffee is too much work. But, um"—Nancy looked around, thinking quickly—"I have some rum. How about a shot of rum? I could use the unofficial welcome."

"As the custom goes, a pirate never says no to rum," Santiago said as he smiled. He nodded to her offer of a shot.

Elated, Nancy disappeared inside the salon and brought back two shot glasses in the shape of cacti filled to the top with spiced rum. Santiago was petting Suzanne, who was now sitting comfortably in his lap. The cat seemed amazingly at ease.

"Okay, here we go," Nancy said as she handed Santiago his shot.

They raised their glasses at the same time, and Santiago quietly said, "Welcome to the neighborhood, Madam Hadley."

"Call me Nancy."

Santiago paused, nodded, and started again. "To our newest pirate. Welcome, Nancy."

She smiled. They toasted and tipped the shots back.

For a moment they remained locked in a mutual gaze, a chord of connection forming out of nowhere, like tuning in to a long static radio station and finally finding music.

A pelican squawked and broke the moment, and Santiago cast his eyes downward. "Well, I must go," he said as he tipped his tam to her and then let himself off the boat and headed down toward Dawson's vessel.

Nancy watched him depart until she was interrupted by a small meow from Suzanne.

"Let's get you settled, girl. Food always helps."

After two hours of organizing the boat, packing everything away, replacing lightbulbs, and setting up Suzanne with her bowls of food and water, Nancy poured herself a crisp, cold glass of white wine and had a seat outside.

She had purchased white-and-navy canvas cushions for the teak benches, and she sat back and let the sun warm her legs as she relaxed, or at least tried to. For the first time in her life, she didn't have anyone to look after, no sandwiches to make, no dry cleaning to pick up, no awful lunches with Roger's business friends to attend—which meant she didn't know what to do with herself. Relaxation came hard for someone who wasn't accustomed to it.

So, she got up and made sure Suzanne was okay, her last mission of caretaking. Problem was, Suzanne had always been an independent sort. After inspecting every single part of the boat while Nancy busied herself with unpacking, Suzanne had found the perfect spot to take a nap. She was happily dozing in the corner of the shower when Nancy interrupted her. The small cat twitched one ear, seeming to know she was needed, and sauntered out to where her human sat on the bench of the cockpit. She cuddled up next to Nancy on the white-and-navy cushions and started purring.

"We did the right thing, right, Suze?"

Suzanne merely squinted into the sun, sighed so deeply that it seemed to signify a contentedness she hadn't felt in years, and proceeded to nap.

"Thank you, my furry Zen master." Nancy took a sip of her wine and felt her shoulders loosen for the first time in two weeks, or possibly thirty-six years.

CHAPTER ELEVEN
SOMETHING NEFARIOUS AFOOT

Roger was in the middle of his back swing on the twelfth fairway at Palos Verdes Golf Course when his phone rang. As a result, he ended up shanking his ball into a lovely pond nestled in front of a grove of eucalyptus trees.

"Goddamn it!" Roger whacked his club down hard on the fairway, sending a local squirrel scrambling back into the ground cover. He reached in his pocket for his phone and saw that it was his attorney, Spencer Raeger, calling.

"Hey Spence, what's up?"

He and Spencer had talked nearly every day this week concerning his wife Nancy—how to freeze assets, how to forestall the divorce she was seeking, which he was trying to prevent entirely. Roger heard a *cha-ching!* in his head every time Spencer called. He had briefly considered changing Spencer's incoming ring tone to a cash register as a gentle reminder that lawyers were maddeningly expensive. But not as expensive as divorce.

"Well, I've found out where Nancy has decided to take up residence."

"Is it Bali Hai Gardens? That sketchy outpost for forlorn divorcees? That's about all she can afford." Roger snickered.

"No, she's about to live on a boat. In King Harbor."

"What? What boat?"

"Oh, I assumed it was your boat, the *Bucephalus*. Which is, by the way, not listed as one of your assets. We need to change that." *Cha-ching!*

"Impossible. She's not on *Bucephalus* because I changed the locks."

"Oh, that's a bit of a preemptive strike, but okay. I'm looking at a publicly registered dock slip contract for twelve months in King Harbor. Signature looks a lot like your wife's."

Roger abruptly hung up on Spencer Raeger. As he was charged by the minute, the need for lengthy conversation or simple phone etiquette was pointless. The financial squeeze Roger had been so masterfully executing over Nancy to bring her back into the fold was failing. There was only one explanation. Those crones had to have come to her rescue with their measly savings from piggy banks and portions of their 401(k)s. He grumbled and thought to himself, *Why me? Is nothing in life fair? Is it too much to ask to have a wife I can completely control?*

Just then his phone rang again. He looked at the screen and saw it was his daughter Stella calling. He sighed and then connected.

"Hi, Peanut."

"Mom is living on a boat?"

"How did you hear already?"

"From Mom! What the hell is going on, Dad? I thought you would be in Kauai by now, buying her some koa wood jewelry and getting everything back on track."

"I know. Things went a little . . . sideways."

"That might be the understatement of the decade. She's moving herself onto *a boat*, and she's taken the cat. Has she completely lost her mind? What fifty-seven-year-old woman leaves her husband for *no good reason* and goes to live on a boat? I think it might be grounds for a psych evaluation. I can call a friend of mine, and we can—"

Roger cut her off. "Stella, she's not crazy. She's just going through something."

Stella remained silent, presumably waiting for more of an explanation.

Roger continued, "Look, if this is what she needs to see how good she has it at home, then I can abide by that. Living on a boat is a lot like camping. It won't be long before she misses her eight-hundred-thread-count sheets, long hot showers, or a toilet that doesn't require her to grind her shit before she flushes it. Not to mention reliable refrigeration for her Chardonnay. Trust me. She'll be back under this roof inside two months."

"I guess, Dad." This seemed to calm Stella for a moment. "But Mom was supposed to watch Charlotte while Sam and I go up the Central Coast for a getaway, which we desperately need. I've already been denied by all of her friends' mothers at Redondo High, even the ones with neck tattoos. I swear they hate working mothers. So now what am I supposed to do? I can't cancel this trip."

Roger, knowing full well he didn't want to spend a weekend with his sullen teenage granddaughter, said, "Sadly, I'm golfing at the country club with the boys this weekend." Roger hoped his excuse didn't sound too hasty. Then he offered, "Why not drop Charlotte at her grandmother's new boat? I'll bet your mom would love it."

"Oh, she would. She already offered. The problem is Charlotte doesn't want to go."

"Why?"

"No Wi-Fi."

Roger considered this for a moment and then added, "Might be good for her. Get some fresh sea air in those lungs of hers. Blow the tech stink off of her. Besides, she's a kid. She has no say."

"You are no help, Dad."

The line went dead. Roger knew his daughter was more at her wits' end with her own daughter than she was mad at him. He sighed heavily, took a deep breath, twirled his new driver under his armpit, and tried to get a handle on the rage he felt behind his eyes. He only half believed that Nancy was going to return to their Hermosa Hills home in two months. In fact, in the bigger scope of his plans, her living on a boat in King Harbor had complicated things nearly beyond his control. Nancy wasn't coming around. Not without a hard shove to get her back into the fold. And if anyone knew how to shove, it was Roger Hadley.

CHAPTER TWELVE
THE EFFING CHARGERS

Chuck Roverson sat at his desk overlooking the marina, his Dodgers baseball hat askew, a spear gun in one hand and a Miller Lite in the other. The King Harbor dock master didn't usually drink until happy hour and certainly never before noon, but the stress of his current situation warranted the numbing effect of alcohol. He felt his fingers tingling, and he wasn't sure if it was the booze or abject fear.

His bookie had left a rather ominous threat on his phone, something about three grand in the red, and if the dough wasn't forthcoming soon, a couple of guys with pliers would alleviate him of his toenails. "Fucking Chargers," he muttered. Chuck had made a bet on the LA Chargers football team, three-to-one odds, and all they had to do was win by three. Things had been looking great until the kicker shanked a measly twenty-five-yarder with seconds to go. The Chargers failed to cover the spread in overtime. Three large was more than he could cover, even if he raided his wife's Lake

Havasu vacation savings. He'd exhausted all his options and even considered stealing part of the money Brad Warren had delivered to him that very morning for a one-year lease on a boat slip for his client, Nancy Hadley. But he could lose his job if he did that. He was guzzling his beer when the phone rang.

"King Harbor Marina, your gateway to the Pacific. How may I help you?" Roverson answered glumly.

"Chuck, this is Roger Hadley."

Chuck immediately sat up in his swivel chair, wiped the sweat off his brow, and set his beer on the desk. "Mr. Hadley, sir, how are you today?"

"I've been better, Chuck. Listen, I was hoping to buy you a drink at the Blue Water Grill. I want to talk to you about a little matter I think you can help me resolve."

Chuck sat there for a minute, trying to work out why Hadley was calling him. The only other time Hadley had spoken to him was when he threatened to have him fired for allowing a visiting yacht to block part of *Bucephalus*'s slip on the Fourth of July.

"Chuck? You there?"

"Uh, sir, yes, sir," Chuck responded.

"How about that drink?"

"Sure, say two o'clock?"

"See you then." Roger Hadley hung up.

Chuck Roverson stared out over all the boats resting in their slips, still trying to figure out what Hadley wanted. Chuck had assumed that Roger and Nancy had simply bought another boat and therefore needed another slip. Then his mind cramped when he thought back to the fine mess he'd gotten himself into. He was enterprising. He had gotten into tight spaces before. He just had to get creative. And that's when it dawned on him. Maybe this meeting with Hadley could lead to more than a drink. Maybe he could blackmail Hadley. After all, he'd seen him fooling around with that other woman, the redhead, the one who wasn't his wife. Plus, he was a rich guy. He had plenty of money. Wouldn't hurt him to part with just enough to keep Chuck's toenails firmly attached. He didn't need to get greedy; he just needed to get clear of his bookie's thugs. He had two hours before their drinks at the Blue Water Grill. He had to think. He wanted to go down by the water.

He grabbed a beer out of the fridge in his office and went outside. A warm breeze nearly blew his hat off, but he caught it and then wrenched it down on his head. He walked onto the platform that led down to the docks and in doing so disturbed a large pelican sitting on the top of a nearby pole.

"Go on!" Chuck barked at the pelican.

The bird lazily flew up and north over the marina and then circled back overhead.

Chuck Roverson felt a large splat on his shirt. He looked down at a big messy glob of pelican poop just above his right pocket.

"Goddamn it!" he yelled as he looked up into the blinding sun, catching just the shadow of a wing.

The pelican hung in midair, coasting on the wind, looking down at his handiwork. Satisfied, he flapped his big brown wings and flew away.

* * *

"We'll have another," Roger said loudly toward the bartender of the Blue Water Grill as he twirled his index finger in a circle, the universal sign for another round.

Roger eyed the birdshit stain on Chuck Roverson's shirt, saw the man's lazy smile, and figured he'd sized him up pretty accurately. A gangly man in his late forties, Chuck likely had at least two failed financial dreams under his belt—being the captain of a booze-cruise catamaran in the British Virgin Islands and owning a money-hemorrhaging sport-fishing operation in some backwater. Roger surmised that both of those shiny hopes had been dashed by the harsh truth of his addictive personality.

Roverson's brow was weathered and furrowed, his nose and cheeks red with gin blossoms, and Roger noticed that Chuck didn't just drink to be social; he gulped his alcohol as if Prohibition were about to be reinstated. Roger had learned of his previous experience as the captain of a whale-watching schooner down in San Diego, which had eventually led him to his job as dock master at King Harbor. Chuck had admitted to Roger that he really was looking for a job at the neighboring, more upscale Port Royal Marina, where the females were moneyed, bored, and flirty with boat personnel. Chuck snorted in an attempt, Roger thought, to laugh. Roger summed up Chuck Roverson in two words: easily manipulated.

"So, Chuck, my wife Nancy Hadley has just recently rented a boat slip in King Harbor."

Chuck's smile vanished. He grew quiet and stared at his drink.

"I signed that this morning," he finally said.

"Yes, then you know. You see, Nancy and I are having a little disagreement on what the future looks like. And well, I was hoping you might be able to help me."

"How so?" Chuck slurred.

"I love my wife."

Chuck snorted and chortled again.

Roger paused for a moment, irritated, and then continued. "I love my wife, and I want her to realize that home, with me, is where she belongs." Roger reached for his wallet. "I was hoping you could help me make her understand that life on a boat can be, shall we say, uncomfortable." Roger stared hard at Chuck to make sure the words sank into his pickled brain.

Chuck Roverson sat there for a second, brow furrowed, trying to grasp the concept.

"I want you to make her life in the marina a little harder than it is for other liveaboards."

"Oh, you mean like cite her for violations and stuff?"

"That's exactly what I mean, but maybe take it one step further."

"I could have someone sink her boat?"

"No, that's a buoy too far, my friend. Somewhere between minor infractions and going down like the *Edmund Fitzgerald*. I just want her to come home, not press charges. Can you do that for me, Chuck?" Roger flashed fifteen one-hundred dollar bills at him and gave him a healthy pat on the shoulder, as if they were devious, scheming comrades.

Chuck hovered in his seat. He stared at the cash.

Roger knew the money would be like catnip.

"How soon do you want the little lady home?"

"Not so soon as to arise suspicion. How about two weeks?"

Chuck looked at his drink and picked it up with a shaky hand.

"I'll do it for three grand. And I need it by next week," Chuck said as he shivered in his seat.

Roger lowered his chin and stared hard at the pathetic loser. "Is that the going rate for intimidation these days?" His voice was oily, dark, more of a snarl.

Chuck froze but remained silent. He stared at his drink sitting on the bar. Then he said, "I saw you and the redhead. It's on the marina security camera too."

This caught Roger off guard. His gaze went from conspiratorial to glowering. *How dare this punk.* However, he relented, knowing he would never pay Roverson the full amount. "Fifteen hundred for now, the rest when I see progress." He held out his hand for a shake to seal the deal.

Chuck wiped a thin sheen of sweat from his brow and then shook Hadley's hand. But as Chuck tried to let go, Roger's grip tightened.

"Don't let me down, Chuck," Roger said in a smooth, even tone as he glared at him. "I'm not a man you want to cross."

Chuck nodded nervously. "I, uh, I won't sir. The broad will come screaming back to you in no time."

"Do not refer to my wife as a broad. It's cheap and tawdry. And she's neither."

"Yessir, sir, I mean, sorry," Chuck stammered, "Won't happen again, sir."

Roger Hadley nodded, and a small smile curled his lip. He let go of Chuck's hand and briskly walked out of the Blue Water Grill, only to discover a large splat of pelican poop on the hood of his just-washed Mercedes.

CHAPTER THIRTEEN
THE MERMAIDEN VOYAGE

Not all animals were suited to boats. Otis, for instance, with his short little legs and squat salami-fed body, didn't have the ability or confidence to jump from the dock platform onto the slightly swaying boat. So, with one muffled whimper, he was hauled aboard in the comfort of Ruthie's arms. At which point Suzanne the Cat sauntered to the stern, steady on her feet and completely at ease after just three days on her new floating residence, to see where the whimper had come from. Suzanne took one look at Otis and, bored with her new visitor, went back up to the bow to scout for more sea life. Otis, who was strapped into a bright-green doggy life preserver with a starfish on it, sat rather unsteadily on the floor of the cockpit as Ruthie and Nancy unpacked groceries.

"I brought rum. That's what sailors drink, right?" Ruthie asked as she wielded a fifth of spiced rum in her left hand.

"I'm making this up as I go, sister, but yes, generally rum and pirates go hand in hand," Nancy said. "But white wine would be fine too."

"We're mermaids. We can drink whatever we want. We make the rules," Ruthie said and winked, as she arranged snacks on the pop-up tray table in the cockpit.

Nancy went down into the salon and flipped on the power to the stereo. She searched for and found a Jimmy Buffett playlist on Spotify. The familiar sounds of the iconic *A1A* album carried over the water from the speakers mounted under the captain's chair at the stern of the boat.

Ruthie looked around at the blue-and-white-striped cushions, the upscale plastic wineglasses and throw pillows Nancy had bought. "Wow, you've really spiffed this boat up, Nance."

"I went kind of gonzo at the Redondo Marine Superstore and the Boat Galley," Nancy said. "But I live here. On a boat. I live on a boat now. Oh my god." Nancy stopped herself and looked around.

"It's great! Stop! Stop worrying. Look, Suzanne has already adjusted."

Suzanne was lying on the port side of the boat, licking her paws in the sunshine.

"She scared off two giant sea lions today that were snoring on our dock. She's fearless."

Ruthie and Nancy looked down at Otis, who seemed to imperceptibly nod that it was the truth.

"Ahoy, mateys!" Lois called as she and Judy walked down the dock toward the boat. They were carrying several bags of goodies. "We brought boat-warming gifts!" Judy exclaimed.

"And Dramamine!" Lois reached the dock platform step and handed over the bags to Ruthie, who was waiting to ferry them to the salon. Then she used her athletic legs to hop up onto the deck with ease.

Judy, far less certain of her boat skills, put one foot on the platform, one on the side of the boat, and took a moment to gird herself for the thrust upward. Ruthie and Lois each gave her a hand and helped pull her onto the boat. Once on, she was the most unsteady.

"Just have a seat, Jude. We'll get everything set up," Nancy said as she readied the boat. She unlocked cleats, prepped the mainsail, and organized the lines for the jib. She double-checked the navigation tech and unplugged the main power line from the dock.

The Mermaids were getting ready for their maiden voyage out of King Harbor. The weather at the moment was cooperating, although there was a hint of fog way off on the horizon. But it was unlikely it would roll in from that distance. At the moment, the sun was warm, the water calm, and the breeze steady. All the makings of a perfect first sail.

"I'm just not used to boats," Judy said, as she nearly fell over getting to the far side of the cockpit. She wound up tucking herself into a corner of one of the teak benches. "I blame my weak ankles."

"I have some calcium supplements in my bag," Lois cheerfully offered.

Judy gave Ruthie a knowing look.

Lois had, over the years, suffered from ailments both real and imagined, but mostly imagined. Hypochondria was Lois's hobby. This mild disorder had manifested itself in her constant fear that she would be struck down with a serious illness like lupus, cancer, encephalitis, or MS, so she specialized in educating herself on every early symptom of every possible disease. Even though all medical tests showed that Lois was as healthy as an organic-eating horse with extremely good genetics, it didn't matter. Lois had no real problems to worry about, so she manufactured something to worry about. An unintended benefit was that if anyone ever needed any possible combination of over-the-counter remedies, including a calcium tablet or Advil, Lois was up to the task.

"I don't need a calcium tablet, Lois, but thank you," Judy said. Still unsteady on the boat and eternally cautious by nature, Judy inspected her seat on the boat and enterprisingly strapped herself to one of the canopy bars with her own scarf for extra security. "There, that's better."

Ruthie was down in the salon, unpacking and stowing various boat-warming gifts. The girls had pitched in and bought Nancy some colorful wool blankets, bright orange and turquoise dishware, wet wipes, garbage bags, and scented candles and brought along Otis's dog bed, which Suzanne adored. Otis watched forlornly as Ruthie put his former bed in the corner for Suzanne. He huffed.

"Oh, I'll get you a new one, Otis. Stop being so selfish."

Otis huffed once more and then buried his nose in his paws.

"Okay, crew, we're about to shove off!" Nancy said confidently.

Ruthie, Lois, and Judy shouted in harmony, "Aye, aye, Captain!"

Lois was by the mast with her muscular arms ready to raise the last few feet of the mainsail. Ruthie stood ready to unfurl the jib. And Judy was safely tucked in the corner of the cockpit, tied to the boat with her own scarf, cheering the rest of them on. Nancy was at the helm, easing their way out of the slip and into the channel.

They motored past the King Harbor Yacht Club, it's floor-to-ceiling windows flashing against the afternoon sun. Nancy glanced over and wondered if anyone inside the club was aware that the *Gypsea*, with its all-female owners, was headed out on a maiden voyage that was about to bring their little marina into the twenty-first century. She felt a surge of personal pride.

Just before leaving the channel, Nancy killed the engine, instructed Lois to pull up the mainsail, and gave Ruthie orders to unfurl the jib. Nothing happened at first. As they were still shielded from the break wall, the wind didn't reach them. Ruthie and Lois looked at each other, wondering if they had done anything wrong. But Nancy stayed steady and watched the wind vane rock lazily at the top of the mast. Three seconds and a hundred yards later, a stiff, fresh breeze filled the sails all at once. The boat heeled to port, and Judy let out a nervous hoot at the sudden pitch of the *Gypsea*. Otis unsteadily slid across the bench to be next to Judy. Suzanne took her leave and headed below to curl up into Otis's dog bed until this was over. Nancy was the only one doing work, so she began to give orders.

"Lois, lock off the mainsail," she said as she pointed to the cleat. She turned to Ruthie. "Use that winch handle to tighten the line on your jib."

"I don't know what a jib is, but I shall comply!" Ruthie began cranking the handle to tighten the sail.

"A little tighter." Nancy observed the sail. "Good."

Once all the sails were properly in place, Nancy set a course heading southwest to the tip of the Palos Verdes peninsula. Lois looked excitedly at the coast and then back at Nancy.

"We're sailing! We're sailing!" Lois said, nearly singing the words.

Nancy laughed. "Indeed we are. Ruthie, one more half turn, please."

"Aye, aye," Ruthie replied. "I might have been born to speak pirate." In an attempt to take the winch handle off, Ruthie wrenched it the wrong way and it popped out, skittered along the railing, and plopped into the sea. It disappeared without ceremony.

"Oh no." Ruthie looked over the side of the boat.

Nancy observed the mishap with only mild alarm and didn't let it faze her. "It's not the end of the world. There's another winch handle down below."

Lois hopped over to the port side of the boat, looked over the side, and said, "Hey, Nance, are the bumpers supposed to be dangling like that?"

Nancy realized they hadn't brought the fenders up. Rookie move. They would be ruthlessly mocked at the yacht club. "Lois, do you feel confident you can bring them up with those amazing biceps of yours?"

"On it." Lois moved forward toward the fender at the bow, but on the way she stubbed her toe on a jib sheet block and yelped. "Ouch! Shit!" She bent down to grab her own toe and then instantly lost her balance. Nancy felt a spike of fear that Lois might roll off the side and overboard. She yelled at Judy, "Judy, take the wheel."

Judy, having tied herself to the boat for safety, was now wasting precious seconds fumbling with her scarf. Nancy let go of the wheel, which caused *Gypsea* to veer severely to the port side, which in turn caused Ruthie and Judy to roll like tumbleweeds to the other. Nancy helped Lois back onto her feet. "You okay?"

"Beyond a suspected broken toe, I'm fine. Just a bruise the size of an eggplant."

"I'm sure Chris will relish in icing it, since it's on your ass," Ruthie said.

"He does have a healer's instincts." Lois winked.

Nancy moved back to the helm and took the wheel from Judy, who looked absolutely terrified to be in control. "Everyone okay?"

Lois and Ruthie both nodded and seemed relatively calm. Otis looked petrified.

"Judy, I know you're still getting your sea legs, but no more lashing yourself to the canopy bars, okay? It's dangerous."

"So is going overboard," Judy replied.

"Right, but tying yourself to a vessel that is going down is also unsafe," Nancy said.

Judy didn't look convinced but relented and undid her scarf. She instead proceeded to wedge herself into the corner of the cockpit as tightly as possible.

Down one winch handle, up one broken toe, but all things considered, she thought they weren't doing too bad. Nancy looked to starboard and realized that the fog that had promised to stay way off the coast was now coming in at a traitorous pace.

"Oh no," Nancy said as she looked out at the approaching fog bank.

"I don't like the sound of that," Ruthie said warily.

"Fog is coming in. Ruthie, we are going to need to tack fast."

"Is fog bad?" Judy asked. "I usually like fog. It makes things quiet."

"Not when we have to navigate through it," Nancy said. "We can't see other boats and they can't see us. No need to panic, though. We'll tack and head back and then motor in safely."

"Oh, good, a motor," Judy said. "I like motors. Very dependable."

"Okay, so when I say *tack*, I mean we are going to change direction. Three moves in this maneuver, and they all go in a specific, swift order."

"Order, got it. I like order," Lois said nervously. She was now in the cockpit right next to Ruthie.

"Ruthie, go get the winch handle from inside the chart table below."

"Copy that." Ruthie hurried down to the salon. She came back with the winch handle and set it next to Lois in the cockpit.

"Okay, great. Give the winch handle to Judy. Don't lose the winch handle, Judy; it's our last one."

Judy reluctantly took it and protected it as if it were the Holy Grail.

Nancy continued, "Listen to me first; then we'll do it together, okay?"

The girls all nodded, worried expressions on their faces. The fog was almost upon them, and the safety of the harbor was in the other direction. They had to get the tack completed so they could turn on the motor and get the hell back to the safety of the channel.

Nancy calmly but firmly explained. "Step one. Ruthie, you're going to loosen your line controlling the jib, that sail right there." Nancy pointed at the sail and the line. "Hold it until I turn the boat, so the sail doesn't flutter."

"Loosen jib. Got it," Ruthie repeated.

"Step two. I will turn the wheel so that the boat comes about; that means I take a sharp right. Judy, I want you to repeat that so you know when to move to the other side."

"Come about and move," Judy repeated.

"Step three. Lois, you pull your line, which also controls the jib sheet." Nancy pointed again so Lois understood.

"Pull jib sheet. On it."

"Loosen jib, come about, pull sheet. That's the sequence; got it?"

Ruthie, Judy, and Lois repeated, "Loosen jib, come about, pull sheet!"

Judy pushed her glasses back on her nose. Otis sat next to Judy. His eyes showed alarm and his tail did not wag.

"Okay, on my count. Three, two, one . . . Loosen!"

Ruthie began to let out the jib sheet out so that it fluttered in the wind.

"I'm coming about," Nancy said, and motioned for Judy to move to the other side of the boat.

The *Gypsea* began turning.

"Lois, pull your jib sheet as fast as you can."

As Ruthie let out her sheet, Lois pulled hers in. The jib moved effortlessly from one side to another—until it didn't. Lois pulled, but the sail was only half in. Lois yanked again. Nothing.

"Must be caught on something." Nancy followed Ruthie's line until she saw that it was snagged on a cleat by the bow. The sheet was fluttering in the wind. "I see it. Judy, can you take the helm?"

"Isn't there someone more qualified?"

"Gotta get your feet wet somehow. Come on, girl."

Judy let go of her death grip on the canopy bar and moved to the wheel, leaving Otis to fend for himself in his starfish doggy life vest. Nancy hopped up on the deck and went all the way to the bow to untangle the line from the cleat.

"Okay, Lois, pull!"

Lois yanked. The line came clean but then fell against Nancy's legs, and she went down hard. All three of the girls stood up to see if she was okay.

"Keep pulling until that jib is tight! I'm fine!" Nancy yelled from somewhere. Then she came limping back to the cockpit to relieve Judy of her duty at the helm.

"Judy, winch handle, please," Lois asked.

Judy handed it to her. Lois put it into the slot and then pulled the jib in until Nancy gave her a nod.

"All right. A few hiccups, but for a first-time effort under some duress, you did good. I'd give that a solid C-plus."

Ruthie and Lois gave each other a high five. Judy stayed where she was and gave an air high five.

"We'll just start the iron horse and head home steadily and surely."

"Iron horse?" Lois asked.

"Sailor's term for the motor," Nancy answered.

Nancy turned the engine on, and it purred as they slowly cut through the water. The fog was upon them now, starting as a veil of mist and then growing thicker by the minute. The temperature dropped, and they all reached for their jackets and sweaters. Nancy realized she needed to train her new sailors. If something had gone seriously wrong, they wouldn't have known what to do. It was irresponsible.

Nancy's heard a small sputtering sound coming from the engine.

It spit and hissed for a few seconds. Nancy smelled something burning and saw a large puff of black smoke come up from the salon just as the engine went dead. She jiggered the key and tried it again, but the motor only kicked out a high squeal, belched up three coughs of smoke, and went completely dead. At that moment, a deep fog overtook them. Nancy broke into a sweat and felt momentarily paralyzed.

"The engine just died."

"But didn't we just buy this boat, engine included?" Judy protested weakly.

Nancy wrestled with panic that threatened to overthrow her thinking. What was she doing out here? She loved sailing and was good at it. But a good sailor didn't always make a good captain. She had always left the actual leadership to Roger. Her role was as the smarter and occasionally mutinous first mate who preferred to question the calls of the captain, not make them. So much could go wrong. She gripped the wheel and steadied herself against her rising anxiety.

"We're going to have to come in under sail," she said as she clenched her jaw tight. "Okay, everyone listen closely to every word I say, as we'll have to work quickly."

CHAPTER FOURTEEN
THE BIG BURP

It took Roger roughly thirty seconds to locate the disheveled shape of Chuck Roverson under a grungy baseball cap within the King Harbor Yacht Club. He was, no surprise, sitting at the bar. A thin sheen of sweat hung on Chuck, as if he were minutes away from suffering a bad stomach flu. Roger jangled the change in his pocket and looked around, assessing who else was in the club, before he approached Chuck.

It was a light crew today, most likely due to the fog that had rolled in right before happy hour. A few old salts were playing cards in the corner. Santiago was quietly finishing a crossword puzzle at the other end of the bar. And finally, there was Turk, the intrepid captain of *Hot Rum*, a rival racing boat, who was sitting by himself, staring out the window, probably contemplating how to take down *Bucephalus* in the upcoming Border Dash sailing race.

The Border Dash ran from Newport Harbor down to Ensenada, Mexico, and it was Roger's exclusive domain. It was his crowning jewel, the feather in his captain's hat, and he had claimed the title four years in a row. Turk had come in second every time, usually by a minute or two. Two years ago, Turk had actually led Roger near the finish, until they butchered their last jibe at the famed final buoy, where all the boats made a hard left toward the finish line. Roger observed Turk from across the room as he ordered another gin and tonic.

"I'll take a bourbon," Roger said to Clyde, the aging, mustachioed bartender. "The good stuff, not that shit you serve to the local drunks." Roger sidled up to Chuck Roverson as Clyde poured a rocks glass of small-batch bourbon.

Chuck, startled by the sudden intrusion, jumped.

"Hey, pal, how's it going?" Roger said as he patted Chuck on the back.

"Oh, hey, Mr. Hadley. Fancy meeting you here," Chuck said loudly and stiffly, as if he were reading from a script.

Clearly Chuck couldn't handle improvisation. Roger's smile faded and he leveled his eyes at him, which clearly flustered Chuck, because he shrank down in his seat.

"What's the good word?" Roger asked in a more hushed tone.

Chuck followed suit and thankfully began to murmur, "I delivered two citations. Both should cost her around eighty dollars. She hasn't addressed them yet."

Roger smiled and said quietly, "That's all fine and well, but we might have to speed things up."

"Well, she's got a cat. That right there might be reason to kick her out of the marina. I left a citation about the cat at her slip on the way over here."

"Now you're thinking."

"Problem is, I already said the cat was okay when we spoke about renting the slip."

"You're the dock master, Chuck. Change the goddamn bylaws, my good man!"

"Well, the problem with that is that it takes a larger committee vote."

"She doesn't know that," Roger implored.

"True," Chuck said. Then he added hesitantly, "Mr. Hadley, about that final installment on the money. I need it."

Roger slowly turned his head, as if all the cogs had suddenly fallen into place. He stared at Chuck, who was slightly quivering. When he spoke, his voice was just above a whisper. "You got thugs after you, don't you, Chuck? What was it? The ponies?"

Chuck nervously took a sip of his drink and didn't respond.

Roger chuckled and said, "I tell you what, I'll give you the rest of the money the minute Nancy is run out of the marina. How's that for motivation?"

"But I need the rest. Fifteen hundred dollars by next week, or—"

Roger cut him off. "Results, Roverson. I pay for results."

There was a sudden sharp crash as Rita, the waitress, dropped a glass from the behind the bar. Chuck and Roger both jerked around toward the sound.

"Hi, guys, sorry about that," Rita said with a sheepish smile. She grabbed a bar towel and began to clean up her mess. "Reflexes just aren't what they used to be."

Roger looked her over once, trying to ascertain if she had heard anything. She continued to busy herself with cleaning the broken glass and then moved toward the kitchen. Roger watched her go.

"Well, I'll be damned," said a deep, gravelly voice from over by the windows. Roger and Chuck turned. It was Turk, and he was pointing out the window.

Roger looked and saw a weather-beaten boat tacking in the channel. The thick fog and shifting wind made it extremely dangerous to navigate the slim channel. Yet, here was a boat coming in. Under sail.

"Engine must have quit on them," Turk deducted.

Roger moved closer to the windows to watch the spectacle. Chuck followed. Even Santiago, who had been quietly sitting on his barstool in the corner, looked up from his crossword puzzle.

"Holy shit, that's her," Chuck said as he pointed in the direction of the boat.

"That's who?" Roger asked.

Behind the helm of the shabby-looking boat was the figure of his wife, looking in all directions as she guided the boat through a series of tacks in the narrow channel. Then he saw Nancy's crew, the goddamn Golden Girls, as they fumbled to help their captain; one even ran into the beam. Things were not going well for Nancy. Roger let out a low chuckle.

The rest of the room was silent as everyone watched the boat slowly navigate the harbor, relying on sketchy wind that would come up, swirl around, and abruptly whisk away again. It made for an awkward line. As the boat got closer, there was a real chance they could run aground on the large rocks right in front of the yacht club. Roger could see the worried faces of the women. But he noticed that Nancy looked stern and determined. It irked him.

"Nothing to laugh at," Turk said gruffly. "Maybe one in ten sailors could pull this off without hitting something. Hell, if we're talking those Port Royal posers, those clueless rich kids would already be crying and calling the Coast Guard. It's impressive, what she's doing."

Nancy and her rookie crew needed to make another tack that would bring them down the side channel that led to their slip on M dock. But it was a dicey move. A swirl of wind came from behind and caused the *Gypsea* to roughly jibe to port, sending the boat directly toward the keel-shredding rocks. Ruthie fell hard, her back hitting the cockpit bench. A palpable gasp was heard in the yacht club. Santiago moved toward the large windows. Turk remained seated but watched intently. Chuck and Roger hung back, watching without saying a word.

Nancy recovered quickly from the unexpected jibe by oversteering the boat in the opposite direction. An unexpected warm wind came out of nowhere, like a gift from Poseidon himself, and spirited the *Gypsea* out of harm's way.

Roger sighed heavily.

Chuck Roverson stood there, shiny from sweat, and said, "That was lucky."

"Luck had nothing to do with it," Turk growled as he got up and exited the club.

"She's a damn fine sailor," Santiago said as he looked out to the boat. "A sailor anyone should admire." He then tipped his tam and also left.

Roger fumed. "Kick her out as soon as possible," he snarled.

Chuck nervously nodded and scuttled away toward the direction of the door.

Roger slammed his drink on the bar. Rita came out of the kitchen, put her phone on the bar, and moved cautiously toward him.

"One more?" she asked Roger.

He didn't even look in her direction, just nodded and glared out at the darkening skies.

Roger wasn't accustomed to being bested, thwarted, or otherwise challenged, and patience was not his strong suit. He had been known to stand in front of a microwave oven, grumbling at the lengthy seconds it took to heat up a sticky bun. But this time there was an added urgency to Roger's normal level of impatience. He had a meeting in three short weeks to prove to his investors that he had an ironclad agreement in place with the Coastal Commission, whose votes were needed to approve his plans to renovate the entire Redondo Beach waterfront.

If approved, Roger's absurdly profitable development would revamp the Redondo Beach pier into an upscale outdoor mall with shops and eateries and an enormous three-story parking structure that would eclipse the ocean views of an entire neighborhood of original beach cottages. The seedier bars on the pier, like Old Tony's Crow's Nest, whose character and decor had been lovingly and locally curated over the last ninety years, would be replaced with high-rent-paying chain restaurants, whose character and decor could be bought on Amazon inside two weeks. He envisioned money pouring into the city from locals and tourists alike. It would bring energy and nightlife and attract a better, more moneyed clientele. Rather than moaning and groaning about losing their views in the name of progress, the lousy residents should be grateful to him. They should make Roger the goddamn mayor. Most importantly, however, the project could elevate Roger's company to a powerful statewide player. And the cherry on the cake of it all was a free boat slip for *Bucephalus* in the Port Royal Marina.

Only problem was, the Bayside Urban Renovation Project was wildly unpopular with damn near the entire population of Redondo Beach. The citizenry hated the idea of their quirky little beach town being transformed into a Rodeo Drive by the Sea. The residents had nicknamed the development project—originally unaware of its own unfortunate acronym—the Big BURP, after the environmental impact report concluded that construction of this magnitude would likely further worsen the natural oil leak directly out in front of the pier. The oil came from a fissure in the sea floor that let natural oil seep up, leaving small deposits of tar on the beaches. If made worse, people would sit in the new upscale restaurants and watch wave after oily wave, along with a dead sea lion or two, crash onto the faux rocks on the beach as they ate sushi rolls featuring tuna illegally caught in gill nets off the coast of Mexico.

Without the votes, there would be no approved plans, and Roger's investors would scatter faster than vampires at sunrise. Roger's newly formed company, Bayside Development, was highly leveraged on this deal and would surely go bankrupt without it. Not the anemic, toothless chapter eleven bankruptcy that merely reorganized debt, but rather the real and painful chapter seven bankruptcy that liquidated all his assets. Bankruptcy judges weren't what you would call sympathetic, especially to developers who came in with big promises and no approved plans. He could possibly lose it all. The great irony—Roger winced and sipped his Scotch—was that Nancy was the key to the entire plan. Unbeknownst to her, of course.

While most city council members could be seduced or outright bribed with lavish fishing trips to British Columbia or vacation villas in Costa Rica, it turned out there were still a few tree-hugging, Greenpeace-supporting hippies on the Coastal Commission who naïvely believed in the beauty and splendor of nature over the sheer pleasure of getting filthy rich. One of those hippies was Glenda Hibbert, a staunch advocate of all forests, sea animals, and most fervently, the beaches where she grew up.

She was also Nancy's old roommate from college.

Back in the day, Nancy and Glenda had protested every manner of environmental exploitation. Roger had shaken his head as the pair chained themselves side by side to redwoods to protect them from logging, stood in front of the governor's mansion to protest offshore drilling, and fought for a law to protect a blue butterfly sanctuary in El Segundo. Roger knew that if anyone could get Glenda to believe that the Bayside Urban Renovation Project was a good thing, or at least not an environmentally disastrous thing, it would be Nancy. And if Nancy got Glenda, he would get the necessary five votes, and the other four hippies on the Coastal Commission could all hop in a VW camper van and get naked together at Burning Man for all he cared.

Not only did Roger have to get Nancy back in this marriage for more personal reasons, like having someone to properly launder his multicolored golf pants, he also needed her back to make this deal happen. He had to convince her that his project was the best possible vision for the future of Redondo Beach, and more personally, for them. He was certain his powers of logic would work on her, or at least wear her down, if only he could get her off that goddamned boat and back under his pitched-beam roof with its spectacular 180-degree view.

CHAPTER FIFTEEN

NO GOOD SAIL GOES UNPUNISHED

After their near disaster, Nancy steered the *Gypsea* peacefully into her slip. It was over. They had returned safely under sail. Nancy took a deep sigh of relief.

"What's that?" Lois asked.

There was a pink piece of paper tacked to her light post. Nancy frowned. It was another citation from the dock master. The third one in as many days. One for adding a bit of carpeting to her dock so that her boarding step didn't slip—apparently a no-no. Her second violation was just as petty as the first—putting a potted palm at the end of her dock. The neighboring boat owner, a very friendly man by the name of Peter Ellis, loved the addition. Alas, no plants on the docks. Another arbitrary rule.

"Oh, it's probably nothing," Nancy said. She could only imagine what the third citation would be. She'd deal with that after the girls left.

With the boat safely tied up, Ruthie, Lois, and Judy sat in the cockpit and waited for a debriefing from their captain as they gave proper gravity to the situation that they had just encountered. They could have crashed into the break wall, been crunched by a tanker in the fog, or the boat could have caught fire. So many dangers, so little experience. The girls were rattled.

Nancy reconnected the shore power plug and hopped back on the boat to witness her somber crew.

"Surviving an emergency situation like that one can only mean one thing."

The girls looked apprehensive and crestfallen, as if this maiden voyage were somehow a failure, or worse, an ominous sign of journeys yet to come. Morale was low.

Nancy gave a stern nod and said, "Fireball shots." She held up a bottle of cinnamon whiskey, and the girls all burst into smiles.

"So, we're keeping the boat?" Judy asked.

"Hell's bells, of course we're keeping the boat. A little fog ain't gonna scare us off," Nancy replied. Judy still wore a worried expression. "Hey, hey, look at what we accomplished together. It was nothing a little ingenuity, skill, and quick thinking couldn't solve. And soon all of you will have those skills." As she said it, she bolstered her own confidence.

"Cheers to that," Lois said as she raised her fireball shot.

"To skills!" Ruthie exclaimed.

They had all downed their shots when they heard a knock on the side of the boat.

All four women turned their heads to see who came calling.

There stood Turk, captain of the *Hot Rum*. Nancy knew him well as Roger's sailing nemesis. She turned pale.

"Just wanted to say good job, ladies. That's the first time I've seen a boat come in under sail in those conditions. That fog was like something out of a Stephen King novel."

"*The Mist*. I read that one. Good stuff," Lois piped up.

Nancy brightened considerably, grinned, and said, "Thanks, Turk. Means a lot coming from you."

Turk merely tipped his hat and sauntered off toward *Hot Rum*. The girls returned to the cockpit. Nancy sighed with relief.

As soon as Turk left, they heard another knock on the side of the boat. This time it was Santiago.

"Good evening, Nancy." Santiago waved. "Well done on the sail."

Good god, Nancy thought. How many people had seen them come in?

Santiago continued, "I came to offer my services. I can take a look at your engine tomorrow?"

"Uh, hi, er, I mean, thank you, Santiago," Nancy said nervously. "That would be great."

Ruthie, Lois, and Judy looked over the side of the boat. All three waved to Santiago as Ruthie lifted one eyebrow. He waved back.

"Roger would shit his golf pants if he saw this," Ruthie whispered, elbowing Lois. Lois snickered, and Judy stifled a giggle.

All the girls quickly went back to their conversation in the cockpit to give Nancy a private audience with Santiago.

"I'd appreciate you taking a look. Not sure what's wrong with it," Nancy said.

"Say ten thirty tomorrow morning?" Santiago asked.

Nancy turned back toward Santiago and said nonchalantly, "Sure. I'll make coffee."

"See you then."

When he was safely out of listening range, the girls hooted, poked fun, and in all other ways relaxed on the back of the boat. This vibe was due in part to the sheer joy of coming in safely, in part to the fact that their maiden voyage was under their belt, and in part, despite Nancy's protests, to the tantalizing development that Santiago, the foxy boat mechanic, was coming over to her boat tomorrow to "check out her engine." Ruthie managed to put a naughty spin on it.

"Stop being so crass! He's my new friend in the marina. That's all."

None of them bought it. And Nancy didn't really either. She tried to repress a smile.

* * *

The sun was setting on the little marina, and after the girls had cleaned the *Gypsea* of all the leftover snacks and empty wine bottles, Lois and Judy carried the trash off the boat. Ruthie stayed for a few extra minutes to finish her wine.

"You did it, kid. You got us back in safely." Ruthie smiled at Nancy.

Nancy answering smile faded quickly. "I was scared out there. I have to do a better job of captaining. And teaching you how to sail. Things could have gone really wrong."

"I know all your tells. I knew you were nervous. But Nance, you got us in, without our help. Imagine what you can do when we actually know what ropes to pull."

"They're called sheets and lines," Nancy corrected.

"See? Always teaching," Ruthie said encouragingly.

Nancy half smiled but remained silent. Her doubt crept in and began to stir up her old demons, like the chills before a fever. She had spent the better part of her life making peanut-butter-and-jelly sandwiches, helping with algebra homework, and ironing golf pants. What was she doing here?

"Stop worrying about all the things that can go wrong. And focus on all the things that are going right. Like that dreamy boat mechanic." Ruthie nudged Nancy and raised an eyebrow.

"Dread is my default mode."

"Did I ever tell you what my airy-fairy hot-yoga teacher said?"

"You have a hot-yoga teacher?"

"For a hot minute. Anyway, she said, 'If you're sad, you're living in the past. If you're anxious, you're living in the future.' "

"You trying to tell me to live in the present?"

"I know it sounds like a load of horseshit, but that old woman is ninety-two and can still do the splits."

"Appalling mental image. But I get your point," Nancy said.

Ruthie went down into the salon to get her purse—and Otis, who had been asleep on the chart table bench since they arrived back at the slip, exhausted from sliding all over the cockpit while trying to stay alive. Ruthie handed her bag up to Nancy, who grabbed it. On the way up the ladder, Ruthie had a sharp intake of breath.

"Aaahhh!" she said.

"What is it?" Nancy asked.

Ruthie winced and handed Otis over to Nancy. "When I took that fall against the bench, I tweaked my back a little. Or maybe a lot."

"It takes a while to get your footing, sailor," Nancy said as she gently took a sleepy Otis into her arms. Ruthie hoisted herself up onto the cockpit and stood upright. "Ice should help."

"As long as it comes in a glass of bourbon," Ruthie retorted.

"Or that. Get some rest."

Ruthie and Otis successfully got off the boat. Nancy waved at them as they walked down the dock toward their car.

Ruthie saluted and called out, "See you tomorrow, 'O Captain, my Captain'!" as she walked gingerly up the dock.

Nancy hopped off the boat and grabbed the pink citation slip tacked to her light post. It was a violation of liveaboard policy. Cats were not allowed pursuant to marina code section 1481.ca.rb. The citation further threatened, *If you do not get rid of the animal, you will be forced to leave the Marina by Monday at 9am.* It was signed by dock master Chuck Roverson.

"What the––" Nancy murmured. She leaned against the light post, looked out over the marina, and thought for a second. She was fairly sure Brad had had a conversation with the dock master about the pet policy when she rented the slip. At that point, the cat was allowed. Had something changed? She'd visit Chuck Roverson first thing in the morning.

Her first few days as a liveaboard in King Harbor had been less than stellar. The welcome wagon hadn't exactly been wheeled out to herald her arrival. In fact, when she'd tried to greet a fellow liveaboard with a friendly wave, all she'd gotten in return was a glare and a grumble. When she had knocked to say hello and introduce herself to another liveaboard and rumored author, Jed Dawson, she got a loud and clear, "Shoo, woman!" That unwelcome greeting sent her back to her own cockpit to sulk. Perhaps he was working on his new crime novel and was annoyed at her intrusion. She had read somewhere that novel writers could get territorial about their alone time.

Then, on another evening, on the way back from the marina bathhouse, she'd seen another liveaboard, the old salt Tom Horn. Tom was better known around the marina as Captain Horny. He was usually a cheerful fellow, but he had unmistakably scowled at her as she passed, despite her commenting on what a lovely evening it was turning out to be.

It felt like she was being shunned. And it stung.

She shuffled to the salon down below, slightly despondent over not making any new friends in her boat neighborhood. She lit a sandalwood candle, poured the last of the wine, and relaxed next to Suzanne, who was fast asleep in Otis's old dog bed. She checked her phone and found she had two missed calls, one from Stella, the other an unknown number. Two messages, too. When she tapped the button, she heard her daughter's impatient tone.

"Hi, Mom. Okay, so you're in. Charlotte has agreed to come stay on the boat with you next weekend, as long as I agreed to up her data plan so she could watch Hulu and TikTok videos on her phone while she's there. Any chance you're getting Wi-Fi? I'll be dropping her off next Friday after school. I'm also packing a bunch of snacks for her because I have no idea how boat kitchens work. Do you even have a kitchen? Or is it like glorified camping? Are you sure you're doing the right thing? Okay, call me, gotta go."

Nancy shook her head. She already had Wi-Fi, and of course she could cook an entire meal in her galley—certainly Charlotte's favorite, pesto pasta with green peas and Parmesan. Instead of calling her back, Nancy decided to take the passive route and let her daughter stew with her unanswered questions for a while. After all, throughout this whole endeavor, Stella hadn't said a single encouraging word or even visited her mom's new floating abode.

Instead, Nancy felt a dismissive intolerance from her daughter, as if she couldn't wait for this ridiculous charade to end so that things could go back to normal. But Nancy had to remind herself that Stella didn't fully know the truth about her father's disgusting indiscretions with that harpy Claire Sanford on *Bucephalus*. To Stella, Nancy's move must have seemed inexplicable, even crazy. Like someone in the early stages of dementia. So, Nancy let her annoyance at her daughter ease. Plus, she was genuinely excited to have her granddaughter come and stay with her. She'd call her in the morning. She tapped the next message, and a familiar voice came on the line.

"Hi, Nancy, this is Rita at the King Harbor Yacht Club. Listen, I was working tonight, and I think I overheard something. Something you should know."

As Nancy listened, her eyes grew dark as she looked over the marina toward her ex-boat *Bucephalus*.

CHAPTER SIXTEEN
TURNABOUT IS FAIR PLAY

Although compact, the galley on the boat was surprisingly well equipped. It had an oven, a stovetop, a blender, a coffeemaker, and everything else she needed to make a batch of her legendary blueberry muffins topped with brown sugar crumble. But the muffins she was currently baking were no ordinary breakfast pastry; no, these muffins had a higher purpose. These were bribery muffins. She tossed the toasty muffins in a basket, fixed her hair, and with shaky optimism, headed toward the office of Chuck Roverson, dock master.

Her next-door boat neighbor, Peter Ellis, was standing barefoot on his boat drinking coffee. Ellis was short and squat, his round belly stretching his *Old Guys Rule* T-shirt to capacity, orange hair sticking out from under his baseball cap. He gave her a gap-toothed smiled as Nancy stepped on to her deck.

"What, pray tell, is that heavenly smell?" His eyes grew wide as he sniffed in the direction of her muffins, like a hound dog getting a whiff of a runaway fox.

"Blueberry muffins. You want one?"

Peter, still dazed by the scent, nodded with a goofy grin.

Nancy walked over and handed him two oversized, still warm muffins with a smile.

"Mmmmm." Peter took a big bite. "I don't think we've ever had a woman live aboard here, Mrs. Hadley."

"Call me Nancy."

"Okay." He paused. "Nancy it is. I think you might wear down some of the old salts if you keep baking things like these miraculous concoctions."

"I'm getting the feeling I'm not exactly welcome here. Is that the case?" Nancy asked tentatively.

"Oh, it's not personal. Some of the more cantankerous old turkeys rankle at the thought of a woman here among them. Means they might have to actually make themselves presentable, shave occasionally, and not fart with wild abandon."

Nancy laughed quietly. But then she thought about how her presence could disrupt the last bastion of the male hangout. This had been their version of a boy's tree fort. In any given marina, ninety-nine percent of liveaboards were men. The women that did reside on boats were usually the better half of a couple, and the ladies usually couldn't wait to get back on land. It was an extremely rare situation for an unaccompanied woman to choose to live on a boat of her own volition.

"Am I seen as the enemy here at the He-Man Woman Sailor Haters' Club?"

"I wouldn't say that. It's more like when a woman moves into your bachelor pad. At first, it's jarring. The fluffy bathroom rugs.

The flowered curtains. The locker room smell replaced by pumpkin spice candles. But then, we secretly begin to love it all. The same will happen with you here. I told you, I loved your addition of the palm at the end of the dock. Feels welcoming."

"The dock master disagrees." She held up her pink citation and then added, "So, I'm not the enemy, but I'm not one of you yet either."

"I think the general consensus is you don't know what you're doing."

"Is there an over/under on how long I'll stay before I go scuttling back to land?"

Peter Ellis looked down at the dock, embarrassed. "Three months."

"I see." Nancy had a thought. "Hey, do any of you guys play poker?" she asked.

Peter Ellis looked at her and cocked his head. "If you can't beat 'em, join 'em? I like your style. There used to be a weekly game hosted by an ex–Navy Seabee, but when Bob 'Bucko' Neighbors moved to Naples, Florida, it sort of petered out."

"Why don't you talk to some of the other guys, see if they'd be interested," Nancy said. "Tell them I'll make homemade pastrami sliders and I have a gallon of Pusser's rum, the preferred rum of the English Royal Navy."

"That oughta reel 'em in." Peter smiled and tipped his hat.

"Thanks, Pete."

"Where you off to with the rest of your blueberry stash?"

"Paying a visit to the dock master. Seems I've gone outside the ever-so-stringent rules. Three citations in the last three days. Hopefully I can corrupt him with muffins."

"Your muffins are strong game," Pete said as he took another big bite out of his. "Strange, though. Roverson is usually on our side. Let me know how it works out."

"Will do. See you later, Pete."

Nancy smiled at Pete and knew for a certainty there was a reason Chuck Roverson was not on her side. And that reason's name was Roger. Rita had told her she had overhead a conversation between him and Chuck—something about a payoff to get her cited and kicked out of the marina. Deductive logic and a close reading of the marina bylaws had led Nancy to believe that the citation over Suzanne was a bluff. One that couldn't be enforced, but there was only one way to be sure.

CHAPTER SEVENTEEN
TO THE VICTOR GO THE MUFFINS

Normally a jovial sort, and someone completely enamored with the technology of his smartphone, Chuck Roverson had begun to hate the device. Mostly because he was being harassed every four hours with texts or voice mail messages threatening to cut off the protruding parts of his body. One message even threatened to put his penis on a stick, roast it over a grill, and feed it to a shepherd–pit bull mix named Lucy. He needed a payment of three thousand dollars to his bookie by next Thursday. Roger Hadley would pay Chuck only after his wife was out of the marina, which had required him to issue the third citation about the cat last night. He'd done all he could do.

So, he popped a beer and poured it into his coffee cup to calm his nerves. He looked out his office window and saw Nancy Hadley walking up to his office with a basket.

Nancy knocked on the glass door as Chuck busied himself by bringing up some random spreadsheet on his computer screen. He heard the knock and looked up.

"Good morning, Mrs. Hadley," Chuck said. The scent of blueberry-infused baked goods wafted his way.

"Call me Nancy," she said. "And good morning. I brought these muffins to you as a, shall we say, goodwill gesture. I can't help but think I've crossed some invisible marina boundary of etiquette, and I was hoping we could talk and get back on the right track."

Chuck stiffened his upper lip and looked down at the basket, trying to stop his mouth from watering. He gently lifted a muffin and tried to remain outwardly stern, although his resolve was weakening with every whiff.

"Well, Nancy, truth is, these rules are in place for your safety. And if you can't seem to abide by them, then we are going to have a problem. You just might have to go." Chuck took a big bite. Brown sugar crumbs tumbled down the front of his shirt. The muffins were buttery and soft. Best muffins ever. It was hard to look tough in that moment.

"Right. About that. I was unaware of the rules on carpet, but it's already removed. And the palm tree is safely back on my boat, not offending either man nor beast. But the last one, the one about pets . . ."

"Tough one. But we can't make an exception."

"I wouldn't dream of asking you to make an exception," Nancy said meekly. And then she bowed her head.

Chuck, sensing victory and a payment that would quell the menacing calls, took a huge bite of the delicious muffin, letting its flavors wash over his tongue.

"Only thing is," Nancy began, after pulling papers out of her bag, "I have a copy of the marina's bylaws as of three weeks ago, and they clearly state that pets are allowed for liveaboards. And then, another funny thing. I checked the contract I signed for the slip last week, and I believe you initialed the portion where it says I have a pet that is expressly allowed by, well, you. If memory serves, you even said Suzanne was a nice name for a cat."

Chuck spit out his muffin in panic. Since when did people come prepared to muffin meetings? The vision of his roasting penis being fed to a crazed junkyard dog caused a nervous shudder.

"The bylaws were, uh, changed recently!" Chuck sputtered.

"I see." Nancy leveled her gaze at Chuck, unflinching.

The heat began to rise up his neck, and he could feel a thin sheen of sweat overtaking his entire face. "As you know, we have the right to change the bylaws at any time—" Chuck started.

"The operative word being *we*," Nancy interrupted. "Chuck—can I call you Chuck?" Nancy yanked the muffin basket back just out of Chuck's reach and frowned at him. "Turns out you alone cannot arbitrarily change the bylaws. They have to be voted on by the entire board. And this morning, with the help of your lovely assistant Ashley, I made a few phone calls, and none of the other voting members seems to recall voting to revoke the pet policy. So, Suzanne the Cat and I are staying exactly where we are."

Chuck sat there dumbfounded, struggling to find a plausible argument that didn't make him come off as a lying slimeball. Nothing bubbled up. Chuck slumped in his chair, defeated. "Okay, you can keep the cat, but I don't know what I'm gonna do."

Nancy's glare softened. She put the muffin basket back within his reach and asked, "This wasn't about the cat, was it? This was about me. What is going on, Chuck?"

Chuck put his elbows on his knees and his head in his hands. He let out a deep, fear-laced sigh, and his resolve, once solid and strong, folded like a cheap lawn chair. "I owe money to some people, and your husband just wanted you to come home. Seemed like a win-win. No harm, no foul."

Nancy nodded, like a detective who had finally gotten his perp to crack. She put a hand on his shoulder. "Look, it sounds like my husband's warped idea to get me back home has forced you into an unfavorable position. You'll never get me out with the marina bylaws, because I've read them three times now, and I am well aware of how to stay within the rules. But I don't like holding grudges. I think it causes cancer. So, I tell you what. I'll make you a batch of those blueberry muffins every Monday."

"Sure," he said with a whimper. For all the devious behavior he had committed against her, Nancy Hadley stood there comforting him. Women. Their capacity for forgiveness and kindness was an eternal spring. But even her amazing muffins couldn't solve Chuck's other problem. The one that required money, of which he had only the fifteen hundred Roger had fronted him and a losing lottery ticket in his pocket. He looked grim at the prospect of a visit from the thugs. He moaned.

Nancy bent down and put a hand on Chuck's shoulder. "How much money do you owe them?" Nancy asked, which brought him out of his stupor.

"Three thousand dollars by Thursday and I only have half," he said glumly.

Nancy stood up and glanced out over the marina before resting her gaze once more on poor disheveled Chuck Roverson.

She put a hand on her hip and said, "You like poker?"

CHAPTER EIGHTEEN
THE GAME IS ON

When Nancy walked back to *Gypsea* from the dock master's office, she made a mental note to call the boat painter today. She looked over at her shabby little vessel with its sun-bleached sides and chipped blue paint and knew that her little boat needed a makeover. As she got closer, she noticed a large figure leaning over the dock toward the bow of her boat where Suzanne was sitting. The hefty man reached out to the cat, and a sudden fear rose in Nancy that he might harm her or wrench her off the boat and throw her into the water. She instinctively started toward the giant man and yelled, "Stop!"

The menacing figure, who was clad in a ratty camouflage overcoat, was startled and turned toward her. Despite his size, he had a gentle face under a white beard, now contorted with a frightened expression. His turn caught him off-balance and he nearly fell off the dock. He used the side of the boat to steady himself.

"Oh, no, it's not what you think," the man said with a high, thin voice.

"Don't harm her!" Nancy moved closer to him, but not too close. Where was her Taser when she needed it?

"Sardines," the man said innocently, and held up two small recently dead fish.

Nancy hesitated, unsure of what to believe. This was the same man that had scowled and grumbled at her three days earlier by the bathhouse. His appearance wasn't doing him any favors. The heavily faded camouflage jacket revealed no shirt underneath, and he wore a pair of huge black combat boots. His appearance was only slightly disarmed by his navy shorts that had little cartoon whales on them. He easily stood six foot five, making the sardines look like tiny minnows in his enormous hands. His wiry white hair swayed in the wind, and Nancy thought this was what Hemingway must have looked after spending a decade drunk in Havana.

"Sardines?"

"For the kitty. Look, she likes them."

Suzanne was rubbing up against the metal railing of the boat waiting for the sardines to come back within reach. The man gently offered up the small fish and Suzanne sunk her teeth into one and dragged it onto the deck.

He turned back and smiled. "She and I are friends."

"Are you sure she can eat raw fish?"

"Cats are true carnivores. They can eat any meat raw," the man said softly as he wiped his fishy hands on his faded jacket and held out one to Nancy.

She hesitated at what her hand would smell like afterward but took his handshake all the same. Best to be neighborly.

"Madam, I am Shepard Wallace. You can call me Shep. I'm a liveaboard over on K dock. Ex-vet." He spoke eloquently, almost regally, when not startled.

"I'm Nancy, and that is Suzanne," she said pointing to her cat. "Where did you serve?"

"Oh no, ex-veterinarian. I'm a pacifist. I thought it might be a good idea to meet the new liveaboard and her feline. I'm a big fan of cats," he offered with a sheepish grin.

"Well, it's nice to meet you, Shep. I'm happy Suzanne lured you over. I'm beginning to think I'm as welcome as a case of syphilis around here."

Shep chuckled. "This cranky old bunch needs a breath of fresh air. So be it that it came in the lovely form of you and your fluffy cat."

Suzanne then leaned over to get an affectionate rub. Shep happily obliged as he continued, "Change is hard for some people. Give it some time. Ellis told me you were trying to get a poker game together."

"Wow, word travels fast around here."

"I blame the boredom. For all those sorts who claim they want to keep to themselves, they can't help getting in everyone else's business. Such is the human condition, I suppose," Shep said with a wink. "Let me know what night and what I can bring."

"Does this mean Suzanne should get used to a steady supply of fresh sardines?"

"As long as they're running. Cats and boats go together. Be careful, though—old Jed Dawson has what we affectionately call a hellhound."

Nancy raised her eyebrows and realized he must be referring to the frothy-mouthed bullmastiff on the other side of her dock. She looked across the way at Jed's boat, which had the lights on. She could smell bacon frying. "Thanks for the tip."

Shep began to amble off.

"Hey, Shep," Nancy said as he turned back toward her. "Thank you for the sardines."

"You're welcome."

"And for the kindness."

He nodded and gave her a wave.

She watched Shep shuffle slowly back to his houseboat on K dock. Nancy had not been aware of how stuck and stagnant she had felt when she was in the business of taking care of her family. The busyness just seemed to take over. She was always so busy. Busy with dirty dishes, playdate drop-offs, and family dinners. Then it was college planning, business building, and couples' dinners. The dreams and passions of her husband and daughter had eclipsed her own by taking tiny bits of her attention each day until Nancy had no time left for her own aspirations. As a young mother, she had put her internal longings on hold, including even finishing her degree, and had convinced herself that watching her child grow up to be strong and independent was her dream. That seeing her husband thrive in business was also, in part, her dream. But there was a terrifying hollowness to her convictions. She had become invisible while cheering on everyone else. Even her capacity for self-reflection had diminished. She knew Roger's favorite drink, she knew her daughter's favorite dinner, and she knew what her granddaughter wanted for Christmas. But she had a hard time really knowing what she wanted. If she wasn't ironing golf pants or cooking a favorite meal or helping to foster someone else's goals, she didn't know how to spend her time. Now there was a burning question that lingered in the recesses of her brain. What did she like? What did she want? Who was she without the familiar titles of Doting Mother and Supportive Spouse to define her?

It was a tough question. Who was she?

She chose one word at a time.

Captain. She was the captain of a boat that needed painting.

Woman. Not wife. Who had just stared down the dock master and won.

Liveaboard. The first female to be one in King Harbor, despite the bristling macho fellow sailors who didn't accept her.

The words came faster as she listed off her very certain likes. Sailing, Chardonnay, Bob Seger, ahi tacos at Blue Water Grill, and a homemade pot of coq au vin. As she sat back creating her canvas of who she was, she added that she was also about to be the host of the hottest poker game in the marina. And right now, that was a damn good start.

* * *

"Hola?"

Nancy looked up to see Santiago, his smile sparkling under his familiar tam. Heat rose in her cheeks.

"Hola! Come aboard. I made coffee." Nancy had readied a pot of Colombian roast and a plate of her muffins for his arrival. A lazy breeze kept the heat at bay and kept the pelicans aloft.

Santiago climbed aboard, and Suzanne instantly came running from the bow to meet him. He greeted Nancy with a kiss on both cheeks. Very European. Or Argentinian? Or Cuban? Nancy resolved to crack that mystery.

"Looks like you've got a fan," Nancy said, as Suzanne brazenly rubbed up against Santiago's hand. Suzanne was wildly purring. Nancy envied her little cat's ability to let down her guard.

"She's a sweet little thing." Santiago petted her head and then reached for the steaming coffee cup Nancy offered him. "So, what happened with your engine last night?"

"I'm not quite sure. When I bought the boat, we had a full inspection on the Yanmar diesel, and it passed with flying colors. The first sail I went on by myself, I only used it in the channel, and it worked fine. But last night it sputtered twice, belched up some black smoke, and went dead."

"This boat, in the hands of a lesser sailor in that fog last night, could have been a real disaster."

Nancy didn't know if that was a compliment or a scolding, as if she might be the subject of a cautionary tale. She decided not to say anything.

"You were very impressive."

Compliment, indeed. "Thank you," Nancy said.

"An engine that has just undergone an inspection usually should run problem-free for at least a year. It sounds like you either ran out of gas or lost your spark. Let me go below and take a look."

She took his cup from him as he went down with his tool bag.

After about ten minutes, Santiago came back up to the cockpit with a little grease on his cheek. "Nancy, I hate to tell you this, but you're completely out of gas."

"Impossible. I filled it the day I bought the boat, and I've used the engine once." Unless there was some type of leak, she couldn't be out of gas. She was almost positive she'd checked the fuel gauge, but in her haste to get the girls settled on the boat, she might have overlooked it.

"It's been known to happen to the best of sailors," Santiago offered generously.

Nancy walked over to her gauge. It clearly read full. "Look, the gauge says I'm full."

Santiago walked over to survey the gauge. He nodded that yes, indeed, it showed full. Then he raised his finger and lightly tapped the gauge. The needle slowly fell to below empty.

Nancy was crestfallen. "But I just filled it up. I know I did. I think I still have the receipt."

Santiago sat there for a second, staring down and thinking. "Perhaps I should look to see if you have a gas leak. Or, is it possible that someone siphoned your gas?"

"Not that I know of." A dark thought crossed Nancy's mind, but then she immediately pushed it out.

"Well, let's get her filled up and you should be fine." Santiago took another sip of his coffee and set the cup down. "I'll call Sandpiper Marine Fuel and get them over here. You'll be good in no time." He dialed a number and sauntered to the other end of the boat.

Nancy sat there puzzling over the gas problem while her coffee went cold.

"They should be here in about fifteen minutes. And I must go," Santiago said, then leaned over and gave her the same two cheek kisses before going on his way.

Butterflies.

* * *

Roger had called Chuck Roverson three times in fifteen minutes. He needed to know if Nancy had been booted from the marina, because Glenda Hibbert was in town and he could have this whole Coastal Commission vote locked up before late next week. He needed Nancy and soon.

"Pick up the goddamn phone, you derelict!" Roger yelled, as he heard Chuck Roverson's cell go to voice mail.

He decided to go down to the marina to see the man in person. Besides, his Nest thermostat was on the fritz, so his house was ten degrees hotter than normal. One irritating issue at a time. He got in his Mercedes and cruised down the hill to Ocean Drive and took a left into the marina.

Roger parked by his dock to check on *Bucephalus* and make sure he had properly hidden the fuel cans and siphon hose he had given to Roverson the day before. Jesus, what a disaster. He'd thought for certain that Nancy, faced with all the unforeseen problems a boat could have, would have reconsidered living on the damn thing by now. But no, instead she'd come off as a hero. Stymied again. By his wife, no less! If he weren't Roger Hadley, he'd think he was losing his edge. Damn her sailing skills. He covered up the fuel cans with an old tarp and stowed them behind a pylon.

He walked up to the dock master's office but found it empty. He peeked in the windows but saw only a few empty beer cans and a basket with a muffin in it. That muffin looked suspiciously like one of Nancy's legendary blueberry muffins. He knew a ploy when he saw one. She must be bribing Roverson with her delicious muffins. He would not be outmaneuvered by baked goods.

He grumbled as he walked back to *Bucephalus*. The boat gleamed in the midafternoon sun; a few gulls were resting on the pristine lifelines. Roger rousted the birds by yelling, "Vermin!" The fowl unhappily flew off.

He unlocked the salon and went down to grab the bourbon. As he snatched the bottle off the teak counter, he stopped momentarily, entranced by the memory of him and Claire Sanford wrapped in their naked, sweaty embrace in the galley. He took a big swig, and a smile curled his lip as he remembered the scent of her perfume on her neck, something spicy with ginger and cinnamon. That fond memory was followed quickly by the nightmare of Nancy's appearance and the sight of her and Faye Woodhall looking down at them from the cockpit. His smile disappeared. Christ. What a fucking disaster. He grabbed a set of travel binoculars, climbed up to the cockpit, and walked to the bow of the boat.

From the top deck, he focused the binoculars to see Nancy's crappy little vessel moored peacefully in slip number thirteen. Suddenly, the head of Santiago popped up from her salon. Roger saw the greasy boat mechanic take a sip of Nancy's coffee and then kiss his wife's cheeks before departing.

"Is that so . . ."

He lit a cigar, sipped his bourbon, and stewed.

CHAPTER NINETEEN
A PIRATE NEVER HAS A TELL

Chuck Roverson was a horrible poker player. If Chuck had a good hand, his tell was so obvious that even Suzanne the Cat knew it. Chuck would take a giant swig of his beer, slam his can down on the table, and grin like a fool. A bad hand would compel Chuck to unknowingly put his right finger in his ear and nervously wiggle it. Nancy had her work cut out for her. Luckily, she had Ruthie, her ace in the hole.

Poker night had commenced on Tuesday evening and had drawn a larger crowd than she expected. There were eight players who sat in the packed salon waiting to be dealt a hand of Texas Hold'em by her boat neighbor, Peter Ellis. To Ellis's right sat the gentle giant Shep Wallace; next to him was Chuck, who was already two sheets to the wind, and then Captain Horny and Turk, the owner of *Hot Rum*. Rounding out the table was Ruthie, and to Nancy's delight, her old crew on *Bucephalus*, Mac and Tony. She had extended the invite in hopes they hadn't chosen sides between her and Roger. They accepted and even brought two bottles of exotic rum as boat-warming gifts.

Mac and Tony knew Turk, of course, but she was surprised that they were also friends with Shep and Captain Horny, as they had all grown up together in Manhattan Beach. They regaled the table with stories of beach volleyball, cheap grub at Bill's Tacos on Pier Avenue, and chasing scantily clad roller skaters on their beach bikes known locally as strand cruisers.

"Shep and I used to work at Mac's Liquor on Marine and Highland," Captain Horny said.

"Still consider it the best job I ever had," Shep said. "Frank Cleary's volleyball crew played on the sand courts right at the bottom of Marine. They used to bet how long it would take a guy to run from the volleyball court, up to Mac's, slap the exact amount for a twelve-pack of Budweiser on the counter, and run back down," Shep recalled.

"Six minutes, eighteen seconds was the record," Tony somehow remembered, as he grinned under his bushy moustache.

"Competition was fierce," Captain Horny added.

Nancy felt she had definitely made some tentative inroads with the liveaboards. It didn't hurt that Tony and Mac had spent the better part of the night highlighting Nancy's sailing skills. The poker crew was welcoming their newest liveaboard.

Overall, the poker game was going well. Nancy's jaw grew tight when she first announced the one-hundred-dollar buy-in, but she was surprised when none of the sailors even flinched as they forked over the cash. Nancy, famous in her social group for her hospitality when hosting anything from a Kentucky Derby party to a full-on clambake, found the boat slightly more challenging space-wise, but the rules of hosting a good party were always the same: good lighting, delicious snacks, and most importantly, ply your guests with large amounts of quality booze.

She had purchased white twinkle lights and put them around the rim of her canopy, and she had lashed one tiki torch to the stern of the boat, a sign that the poker game was on. In the background, jazz great Bill Evans's mellow piano emanated from the boat stereo. Ruthie shuffled and Nancy refilled drinks as the crew knocked back painkillers made with Pusser's rum, pineapple juice, cream of coconut, and a dash of nutmeg. Shep especially liked the concoction and apologized for asking for a third.

"Brings back my island days," he said sheepishly as he politely handed his cup over.

"What island?" Ruthie asked.

"I lived in Tahiti for about ten years. Married one of their princesses," Shep said with a quiet grace. "Just like Captain Cook. She was the light of my life, and I shall love and remember her until we meet up among the Polynesian gods." He smiled.

Ruthie smiled warmly back at Shep, a clear sign of acceptance.

Nancy had two goals for this poker party. The first was to make friends with some of the liveaboards in the marina, all of whom were men. A batch of hot pastrami sliders seemed to be doing the job so far.

Before the game started, Nancy had had a brief chat with every one of them. As gruff as they'd all appeared at first, the guys were surprisingly open about their lives when she asked about the circumstances that had brought them here. All of which gave Nancy the impression that no one asked them about anything much anymore. A sailor's life could be a lonely one. Each had a story that had landed them here, living on a boat, floating on water, loosely tethered to the docks of civilization instead of living on solid ground—divorce, failed businesses, bankruptcy, widowerhood, or a combination of those reasons. It seemed, at least for this crowd, that the reason for living on a boat was born of loss, a broken dream, or a failure. Nancy realized that was her truth as well. This brand of resigned sadness in her fellow boat dwellers might eventually come skulking in her direction too. It wasn't doing much to tamp down her own deeply held anxiety.

"Shuffle up and deal, Turk," Captain Horny said, his thick Southern Georgia accent becoming more pronounced with every sip of his painkiller. His baseball cap had a Georgia Bulldog on it, and he had a gentle, disarming smile.

Not all who lived on boats were a sad sort, however. Peter Ellis was joking about a greenhorn who had just put a for-sale sign on his Hunter thirty-nine-foot.

Turk said, "He only lasted seven months. Who had seven months, Ellis?"

Ellis pulled out his phone and checked. Then he answered, "Dawson had six months, three weeks."

The owner of said boat was what the guys called a short-timer. Every year, there were always a couple of guys in their late thirties or early forties who came down breathless and excited, new boat keys in hand, who couldn't wait to toss convention aside and live like Jimmy Buffett, free and easy. Some newcomers even hauled a ukulele on board. But it never lasted long. Within six to nine months, the boats of the greenhorns were left to sit alone in their slips, their owners returning to their drab cubicles and cute girlfriends, back to climbing the pointless ladders of success, with no deeper understanding of life, their only trophy being able to say romantically, even wistfully, "Yeah, I lived on a boat once." But that was the equivalent of singing karaoke in a dive bar and claiming you were once a rock star. Ellis explained that when the for-sale signs went up on the short-timers' boats, every liveaboard would share a wry smile. Boat living wasn't meant for everyone, and Nancy got the sense they thought the same of her. She knew the over/under on her making it here was three months. For a moment, she even considered betting.

Nancy's second and more pressing short-term goal was to assist Chuck Roverson in winning the night's loot so he could pay off his gambling debt, keep all of his protruding body parts, and void Roger's control over him. At present, Chuck's pile of cash was going down quicker than the *Titanic*. He had eighty-two bucks left, which wouldn't be considered too bad, except he'd already had to buy in twice more at a hundred dollars a pop. Ellis and Captain Horny were both up, and Ruthie had been playing close to the vest. Turk was dealing and they put in for the blinds.

Turk dealt each player two cards facedown, and they all made a round of bets. The flop revealed a pair of sixes and a jack of hearts. As Nancy got up to ostensibly check the tiki torch, she glanced at Chuck's hand—he had a four and a queen. No bueno. She scratched her eyebrow as Ruthie looked up at her. The dipshit would likely stay in. He had stayed in on horrible hands the entire night, foolishly thinking he'd beat the odds. Only he never, ever did. But that's what Ruthie was for. She stayed in. Ellis stayed in, as did Shep, Mac, and Tony. Captain Horny folded, tapped out. It was the last hand of the night, so the big and small blinds were the largest so far, and you could feel the energy level of the table kick up a notch.

The betting began with Shep.

"Raise twenty," Shep shyly said.

Everyone put in twenty, including Chuck.

Mac raised another twenty, and Tony checked.

Surprisingly, everyone stayed in again. Turk flipped the fourth card, the turn. A jack of diamonds. Another round of spirited bets. Turk then flipped over the final card, the river, which was a three of hearts.

Chuck wiped sweat from his brow, nervously coughed, and went for his ear again. Anyone with an ounce of poker skill or basic poker knowledge would fold. But alas, he did not. Ruthie paused and looked at each player. She led them deeper into the muck. "Time to separate the boys from the broads. I'm in for a hundred more."

A bet like this would normally scare off lesser sorts, but these were liveaboards and they'd proved over the course of the night to be crusty, daring, and hardened from a steady diet of rum and boredom. They lived for this kind of bare-knuckle action. Ellis called. Shep threw in the last of his money. Mac and Tony tossed in their cards. And Chuck Roverson pushed the last of his sweaty dollars into the pot and said he was good for the rest. It all came down to this one hand. Winner take all. The pot was at eighteen hundred dollars.

Shep revealed a pair of tens, his lucky number. Turk showed his hand next. He gave a shy grin and turned over the six of hearts. With his six, he had a full house and what looked to be the winning hand.

Ellis sighed heavily and threw his pair of kings into the middle. Not good enough to beat Turk.

Chuck threw in his pathetic four and queen. The idiot. Nancy saw a shadow of shock cross Chuck's face as he realized he was all but assured of losing an appendage in the very near future. He suddenly grew pale.

"Sorry, boys," Ruthie said as she turned over her cards to reveal she had the jack of clubs. She also had a full house, but better than Turk's. The pot was all hers.

There was a collective groan.

"I don't usually play with amateurs. I'll go easier on you next time," Ruthie said with a wink as she raked in all the cash with her arms.

"Not bad for a broad," Turk said as he got up, chewing on the last bit of a cigar in his mouth.

Mac and Tony each gave Nancy a big hug, said they'd see her soon, and asked her not to hold it against them if they sailed with Roger.

"Never," Nancy said.

Peter Ellis stood, gathered his sunglasses, and downed the rest of his painkiller.

"Well, I'm going to go sip bourbon on the back of my boat and get a little more comfortable with my loss," Ellis said. Then he gave a salute to Turk, Shep, and the rest of the boys and turned toward Ruthie and said, "Wanna join me, hot stuff?" He smiled to reveal a dimple in his cheek and a twinkle in his eye.

A smile curled up on one side of Ruthie's face. "You old salty dog," Ruthie said. "Is it good bourbon?"

"Life is too short to drink any other kind," Ellis answered as he held out his hand to her to join him.

Ruthie stacked the cash together and handed it to Nancy. "See ya, sister." She took Pete's hand and hopped off. Nancy could hear Ruthie giggle at something Ellis had said. She couldn't help but smile.

"Welcome to the neighborhood, Nance," Turk growled in as friendly a manner as he could muster after his poker beatdown. He shook her hand and found his way off the boat.

"I'm a sucker for pastrami sandwiches. Much appreciated," Captain Horny said as he munched the last one, gathered his things, and also wandered off the boat.

Shep was giving Suzanne one last pet and reached into his pocket for a sardine he had wrapped in a plastic bag for her.

"Alas, it is time for me to depart, fuzzy one," he said to the cat. Then, to the humans, "Until we meet again, ladies and gents." Shep quietly departed.

Nancy began cleaning up the boat and looked over at Chuck Roverson, who looked ashen and drawn.

"Oh god," Chuck muttered, his head in his hands.

"Chuck—" Nancy tried to interrupt.

"No, you don't understand. There's a pit bull–shepherd mix named Lucy!"

"Chuck, calm down."

"They'll be waiting for me!" Chuck stood up, ready to bolt. But Nancy put a firm hand on his shoulder and sat him down on the cockpit bench. She handed him eighteen hundred dollars from the poker game, all the winnings. She had also given Ruthie a bottle of bourbon for her skills.

"It's all yours," Nancy said.

"But Ruthie won all that. It's hers."

"No, no, you don't have to worry."

"She doesn't have a crazed junkyard dog, does she?" he asked, suspicious.

"Ruthie did this as a favor to me," Nancy said, reassuring him.

Chuck squinted at her, obviously trying to work it out.

"But how did you know she would win?"

"Ruthie has a master's in psychology and she's a woman. Never underestimate our intuition. Plus, she won a poker championship in Morongo Casino back in the day. Odds were in her favor."

He stared down at the money she had just given him. "So, you did this"—Chuck's brain was processing, albeit slowly—"for me?"

"Technically, I did it for me. You needed money for reasons I do not need to know. Roger was paying you to run me out of the marina, right? Well, now you don't have to run me out of the marina, you can still pay off your thugs, er, debts, whatever they may be, and Roger is off your case."

"You mean I don't have to deal with Roger anymore?" Chuck sounded relieved.

"Nope."

Chuck hesitated but then added, "He's mean, ma'am. Like a snake. He scares me."

Nancy nodded. Roger didn't play nice. He claimed it was his reason for success in business. Balls and brains. But there was real fear on Chuck's face.

"You don't have to deal with Roger anymore, Chuck." Nancy patted him on the shoulder and gently lifted his elbow so he knew it was his cue to leave.

Chuck stood up, wadded up the money, and put it in his pocket.

"You have no idea how excited I am to keep my penis," Chuck said weakly as he sniffed, his eyes wet with tears and relief.

"I, uh, can only imagine," Nancy said as she grimaced. "Now, go pay off those thugs, er, debts, and try to behave."

"I will, ma'am. I will. I promise. No more. Screw those loser Chargers!"

Nancy had no idea what he meant, but she took it as a good sign that Chuck was going to turn over a new leaf. Or at least remain physically intact and gainfully employed.

Chuck Roverson nearly tripped on the power line lying on the dock as he stumbled back to the dock master's office. This clumsy move only cemented in Nancy's mind that Chuck wasn't a bad man but rather just a well-meaning, lovable doofus who could stand to lay off the sauce a little.

Nancy watched him go and then took a moment to wipe down the table. She poured herself a small glass of wine and sat down on the bench. She felt that same balmy breeze come into the marina, and as it flooded over her, she faced its warm energy and let it fill her up. She breathed it in and reflected on a lively evening of making new friends, helping a poor soul in need of a leg up, and genuinely having fun. For the first time, she felt safe and as if she might belong here. Plus, her plan had worked. Roger had no hold over her now. Suzanne was happily gnawing on her sardine, and the last thing Nancy heard before she dozed off was the tinkling of ice cubes and the laughter of her best friend Ruthie coming across the water from Peter Ellis's boat.

CHAPTER TWENTY
A DEBT FULLY PAID

It was nearly one in the morning. Chuck Roverson's thumb hovered over the send button on his smartphone as he read and then reread the text he was about to send to Roger Hadley:

> Thank you, Mr. Hadley, for our arrangement, but I can't go through with our deal. I can pay you back next month after the Chargers Browns game. Hope we can have a beer soon! ☺

Seemed friendly enough. He took a swig of warm beer, which gave him the liquid courage he would need to hit send. It wouldn't be that bad. He was just politely asking to be let out of their arrangement. No harm, no foul. And besides, Nancy was a nice lady and a good addition to the marina. Even the crustiest of liveaboards couldn't resist her otherworldly muffins and poker nights. Hopefully Roger Hadley would let bygones be bygones.

Now that he had dealt with the Roger issue, Chuck turned his attention to cleaning up his not-so-little gambling debt. He wadded up the money Nancy had given him plus Roger's share, a cool, even three thousand dollars, put it in a brown paper bag as instructed, and waited for the headlights to flash from the parking lot. The marina was unnaturally dark. There was no moon in the night sky, plus some of the dock lights were out. Chuck had been so embroiled in his personal problems that he hadn't had a chance to replace the three broken lights on the dock posts outside. Bright side of that was it would make it easier to see the flashing headlights. He prided himself on how his preoccupation with sports betting and his commitment to procrastination had played to his benefit. Everything happens for a reason, he thought.

Sure enough, about a minute later, a pair of headlights flashed twice from the parking lot. Chuck took a last swig of beer, put his phone in his pocket, grabbed the brown paper bag, and headed down the dock toward the lot.

Unfortunately, the ill-lit dock, combined with the inky darkness of a moonless sky, made it hard to navigate. Chuck hurried along and, in his haste, tripped over something thick and wet. He fell flat on his belly, splayed out like a grounded flounder. He got up, the money still tightly held in his fist, and went over to inspect what had caught his foot. He heard a loud snort and suddenly felt a bolt of pain in his ankle. Something bit him.

"Aaaaagh! Damn it!" Chuck screeched as he yanked up his ankle.

He inspected himself and saw a large bite mark with a little blood. He looked down at a very large, very agitated harbor seal.

"Schnoooooft!" The seal huffed a warning that sounded like a foghorn. "Mawwwwr!" A seal's version of a growl. The seal took an aggressive lunge toward Chuck.

Chuck freaked out and hopped on one leg forward to try to get away from the seal. Cradling his mangled ankle, his next hop landed him on an errant kayak paddle left on the dock. The paddled rolled and sent him off-balance. He fell backward off the dock and into the water with a giant splash.

When he stood up, he was in neck-deep water. He checked for the bag of money—no longer in his fist—and desperately searched around in the water as the seal sounded another warning that made Chuck scream like a little girl. Then he spotted it. The brown paper bag full of cash was floating out to sea. He frantically swam to it, grabbed it, held it in his teeth, and crawled up the nearest ladder and back onto the relative safety of the dock. Out of breath and roughly ten feet from the angry seal, Chuck got up, soaking wet, and limped quickly past the seal toward the parking lot.

"Christ, what else?"

Chuck stumbled forward and didn't look back into the black water where he had taken his untimely dip. If he had, he would have seen the fading light of a text from Roger Hadley that read, You will pay, Roverson.

CHAPTER TWENTY-ONE
AHOY, TEEN MATEY!

It was noon on Friday, and a low marine layer of clouds was threatening rain. Nancy frowned. She didn't want bad weather to cast a pall on the first day her granddaughter was visiting the boat. Stella was on her way to drop off Charlotte for the weekend. Nancy had taken great measures to make sure Charlotte would not only be comfortable but would actually like it on the boat. She'd stocked the galley with her granddaughter's favorites: cheese sticks, Flamin' Hot Cheetos, and KitKats. She'd made her bed and put a small stuffed orange fish pillow in her berth. And she'd double-checked that the Wi-Fi was working. She was nervous but excited.

Nancy, however, had been warned that the charming, sweet granddaughter she knew and loved had recently been replaced by a new teen doppelgänger. She looked a lot like Charlotte, but instead of having an easy smile, a cheerful attitude, and a wardrobe that included koala bear sweatshirts, she now wore black T-shirts, a pair of black-and-white-checkered Vans, and a perpetual expression of disapproval under her dark-purple-dyed hair. Her vocabulary had been reduced to one-word answers that Stella classified as glorified grunts. "She's difficult right now, Mom," Stella told her before she left the house.

"I have some experience with teenagers. You were one once."

"It's different now. Smartphones are ruining our kids."

"We used to say that about TV with your generation."

"Yes, but I grew up addicted to *Friends* and *Seinfeld*. These kids watch vlogs about suicide and school shootings. It's *dark*."

"I'm up to the challenge. See you soon," Nancy said. She silently wondered how surly her granddaughter could really be.

Stella pulled up in the marina parking lot just as Nancy walked up from the dock to greet them. Charlotte got out of the back seat armed with a stainless-steel water bottle, a backpack, and a scowl. She was dressed in ripped jeans, a blue Tillys sweat shirt, and, true to Stella's word, a pair of black-and-white-checkered Vans. Her naturally golden hair was now an unnatural shade of dark purple, and she was wearing black eyeliner that only made her pale skin look more ghostly by contrast. Nancy was alarmed for a split second but hid her shock.

"There's my girl!" Nancy opened her arms to hug Charlotte, who remained stiff and barely managed to lift one hand to receive the hug. "Just me and you this weekend, kiddo. You ready?"

"Mmmm," Charlotte grunted, as if resigned to her fate. Nancy looked over at Stella, who gave her a thumbs-up and a look of exasperation.

"Okay, I'm off. Be good to Gran, and I'll be back on Monday," Stella said. She gave her daughter a quick, dismissive kiss on the forehead. Charlotte made no move to return the affection.

"I'll text you with updates. Have a good trip!" Nancy waved as Stella pulled away.

"This way, kiddo." Nancy ushered Charlotte and her sullen attitude, which was big enough to make it seem like a whole other person had joined them, down the dock toward *Gypsea*. As soon as they got to the slip, Suzanne came out to greet them. She ran up to Charlotte and began to purr.

"Oh my god, I didn't know Suzanne was going to be here!" Charlotte exclaimed with no hint of sarcasm. Charlotte was a huge animal lover. She adored all living creatures, from the soft, furry variety to the lesser appreciated critters like scaly lizards and milk snakes. If it was of the animal world, Charlotte wanted to bond, and none would escape her attempt at affection. Nancy had asked her once about her love of animals, and Charlotte had replied, "Animals are better than people. They don't hurt others unless they have to, and they don't lie." Nancy thought her answer was both wise and telling. The purr from Suzanne seemed to melt away all the angst that Charlotte had been carrying with her. For a split second, she was gentle, sweet Charlotte again.

"Of course Suzanne came with me. Couldn't imagine being here without her. That little fur ball and I are in this together."

Charlotte picked Suzanne up and nuzzled her face and neck. Suzanne purred even louder.

"Aren't you afraid she might fall in? Or get attacked or something?" Charlotte asked.

"She's got better footing on this boat than I do. Plus, she's made some friends."

"Friends?"

"Sure. There's Leon the pelican that visits every morning after his breakfast. He sits on that pole right over there while Suzanne suns herself on the back cushions. They basically watch each other. And of course, there's the dolphin."

"What dolphin? You have a dolphin?" Charlotte's eyes got wide.

"No, but there's this one dolphin who visits once in a while. He comes to the back of the boat and sort of bobs up and down in the water until Suzanne leans over the railing and sniffs his snout. Her whiskers must tickle him or something, because after a few touches, he nods and makes a high-pitched noise. It lasts for a couple of minutes, and then he takes off again. Or at least I think it's a he."

"Wow," Charlotte said with genuine awe. She looked at the back of the boat, as if the dolphin would appear at any moment.

"You never know when he'll show up. Come on, let's get you settled below. I made up the berth for you."

"Berth?"

"It's what we call a bedroom on a boat."

"Oh," Charlotte said. "Sav."

Nancy had no idea what that meant, but she showed Charlotte the basics around the boat. How to turn on the lamp in her berth, where the fridge was in the galley, and how the toilet worked in the head. Throughout the tour, Charlotte didn't say much. Finally, Nancy added, "Oh, and I have Wi-Fi. You want the password?"

"Maybe later," Charlotte said. She looked around and finally offered, "This is lit, Gran."

Nancy hesitated for a moment, shocked at the lack of fire for the Wi-Fi code and not entirely sure if *lit* was a good thing. Then Charlotte smiled and said, as if translating, "This is pretty cool, Gran."

Nancy's heart skipped a beat at these five small words of praise. She smiled brightly and said, "Plus, I have your favorite treat. Ruffles and French onion dip. Let's go up top and indulge."

"Sweet!"

Nancy and Charlotte snacked on chips and dip up in the cockpit while they watched Suzanne intently eye the sea gulls. The clouds lightened and the sun began to peek through the layer of gray. It warmed enough for Charlotte to roll up her sweat shirt sleeves and bask in the sun as they listened to music. Nancy had her system set up so that anyone could connect their smartphone and play music. Currently, Charlotte was introducing Nancy to the musical stylings of the Imagine Dragons and Ed Sheeran.

"I like this guy," Nancy said as she crunched a potato chip.

"Mom thinks he's whiny," Charlotte said as she made a smirk. Then she sighed and said, "She doesn't like my music. Actually, she and I don't agree on much lately."

Nancy gently offered, "Well, for what it's worth, I didn't like Stella's music when she was growing up either. I think it's a rite of passage to hate the younger generation's music. Otherwise though, are you guys doing okay?"

"I don't know. She nags me a lot. I can't do anything right."

Nancy nodded. "Well, it's hard not to nag as a parent. It's like our chief duty. She's got a lot on her plate. Not that I'm making excuses."

"It's more than that. She's never around, Gran. And when she is home, she yells at me, she yells at Dad. It's just loud and tense at home. That's why I stay after school so much. I don't feel like going into the war zone otherwise known as our kitchen."

Nancy paused and remembered. "I hated hearing my parents fight."

Charlotte studied Nancy. "I've only ever heard about my great grandma, never great grandpa."

Nancy took a deep breath, "Well, we don't talk about Karl much. He had his own demons, I guess you could say. He left when I was a little younger than you. Around twelve."

"He just . . . left? Like, just up and left?

Nancy nodded slightly, thinking back to that time.

"Why did he leave?"

"Oh, I think things just got a little too hard for a man like him. Money and jobs were scarce. And the pressure got to him. I always thought of him as this larger-than-life character. He was tall and muscular, with big shoulders, and he was so handsome. Had a dimple in his chin, and when he smiled, he lit up the room. When his charm was blazing, people were simply drawn to him. Women, little kids, even dogs. I thought because of all that inner glowing energy and all that outer strength, he could handle anything. But that's not how it worked out. The kind of strength my mom and I needed wasn't the kind he had."

Charlotte quieted and munched on her potato chips as she gazed out over the marina. Nancy watched her and wondered what she was considering behind those cornflower-blue eyes. Charlotte's eyes reminded her of her mom's. Blue with a hint of gray in them, like the clouds just after a fading storm, calm and gentle. Nancy had never forgiven her father for stealing that little spark of life in Grace, for letting her vibrant colors fade.

The crunch of a potato chip brought Nancy back, as did a question. "My dad won't leave, will he?" Charlotte asked in a small voice.

"No, sweet girl. Your dad is nothing like Karl. He's devoted to you and he loves you more than anything in the world. I'm afraid you're stuck with him for good."

"Good. I don't want to be alone with Mom. That's when she's the meanest."

Nancy looked at her granddaughter, trying to ascertain if this was true or if this was a teen dramatizing a situation.

Nancy and Charlotte spent the rest of the afternoon and evening settling into conversation about music, the best things about Suzanne the Cat, and Charlotte's favorite subject, Social Studies. A lazy breeze drifted in, but the waters of the marina remained beautiful and calm, and Nancy realized this was the calmest she had felt since she'd been out here.

Grandmother and granddaughter drifted off to sleep, listening to the occasional seal bark in the distance.

CHAPTER TWENTY-TWO
FIRST SAIL, FIRST LOVE

By morning, Charlotte had settled into boat life. Kids adapted quickly. She and Nancy had enjoyed a cheese omelet in the cockpit when they heard a familiar voice bellow across the marina. "Hello? My key won't work! Come and get me!"

Nancy looked up and saw Ruthie, dressed in a bright-yellow frock with sparkly gold earrings dangling from her ears. She was locked behind the gate.

"Is that Ruthie?" Charlotte asked.

"Yep, that's her. Do you mind opening the gate for her?"

"No prob." Charlotte hopped off the boat and ran down the dock to retrieve her.

"Is that my favorite kid?" Ruthie asked through the gates.

Charlotte smiled brightly and opened it. Ruthie enveloped her in a gigantic hug in her yellow jumper, which made it look like the girl was disappearing into the sun. Otis let out a small *arf* of joy. Suzanne the Cat went to the edge of the boat to see what all the commotion was about, and her ears twitched with irritation at the sight of Otis.

Ruthie climbed aboard, put Otis down, gave Nancy a quick hug, and put Charlotte at arm's length. "Let me take a look at you. That's a radical move with your hair, kid, but I like it!"

Nancy grimaced. She hadn't wanted to mention the hair yet. But judging by Charlotte's expression, the teen didn't seem to mind.

"Really? It's just a temp thing. I wanted to tweak my parents," Charlotte said impishly to Ruthie. Then she gave Nancy a look. "Don't tell them though, Gran, okay?"

"Your hair-dyeing secrets are safe with me." Nancy smiled and Charlotte smiled back. Nancy handed a winch handle to her granddaughter, who frowned as she took it.

"What's this?"

"It's a handle to help you tighten a winch so you can bring in the sail."

"Oh shit, we're sailing?" Charlotte froze.

"Language, please," Nancy admonished. "There's always a chance we'll go sailing. Besides, you gotta get your sea legs sometime." Nancy winked at her nervous granddaughter.

Charlotte relaxed about the swearing but remained wide-eyed at the prospect of heading out to sea.

"Don't be nervous, Charlotte. I was a novice just last week, and despite almost crashing onto the rocks, I think we did really well!" Ruthie offered with a reassuring pat on the young girl's shoulder.

Charlotte's face turned even more pale at this news. "Wait. You almost crashed into the rocks? That doesn't sound safe at all. I'm just a kid," she protested weakly. "What if I get seasick?"

"I brought Fritos," Ruthie announced as she held up a bag of the salty corn snacks.

Charlotte eyed the bag of Fritos with utter confusion.

"Salt helps with seasickness. But if you do sense it coming on, we'll just turn around," Nancy said, smiling at her granddaughter.

Charlotte sat down on the cockpit next to Otis, who looked up at her with the same resigned fate.

"Ahoy!" Lois yelled. "Can I get a hand with these bags?"

Nancy hopped down to help Lois with the groceries and a bottle of wine.

"Hey, sister, where's Chris?" Nancy asked, referring to Lois's husband and honorary member of their girl tribe.

"He's coming. He's trying to stuff dollar bills into that ancient rusted parking valet box," Lois said as she hauled herself up on the boat.

Nancy looked up toward the parking lot and saw Chris patiently shoving rolled-up bills into the parking machine. But that wasn't all she saw. She also saw the blue-and-white vans from U.S. Immigration and Customs Enforcement, otherwise known as ICE, slowly rolling by. Strange. Why would they be here, of all places? The vans slowly stopped at H dock, a few docks over. Four men got out and forcefully walked down. The only people she knew over in that part of the marina were a boat cleaner from San Diego named Jeff and . . . Santiago. Her view to Santiago's slip was blocked by a large powerboat. She couldn't see if the ICE agents were at Santiago's boat or someone else's. She strained to see what was going on, but to no avail. Just then she heard a tussle as she saw Judy arrive.

"Hi! Sorry I'm late. I had to haul all this stuff here," Judy said as she started handing canvas bags onto the boat and into Lois's waiting hands.

"Jude, what is all this?"

"Oh! I found some great books on sailing for beginners, plus a novel or two so we can learn about the philosophy of sailing, plus one on knots, and another on nautical navigation by the stars."

Lois looked in the bag. There were at least fifteen books. "Couldn't decide on just one or two, huh?"

"It's practical information that could prove useful," Judy quipped. She plowed on, "I was flabbergasted at how many books there are on sailing! I mean, who knew!"

Judy climbed aboard and settled next to Charlotte and Otis. Chris finally came ambling down the dock armed with a paper bag. "Argh! Aye, aye, Cap'n!" Chris warbled in a pirate tone. His smile was always bright and mischievous under his warm brown eyes. He wore his hair in a seventies shag style that somehow kept him looking perpetually young and hip. He had an easy manner, existing effortlessly, as if he were a leaf on a river, simply floating by. His energy always managed to put a smile on her face.

Nancy chuckled and said, "We were wondering when our bartender was showing up."

"Aye, Cap, I had to search out many a pirate haunt to get the right hooch! I come bearing jalapeño margaritas! Permission to come aboard?"

"Granted."

He hopped on the boat, found Lois, and gave her a quick kiss. He greeted Charlotte with a friendly tousle of her hair and said, "Hey, half-pint! I thought you were blond."

Charlotte smiled at Chris and gave him a hug. "That was last month." He nodded and handed the bag of hooch to Ruthie down in the salon.

"Change is the only constant in life." Chris smiled, well aware of the ever-varying moods of a teenager and the continual restyling of their hair, having lived through the teen years with his own kids.

"What am I supposed to do with this?" Ruthie asked, referring to the bag of hooch.

Lois turned to Chris and said, "Honey, we're prepping the boat. Can you make the margaritas?" She blinked her eyes lovingly at him.

Chris sighed heavily, shook his head, and said, "You are a full-time job, woman."

"I'm the best job you ever had." Lois kissed him on the cheek.

"True." Chris hesitated and added, "But you're lucky you're cute," before heading down into the galley to begin making drinks. Lois readied the sails and lines along the boat. Ruthie and Charlotte prepared snacks while Judy unpacked her books down below. Nancy unplugged the shore power and checked her navigation instruments. Then she tapped the fuel gauge three times. It stayed full. After a few minutes, they were ready.

"All hands on deck!" she shouted.

Lois and Chris were at the bow and stern, ready to throw off the mooring lines. Ruthie had the mainsail sheet in her hands and was ready to bring it up when commanded. Judy tucked herself into her corner under the canopy. Charlotte was on the far bench with a jib sheet in her hands.

"Charlotte, you're going to unfurl the jib when I tell you, okay?"

"Are you sure I'm ready for this?" Charlotte shuddered and looked pale. Nancy couldn't tell if it was scared pale or her normal pale, offset by her purple hair.

"I've got your back. You're ready." Nancy gave her a look of confidence and nodded. "Okay?"

Charlotte nodded back, uncertainty being the main expression on her face.

Nancy started the engine and gently eased the *Gypsea* out of her slip. As they were backing up, she cleared the large powerboat that had blocked her view of Santiago's boat. At that moment, she saw Santiago talking with the ICE agents. She froze. *Gypsea* was drifting back so far that she was coming dangerously close to another vessel.

"Uh, Nance?" Judy asked, "Aren't we getting a tad too close to that boat?"

Nancy quickly looked behind her and instantly put the boat in forward gear, all the while craning her neck to see what was happening with Santiago. The last thing she saw was an ICE agent taking into his walkie-talkie and what looked like a pair of handcuffs.

"Shit," Nancy mumbled.

"Language, please," Charlotte said.

Nancy picked up on the sarcasm delivered deftly by her granddaughter, turned to her with a smile, and said, "Thank you, dear."

She glanced back in the direction of Santiago as she steered her boat into the channel, deeply concerned about the fate of her friend.

* * *

"C'mon, Lois, where's that Finnish strength!" Nancy shouted with a smile.

"Suutele persettäni, paskahousut!"

Ruthie, Judy, and Nancy all chuckled as Lois struggled with bringing up the mainsail the last two feet, which were the hardest. They all knew her Finnish insult well. Nancy even knew it from her own childhood. Her mother, Grace, on occasion, would hurl it out.

Lois had been using it since they were kids. In English, it roughly meant, "Kiss my ass, shit pants!"

"I thought she only used that on me!" Chris said, delighted.

Charlotte was ready to unfurl the jib, and Nancy gently told her it was almost time. She looked nervous, but Nancy hoped that once Charlotte understood how a boat moved on water, how natural it felt to be powered by wind instead of an engine fighting against the sea, she'd relax a little.

Lois finally got the mainsail up and came back to the cockpit, where Chris handed her a margarita. Ruthie and Judy both turned their faces toward the sun and started spotting seals.

"Okay, kiddo, you're almost up," Nancy said to Charlotte, whose knuckles were turning white from holding the lines. "Now, gently loosen the jib furling sheet right behind you."

"Here we go."

Nancy steered *Gypsea* through the calm waters of the channel, past the break wall and into the undulating sea. A steady swell was running, and the wind instantly filled the mainsail and heeled them over to port. Everyone held on tight, especially Charlotte and Otis, who weren't quite expecting it, and both let out a small yelp of fear.

"It's all right, honey; completely normal. We're going to unfurl the jib. Let the line out slowly, and Ruthie will be pulling the jib open from the other side at the same time."

"On it!" Ruthie said, and gave a thumbs-up.

Charlotte nodded, although her expression was still grave. She tentatively let the sheet out, then Ruthie pulled her end, and the jib came rolling out.

The boat started to pick up speed as Nancy found her line against the wind. Judy handed a winch to Ruthie so she could trim the jib. Charlotte's job was over.

"Good job, Char," Nancy said, as she killed the motor and let the *Gypsea* cut through the rolling swell with ease. "We're under the power of the wind now."

"Wow," Charlotte said. "That was easier than I thought."

"Want to learn more? Come over by me." Nancy shifted at the helm and handed Charlotte the wheel. Charlotte hesitantly took it, and Nancy helped her. She could tell that Charlotte was beginning to feel how the boat moved and why. "Steady now, we're heading due southwest. Look up."

Charlotte looked to the very top of the mast, where the wind vane told them exactly where the wind was coming from. "If you head straight into it—sailors call that the irons—you'll lose all your forward motion. The trick is to catch the wind at the right angle, so it fills your sails and moves you forward. Too much wind and you keel too far over to one side and you'll be fighting it. Too little and you go nowhere. When you get it right, you feel the boat pick up speed, and she'll almost steer herself." Nancy and Charlotte played around with the wind for a bit as Nancy passed on other sailing tips, prompting Charlotte to ask questions as she started to grasp the concept. The rest of the crew sat back and enjoyed the breeze and the sunshine. Judy even felt so comfortable that she and Ruthie hung their legs over the high side as waves splashed against their feet. Lois snuggled into Chris, and they talked quietly as they looked out at the coast slowly passing by. Soon the Palos Verdes peninsula was looming ahead of them.

"Okay, almost time to tack. Ruthie?"

"At the ready!" Ruthie moved back into position.

"Okay, Charlotte, the blue line is your jib line. On a tack, Ruthie is going to let go of her line, and you will quickly pull your jib while I come about. Got it?"

Charlotte nodded, a look of determination and seriousness on her face.

"Tacking!"

Nancy turned the boat north, and Ruthie and Charlotte dealt with the jib lines and sails like pros. They were getting better.

"Wow, that was pretty good," Chris said, impressed.

"Nailed it!" Ruthie exclaimed. "Nice going, rookie!"

Charlotte beamed.

They were headed north toward the Hermosa Beach pier, the wind strong and steady, when, after about ten minutes, they heard a series of splashes.

"What is that?" Charlotte pointed to the thrashing ocean.

"Ah, the locals are out for a swim!"

A huge pod of Pacific two-sided dolphins swam up and around their little boat. On both sides, hundreds of dolphins jetted out of the water before dipping back down, diving and coming up for a breath. A few even jumped clear out of the water and flicked their tail fin before plunging back into the ocean. They were fast and playful, and they loved boats. "Lois, take Charlotte up to the bow. Show her what they can do."

"Come on, kid!" Lois helped her up and then carefully told her where to hang on and where to place her feet to get safely to the bow.

Once there, Lois and Charlotte got on their knees and looked directly down into the water. Three dolphins were racing with the boat, swimming just inches ahead of the hull. The dolphins would come up for a split second to catch a breath and then hurtle back down to stay just ahead of *Gypsea*'s bow. The dolphins were playing. It was a big game. And they loved it. Charlotte laughed and exclaimed, "That is *lit*!"

Judy looked back at Nancy with a quizzical expression. "Lit means cool," Nancy affirmed, and gave a thumbs-up.

A few magical minutes passed, and the dolphins finally headed out toward open water and out of sight. The entire crew was left glowing and enlightened from the experience. No one could stop smiling. Charlotte looked relaxed and, if Nancy wasn't mistaken, also smitten by the sail. She watched her granddaughter monitor the wind vane, check speed and direction, and finally let her head hang back and take in the breeze. She got it. What it was all about.

As they headed back into the channel, the ladies got busy bringing in the jib and dropping and folding the mainsail as they came into port. Chris sat there feeling useless but in awe, watching the girls bring *Gypsea* in. Charlotte stood on the side deck, holding a halyard, and looked up to see a pelican lazily hovering on the wind right above the boat. "Hey, Gran, is that our pelican?"

"Yep, that's Leon."

The pelican looked down briefly and then flapped off in the direction of their slip. Charlotte smiled at Nancy, and in that moment, as she caught a glimpse of her granddaughter in a state of sun-kissed happiness, all was right with the world.

Nancy motored into the slip without incident while Lois hopped off the boat and tied the mooring lines to secure it in place. When everything was settled, the girls came back to the cockpit with big proud smiles. It had been a good sail, and they knew it.

"I think we're ready for the beer can races, ladies."

"Really? Do you think we're ready?" Judy asked.

"Judy, you're an expert at winch handle delivery. Ruthie, aka Jib Queen, job well done. And Lois, no one handles a mainsail like you, champ. And besides, the beer can races aren't that serious. It's recreational. We're ready."

"Beer can races?" Charlotte asked.

"Every Tuesday night the locals race their sailboats out in the bay. It's casual and fun. Usually someone ties beer cans to the farthest buoy, and that's the turning point to come back home. And obviously it's named for the beer you drink while sailing. The only thing we take seriously is safety. Just a little local race with big bragging rights."

"I believe one of the ten commandments of beer can racing is *Thou shalt belly up at the yacht club bar afterwards*," Ruthie added.

Chris piped up, "Well, judging by what I saw today, my money's on the Mermaids to win."

"Who are the Mermaids?" Charlotte asked.

"That's us, kid," Ruthie said as she nudged her. "We are the last of the wily mermaids, the free-spirited sirens of the sea that frolic and play."

Charlotte looked at Ruthie and then at Nancy. "Can I be a Mermaid?"

Ruthie asked, "We don't have an age minimum, do we, Nancy?"

"Nope. But we all have to agree." Nancy looked at her best friends, who all instantly nodded, and said, "You have to pull your weight with the crew."

"Yes, ma'am," said Charlotte, with an enormous grin.

"And you have to obey the captain." Nancy winked at her.

"Aye, aye, Captain!"

"And you have to have fun," Ruthie chimed in. "Thou shalt not worry; thou shalt be happy."

"I can do that!" Charlotte said.

"Consider yourself an honorary Mermaid. First race is five thirty PM on Tuesday. Think you can do that?"

"Aye, aye, Captain," Charlotte said again as she gave a formal salute. Suzanne meowed and wandered to the back of the boat toward the pelican. "Oh, hey, Leon." Charlotte waved at the pelican who sat atop the post nearest to them. Leon shook his head and stretched out one wing.

Ruthie was massaging her back as Chris delivered a final batch of victory margaritas. Judy was munching on some cheese and crackers and Lois was organizing the lines.

Nancy sat down and sipped her margarita. Ruthie looked over at Otis. "I think he's getting used to it," she said, but Otis looked as wide-eyed and terrified as ever and then peed on the floor. Ruthie looked down at the pee and frowned. "Okay, okay, it's a process." Ruthie quickly got up and hosed off where Otis had done his business.

Lois observed the little dog and said, "Some dogs are shining examples of their breed; some dogs are cautionary tales."

"Oh, don't get so uppity; Otis has a weak bladder," Ruthie said. "Come on, Otis, we're going to stop in and see Pete for a few." She winked at Nancy.

"That seems to be going well," Nancy said

"What can I say? He's got a thing for lady sailors."

"Be gentle with the poor man," Chris added.

"Be careful," Judy said to Ruthie before she hopped off.

"Of what? What could possibly happen? We're too old to get pregnant or arrested. Hell, if we did get into trouble, the cops would chalk it up to us being Alzheimer's patients and let us go. About the worst thing that can happen is we run away from home or get an STD."

"Are you planning on going AWOL?" Judy inquired.

"I don't know. Anything's possible," she said, and gave a casual shrug at the idea.

"Have you contracted an STD?" Lois quipped.

"Whoa, I don't think this is appropriate conversation for a fourteen-year-old," said the fourteen-year-old.

"No STDs," Ruthie said indignantly. "I use condoms."

Lois spit out her wine. Judy put the back of her hand to her head in a fainting motion. Charlotte plugged her ears with both fingers. Chris groaned as the too-much-information line had been thoroughly crossed.

Finally, Nancy said, "Honey, I don't think they make condoms for your heart."

"Oh, hell, don't worry about me, you old biddies. I'm going to get my kicks before I break a hip or something."

"That's true," Lois piped up. "Break a hip and you're a goner. Take Doris Newsom. Healthy as a horse, slipped on an avocado in her own kitchen, fell, and broke her hip. Dead as a doornail two months later."

"Jeez, Lois," Chris said. "Is this why you won't let me eat avocados anymore?"

Lois ignored the question and took a sip of her margarita.

Ruthie tucked Otis under her arm and headed off in the direction of Peter Ellis's boat. Ruthie's leaving broke the spell of their little cabal, and everyone decided to call it a night. Charlotte went down to settle into her berth to read a book on knots. Chris and Lois hopped off the boat, hand in hand, leaving Judy to pack up the numerous cheeses she had brought along.

As Nancy watched Judy walk down the dock, she realized she didn't know what had happened to Santiago and the ICE agents.

"Hey Charlotte, you okay if I leave you for a few minutes? I have to check on something."

Charlotte nodded as she munched on a cracker with Suzanne in her lap. "What's going on?" she asked.

"I've just got to check on a friend of mine."

"No worries."

Nancy blew her a kiss and stepped off the boat.

CHAPTER TWENTY-THREE

DREDGING UP THE PAST

Nancy headed over on foot to Santiago's slip, texting him on the way over. Worry clouded her head as she waited for his return text. She hustled over to his slip and leaned over the side of the boat.

"Hello? Santiago?"

All was quiet except for the small splashes of a stand-up paddle boarder who was slowly paddling by.

"Anyone here?"

"They took him away," the paddle boarder said.

"Who took him? And where?"

"Guys in white vans."

Nancy stood there for a moment, not believing it. ICE had taken Santiago? Why? Nancy then realized that she had no idea if he was a citizen, if he had a Green Card, or if he was illegal. That was the problem when one's life was shrouded in mystery. No one knew how to help you.

Nancy walked down the dock to the bathhouse and in the direction of the dock master's office. Surely Chuck Roverson would know what had happened. But when she arrived at his office, it was locked. She peeked through the blinds and saw that his normally messy desk was neat as a pin. Weird.

Nancy walked back to her boat with her mind reeling with the confirmed news of Santiago's disappearance.

When she returned, Charlotte had made them both tea—a sweet gesture—as the moon rose over the stern. Nancy took the cup of tea with a biscuit on the side and sensed a seriousness come over the girl.

"Gran?"

"Yes, honey?"

"What happened with Grandpa Rog?"

Grandpa Rog was what Roger had asked to be called by his grandchild because he was under the impression it made him sound hip. He was sorely mistaken.

Nancy took a deep breath, not quite certain of how much truth she wanted to share with her granddaughter, who was still innocent in the ways of love. Luckily, she had yet to suffer the agony of heartbreak or the slap of embarrassment that came with a cheating lover.

"Well, it's complicated," Nancy began as she took a small bite of a biscuit.

"Was he boning someone else?" Charlotte said bluntly.

Nancy choked on her biscuit and coughed to clear her throat.

"You can tell me. It's not like it's going to totally destroy my vision of Grandpa Rog."

Nancy hesitated, not knowing if she should confirm Charlotte's guess or not.

"My friend Kaylynn liked this kid named Jonas, but then she found out he was 'Netflix and chillin' ' with someone else. She doesn't like him anymore."

"What is Netflix and chillin'?"

"Well, when some boy texts you and says, 'Hey, do you want to come over and watch Netflix and chill?' what he really means is that he wants to have sex five minutes into the movie."

"Charlotte, you're fourteen." Nancy tried to hide how appalled she was at her granddaughter's knowledge of such things as she realized, with growing alarm, that she could *not* handle it if her sweet grandbaby was going to announce that she was sexually active. Charlotte must have seen Nancy's expression.

"Oh no, Gran, not me! Good god, no. Not Kaylynn either. Or any of my close friends. I still play trumpet—not exactly a cool factor in high school. We're not ready for that kind of thing. Gross."

"Oh, thank god. But some of your friends are . . . er . . ." She paused, unsure how to ask.

"Boning? Yes," Charlotte confirmed. "But only two. And they're both pretty damaged. One's dad went to prison, and the other already has a tattoo. On her thigh. Double gross."

Nancy allowed herself to breathe as she rejoiced in the knowledge that Charlotte was still just a girl in many ways. Still innocent. At least for now.

"So, that's why you left him?"

Nancy shifted in her seat, uncomfortable answering questions like this from her fourteen-year-old granddaughter, especially since she and her daughter hadn't talked about it yet. "You could say that is what pushed me to leave, yes. But it turns out I had other reasons that I didn't even know I had until I got here." Nancy gestured at the boat and water that surrounded her.

Charlotte nodded and stared out into the marina. "I think you're figuring out who you are without Grandpa Rog. And it seems to me like . . . you like *you* so far."

It was Nancy's turn to gaze into the distance and take in the unexpected wisdom of the girl's words.

Then Charlotte added, "I don't understand why people cheat. I mean, if you don't want to be with someone, isn't it better to be honest and leave? Cheating is just a cheap way to hurt someone. So lame."

"I think people cheat because they want to live another life, but they don't have the courage to stop the one they're in. It can be hard to do the right thing," Nancy softly replied.

"I'm sorry that happened to you."

"Is there any way we can keep this between us, Char?"

Charlotte gave Nancy a hard look. "Mom doesn't know, does she?"

Nancy shook her head and found herself ashamed that she couldn't be honest with her own daughter yet.

"I won't tell, Gran. It's your story. Not mine."

Nancy went to give Charlotte a hug, anticipating her typical pull away, but instead Charlotte grabbed her with both arms and hugged her tight.

CHAPTER TWENTY-FOUR

A SQUALL OF LINGERING REGRET

That night, after she had tucked Charlotte into her berth and left her to snuggle with her orange fish pillow, Nancy went above and sat on the back of the boat. Suzanne soon wandered up and sat next to her as they both watched the lights of the beach town reflect on the water.

Nancy felt uneasy at the whereabouts of Santiago and Chuck Roverson. But upon deeper reflection, she thought about the day with her granddaughter and the relative triumph of nature over Wi-Fi. She couldn't wait to tell Stella how well Charlotte had done on the water. It wasn't so long ago that Stella used to love to sail with her too. She and Roger would take Stella out on Thursday nights for sunset sails. There were plenty of good memories with Roger that she had to tuck away in her mind so she could deal with the current pain. But sometimes the memories came bubbling up anyway.

She dialed Ruthie's number and heard the phone ring a couple slips down. Nancy remembered that she was with Ellis. But just when she was about to hang up, Ruthie answered.

"You okay?"

"Ruthie, I'm sorry. I forgot you were over there."

"Totally okay. Pete's making us another drink and trying to find the Tito Puente playlist on his phone. What's up?

Nancy launched right in. "I'm just sitting here thinking. And I'm . . . I'm missing Roger."

Momentary silence from Ruthie and then, "It's okay to miss him, Nance."

Nancy could feel the hot tears in her eyes as she tried to explain where this was coming from. Even she didn't quite know. "I just remember how he used to make me feel so safe, how he was so sure that everything was going to be okay. How he would make sure we had everything for a sail. How he would just take care of everything. Having Charlotte here, it makes me feel like I'm not doing all the right things."

"Nance," Ruthie said flatly, "it was you who always made sure you guys had everything for the sail. Not Roger. You got the wine, the sandwiches, the jackets and sweaters. You took care of everything. Hell, didn't you even change the burned-out light fixture in the boat bathroom?"

"It's called a head," Nancy quietly corrected.

"Roger had a habit of showing up late or not at all. And when he did, he mucked things up, yelled at his guests, and then blamed you for whatever went wrong. If you're going to tell stories from the past, at least tell the truth."

Nancy sniffed and wiped away a tear. That confused her. She had to think.

"Nance, it's okay to miss Roger. Christ, he was your husband and partner for over thirty-some years. But don't give him hero status in hindsight. His presence might have lent you some feeling of safety, but in the end, it was you who made you feel safe. Roger may have provided the means, but you provided the feeling of safety. He just stole the glory."

Nancy smiled and heard a trumpet pipe up in the background. Pete had successfully navigated his phone and located the Latin mood music of Tito Puente. Nancy took the hint and said, "That's my cue to let you go. I'm okay. Love you, Ruthie."

"Back at you, kid," Ruthie said, and hung up.

Nancy meandered back through her memories with Roger, only this time she took the rose-colored lens off and tried to see the truth in those recollections. It was true that Nancy had always packed the bag for sailing, and she remembered Roger's footsteps coming down the dock back then, always rushed, and how it always made her nervous, like a drill sergeant coming for inspection.

"Did you remember my sunglasses? No, not those ones, the good ones," he would bark.

Nancy would quickly dig in her bag and find the good pair. Roger would then snatch them away without a thank-you.

"All right! Let's head out! Stella, come up here and sit with me. Get me a drink, would ya, Nance?"

"Mom, I want a lemonade!" Stella mimicking Roger's bark.

Nancy would obey, and by the time she returned with refreshments, Roger and Stella would be talking in shorthand. She would try to interject with questions on what they were talking about, but they always left her out. She made drinks, got sandwiches, and pulled lines, but she couldn't suggest what music to play without a snide joke or comment from the two of them. She felt isolated on those sunset sails, even though she tried tirelessly to fit in with her own family. When the sail was over, the mess was always left for her to clean up. She had always felt like a servant on her own boat.

Nancy came out of her fog, it seemed, at long last, and began reconciling the Roger of her memories with the Roger of reality. The Roger she thought she knew versus the Roger everyone else knew. Chuck Roverson's comment echoed in her head: "He's mean, ma'am; he scares me." A crystallization of Roger slowly began to appear as she combed through her memories. It was as if someone had gone into her mind and cleaned all the windows at once.

CHAPTER TWENTY-FIVE
PIRATE'S CODE OF DISHONOR

It came as no surprise to Roger Hadley that he got Glenda Hibbert's voice mail instead of a live person. No one answered their phones anymore, even when they could plainly see who was calling. Ideally, he would be calling from Nancy's phone, thereby greatly increasing the chances that Glenda would answer, but he didn't have that luxury. The call went directly to voice mail. Where could the nut ball tree hugger be? Roger took a quick sip of his old-fashioned on the barstool at his favorite local watering hole, Laurel Tavern.

"You've reached Glenda Hibbert with the California Coastal Commission. Please leave a detailed message, and I'll return your call. Complaints can be addressed via email to Ghibbert at CCC dot com."

Roger put on his warmest, friendliest voice. "Glenda! How are you on this fine evening? Listen, I was wondering—well, we, we were wondering, Nancy and I, that is, if you're free for dinner over the next couple of days. Would love to catch up and talk about . . . um, catch up, really. Give us a call back."

Roger hung up and reviewed his performance. Friendly, engaging, just a couple of old friends reaching out. She'd call back shortly, he assumed. He looked at his watch and realized he was comfortably ahead of schedule. It was only Tuesday, and just this morning he had successfully kicked the ass of his pompous neighbor at pickleball, sent that smug tam-wearing boat mechanic Santiago to an ICE holding cell, and had Chuck Roverson fired. Served lover boy and that bumbling drunk right for crossing him. But even with all those successes, he still hadn't secured that absolutely crucial fifth Coastal Commission vote.

He pushed that thought aside and chose to focus on the positive. He was looking forward to the beer can races that evening, especially since he had heard a rumor that Nancy and her band of harpies were entering her crappy boat. He and *Bucephalus* would crush them. He relished the thought. Plus, there was a warm wind driving up from the south. Same damn wind that had been blowing all month. Odd and off-putting, but not wholly unfortunate. Made for great racing conditions.

But while that warm breeze had managed to sweep away the stilted haze that had been hanging around Hermosa for most of the spring, this new wind also made Roger uneasy. He normally remained in complete control of all his endeavors, but somehow the constancy of this breeze had thrown him off a little. Just as the wind had not been still, nor had his mind. He had begun writing lists of things to be done and ticking them off so as not to miss anything. He chalked this up to Nancy's reprehensible move to play castaway like some reject from Gilligan's Island, leaving him to fend for himself. Now, along with *Get Chuck Roverson fired*, he also added *Buy deodorant* and *Iron golf pants* to his list of chores to be done.

He took another sip of his old-fashioned and watched the four PM hot-yoga class empty out onto the sidewalk in front of him. The sun reflected perfectly off the impossibly tight activewear the twentysomething babes wore as they left their class. Roger congratulated himself for living in a town where a guy could have a stiff cocktail while watching perfect asses prance around in front of him. It was another glorious day in sunny Hermosa Beach.

Roger's cell phone rang, and he looked at the number and cursed. His investors. He stared at the ringing phone without picking it up. He let the call go to voice mail. A tiny bead of sweat formed on his temple. He needed to make some guarantees that he couldn't quite make yet. Time was running out, and it was becoming clear that Nancy wasn't going to make it easy on him. So, he might have to play a little hardball with her after all. He stared into space in the direction of Pier Avenue and had begun to formulate a plan when he heard a familiar sultry voice.

"What's a scalawag like you doing in a fine establishment like this?"

Roger blinked and looked in the direction of the voice. There in the doorway of Laurel Tavern stood the slim, sinewy silhouette of Claire Sanford, her red hair backlit by the sun, making her appear like a life-sized parrot. She sauntered over to him, lifted his drink, and took a long sip. She never took her eyes off him. Roger, no stranger to hardened gazing, took in every inch of Claire and then took the glass back.

"Blanton's?" she asked.

"Best bourbon in town," he said.

"I expect nothing less," Claire purred. "Did you transfer the money to Dunhill?"

"Landed in his account today at eleven ten AM."

"And you used a third party so it can't be traced to you?"

"You don't have to check up on me. This isn't my first bribery rodeo."

"Of course," Claire said. She touched Roger's forearm, which remained stiff instead of softening at her touch. "You seem tense."

"We need to start thinking about plan B. If Nancy doesn't bring Glenda around, and this moment she might be spectacularly disinclined to, we need another way in. Are you sure the vote is resting on her?"

"My information is solid. There are nine commissioners. Glenda Hibbert is the swing vote."

"We got any dirt on her?"

Claire hesitated for a moment. "Roger, bribery is one thing, but if you're talking blackmail . . ."

Roger chuckled at her hypocrisy. "Suddenly one sin is worse than another? Come on, Claire. Don't feign scruples now. Your casual ruthlessness is one of the main reasons I find you so attractive. Willing to do almost anything to get your way. Outside of murder, I suppose. Which reminds me, how did your third husband die?"

"Heart attack," she answered flatly. Claire yanked his drink away again, sipped the last of the bourbon, and tilted her head as if considering the remark. She said, "Point taken. I'll see what I can find on Glenda Hibbert. Now, are we going to get out of here or what?"

Roger left money on the bar for the drink, no tip, and said, "Plans changed. I've got to get to the marina. Beer can races are tonight."

By her expression, he could tell that Claire was not pleased.

"A sailing race—over this?" Claire gestured to her ample cleavage. "Don't you think we should iron out the finer details of our bribery and blackmail schemes while drinking margaritas naked in your hot tub?"

"As enticing as your planning session sounds, tonight's race is part of the plan. Rumor is that Nancy is racing. And I plan on taking her down a notch or three. I'll call you after we're docked."

CHAPTER TWENTY-SIX
A POOR, UNMOORED SOUL

As Nancy was walking back from the local marina market armed with snacks and beer for that night's beer can races, she saw Chuck Roverson shuffling across the parking lot carrying a cardboard box with files and a plastic Ficus tree, its dusty leaves sticking out of the box top.

"Chuck," Nancy called out and waved.

Chuck's shoulders sagged, and he put down the box. Much to Nancy's surprise, he started to weep. She walked over to him and put her bag down. She hugged the man. He calmed down a little, and they stood there. Nancy looked at him, then the box.

"What's this all about?" she asked, gesturing to the box, which held, besides the plant and files, a stapler and a framed picture of his wife.

"I got canned!" Chuck blustered as he stifled another cry. "Eleven years, and they don't even take me at my word. They said I was drinking on the job. I've never had a drink on the job. Besides beer, I mean. But I was never impaired."

"Oh, Chuck, I'm so sorry." Nancy crossed her arms. "If you were never impaired on the job, then how did they fire you for it?"

"They found two airplane bottles of bourbon open and half-empty on my desk, and I swear they weren't mine. I don't even like bourbon. I'm a rum guy. Mai tais. My eternal weakness."

Nancy nodded. And then a memory hit her sharply. She and Roger had recently taken a trip up to Mendocino. Roger had promised it was a weekend getaway for the two of them, but it soon became glaringly apparent that he had an ulterior motive when they "bumped into" a real estate investor Roger was doing a deal with. The two men ended up golfing both days while Nancy was left to peruse the bookstores and boutiques of utterly charming Mendocino all alone. So much for romance. Jesus, the shit she had fallen for. But then she remembered watching Roger open his satchel on the plane and take out two airplane bottles of Four Roses bourbon during the flight.

"Where did you get those?" Nancy asked as she watched him covertly pour the airplane bottle into the plastic cup provided by the unknowing flight attendant.

"I'm not paying airline prices for booze."

"How many of those things do you have?"

"They had a deal if you bought six. Don't judge me."

"Too late. You do realize we are not destitute, right?"

"I'm not going to let an airline pick my pocket every time I'm parched. If you made any money of your own, perhaps you'd understand the value of it," Roger said dismissively. He sat back, satisfied with himself, as he sipped his bourbon neat.

Nancy glared at Roger but said nothing. She cast her attention out the window and found solace in trying to work out ways to murder your spouse and get away with it.

Chuck's pathetic sniffling brought her back.

Nancy stood and looked at the sad state of her former dock master standing in the middle of the parking lot. "I'm so sorry, Chuck. Did you say it was bourbon they found? Any chance you remember what brand?"

Chuck's eyes were downcast, shoulders slumped. He looked like an abandoned teddy bear. "Yeah, Four Flowers or something . . ." He checked his memory. "No, it was Four Roses."

Nancy pursed her lips and shook her head in grim realization. *Roger.*

CHAPTER TWENTY-SEVEN
THE BEER CAN RACE

Lois and Judy pulled up in Judy's sensible Honda Accord. Lois had the window rolled down, and Nancy could hear Lois losing patience with Judy.

"Just park right there! What's wrong with that spot? You have to pick a spot!"

Finally, Judy pulled into one of the many parking spaces, and they got out of the car.

Nancy stood with her armed crossed, a scowl on her face.

"What is it?" Lois asked.

"You are not going to believe what Roger has done, the snake," Nancy said.

"Boat life is so much more exciting than sofa life!" Judy said as she gathered her things.

"Roger, gossip, and the first beer can race of the season. It's already awesome," Lois added.

Judy opened the back door and grabbed a bag of goodies and her sweater. They walked to the gate, and Nancy unlocked it.

"Where's Ruthie?" Lois asked.

"She's already here. She's over on Pete's boat," Nancy said.

"Good for her," Lois said lovingly. "The tramp."

"I can hear you, you old crone," Ruthie said as she walked up the dock from Ellis's boat. "I'll take that as a compliment."

"It was meant as one."

"I got here just in time," came a small voice. Charlotte came rolling up on her bike after school. She wrestled with her bike lock, grabbed her Gatorade and a small paper bag, and caught up with Nancy and the girls.

"Good to see you, kiddo," Ruthie said.

"Hi. I brought this." Charlotte took something out of the brown bag and held up a small brass plaque that read *Beware the Mermaids*.

Nancy held the plaque and ran her fingers over the letters, very touched by her gift. "Where did you get this?"

"It was the weirdest thing. I was riding my bike yesterday, and I rode past the garage sale of our cranky neighbor, Irene. It was just lying there, calling my name in the sunshine. I guess her husband who died last year was an old sailor."

"It's perfect," Nancy said as she put a hand on Charlotte's shoulder. "Poseidon would be pleased. Thank you, Char." She gave her a kiss on the top of her head, and Charlotte smiled and trotted off down the dock. "Come on, Mermaids, I have a surprise for you!"

The Mermaids, plus one junior Mermaid, looked at each other, excited at what Nancy might have up her sleeve. She led them down the dock, and when they were about ten yards from the boat, Nancy stretched out her arms as if presenting a grand award.

Charlotte exclaimed, "Wowza."

The group stood there observing the gleaming, newly painted *Gypsea*. The chipped paint along her beam had been freshly redone in navy blue. Her name, once faded and peeling away, was now slightly raised in bright gold letters with a navy drop shadow. On each side of her name were two beautiful mermaids painted in gold and blue. The boat sparkled in the late-afternoon sun and Leon the pelican, who was resting on his pole after a late lunch of mackerel, seemed to lift up his large beak, impressed.

"Wow. We look legit," Ruthie said.

"And fast," Lois remarked.

"I love it, Gran," Charlotte said.

"I knew I should have brought the champagne." Judy cursed herself for not deciding sooner.

"Luckily," Nancy said as she produced a bottle of Veuve Clicquot from her bag, "we have one courtesy of my boat broker, Brad!"

"You're full of tricks, old girl." Ruthie gave a wry smile. "Let's pop that baby and christen our *Gypsea*!"

Nancy and the girls assembled on the dock near the bow of the boat. She held the champagne bottle high and said, "I christen thee *Gypsea*! We sing to your spirit of freedom and of new beginnings."

"To the *Gypsea*!" said the girls in unison.

Nancy removed the foil, and with a deft twist and yank, the champagne bubbled out of the bottle. She splashed some over the bow hull of the boat, then poured some into the water to appease Poseidon, god of the sea. When she finished, she took a swig herself and passed it to her girls, who each took their own drink. When the bottle came to Charlotte, she politely declined, instead toasting with her Gatorade.

The Mermaids readied the boat for the race. It was just past five o'clock and the warm breeze was picking up. A perfect night for a race. And beer.

* * *

There were no written rules for beer can races, but there were several unwritten rules. The first and most essential was to have fun. The second was to stay out of trouble while having the aforementioned fun. Loosely translated, this meant try not to crash, collide, or capsize. Pretty straightforward. The third and fourth rules also seemed obvious: try to be first to the starting line, and more importantly, try to be first to the finish line. But, as Nancy explained to her novice crew, who were paying rapt attention, it was amazing how hard those last two rules were to execute.

The starting line in any sail race was a straight line between two markers. You just sailed across the line as the starting horn went off. Pretty basic. Until you added a flotilla of other boats all trying to cross first too. All of whom were madly jockeying for position while trying to avoid colliding with each other. Cross the line too early, you'd be forced to circle back and make another pass. Too late and you'd be starting the race behind everyone else. It took tricky maneuvering of your boat to be in just the right place at just the right time.

It was ten minutes to the race start time, and the Mermaids headed out of the channel on the *Gypsea*. Two boats behind her, Nancy saw *Bucephalus* enter the channel. She recognized Mac's familiar moustache as he hoisted the mainsail. Tony was bringing in the fenders. Roger was at the helm, a stern, crabby scowl on his face, as if he were heading into war. Which, in a way, he was. Nancy knew that while everyone else loved the casual nature of the beer can races, Roger was out to win.

* * *

Roger was most at home at the helm of *Bucephalus*, named after Alexander the Great's horse. He carried on as if he were Alexander the Great himself, unwavering in his relentless pursuit of victory. His cheerless leadership made certain his jovial crew remained miserable. Little did he know that Nancy, Mac, and Tony used to sneak shots of Black Seal rum in the salon between tacks; it was the only way to enjoy Roger's ship of misery. Roger was unbending in his strict rule of no booze during races so as to stay sharp for competition. He perceived every competitor as a mortal foe and treated them as such.

Which was why, when he glared over at Nancy's boat, he was likely taken completely aback by the sight of his slight, beautiful, purple-haired granddaughter on board Nancy's freshly painted vessel. He nearly dropped his binoculars. There was a noticeable hiccup in Roger's mind that disallowed his fervent rancor for the *Gypsea* and her crew. Seeing Charlotte on someone else's boat didn't quite compute in Roger's brain. He was having trouble. But it didn't take long for his psychopathic tendencies to kick in and remind him that even though she was his granddaughter, she was also, at the moment, his competition. Compartmentalization was his special gift. His conscience cleared, he forged on.

* * *

The late-afternoon sun glistened on the water, like liquid diamonds. Nancy looked at her girls on the *Gypsea* and realized the only thing missing was Roger's surly attitude. On her boat there was a jubilant, anticipatory energy among her crew.

Once they were on the open water, they headed beyond the R10 buoy to get positioned for the starting line. Peter Ellis's boat came up right next to Nancy's. Ruthie stood up and waved shamelessly.

"Play coy!" Judy whispered.

"I'm too old for coy. I'm just the right age for 'Come 'n' get me!' "

Pete winked at Ruthie and blew her a kiss. "Good luck, Mermaids!"

The wind was running ten to twelve knots and threatening to increase. Off their starboard was *Hot Rum*, captained as always by Turk, who acknowledged Nancy with his signature grumpy nod. She nodded back, feeling more secure in her place, not just on the water but also in the marina. There were eleven boats in the race, and at that point they had all sailed away from the starting line with thirty seconds to the starting time. Nancy squinted into the sunlight and saw the sleek and speedy *Bucephalus* off to her port. She could sense Roger scowling in her direction.

All the boats either tacked or jibed back toward the starting line.

The starting horn blew. The race was on.

Turk and *Hot Rum* were the first across the line, which wasn't a surprise. Turk and his team had been together so long, they spoke in shorthand and were able to smoke cigars and down rum drinks while pulling ahead of everyone else. Nancy was behind *Hot Rum* by about ten meters.

"Ruthie, pull the jib tighter!"

Judy handed the winch handle to Ruthie with nurse-to-surgeon efficiency. Ruthie inserted it and instantly cranked on the winch and trimmed the sail. The wind caught the sails of *Gypsea* perfectly, and they felt a jolt of speed. They started to gain on *Hot Rum*. To her right was Pete's boat, *My Favorite Mistake*, coming on at a steady clip. Nancy looked for the *Bucephalus* and finally spotted her out deep. If he went way out, he'd take one tack and be headed back. Nancy knew that maneuver. It was hers. If Roger got lucky and he got a favorable wind shift, he would likely win. She looked up at her wind vane and concluded that there would be a shift. And if the wind didn't shift, Roger's outside line would be a bust and he would come in last. She decided her present course of action was the right one. She kept on her line.

Most of the boats rounded the beer can buoy and were on a good line back to the finish, but a few had troubles, likely beer or rum induced. and lost ground. Nancy and the girls had no such trouble and did a fairly solid job executing their tacks. She and *Hot Rum* were leading. Ellis was thirty meters behind, and Roger was still on his long tack to the west.

As the boats came hurtling back with a strong warm wind behind them from the south, Roger had tacked and sent *Bucephalus* screaming back from his outside line. Turk's unfortunate decision to tack a moment later had allowed Roger to gain ground on *Hot Rum* and then on Nancy. She saw him coming, glowering from behind the wheel. She had one move left.

"We're going to jibe! Lois, Ruthie!"

The women almost jumped when Nancy gave her order.

"Winch!" Lois said.

"On it!" Judy said.

Ruthie released her sheet as Lois madly cranked the sail over. The jibe appeared to take them out of contention for the win, and it confused the girls as they watched the other boats head for the finish line as the *Gypsea* headed out west.

"Gran, are you sure about this?"

"Trust me, kiddo."

Ten seconds later, Nancy said, "We're coming back about! Get ready to tack!"

"Again? So soon?" Judy said.

"Now!" Nancy ordered.

Lois grabbed her line and let go as Ruthie pulled the jib to her side.

"Tighter on that sheet!" Nancy yelled.

Judy handed her winch to Lois, and the sail tightened. They were headed back to the finish line at a crazy angle, but now they had the right of way, which meant no other boat could cut them off. The sails were taut, and they were flying over the water.

"We're going eight knots!" Charlotte exclaimed as she looked at the knot meter.

"This oughta get us there," Nancy said to herself as she gauged the wind.

Hot Rum was heading straight for the finish line and would cross in about a minute. *Bucephalus* was slightly ahead of *Hot Rum* and looked like the clear winner. But the *Gypsea* was gaining ground from a sharp starboard angle. If all things remained the same, Nancy would cross the finish line first, by a boat length.

With a hundred meters and thirty seconds to go, Nancy held her line and allowed herself a smile.

But then she saw the bow of the *Bucephalus* turn toward her and away from the finish line. It defied logic.

"Hell's bells, he's tacking," Nancy said, alarm in her voice.

"Why is he turning? The finish line is that way," Lois asked.

It was like playing a game of chicken on the water. And it went against the number one rule of safety. Roger knew Nancy would always play it safe. In fact, he counted on it. Given where they were in the water, the *Gypsea* technically had the right of way. But Roger's gambit worked. Nancy flinched. She had no choice but to change her line or risk running directly into Roger. She turned the wheel to avoid a collision with *Bucephalus*, and her sails instantly fell slack. The *Gypsea* virtually stopped in the water.

"What happened? Why are we stopped?" Judy asked.

"It's a safety issue," Nancy grumbled as she glared at Roger.

"My ass," Ruthie said as she caught Roger's wicked smile. "He did that on purpose."

Turning *Bucephalus* in the direction of Nancy had slowed both boats. Meanwhile, Turk and *Hot Rum* sailed happily over the finish line, winning the race in a cloud of cigar smoke and the sound of rum tumblers clinking in victory.

Nancy and Roger glided over the finish line in a disappointing second and third, respectively.

"Gran, what was that about?" Charlotte asked.

"The first rule in boating is always safety. Always," Nancy said earnestly. "And it's not like we get a trophy for the beer can races anyway. We did well."

But Lois plainly translated the events. "Roger would rather lose than let us win."

"That can't be true," Charlotte said, surprised. "Gran?"

Nancy just kept staring out at the sea, not wanting to confirm her granddaughter's suspicions about the absurd behavior of her grandfather.

The girls sat in the cockpit, dejected. They let out a collective sigh. The rookies had come so close to a tantalizing victory in their first race, only to have it ripped away in such an underhanded fashion. Nancy glanced over at *Hot Rum* just in time to see Turk, cigar clamped between his jaws, beat on his chest like Tarzan at the helm of his boat, while his cheerful crew downed chalices of grog. He saluted Nancy and gave her the peace signs on both hands, which was sailor shorthand for victory cocktails back at the yacht club. Nancy smiled and gave him a thumbs-up. Nancy looked over at *Bucephalus* and saw Mac and Tony grimace when she gave them a halfhearted salute. They knew what they had done under Roger's orders. Roger's back was turned when Mac and Tony gave her a sad wave in return.

The warm breeze that had kept them on a sure course during the race died down just as they limped back to their slip.

CHAPTER TWENTY-EIGHT
VICTORY COCKTAILS

Swagger. That's what the winner of the beer can races got upon entering the yacht club. And that's just what Turk and his veteran crew had that Tuesday evening. He was greeted with many congratulatory pats on the back and raised drinks, and he loved every minute of it. It was one of the rare moments when Turk's cranky demeanor melted away and threatened to expose the kind, happy man underneath. Winning looked good on him. Everyone tried to buy him a drink, but in true Turk fashion, he ended up picking up the entire bar tab that evening.

Nancy and the girls took up residence at a table by the floor-to-ceiling windows that looked out over the channel. Charlotte sipped her lemonade and watched the sea lions hanging out on the docks, warming themselves with the last rays of sunshine. The rest of the ladies were on their first bottle of wine, knee-deep in a group sulk. Roger, Mac, and Tony had yet to arrive. Turk was busy celebrating when Peter Ellis came over and squeezed Ruthie's shoulder.

"Shame about tonight, girls. I think you could have won it."

"Thanks, Pete," Nancy said.

"Thanks, babe," Ruthie said as she touched his hand.

"We were robbed," Lois piped up. Judy and Charlotte nodded in agreement.

"You'll get 'em next time." Then Peter looked at Ruthie and said, "If you need some extra support after your loss, might I offer up my excellent listening services?"

Ruthie smiled at him. "Your listening services are legendary. Meet at your boat in a half hour?"

Pete winked. "Can't wait." Then he walked over to the bar to hang with his crew.

"Gross." Charlotte rolled her eyes.

"Hey kid, trust me, when you get to my age and someone offers up 'listening services,' you take them up on it."

"Well, we should hit it soon. Otis and Suzanne are still on the boat and likely plotting their escape."

Just as Nancy was getting up from her chair, Roger walked up to their table, his chest puffed out. He let out a deep and posturing sigh. "Tough loss out there today."

No one said anything for a long moment. Finally, Nancy looked up at him with a lava-hot glare that would have melted a less iron-clad soul: "Rotten luck, I guess."

Roger mouth grew into a thin line. "Well, it takes knowing the right line."

"It sure as hell does," Lois said. "And we had it."

"All evidence to the contrary," Roger said coolly. "But I'm sure you'll eke out a win one of these days. Count yourselves proud of your second-place finish, hens," he said and then as he turned to go back toward the bar, a small, strong voice piped up.

"We're not hens." Charlotte stood up. "We're Mermaids."

Nancy, Lois, Ruthie, and Judy all sat there, stunned at her strength, but also because it was the first time their name had been said in public.

Roger looked puzzled. "The what?"

"And we're going to beat you next time, Grandpa Rog," Charlotte said, her chin jutting out rebelliously.

"I see your grandmother has been serving as a poor role model," Roger said, irked by his granddaughter's audacity. Then he chuckled slowly. "I look forward to it, Charlotte. The old hens, er, mermaids, renew my vigor. By the way, does your mom know you're here?"

Charlotte sat back down quickly, suddenly nervous, and didn't say a word.

"Of course she does," Nancy answered for her. Then she looked at Charlotte. "Right? Your mom knows you're here?"

Charlotte turned a shade of red and said, "I forgot to leave her a note."

"Oh god." Nancy immediately got out her phone and texted Stella. "*Just so you don't worry, Charlotte was sailing with me tonight. She forgot to leave a note. All is well.*"

After a few moments, Stella texted back. *I'll be there in fifteen minutes.*

Nancy looked back at Roger who was near the bar now. She stood up. "What makes you think we can't beat you, Roger? I mean, if we're being honest, I did most of the sailing on the *Bucephalus*. You merely barked orders and took the credit."

Snickers and murmurs came from the rest of the crowd as they quieted.

"Orders that you blatantly ignored most of the time!" Roger snapped.

"Which resulted in winning most of those races!" Nancy came right back.

Roger stood there, twirling the straw in his drink. Nancy could almost feel the heat radiating from his fuming face. Finally, he brushed off her comment. "Fine, fine. You won us a bunch of beer can races. You realize those aren't real races. Not even close. It takes a true sailor, a leader, to win the *big* races." He dismissed her with a wave.

Lois got up out of her seat with her fists clenched, ready to punch Roger in the throat, but Judy held her back. Ruthie stopped chewing on the cherry from her old-fashioned and glared at him. Charlotte joined in the glaring.

Given the fact that everyone knew Roger and Nancy were having marital issues due to Roger's naked boat charades with Claire Sanford, they all listened intently to the increasingly hostile exchange at the table. Nancy became aware of all of the faces looking in their direction. Her face grew hot. Still, she stood her ground.

Nancy leveled her gaze and said, "Roger, I'd be willing to bet serious money my crew could beat your crew in any race, any day, any time."

Roger chuckled, "Do you have serious money anymore, Nance?"

Burn.

"Name the race," Nancy challenged him.

Someone from the back of the room, who sounded suspiciously like Pete Ellis, piped up, "The Border Dash!"

A couple of hoots from across the room made Roger's neck turn red. The Border Dash, the storied yacht race from Newport Harbor to Ensenada, Mexico, was *his* race.

Nancy raised her eyebrows and then gave a single nod, acknowledging the call. *Your move, big guy.*

"You wouldn't stand a chance against *Bucephalus* in that pathetic bathtub of yours."

"Her name is the *Gypsea*. And are you saying it's on?"

Ruthie, Lois, and Judy hadn't moved.

Roger stood still, like a snake before a strike. All eyes were on him when he finally let the words slither out of his mouth. "It is on, you silly woman."

"That's mermaid to you," Nancy shot back.

Roger growled, slammed his drink on the bar, and stalked out of the yacht club in a rage. He tried to slam the door behind him, but because it had been under repair, the door just swished back through. Very unsatisfying.

Once Roger was gone and the coast was clear, a roar of applause started up.

Nancy let out her breath, unaware that she had been holding it, and nearly fell over. Everyone was looking at her and their table. Turk, who was leaning up against the bar, came over and offered a toast. "It's about time someone knocked that old turkey off his roost. Seems rather poetic that it would be you. To the crew of the *Gypsea*!"

"To the *Gypsea*!" The entire room raised their glasses to Nancy and the girls. Then, led by Turk, they added, "To the Mermaids!"

Ruthie let out a laugh, and Judy and Lois grimaced. Charlotte shrunk from the attention but still managed to raise her glass. Nancy stood up. "Thank you all. We'll do our best."

And just like that, the *Gypsea* and her crew were slated to enter the Newport to Ensenada Border Dash. Nancy appeared calm, but inside, panic barreled through her like a tsunami.

That was the bluff of all bluffs. My god, what have I done?

When she took the last sip of her Chardonnay, it went down like battery acid.

CHAPTER TWENTY-NINE

OLD GRIEVANCES LAID BARE

Fifteen minutes later, flush with nervous but excited energy, Nancy and Charlotte were walking to the dock just as Stella was pulling up in her SUV. There was a quiet understanding between Nancy and Charlotte that they were "in trouble" with "Mom." Stella had likely been hysterical thinking Charlotte had been abducted by a serial killer, or more likely, smoking weed somewhere with her aimless friends. Nancy assured Charlotte it would be okay once she got a chance to explain everything. But judging by the way Stella slammed the car door and marched down the gangplank to meet them, the hope of a smooth apology suddenly vanished like sea mist at sunrise.

"Get in the car," Stella snarled to Charlotte.

"But I've got my bike," Charlotte weakly protested.

"It's locked; leave it. You can get it another time."

Charlotte obeyed and headed to the car. She looked back at her Gran, looking like someone being led to the gallows.

Once Charlotte was safely ensconced in the glass and steel of Stella's BMW, Stella let loose on her mother.

"What the hell do you think you're doing, Mom?"

"Stella, calm down. We went sailing. It was the beer can—"

Stella cut in. "Do you have any idea how irresponsible this was?"

"Look, I know she forgot to tell you, and I can imagine your worry, but everything is fine. We had a great day."

"No, Mom, everything is not 'fine.' She completely missed her study group!"

Stella stood there, facing off against Nancy.

"Didn't she just get out of school? It's the start of summer."

Stella shook her head, disgusted. "Why would I expect you to know any of this? She's in an advanced-placement study group that helps with college admissions."

"She's fourteen. Does she really have to start thinking about college?"

"Only if she wants to have a future," Stella said, with biting sarcasm.

Nancy relented. She didn't like seeing her daughter so upset, but she had the feeling this wasn't just about taking Charlotte sailing or the study group.

"Okay, okay, I'll make sure Charlotte only goes with us when she doesn't have important stuff going on."

"Mom, you're not getting it," Stella said, frustrated, and then she blurted out, "I don't want her sailing with you at all."

Nancy was taken aback. "Why?"

Stella stammered on, still in the grips of anger. "She should be making connections and hanging out with the right crowd!"

It was Nancy's turn at sarcasm. "Right, I can see your concern. The inherent dangers of hanging out with her grandmother. And since when do kids make 'connections' instead of friends? I was just trying to introduce her to something new, to conquer a fear. It seemed to make her happy."

"Yeah, well, happy is all fine and good, but it's not going to get her into Stanford."

"Is that what's important to you? Because I'm pretty sure it's not important to her, not yet. Which is fine, because she is *fourteen*! And I don't see your Ivy League education increasing your happiness to any great degree. Life is about more than money, Stella."

"Oh, I know that, Mom. It's about achievement, and I want Charlotte to have opportunities."

"And you don't think sailing is a good life skill to open up 'opportunities'?"

"Stop!" Stella shook her head, almost turning red with frustration. "I want her to have role models that actually do something with their lives, Mom. I don't want my daughter thinking it's okay to not have any goals other than 'being happy.' " Stella used air quotes.

A pit opened up in Nancy's stomach.

"What are you saying?"

"You never had the guts to go out and do anything on your own, Mom. What can you teach Charlotte about the real world? You've never lived in it. You never had to pay rent or get a job. Do you even have a dream to do anything? Forgive me if I want more for my daughter. I was too young when I had her. Just like you were too young when you had me. It's ironic that the one thing I have in common with you is the one thing I regret. And let's not forget that you literally walked out on Dad—I'm not sure that's the best thing for Charlotte to see either!"

It stung, hard and long, like a blinding slap to her face. So, there it was. This is what her daughter thought of her. All the love and work of raising her daughter amounted to her believing that Nancy was a silly old woman who never had the courage to do anything on her own. Her own daughter had rendered Nancy and her path in life meaningless. She could tell that Stella knew she had breached a boundary that she couldn't cross back over.

"I see," Nancy said quietly.

Stella stood there defiantly, so much like her father, ready to take on whatever else came out of Nancy's mouth. But Nancy saw her chin quiver. A sign that even Stella might not feel as strongly as she sounded. The damage, however, was done. Nancy's shoulders sagged and she looked at her daughter. Maybe Stella was right. Maybe Nancy had very little to offer her bright, promising young granddaughter. Nancy gave Stella a weak smile and said, "Well, I have to go take care of Suzanne. She's hungry. You two should get going."

"Mom, I didn't—" Stella began, but couldn't bring herself to finish the sentence.

Nancy, looked back at her daughter, all the light in her eyes gone, and said, "It's okay, honey."

"Mom, wait!"

Nancy turned toward the dock and walked away, her daughter stilted and pleading for her to come back. Nancy kept walking.

* * *

When Stella got back into the car, she found an irate daughter facing her.

"What did you say to Gran?"

"Don't worry about it. It's between me and Gran," Stella said sullenly.

"Mom, stop treating me like I don't know what's going on! What did you say to her?" Charlotte demanded. "You hurt her! I can tell."

Frustrated, Stella snapped, "Don't you think it's time for you to hang out with people your own age? Go with your friends. Play a little volleyball."

"Volleyball?" Charlotte held out a handful of her purple hair. "Mom, do you even know who I am?"

"Listen, Charlotte, it's summer. At the beach. Most kids would die to live where you do. And I would rather have you hang out with your friends. Whatever happened to Joanna Craven? You guys were tight for a long time. Plus, I think she's smart enough to get into Stanford."

Charlotte looked at her mom like she was a loon. "What does Stanford have to do with anything?"

"Joanna has been your friend since kindergarten. I'm just saying, hon, connections are what make the world go round. With the right connections, you can be highly successful in your future life. Plus, maybe you can learn how to golf. A valuable life skill like coding."

"Golf. Coding. Really." Charlotte's deadpan delivery was potent.

"I'm just looking out for you," Stella said with concern, as she touched her daughter's knee.

"No, you're not." Charlotte removed her mom's hand. "My success or failure reflects on you, Mom, and you care way too much about money."

"That's not true! I just want you to be happy."

"When you say happy, though, you don't mean happy. You mean rich. You mean 'connected.' " Charlotte used air quotes.

"I do not," Stella sputtered.

"You think it's about salaries and titles and home values and 401(k)s. But guess what, Mom, you have all of those things. And you're not happy."

"I am happy!" Stella roared.

"Sounds like it." Charlotte stared out the window.

Stella caught herself and took a deep breath. She continued, "Listen, I just don't want you to screw up your life."

"How am I screwing up my life by learning to sail with my *grandmother*! Mom, you are clueless! She's surrounded by her best friends, she knows exactly who she is, and she is not afraid of anything. Gran is rich, but not because of money. She's happy. And you want me to hang out with Joanna. Weed-vaping, sex-having Joanna Craven." Charlotte then abruptly stopped her tirade. She had said too much.

Stella sat in the driver's seat, mouth agape. "Joanna Craven is having sex and smoking weed?" she asked with genuine astonishment.

Charlotte shook her head. "Not everyone is who they seem, Mom. And that includes Grandpa Rog."

Charlotte reached for the door and got out. She announced, "I'm riding my bike home."

Stella was dumbfounded by Charlotte's outburst and her revelation about Joanna Craven. Not to mention whatever Charlotte meant about her dad.

Stella knew she had hurt her mother with her words. But damn it if it wasn't true. There was no way she was going to let Charlotte waste her potential. Her father had taught her to be strong, to succeed, to achieve. These were the very attributes that had led her to be able to create a life of privilege for her daughter to enjoy. It was disturbing that Charlotte didn't think she was happy. Of course she was happy. Who wouldn't be, with a gorgeous home in Manhattan Beach, a newly leased Porsche Cayenne, and a vacation condo in Kauai, all of which was reflected in her annual Christmas letter? Still, something prickled at the edges of her mind. Or was it her heart?

CHAPTER THIRTY

IT NEVER RAINS IN SOUTHERN CALIFORNIA

It was late afternoon when Nancy heard the gentle patter of raindrops on the deck of the boat. The rain falling on the surrounding water sounded like the tinkle of piano keys all around her, quieting the usual sounds of the marina. The low-hanging gray clouds created a soothing light inside the boat. The familiar squawk of sea gulls was muted as they holed up in their hiding places. The usual din of boat motors in the distance was absent as well. Even Leon the pelican was nowhere to be found. Nancy got up and made coffee. Rain being a rare and wonderful thing in Southern California, she grabbed a blanket and sat under her canopy.

It had been drizzling most of the day as she sat with her thoughts and sipped her coffee. She'd let Suzanne snuggle in next to her as she ruminated on her conversation with Stella. She had long understood that she and her daughter weren't alike and that it lent itself to a certain distance between them. They weren't close like some mothers and daughters. They didn't get together for the random glass of wine on a Tuesday night to talk about love lives and little things. They didn't get their nails done or plan spa treatments together. Nancy felt deprived of that vital bond. But even though she hadn't experienced it, it hadn't stopped her from trying. That was the thing about moms and daughters, she thought. Even when it seemed like you were worlds apart, the bond remained, like a fine, unbreakable thread. Nancy loved Stella more than anything in the world. She knew her daughter needed a mother, even if Stella didn't know it.

But it hurt to know that Stella thought she was a failure at her own life. It was a jarring and painful realization that being a good and devoted mother to Stella had not been nearly enough. While Nancy had Stella young, she had never thought that her surprise pregnancy was a mistake. She didn't think about what she had given up. It was in Nancy's nature to forge on with motherhood and embrace its gifts, to make her daughter feel intended and totally loved, just as her mother Grace had done for her.

But Stella was different. Stella, also pregnant young, resented the mistake of becoming a young mother. Somehow it had made her feel stupid. She'd also made it sound like she hated it more because she was following in Nancy's footsteps. Perhaps that was why Stella put her career first—to undo the damage of her young pregnancy, to prove that she was more than her mother. As a result of Nancy's lack of accomplishment, Stella was now forcing her ambitions onto her own daughter, not realizing that Charlotte might not exactly consider Stella a living inspiration.

She sighed heavily, wondering if this entire new chapter of her life might have been a big mistake. So far, her presence in the marina had caused nothing but problems. Stella was mad at her; Charlotte was mad at Stella; Roger was furious at everybody, including Mac and Tony; Santiago had been allegedly hauled off by ICE; and Chuck Roverson had gotten fired. All ostensibly because of her. Nancy wondered if it was too late to undo the damage.

She heard quiet footsteps approach. To her great and delighted surprise, Santiago appeared in front of her in a green canvas coat, wet from the rain. He was smiling under his usual navy tam, coffee cup in hand.

"Permission to come aboard?" Santiago said with a twinkle in his eye.

Nancy broke into a huge smile of relief and waved him up.

As soon as Santiago climbed into the cockpit, Nancy gave him a huge hug. "You had me worried, Santiago." Then she released him and scolded. "It's not good to leave a woman at my age alone with her worry."

Santiago chuckled. "My apologies indeed. My friends over at Immigration wanted a word with me."

"What happened? I knew you were in trouble, but I had no way to reach you."

Santiago sighed and then said, "It is a long story."

"How about a drink?"

He nodded.

She went to the salon and returned with two glasses and a carafe of chilled white wine. They toasted.

"Thank god you're back and safe. I missed you—I mean, we missed you," Nancy said, trying to lessen her overenthusiastic concern. "What happened exactly? Does this mean you're being deported?"

Santiago chuckled. "No, no, madam. I have been a citizen since 1977."

Nancy shook her head slightly. "There's a lot about you I don't know, Santiago. That should change."

He agreed. "Indeed. I am a quiet man."

"A quiet man from, say, Cuba?"

"Wrong country," Santiago replied, his sea-green eyes squinting just so.

He switched topics. "Odd though, don't you think, that ICE showed up out of the blue, no?"

Nancy acknowledged it. "True. It's not like King Harbor is a haven for illegals."

Santiago took a sip of wine. "I have a friend in a very high place. After I was interrogated for over four hours by two rather green and unfriendly ICE agents who considered my paperwork fake, they let me talk to a supervisor, who quickly figured out who I was and my legal status as a citizen."

A warm breeze blew up the channel, ruffling the napkins on the table and mussing Nancy's hair. She looked into the direction of the wind, breathed it in, and then let out a long, slow exhale.

"This wind, it's so unusual for this time of year."

Santiago nodded knowingly. "Ah, the Winds of the Yamagaia."

"The who?"

"An ancient Mayan wind. The Yamagaia, as she is known. The wild spirit of change."

"I've never heard of the Winds of Yamagaia."

"The legend says the winds come around once every few decades to unsettle things, to mix them up, to challenge what has been. The legend says that it also brings strength to those in need."

That wonderful wind. Nancy sat silent for a moment, contemplating a force beyond her control. She thought of all that had transpired over the last few weeks. Perhaps the Winds of Yamagaia had been helping her all along, as if clearing the way.

"Maybe I needed that wind."

She and Santiago quietly took another sip of their wine, the silence comfortable between them.

Then Santiago cleared his throat and said, "I made a phone call to my old friend. I found out that someone tipped the ICE that I was illegal."

"Who would do that?"

"Who indeed." Santiago stared at Nancy.

Nancy looked back at Santiago, her brow furrowed, thinking. She didn't know anyone who would put in a false call with the intention of ruining someone's life. But then a previously hazy window in her mind became clear. A small flutter of fear leapt in her chest.

"Roger?" She whispered his name, hoping Santiago would refute it.

Santiago said nothing.

Nancy seemed to sink in her seat as she realized the truth. She was well aware of Roger's ruthlessness. But this was next-level despicable.

"Why?" It was all Nancy could say as she sat there clutching her wineglass.

"Roger Hadley strikes me as a man who always gets what he wants."

"That's true." She paused. "So, what does he want?"

"You. Back."

"No, he doesn't want me. He wants to win." Roger had unleashed his wrath upon her friends, neighbors, and the harmless dock master. She felt guilt, followed by a need to make everything right.

Santiago sipped his wine and nodded sadly. "Whatever he wants, it appears he will stop at nothing to get it. He is not a man who backs down from a fight."

"Then there's only one thing left to do," Nancy said quietly.

She fiddled with her wineglass and then lifted her eyes to Santiago's.

"Fight back."

CHAPTER THIRTY-ONE
ROGUE WAVES

Having walked up three flights of stairs from the garage with a fresh bottle of bourbon, Roger huffed his way into the kitchen and retrieved a rocks glass. He was daydreaming about how he would reward himself with an elevator after his blockbuster deal, the Bayside Urban Renovation Project, aka the BURP, closed, when his phone rang. It was Claire.

"Hello, lover," Claire purred. At the sound of his heavy breathing, she changed her tune. "What's wrong? You sound like you've been hauling a water buffalo up the stairs. Was her name Nancy?" Claire chuckled at her own joke.

"Funny," Roger managed to get out before bending over to catch his breath.

"Roger?"

"I'm here. I'm just a little winded."

"Well, I'm about five minutes away. Can you come give me the parking pass?"

This request, while seemingly small, felt like the equivalent of climbing back down Mount Everest in his current winded state. His chest felt tight, heavy. "For fuck's sake, just park in the driveway and you can grab it later."

"Don't be so grouchy."

"The investors called. They need an assurance by next week or they're pulling out. They said it felt like we were being 'disingenuous,' " he growled.

"Shit."

"That's not very helpful, Claire."

"I don't know what to tell you, Roger. You were the one who was supposed to get that hippie woman to vote in favor of our entire pier renovation. Otherwise it's curtains."

"I'm working on it!" he bellowed. He was still trying to catch his breath.

Roger sat down on a barstool and felt a slight flutter in his chest. Was that a palpitation? Nah, he'd just had a stress test.

But then Roger recalled all those horror stories his golf buddies had told him about some poor bastard who had been confidently pronounced fit as a fiddle by his doctor, only to croak on the fourteenth fairway the very next day. Roger was sweating too but he blamed that on his insane thermostat, which had a mind of its own. He'd made a note to get that thing fixed or destroyed. He fumbled with the plastic wrapping on the bourbon and finally got it open with the help of a nearby steak knife. He poured a finger of the golden-brown liquor into his glass. Before he took a sip, he tried to take a deep breath. A sharp pain, like an ice pick in his ribs, gripped him.

At that moment, Claire came up the stairs wearing a dress with pieces strategically cut out of the shoulders and waist, her gold hoop earrings almost as big as her head. Roger took one look at her and fell off the barstool, clutching his chest.

He heard Claire gasp and then fumble with her phone. "Hello? Hello? Is this nine-one-one?" he heard her say. "What's your address, Roger?" she screamed at him.

He lay on his side as the ocean view darkened in front of him. Either he was dying or a storm must be forming just off the coast. All he could think about was how he was surrounded by idiots. A bizarre last thought for a dying man.

* * *

Back on *Gypsea*, the rain had stopped. The temperature had cooled, prompting Nancy to bring up two light blankets for her and Santiago. The moon peaked out from silvery clouds, and the air smelled like minerals and salt. Nancy lit a small candle and put it in the center of the table. They had just finished the carafe of white wine and were considering another when Santiago reached out and gently touched Nancy's shoulder. It was electrifying. She leaned in, as if drawn by a magnetic force toward Santiago's sparkling blue eyes. He came forward too.

Nancy's cell phone rang.

Santiago moved back to his original position, and the moment fizzled like a lame firework.

She picked it up and saw that Stella was calling. She immediately answered. "Hey, what's up?"

"Mom, Dad's in the hospital. They think it's a heart attack."

"You're kidding. I can be there in fifteen minutes."

Nancy hung up. She looked at Santiago and his ever-patient gaze and said, "I have to go."

"You do?"

"Yes, Roger's in the hospital. They think it's a heart attack." Nancy looked at Santiago almost a beat too long. He had to know what she was thinking. "Don't get me wrong; there's a part of me that thinks the shit got exactly what he deserves, but I wouldn't be me if I didn't at least check on him. Thirty-six years of marriage is hard to ignore." She shrugged helplessly.

"It's your kindness, Nancy. You have a good heart."

"Ruthie says I have a guilt complex and an outsized sense of duty."

"Maybe. But it's a lucky man who has you by his side." Santiago placed his empty wineglass on the table and got up. "Go. I'll clean up."

"But," Nancy faltered, "maybe we can pick up where we left off later tonight?" she asked, hoping to not totally chill the moment she never thought would happen.

"Take care of your family." Santiago kissed her hand and picked up the glasses.

Somehow that sounded like a no. Nancy sighed heavily before alarm mode took over. She gathered her rain jacket, grabbed her key, and headed to the hospital.

As she was walking up the dock, Nancy saw a bolt of lightning hit somewhere out at sea and light up the early-evening sky. She felt the rumble of thunder, as if the gods themselves were giving her an ominous warning.

CHAPTER THIRTY-TWO
BAD MOON ON THE HORIZON

Nancy hated hospitals. The scent of industrial-strength cleanser, the beeping and whirring of machinery, the moans of patients in varying degrees of pain and discomfort. Remembering her mother's blithe spirit moving between planes under the glow of fluorescent lights made her stomach tighten the minute she walked through the automatic doors. She quickly located Roger's room and gently knocked on the door.

"Come in," she heard a female voice say.

Nancy entered and saw Stella, her eyes red and swollen, a tissue clutched in her hand, standing in the corner. Nancy opened her arms, and her daughter rushed over. She embraced her as she always did, with uncompromising love.

"Mom, I'm so sorry." Stella's tears flowed quietly.

"Shh, now. Hush, baby. Everything is okay."

Stella melted into her mother's hug and stayed there for a minute until a nurse came in and tended to the machines. Stella stood up then and looked at her father in the hospital bed.

Nancy looked over and saw her nearly-ex-husband hooked up to an IV with oxygen tubes stuffed up his nose. He was asleep. Nancy went over to Roger. She smoothed his hair and touched his forehead with the back of her hand. "You old goat, what have you done now?" Nancy murmured.

Roger woke up briefly and saw her. He gave her a wan smile and asked weakly, "Where have you been?"

"I'm here now."

Roger looked at her with a rare gaze, vulnerable and open, the one he reserved only for her, the one that had made her fall in love with him in the first place. She softened when she saw his need for her again.

"I'm going to leave you two, but I'll be back in the morning," Stella said.

"Okay." Nancy settled into the seat she had occupied. "I'm going to stay."

Stella nodded, and Roger gently squeezed Nancy's hand before he closed his eyes and fell asleep again.

As the evening passed and the light in the hospital room grew dim, Nancy fell into the same routine from a lifetime ago. She found the cafeteria and got herself a cup of tea, bought a bag of potato chips out of the vending machine, and settled in for the night in a chair by Roger's bed.

The first and only time she had been in the hospital with Roger, beyond the happy birth of their daughter, was after a sailing accident in which Roger nearly drowned. It was the summer before Roger was heading into his senior year and Nancy her junior year at UC Davis. They had gone sailing with their friend, Tim Sheldon, on his family's yacht in the San Francisco Bay on a wild and windy day. Roger, claiming to have much more sailing experience than he actually had, was standing on the side of the deck when the wind gusted and the boom swung over hard and fast. It hit Roger square in the head and launched him off the boat. Semiconscious, Roger struggled in the water while the entire crew, including Nancy, went into emergency lifesaving efforts. Someone threw him the life ring, and he clung to it weakly until the boat was able to maneuver back to him. The crew dragged a dazed and bloodied Roger back onto the boat and motored back to the harbor, where they were met by an ambulance that whisked him off to San Francisco Memorial Hospital. Nancy was traumatized by the thought of losing Roger, partly because she was in love with him and partly because she wasn't sure she could handle any more loss. Her mother had died at the beginning of her sophomore year. It didn't take much to send her reeling.

When Roger Hadley came into her life, she would never have guessed that he would offer her safety. He had been the captain of the football team at UC Davis, head of the chess club, and he knew how to surf. He was like the West Coast version of JFK—dashing, handsome, and in very high demand by the female contingent on campus. So, when Roger came courting her, Nancy was at first stunned by his attention but quickly found it suspicious and scoffed at his invitations. She was sure he viewed her as a conquest. Along with his popularity came his rather salty reputation. Roger liked to win. And that included women.

Nancy held out her affections longer than any other woman on campus. So, when Roger took the drastic step of joining her study group in nihilist literature, not the most popular of electives, she knew he was serious. No one talked Kafka for the fun of it, but there he was, going at it with the bookish Donovan Cartwright, another one of Nancy's suitors and an expert on the Bohemian novelist. Roger got into a heated debate with Donovan over whether or not Kafka was really that grim or if he was just trying to get in the pants of a pretty wench at his local watering hole in Prague. Donovan ended up calling Roger a Philistine before he skulked away to lick his intellectual wounds. And in that moment, when Roger had bested Donovan in an effort to win her favor, she succumbed and agreed to go on a date with him. After a few short months of dating combined with some dubious contraceptive advice, Nancy found herself pregnant.

Roger graduated with honors while Nancy put off her last semester to get ready for the birth of their unexpected daughter. They landed in Cow Hollow, an affordable and bustling neighborhood in San Francisco that boasted a park with stunning views of the Golden Gate Bridge. They, however, lived in a two-story walk-up flat that boasted an unimpeded view of a Safeway supermarket sign. It was here that they awaited the birth of their daughter and began to settle into the idea of becoming young parents.

One late night, Roger got home after a night out with the boys. Alcohol having removed his inhibition, he admitted that he had always pictured himself as the father of a strong, capable, handsome boy, a mini version of himself whom he could teach to throw a football and swing a golf club. "What do you do with girls?" he asked Nancy before they drifted off to sleep. She reassured him that she wouldn't be just a girl, but *his* girl, which seemed to soothe him.

Roger worked hard, putting in longer days and nights. It was after one of those long nights at the office that Roger came home and carelessly left his suit coat in the kitchen. When Nancy went to hang it up, she found a bar napkin with a phone number on it with the name *Lisa*. Surprisingly, it wasn't anger Nancy felt. It was fear.

The one devastating and lasting effect of trauma experienced too young was that her feeling of dread had never really left her. It was always there, lurking under the surface of her consciousness. It would fill her head with all the worst possible scenarios in vivid, full-color clarity. Hear a siren? Roger had gotten hit by a bus and was bleeding to death in the street. Doctor calling? It was stage four cancer. She always expected calamity, and she was acutely and painfully aware that everything could change in an instant.

So, in that instant, Nancy touched her growing belly, thought of her future, and decided to ignore this potential transgression. She tossed the paper down the garbage disposal, mulching up any chance of it ruining her life, and got on with her wedding plans.

But there were other notes over the years. Unlike a shocking diagnosis or a sudden death, Nancy learned that these transgressions slowly eroded love and trust, the heartbreak almost imperceptible but always there, until one day she couldn't quite remember what real love felt like anymore.

At dawn, she woke with a start in the chair facing Roger's hospital bed and instantly felt the soreness in her neck. She got up and wandered down the hall for coffee. When she came back, Roger was awake.

"Hey, you," he said softly.

Nancy came over and smiled at him. He grabbed for the coffee, but Nancy pulled the cup back. "No, no, not until the doc gives his approval and you're cleared for takeoff."

He started to grimace but then switched gears, offering her a smile followed by a "Thanks for coming."

"Of course, you're technically still my problem."

Roger smiled wider at the joke.

"So, what happened?" she asked.

"They think it was a myocardial infarction."

"A heart attack."

"Yes," Roger said as he grabbed the sheet and started to wring it in his hands.

He seemed genuinely rattled by his situation.

"They're still running tests, and I'm on blood thinners in case of clotting in the lungs. He said I have to stop drinking so much."

"Good advice," Nancy said, taking a sip of coffee.

Then his voice changed, and he added more sharply, "He also said it could be stress related. He asked me if anything had changed lately." Roger looked Nancy dead in the eye.

Nancy stiffened. Was he blaming her for his heart attack? "And . . . what did you tell him?"

"Well, I told him that you had absconded away from the house and were living on a boat."

"So, not the whole truth," Nancy said flatly.

"Goddamn it, Nancy, do we have to get into details right now?" he growled, impatient.

"If by details you mean what Claire Sanford's ass looks like naked, then no."

"I've just suffered a heart attack!" he bellowed.

Nancy felt the muscles in her shoulders tighten as a familiar anxiety came over her. Before she knew how to stop them, the words came out. "I'm sorry." She shouldn't get him riled up.

Roger shook his head. "I need you, Nance. I need you to come back."

Nancy sighed and got up. She started pacing around the room.

"Besides," Roger added, "that thing with Claire meant nothing. It was over before it began."

"Is that so? Because you seemed pretty into her. No pun intended."

"Yes. I mean, no. She plainly saw how important you were to me and decided to go sniff around Larry Bland instead. She is not you, Nancy. You're the only woman I've ever loved." He stopped and let that sink in. "The life we've built, the memories we have, it adds up to something." He threw up his hands in mock defeat. "I can't do this without you. Look at me, I'm falling apart!"

She looked at him. He wore a joking frown, one hand with an IV stuck in it, the other with a heartbeat monitor on it. He was a mess. But he still had that sparkle in his eye.

"What shape is the house in?"

He smiled ever so slightly and said softly, "Barely holding up without you."

She smiled at that. She'd always loved to be needed. She thought about how safe and happy she had been in that house. How easy it would be to slide back into it. The boat was a lot of work. She'd made some friends, but she'd also hurt some people. Chuck Roverson, for one. And there had been too many nights on the boat when she would wake up alone and feel utterly terrified. The loneliness of her situation seeped into her bones, as if it were a slow-working poison. The dread would last until sunrise. Maybe she wouldn't feel that way if she went home, if she went back to Roger.

Roger went in for the kill. "It'll be different this time, Nancy. I got my first taste of life without you and I don't want seconds. Please come back."

He reached for her, his arm begging for her to come to him. She hesitated ever so briefly but found herself alarmed at how swiftly the life she was building collapsed like a house of cards at the prospect of the safety her old life offered. They embraced on the hospital bed before the nurse came in. She was clad in scrubs that had little red ladybugs on them.

"Good morning, I'm Amber. You must be family. Sister?"

Nancy shook her head, "No." And then she looked at Roger with a smile. "I'm his wife."

Roger smiled at Nancy and then he looked at the nurse with a worried stare.

Amber the nurse seemed slightly confused but then brightly said, "All righty then! Well, there's a good chance this guy will be released by three PM today!"

"Oh, already? I mean, don't you have to run more tests or something? Check for a clot?"

"Nope, the doctor will make one more round this morning, and he should be free."

Nancy looked at Roger and smiled. "Then I'm going to go home, take a shower, and get some fresh clothes for you. I'll be back. We'll go home." She meant it warmly, but there was something stirring inside of her, a feeling like a limb being caught in a bear trap. Her smile faltered. The gravity of her admission hung in the air like a foul smell.

"That's my girl." Roger smiled and kissed the back of her hand.

Nancy robotically leaned over and kissed Roger, something she hadn't done in months, and it felt like it always felt. It felt like home. But maybe this time that wasn't a good thing.

CHAPTER THIRTY-THREE

THE SMILING BARRACUDA

That morning on her way back to the boat from the hospital, she saw Shepard Wallace.

"Hey, Shep, how are you?"

"I am very well, my lady. I went fishing this morning and thought I'd share the wealth." He held up a small bag of dead fish.

"Ah, she'll be happy to see you," Nancy said as the two of them walked toward her boat. When they came closer, Suzanne was already waiting for them, meowing expectantly.

Nancy smiled and then addressed her cat, "No, Suzanne, you cannot go home with Shep. You belong to me."

Suzanne flicked her tail twice to let Nancy know she wasn't the boss of her and went up to Shep, gently took her fish treasure out of his fingers, and trotted off to enjoy her feast.

"If I may be so bold, I also wanted to let you know what went on last night, here at the marina."

That was the night she had been at the hospital. Nancy thought he spoke like a weary knight from the Middle Ages—proper, measured, and ever articulate. When he moved slowly toward her, she could almost hear his bones creak, like rusted armor.

"Did something happen to *Gypsea*?" Nancy asked, alarm rising in her voice.

"No, no, not at all. Our fine ex–dock master, Chuck Roverson, paid a visit and called a meeting with those of us he deems friends. Ellis, myself, and a few others. He intended on you hearing it as well, so I have taken it upon myself to be the bearer of such news."

"What's going on?"

"It seems there are plans by a developer to renovate the entire Redondo pier and marinas. Chuck, while employed at the marina and under a nondisclosure agreement, could not discuss the rather disastrous details of the plans. But since he has been, shall we say, liberated of his employment shackles, he told us what is at stake."

"I've heard a little about the pier project—they call it the BURP, right? I thought it only affected the pier itself and some of the lesser outbuildings."

"Yes, the Bayside Urban Renovation Project. And no, my lady, it seems as though it is much more far-reaching than that. A company called Bayside Development is the lead on the project, and their plan is to demolish the entire pier and replace it with an upscale mall and, I shudder to think, luxury condominiums. But the most concerning part is that they intend to expand the Portofino Marina and . . ."

Nancy nodded to prod the gentleman on.

"It pains me to say it, but they want to backfill King Harbor for parking and build a neon-ensconced pier not unlike the one in Santa Monica. A tourist trap, complete with restaurants, bars, and amusement rides." Shep mimed a roller coaster dropping with his hands that mimicked what Nancy's heart was doing in her chest.

"What? They want to pave over our marina?"

"Indeed. And they also intend to take the public boat launch out and replace it with Jet Ski and powerboat rentals. Evidently, our little marina only brings in a meager profit, whereas the daily parking fees and lease agreements from the new pier would fill up the coffers for Bayside Development and the city of Redondo Beach for decades to come."

"This cannot be happening. Don't we get to vote on it or something? Do we need to mobilize? How do we stop this?"

"That's part of the problem. It's been done under a blanket of secrecy for precisely the reaction that you are having now. The development company is in the process of doing an environmental impact report, but Peter Ellis is quite adamant that those results can be manipulated to be in favor of the highest-paying party."

"Jesus, it's like Congress." Nancy stood there, shocked at what she was hearing.

Shep said one last thing. "It seems our last line of defense is the California Coastal Commission. In order for the project to get a final green light, they need a majority of the nine members to vote for it."

"Well, that's a relief," Nancy said. "The commission will never allow this to happen. Its main responsibility is to uphold environmental protections. They're famous for it. This Bayside Urban Renovation Project will never get a majority of the votes."

"Or so we thought," came a voice from behind her. Nancy turned and saw Pete strolling over from his boat. "They've already got four votes," he said gravely.

Nancy was incredulous at this news. "Impossible. How?"

"Three of the commissioners are new. Appointees from the current Republican administration are hell-bent on seeing California abandon its frivolous environmental ways in favor of unregulated capitalism. Offshore drilling, old-growth logging, and in our case, marina backfilling. These three new appointees are even threatening to overturn protections for the Monterey Bay Marine Sanctuary so British Petroleum and other enormous oil companies can build offshore oil platforms." Pete shook his head and looked out at the bay.

"What about the other six commissioners? Most of them are as liberal minded as it gets," Nancy said.

"*Most* is the imperative word there. Calvin Eldridge is a longstanding Reagan Republican who is pro-business. He's indicated that he feels the development will bring in much-needed revenue and is good for the local economy. That gives them four solid yes votes, and they only need one more." Ellis frowned before continuing. "Right now, there are only four confirmed environmentalists on the commission."

"That's eight, so who is the last and deciding vote?" Nancy asked.

"We're not sure. It's someone who was just appointed, and the name isn't public yet."

Nancy shook her head, incredulous at the news. "I know how developers work. My husband was one. I know for a fact that they have to get the city's approval through a vote. Especially if they're out-of-town developers. Surely we can still have a say."

"That's the worst part. The developers aren't out-of-towners," Pete said. "They're based right here in Hermosa Beach. Turk had his grandson dig up anything he could find on them. Kid is a tech whiz, although I have calluses on my big toe that are older than him. Turns out Bayside is a newly formed development company working out of offices on Pier Avenue. They've got Marlin Equity bankrolling them too. Small potatoes they are not. We're talking serious money. And that kind of money almost always gets its way."

A memory deep inside Nancy's brain struggled to the surface. Bayside Development. Why did that sound familiar? She racked her brain but came up with nothing. She made a mental note to research it later.

Shep interrupted them. "Sorry to be so rude, but it is time for me to bid adieu. It's almost time for *Jeopardy!,* and I haven't missed a show since the late eighties."

He nodded to Nancy and Ellis.

Nancy patted him on the shoulder. "Thank you, Shep. I appreciate your taking the time to tell me yourself."

"Of course, my lady," Shep said, and shuffled down the dock toward his nightly ritual of watching the trivia show via satellite TV on his Catalina 30.

That left Peter and Nancy on the dock. She changed the topic and asked, "So, you going to see Ruthie?"

Peter looked surprised by the question. "No, actually. I haven't seen her. She's been busy, she says."

"Oh. I thought when I talked to her earlier that—never mind. My mistake."

"Tell her to call me?" Peter said earnestly with a hangdog expression, like a heartbroken cowboy in a country song. He headed back toward his boat.

"Will do." Nancy hopped on the *Gypsea*, her mind already working on the puzzle of what seemed so familiar about Bayside

Development. She got out her computer and tapped a few keys. She looked up any public documents and news stories about the Bayside Urban Renovation Project at the Redondo Pier. The BURP, the nickname given to the project by its detractors, had been aggressively fought against by a small group of feisty locals keen on keeping their beach town authentic and slightly grungy. They were hell-bent on stopping the bulldozers from taking down Old Tony's and would do anything in their power to stop the bulldozers from backfilling King Harbor too. But while they were very vocal, they were not well funded.

The fate of King Harbor and the pier was going to be decided by one person—the newly appointed commissioner—someone who hadn't even been publicly identified yet. That vote was just two weeks away.

Nancy continued her investigation and opened the sparse website of Bayside Development. There wasn't much information about the company itself, beyond its being headquartered in Hermosa Beach. They knew how to hide their venture capitalists. The website had a line that cheerfully read, *The most upscale beach living under the sun! Bayside Urban Renovation Project in Redondo Beach coming soon!*

Nancy frowned. In the lower right-hand corner of the page was a cartoon drawing. A barracuda, presumably the logo of Bayside Development. A bright, silvery barracuda wearing sunglasses and smiling. One of his sharp teeth even had a glint on it. Only problem was, Nancy had seen that barracuda before.

She poured herself a cup of coffee and pondered what this meant. Then she checked her watch and realized she still had to go to her house and get Roger a fresh change of clothes.

CHAPTER THIRTY-FOUR
RUTHLESSNESS HAS A NAME

As soon as Nancy hit the doors to the hospital, she nearly ran into Dr. McGowan, who was shuffling through papers on a clipboard. Nancy, armed with fresh clothes for Roger, sent them flying all over the reception area.

"Oh dear, I'm sorry," the doctor said as he retrieved a pair of errant socks. Dr. McGowan was young, tall, and lanky with light brown hair. He wore silver rimmed glasses that sat on the edge of his long, slender nose. His shy nature was complemented by a faint Irish accent, which instantly likened him to a young Liam Neeson. Nancy looked at his name tag and remembered it from Roger's chart.

"Oh, you're Dr. McGowan. I'm Nancy Hadley, Roger's wife. I just wanted to say thank-you for looking after my husband. He had quite a scare there."

Dr. McGowan looked momentarily confused. "You're Mrs. Hadley?"

"Yes." Nancy nodded and reached out to shake his hand.

He shook her hand politely but offered nothing else.

"So, is there anything I need to know before I take him home? I don't want to stress his heart further."

"I'm sorry, what do you mean?" Dr. McGowan looked even further confused.

"Well, I mean, his heart. Given its weakened state due to the heart attack, I just want to know what limitations he has until he heals. Cut out red meat, salt, no coffee, no overexertion. I can take notes. Also, I'm curious to know if he will eventually need surgery."

"We're talking about Roger Hadley, right?"

"Uh, yes, room two thirteen? Tall guy. Silver hair. Big mouth," Nancy added. She expected the doctor to remember the heart attack patient he had visited a mere twelve hours ago.

"Forgive me for my confusion, Mrs. Hadley." Dr. McGowan stared as he shook his head, as if coming out of a trance.

"I'm sure you have a lot of patients; it's understandable."

"No, that's not it." Dr. McGowan took off his glasses and rubbed his eyes. "Before I disclose patient information, do you mind if I see some identification?"

Nancy, processing the request, squinted at the doctor as she reached for her wallet.

* * *

Stella was standing outside her father's hospital room, taking a conference call, when Nancy marched up. She reached Stella, hands on hips, and stared at her for a good long minute while Stella muttered to the person on the other end of the phone.

Stella covered the receiver with her hand and said, "I'm on a call, Mom. What is it?"

"Did you bring your father to the hospital when he had his heart attack?"

"No, he texted me when he was here. I think an ambulance brought him. He was alone," Stella said with a hint of snide sarcasm.

"Wrong." Nancy turned on her heel, left Stella in the hallway, stomped into Roger's room, and ripped off his blanket.

"Hey, honey, I— "

"Gas. You had a bad case of gas," Nancy growled.

Roger started to stammer. "Uh, well, the doctor said he, uh, didn't know for sure, and I, er, just found out this morning."

"Nope. Try again, Rog." Nancy glared at him. "Dr. McGowan ascertained and reported to you sometime last evening, before I even *got* here, that you did not, in fact, have a myocardial infarction but rather a bad case of deep-bowel gas. Your heart was never in danger. Your farts backed up. Probably because you're so full of shit."

"I would think you would be pleased that I am not keeling over from a major coronary!"

"You lied. You're a liar. *L-I-A-R*." She spelled it out for emphasis.

Roger shifted his weight uncomfortably in his bed, evidently trying to shake off the insult.

"And to think you almost had me. I almost fell for your line of shit again. And I would have had I not run into Dr. McGowan."

"Isn't that an invasion of my privacy? I should sue him!"

"Not if I'm your wife, it's not. But that's the problem, isn't it, Roger?"

At that point Stella came back in after hearing the raised voices. She said in whispered tones appropriate for a hospital wing, "Hey, hey, what's going on? The nurses are threatening to dose you if you don't bring the noise down. I thought you guys were back together?"

"I would sooner step into a pit of starved alligators than move back in with your narcissistic, lying cheat of a father."

"Mom! Easy!"

"Oh, stop it. It's no secret you'll always take his side," Nancy said to Stella. Then she turned to Roger. "How could you be such a snake?" She searched his expression but found only defiance.

She could see his eyes moving rapidly back and forth, trying to come up with something that might redeem him. But no words came.

"You know, it makes sense that it was gas. A huge pent-up fart can only come from a giant asshole."

"Mom!" Stella moaned.

"You can't talk to me that way!" Roger bellowed.

"Oh, shove it, you old goat. I can talk to you any way I please. You're not in a weakened state; you're not ill. In fact, you're sharper and more ruthless than ever." Nancy shook her head. She looked at Stella, who seemed stunned by this turn of events. "Are you going to tell your daughter who brought you here?"

"I thought an ambulance . . ." Stella muttered, apparently in shock at the strength of her mother's voice.

"No. Oh no. Your father was allegedly brought to the hospital by his wife, a Mrs. Hadley. Only the Mrs. Hadley Dr. McGowan remembers had short red hair and a slight New Jersey accent. He didn't check her ID, but I can guess who it might have been."

"Oh shit," Roger muttered.

"Who? What are you talking about, Mom? You're not making any sense!"

"I'm the *only* one making sense." Nancy went over to the table next to Roger's bed. It held a cup of ice chips, tissues, leftover banana pudding, and Roger's cell phone. She snatched the phone from the table just before he could lunge for it. She opened his last text and there she found what she was looking for. A text from Claire Sanford.

Nancy read it aloud. "*Let me know when the coast is clear, tiger. I'll come pick you up. Let's make margaritas and mess up the sheets tonight.* Smiley face. And the eggplant emoji." Nancy tossed the phone onto Roger and shook her head in disgust. "Jesus Christ, what a classless tramp. I want a divorce."

Roger crossed his arms and said, "Nope."

Nancy, mystified, turned to him. "You can't just say 'nope' like I'm some indentured servant. I know this may come as a shock to you, but I have rights to exactly half of everything you have."

"Who?" Stella, obviously reeling, interrupted. "Who is a classless tramp?"

"We'll see how many rights you have when you can't cover the cost of a decent divorce attorney," Roger chided.

"Roger, not only am I not coming home *ever*, but I'm going to kick your ass in that Newport to Ensenada race. I will take that money and hire the best goddamn divorce attorney in town." Nancy started for the door. "Yours!"

Roger smiled at her sharply, like a shark, and said, "You want to know how likely I think it is that you can win my race? I'll bet on it."

Nancy stopped in her tracks. She saw a pinhole of a possible way out. She turned around, put her hands on her hips, and faced Roger. "What are the terms of the bet?"

Roger sat up and rubbed his hands together as if sharpening his tools. He cocked his head as if trying to read Nancy's mind. "If you beat me, I'll grant you the divorce you so desperately want, which, I'm sure you are well aware, will entitle you to half of everything we have."

"I'll get that anyway. I want *Bucephalus*."

His mouth fell agape. "Never!"

"I'm not going to win anyway, right, Roger? If you're so sure, then why not put your boat on the line?"

Roger closed his mouth and sat still as a statue, his brow crimped and his eyes calculating. "Fine," he growled, "*Bucephalus*."

Nancy stood with her chin out and gave a simple nod of acceptance. There was no way he was going to make this easy on her. She waited for the other half of the bet.

His smile got sharper. "But if I win? I get you back. You will sell that crappy little heap that floats, and you will come back under my roof where you belong. Ruthie, Lois, and Judy are not allowed in the house. You'll smile nice, go to my luncheons, do exactly as I say, and you'll iron my golf pants with glee. And you'll never ever pull a stunt like this again." Roger rested his hands in his lap and waited for her reply.

Stella stood with her mouth agape.

Nancy peered at him, knowing some devious plot was brewing inside his twisted mind. Obviously, this was about his psychotic need to control, but there was something else. He needed her. But why? Nancy knew Roger couldn't resist a bet. She had no choice but to bet on herself. She thought about the high stakes and the shortcomings of her situation: a heavy boat, a novice crew, an unfamiliar route. Her chances were as a good as an old gray mare winning the Kentucky Derby.

"What's your angle, you conniving old goat?"

"No angle. Just trying to put things back in their rightful order. You're not fit to be in charge."

They were at a standoff.

Roger saw her contemplating and interjected, "Or we can keep doing this dance, Nancy. A long, protracted divorce that will surely bankrupt you. Eventually I will get what I want, either way." Roger looked so smug, so satisfied sitting there after faking a heart attack.

Nancy's shoulders tightened at the sound of his certainty, his sheer cockiness. She took a deep breath and let it out slowly. She bent down to his level and said, "You're on, putz."

Nancy turned on her heel, tossed the bag of fresh clothes in the medical waste bin, and began to stalk out of the hospital room.

Roger's eyes grew dark, like a malevolent king betrayed by his peasant queen. His face turned red and he bellowed, "I will crush you!"

Nancy poked her head back into the room. "Better watch that blood pressure, Rog." She pointed to the machine that had started to loudly beep. "Claire's making margaritas."

Nancy disappeared down the hospital corridor.

Roger threw his cup of ice chips across the room and roared like a trapped lion.

* * *

"Never tell me the odds," Ruthie said, after Nancy had told her about the bet on the Border Dash and the sad shape of their boat and crew.

All the girls, plus Lois's husband Chris, had gathered for an emergency code red barbecue on the boat to discuss the upcoming race and the relative outcomes. Chris was attending to his teriyaki

Kobe beef skewers on the small charcoal grill on the back of the boat. Ruthie, Lois, and Judy sat on the starboard side of *Gypsea* with their legs hanging over. The tasty smell of grilling meat wafted through the air, making Otis's mouth water, the evidence dripping onto the gleaming deck.

"It makes me nervous," Judy added. Ruthie and Lois silently scowled at Judy, who then quickly added, "But buying soap makes me nervous, so don't let me be your guide."

Ruthie sighed as she summed up the situation: "So, you have to earn your freedom. Like an indentured servant."

"You make it sound so glamourous," Nancy retorted.

"It's just that we're not exactly spring chickens," Lois said, as she rubbed her thighs nervously.

"Aw, come on. We'll need a little *sisu*, that's all," Nancy implored.

Lois acknowledged the word and explained to Ruthie and Judy. "*Sisu*. Means a combination of strength, know-how, and guts in Finnish—the Finnish equivalent of a can of whoop-ass."

Judy adjusted her glasses and nodded. "Finns did win the war against the Russians. And they were on skis."

"Hell's bells," Ruthie added. "Might as well go out in a blaze of glory."

"That's the spirit," Nancy said.

They all cheerfully toasted.

Chris piped up. "Chow's on."

Each of them got up to go in the direction of dinner while Nancy stayed behind and wished on the first night's star for a miracle.

CHAPTER THIRTY-FIVE

SHE MAY BE SMALL, BUT SHE BE FIERCE

Nancy sat on the stern of *Gypsea* and considered her odds of winning the Border Dash, and it made her nervous. The 125-nautical mile race began in Newport Harbor and ended in Ensenada, Mexico. It was the premier regatta on the West Coast. It had a storied and colorful history that started with Humphrey Bogart, who had instigated the first race in 1948 when he sailed against his buddies Errol Flynn and Spencer Tracy.

Every year, die-hard sailors from across the globe came out to prove their skills. The race included a broad range of sailboats and yachts each with their own rating and class. Besides attracting hard-core racers, the Border Dash had a long history of encouraging recreational sailors to enter and compete.

Nancy had received a favorable race rating from the International Racing Conference (IRC), basically like getting a handicap in golf, which placed *Gypsea* in the same race class as *Bucephalus*. She and Roger would be racing head-to-head. It was going to be a tall task to beat Roger, as her boat was heavier and more squat than the sleek *Bucephalus*. She pondered this disadvantage while filling out her race registration. Loyal to the end and helpful as always, Suzanne was comfortably sprawled on half her paperwork.

The purse in the Border Dash for their class was a cool fifty thousand dollars. That was serious money for most people but would be a drop in the bucket in a nasty divorce, where she could never outgun Roger. Plus, she figured she would burn through fifty thousand in less than a year if Roger welched on the bet. On the surface, that was why she had to win this race. But the real reason was much more personal.

At the ever-ripening age of fifty-seven years old, roughly two months prior, Nancy had found herself quietly diminished, fading, and unfulfilled. Sure, she could blame part of that on Roger, but she was painfully aware of her own culpability in her life's result too. After all, she'd grown up in the mid to late 1970s, just a few years after formerly well-behaved housewives took to the streets of American cities demanding equal rights. Women shed their coy, meek personas and fearlessly protested in the streets, brazen and braless, swinging pink baseball bats at the heads of the patriarchy. If ever there was a time to break away from the doldrums of prim and proper womanhood, 1970 was the time to do it.

Nancy was too young to march but marveled at the courage of her older female compatriots. She couldn't wait to fight for women's rights when she got to college. Of course, that was before Grace died, before she met Roger. When her time did come and there was a rally on her college campus, Nancy's views had dramatically changed. She was finally in a situation that let her feel safe again, with a husband and a baby on the way. Roger took turns bitching about the protests, but Nancy privately rooted for the women in their struggle while she crocheted little pink hats for her baby girl to come. She wasn't part of the movement, but it saddened her when it came apart all the same.

As with all movements, it wasn't long before the dynamic energy of the women's movement deflated like a slow-leaking balloon. They won some ground but lost some too. Nancy witnessed some of her friends, the very same women who marched on campus, finding themselves at odds with their own ideas. Love came calling. In some cases, fear came calling. For every successful Mary Tyler Moore or Laverne and Shirley, there was an unnamed divorced woman who was on the verge of poverty, hanging on by her unmanicured fingertips, unable to get a decent job to feed her children, unable to open a checking account on her own, unable to survive without help from family or a man.

So, some put down their signs and walked into marriage. They hid their battle scars and their pride, bowed their heads, and towed the line. They had children and mortgages and school plays to attend. Before they knew it, they were making meat loaf, sewing Halloween costumes, and setting their dreams adrift, just like their mothers before them. Their ideas and hopes for change faded like construction paper left out in the sun. It was all so depressingly inevitable. Once in a while, a woman just like Nancy Hadley, part of a legion of unfulfilled housewives, would drink too much Chablis after making another tuna noodle casserole and remember her once bright and burning desire to be more.

And that was why she had to win this race. It represented a larger, long-forgotten struggle. She wasn't there for that first public fight. But she was here for this personal one.

She had to stand up to Roger. Face-to-face. Or, in her case, bow to bow.

She needed Roger to know that she could.

She needed to know it too.

CHAPTER THIRTY-SIX
ALLIES UNITE

Nancy was deep in thought when she saw Suzanne the Cat hop up and walk on the edge of the boat, alerting Nancy to an impending visitor. She rose up to look over the side and saw the small frame of her granddaughter, clad in a hoodie, denim shorts, and her checkered Vans, walking toward the boat. She waved and then hopped up. She took a seat across from Nancy.

"So what's the plan?"

"I take it you heard, then."

"I heard that Grandpa Rog faked a heart attack to get you back and that it ended in a massive fight and winner-take-all bet on a sailing race."

"That about sums it up," Nancy said with a heavy sigh.

Charlotte sighed too. "Well, bright side is that the truth is out there."

Nancy nodded. *Truth can set you free. And completely destroy a family in the process.*

As if sensing Nancy's guilt, Charlotte said, "Gran, this isn't on you."

Nancy sat there petting Suzanne, not buying Charlotte's point of view. "It doesn't matter. Things will never be the same again."

"First of all, if this is your fault, I'm the Queen of TikTok. Which I am not. And second, as any teenager can tell you, that's the thing about life. It changes. Take me, for instance. One day you're playing trumpet in the school band with your nerdy best friend Janey; the next you're trying out for a jazz band with the coolest kids in school. Change isn't always bad, Gran."

"Are you telling me you tried out for a jazz band?"

Charlotte grinned.

"And you got in?"

"I'm lead trumpet! We call ourselves the Low-Key Love Trio."

"I love it." Nancy reached out and hugged her granddaughter.

"But I digress." Charlotte grinned as if she knew exactly how smart she sounded—and was. "I ask you again, what is the plan?"

Nancy slumped back in her seat. "I don't know what I was thinking. My boat isn't as sleek or as fast as *Bucephalus*. Roger has Mac and Tony, who know each other so well they speak in shorthand, and I've got the girls, who have never been sailing further than Palos Verdes point. The odds are against me."

Charlotte sat and thought about that for a moment. She looked out at the horizon and then shook her head at Nancy. "That may all be true. But you have something Grandpa Rog doesn't have."

Nancy squinted at her Charlotte, waiting for her to finish the thought, at a loss to what she could mean. Roger had every advantage.

"You don't know what you're capable of."

"Go on."

"It's all new. Grandpa Rog is going to do his same race. You can tackle it with new thinking. Isn't that how some teams win the Super Bowl or the World Series? By doing it in a way that no one ever has. Plus, you've got the heart of a lion, Gran."

Nancy's smile grew slowly.

And then Charlotte added, "You just need a plan."

CHAPTER THIRTY-SEVEN
HOW TO LIGHTEN UP

The familiar, warm breeze rustled the nautical map Nancy studied as she tried to figure out the fastest route to sail to Ensenada. She had ordered stiffer race sails for the main and the jib. She had ordered a special spinnaker too, had her keel inspected, and scrubbed off any latent barnacles that might slow her down. Now she was trying to ascertain if her boat, given perfect conditions, could actually beat Roger in the Border Dash. She tossed the map down in frustration just as Suzanne headed above. Nancy looked up and heard Santiago softly speaking to her.

"Hello, little love," Santiago cooed to Suzanne.

"Santiago," Nancy said warmly as she went up.

"Good morning, Nancy." He smiled, and the dimple in his chin disappeared as he did so.

Nancy relaxed as soon as she saw him. Santiago picked up her cat and gave her head a rough, loving rub. Nancy could hear the cat purring from across the cockpit.

"I'm glad to hear that Senor Roger is okay after his . . . incident."

"How incredibly civil of you. I think Ruthie put it more accurately when she said Roger's bullshit finally caught up to him."

Santiago chuckled and sat down in the cockpit. Suzanne nestled in his lap.

"So, I take it you've heard about the bet," Nancy stated.

"Ah, yes. Good word travels fast. Good bets travel faster where I'm from."

"Where is that again? The Yucatan?" Nancy said, angling for any inkling to Santiago's past.

"No, not the Yucatan, Señora," he replied.

Thwarted, Nancy changed topics. "I don't know what I was thinking in the moment, a bet like this, with the crew I have. But I've no choice now. I have to find a way to win."

"You are far from a long shot, Nancy. Your skills and your instincts are strong. Your crew is green, but they respect you and they can learn fast." Santiago looked around at her boat, then added, "But the *Gypsea*, she needs to get in racing shape."

"What do you mean?"

"She needs to lose a little weight."

Nancy was a mixture of hopeful and skeptical. "My sentiments exactly. But how?"

"I have an idea," Santiago said with a wink.

Nancy went below to get them some wine.

CHAPTER THIRTY-EIGHT
ALLIES ABOUND

After Santiago left, Nancy felt a glimmer of optimism for the first time since she had challenged Roger to the race. She was also a little giddy from the wine. Or maybe it was Santiago and his penetrating gaze. Or *both* Santiago and the wine. Either way, she was feeling great, polishing off some leftover Thai food from the galley fridge, when her cell phone rang. She looked down and grinned at the name that came up. She picked up before the second ring. "Pray tell, *mi amigo*, what crusade are we going on?"

"God, it's like having my own bat phone. You are always at the ready," said the steady, low voice of Glenda Hibbert. "I was going to ask you the same thing, old friend."

"However long it's been, it's been way too long. The last time we spoke, you were heading up the Heal the Bay Foundation and had begun a quest to save the marine sanctuary around Monterey."

"Ah yes, Monterey Bay. That was three years ago. We managed to expand the sanctuary to six thousand square miles right where

Exxon wanted to drill for oil. Those were better times for us environmentalists, when the feds really stood by us. It's now the biggest marine sanctuary in the world. Although, with the new administration, there has been talk of offshore drilling again, but I don't want to bore you with my problems."

Nancy sat back against the couch in the salon and smiled and sighed. Ah, the memories of their younger days as passionate firebrands out to save the world. "Damn, that's impressive. They should have named it after you."

"I'm not that noble. I'm just a sucker for the otters. And the marine sanctuary has been my one true passion for a long time."

"So, what's up? Are you in town?"

There was a pause before Glenda responded and then said awkwardly, "Actually, Nance, I'm returning your call."

"What call?"

"You called me a few days ago. Or I guess technically it was Roger who called me, but I was under the impression you two wanted to get together for dinner with Donnie and me?"

"Oh, no. I wasn't aware that Roger called you. I wonder why?"

"Beats me. Maybe he was hungry? Anyway, I'm coming down to the beach next week for a series of meetings in your area—perfect timing for a catch-up."

"Uh-huh," Nancy said, distracted. Why would Roger call Glenda? He didn't even like Glenda. He incessantly poked fun at her hippie, tree-hugging, otter-saving ways.

"Nance, what's up? Why are you being so weird?"

Nancy paused for a second before realizing that this moment was as good a time as any to spill her news. "Roger and I split up."

There was silence on the other end of the line. Then Glenda said, with no small hint of astonishment in her voice, "You left Roger?"

"I can hardly believe it myself as I stand here with this carton of pad thai in my hand, but yes, I'm filing for divorce from my husband, who was, as it turns out, a cheating, lying dirtbag. But first I have to win a boat race so I don't have to hire his divorce attorney. Oh, and I also own a sailboat with Ruthie, Lois, and Judy that I live on now with my cat."

"And I was going to tell you about my new succulent garden," Glenda said.

Nancy laughed quietly and then sighed. "Yes, well, as you know, Glenda, one can only be complacent for so long before one loses one's shit."

"I daresay, I'm a bit proud of you." Glenda said, then added, "It's brave."

"Thanks," Nancy said rather quietly, because the last thing in the world she felt like was brave. "So, how are things with the Heal the Bay Foundation?"

"Oh, I guess you wouldn't have heard. I'm no longer there."

"No, I hadn't heard. What lucky critter has you on their side now?"

"I've just been appointed to the board of the California Coastal Commission."

"You're kidding."

"No, and ironically, my first assignment is in your own backyard, Redondo Beach," Glenda said. Then there was a long pause. "Nancy? Are you still there?"

Goddamn that man.

CHAPTER THIRTY-NINE

FULL STEAM AHEAD

"So, did you tell her what he was up to? Jesus, he's like a Bond villain," Ruthie said as she cranked the winch to tighten the jib.

"I told Glenda Hibbert the entire ugly truth, not only about our split but also what Roger was up to behind the backs of all his friends and fellow sailors. The greedy fool. He's willing to forsake everything and everyone for money."

"She had to have been appalled," Judy said as she stowed Ruthie's winch.

"She was. And I can assure you, her Coastal Commission vote is not going in favor of Roger and his hideous project."

"I mean, *Pave the Bay* can't be a good slogan, right?" Lois asked, as she tied off the mainsail sheet.

"So, the marina is safe? She told you that?" Ruthie asked.

"I've known Glenda Hibbert for thirty-seven years. She and I used to stand together to protect every otter and giant sequoia from San Diego to the Oregon border. Protecting the California environment is in her blood. There is no way she would vote to destroy King Harbor for more parking. Ain't happening."

"That's a relief," Judy said, "I love our little marina."

Nancy had set up a training schedule for her crew in the twelve short days they had left before the Border Dash. The plan was to sail out beyond the buoys every evening so that her crew could practice drills on handling the sails and get more comfortable with the much faster pace that the Border Dash required.

On the first night of training, Ruthie, Lois, and Judy arrived at the marina, ready to sail. At the end of the dock they saw Nancy standing next to a handsome young man no more than thirty years old, wearing a pith helmet, a hat usually reserved for those headed on safari.

Nancy began the introductions. "Ladies, I'd like you to meet Jerome Temple. He was the sailing instructor at the Bitter End Yacht Club in the North Sound of Virgin Gorda for the last five years. Unfortunately, the Bitter End was completely destroyed by Hurricane Irma, but nature's havoc is our good fortune. While it's being rebuilt, Jerome here is going to help whip us into sailing shape over the next ten days."

"What makes you so special, sport?" Ruthie asked, a hint of playfulness in her tone.

In a soft-spoken, Maine-tinged accent and with a hint of pride and a touch of good humor in the curve of his mouth, Jerome answered, "I solo-circumnavigated the globe last year on a thirty-two-foot sailboat past the five southern capes."

Lois whistled low and said, "I guess you'll do."

Ruthie raised her eyebrows and murmured, "Great. An over-achiever. We shall go forth and disappoint you."

Judy loved the idea of professional training, anything so that she didn't have to tie herself to the boat in abject terror. "Welcome, Jerome! I love your hat!"

Jerome smiled and tipped it her way. "My pleasure, ma'am. I'm here to share little tips and tricks that make sailing joyful, easy, and intuitive instead of clumsy and scary. That's all." He paused and looked the women over. "Oh, and also to help Nancy here kick Roger's ass."

The women all hooted at that.

"I like him," Ruthie offered.

"Honorary merman," Lois quipped.

"He's just what we need," Nancy said with confidence.

"In ten days, I'll help you develop your own sailing style, and you'll be able to read each other's cues to work together seamlessly," Jerome added. "That's the plan."

They all climbed aboard *Gypsea*, and Jerome assigned each woman her tasks on the sail. Lois was strong and fearless, so she worked the mainsail and the rigging. Ruthie was a little calmer and slower, so he put her on tacking with Judy. Nancy was at the helm and in charge of decision-making on the water.

"Okay, let's see how we do," he said, and then began to whistle the tune to *Gilligan's Island*.

"Not exactly reassuring, Jerome," Ruthie quipped.

He changed his tune to "Son of a Son of a Sailor" by Jimmy Buffett.

"Much better."

They headed out into the bay, past the breakwater, and cut the engine. On their first tack, things went haywire. Lois had cleated the wrong line, so the mainsail fell slack. Ruthie had arranged the jib lines counterclockwise, so when she let it out, the lines were instantly tangled. Judy panicked and dropped a winch, which fell into the galley. She scrambled below to get it, and upon her return, Jerome merely gave her a thumbs-up and continued whistling.

Nancy knew it was messy. It was the worst they'd had since their first sail.

After the minor disasters were corrected and the *Gypsea* was on the right tack, Jerome assessed their performance. "Okay, not altogether terrible. From what I can tell, you need to get more familiar with the equipment, but more importantly, you need to trust in yourselves and each other. Sailing should feel natural. Just like your friendships. Trust it."

Ruthie looked at Nancy for the first time and mouthed the words *not bad*.

The practice went fairly well after that. The girls began to understand the basics of sailing by feeling rather than instruction. They pulled lines and took tacks smoothly and eventually sailed with a gentle poetry intertwined with the sun, wind, and waves.

Nancy's novice crew were shaping up to be seaworthy sailors. She knew that the competition was not only going to be fierce, it was also going to be personal. Roger was gunning for her. Rumor around the yacht club was that he had denied Mac and Tony their customary places on his boat this year in favor of a couple of ringers. Apparently, he'd found a pair of Swede racers who had just crewed for an America's Cup team in Bermuda the previous year. Nancy groaned when Pete told her the news.

Her team had to work like a Swiss clock. Every tack had to be fast and clean. Every sail flawlessly trimmed. And the wind had to be on her side. Everyone and everything had to be perfect. It was a tall order for a small group of women in their late fifties. Even if they were faultless, Nancy knew it might not be enough to keep up with the younger and stronger men. She would need a daring plan if the Mermaids were going to pull this off. They couldn't outmuscle the men, but they could outthink them.

The *Gypsea* returned to port with a happy crew singing the words to "A Pirate Looks at Forty" while Jerome whistled along.

"Yes, I am a pirate . . ." Lois crooned. Judy and Nancy joined in the next line, singing with a fervor usually acquired only after a few rounds at the bar. Today, sailing was all the shots they needed.

Ruthie looked over at Jerome, gave him a wink, and said, "Impressive, kid."

"Aye, you had it in you all along," he replied.

They tied up to the dock, and Jerome turned to the crew of the *Gypsea*. "I'll see you tomorrow evening, where we will deal with the dreaded spinnaker. Until then, ye mermaids."

The physical nature of pulling lines, cranking on winches, and unleashing jib sails made even the sturdiest of them, Lois, moan as she stretched her hamstrings. "Damn. The only thing that's going to sooth this weary body is a hot tub and a margarita."

"Margaritas. My favorite part of sailing," Ruthie said.

"The only muscles that aren't sore on the ones on my face," said Judy.

"Lead the way, Lois," Nancy replied.

Lois called ahead and had Chris fire up the blender and ready the hot tub at their Manhattan Beach house. The Mermaids wandered in, exhausted, at eight PM. It became a nightly ritual over the next ten days. With every training sail, the girls became more comfortable being tossed on rough seas while executing Nancy's orders—*flawlessly*. It turned out you could teach old dogs new tricks.

At the end of those evenings, sitting in the hot tub under the stars, the soreness melted and gave way to laughter as the Mermaids recounted their funnier moments on the water. The long days of working toward a common goal seemed to turn back time. Instead of recalling old memories, they were making new ones. It felt like the best time of their lives.

But on the last night of training, Ruthie didn't show. Nancy waited at the dock, ready to go, along with Judy and Lois. She checked her cell phone twice, but there was no message. She rang Ruthie, but it went straight to her voice mail. She finally called Pete, thinking perhaps Ruthie had gotten seduced by drinks on the back of his boat. His phone rang twice and then he picked up.

"Hi, Nance," Pete said. "What's up?"

"Hiya, Pete. Any chance Ruthie is with you?"

"No." There was tinge of sadness in his voice. "Haven't seen nor heard from her in a fair bit."

Nancy frowned. Weird. "Tell her I'm looking for her if you see her."

"Yep. You do the same."

Nancy hung up the phone and looked at Judy and Lois. "She's not home. She's not on Pete's boat. Any clue?"

Judy and Lois looked at each other and shook their heads. Then Lois said, "She bailed on me last week because Otis had to go to the vet. Maybe it's something with the pup?"

Nancy nodded. That dog was Ruthie's life. If Otis was sick, the world could stop spinning and Ruthie wouldn't notice. "Yeah, that's probably it. Well, we need a backup."

"How about Charlotte?" Lois offered.

"We could ask her." Nancy hesitated. She could call Charlotte directly. Or go through Stella. After the spectacle at the hospital, she wondered if she should. She stared at the phone and finally hit Stella's contact number. She cleared her throat.

Her daughter picked up on the second ring. "Hey, Mom." She sounded sullen, sad.

"Hi, Stella." There was silence between them for a moment. "Hey, I was just wondering if Charlotte could come for a sail with us tonight."

"Oh. I thought you were calling to—doesn't matter. Um, I don't know. You'll have to ask her." Stella called out for Charlotte, and Nancy could hear Charlotte bounding down the hardwood stairs. She came to the phone breathless. "Hi, Gran!"

"Hey, kiddo," Nancy said. "Was wondering if you wanted to join the Mermaids on their last training sail before the big race. If it's okay with your mom, that is."

Nancy heard Charlotte cover the phone and mumble something to Stella. Then she came back on. "Wouldn't miss it. I'm hopping on my bike now." Charlotte handed the phone back. Nancy stayed on the line.

"Thanks for letting her come, Stella." She paused. "I know we have a lot to talk about."

"Maybe we can talk this weekend?"

Awash with tentative relief at the return of her daughter's gentle voice, the one without the edge in it, Nancy said, "Of course we can." But then she remembered the race and added, "Oh, wait, no. We leave Friday morning for Newport. The race starts Saturday afternoon."

"Oh, of course. My head is a mess. I forgot about the race."

"Will you be there to see us off?"

"I don't know," Stella said. "Sam and I have counseling."

"I think that's good, honey." She knew that was a big step. Stella and Sam had talked about going for a year, but making an appointment and actually showing up was another story. It could mean things were getting better between them. Or it could mean things had gotten much, much worse.

Stella sniffled on the phone; it sounded like she'd been crying. "Thanks, Mom."

"You're going to be okay, hon," Nancy said.

Silence.

"Hey, maybe I can be in Ensenada when you guys come in," Stella offered.

"I'd love that."

"Charlotte's getting on her bike now. Have a good sail."

"Love you," Nancy said, but Stella had already hung up.

Nancy turned to the girls. "Charlotte is on her way."

"Everything good with Stella?"

"No." Nancy hesitated for a second and answered. "But it's not hopeless. Seriously, Ruthie can't even call?"

* * *

On the final training sail, Jerome declined to join, letting the crew understand they could sail just as well, maybe even better, without his guidance. Their youngest Mermaid protégé, Charlotte, showed off just how aptly she was suited to the job. Apparently, a good haul of the sailing books Judy had acquired weeks ago had ended up in Charlotte's possession, and she'd put them to good use too. The girl knew what she was doing, and just like her grandparents, her gift for sailing was as natural as breathing.

Once safe back in their slip, Nancy raised her glass and said in a thin, unsteady voice that she and the crew of the *Gypsea* were "as ready as we're ever going to be."

"Praise indeed," Lois said wryly, as she sipped her wine.

"My nerves are getting to me." Nancy shook her head, as if to shake off the bad mojo.

Judy said, "I think Jerome really brought our sailing to the next level."

"That's oddly reassuring, coming from you," Lois said.

The crew put the sail covers on, organized the lines, and got ready to take off for the evening. Judy and Lois headed off for their well-earned hot tub at Lois's house. Charlotte stood on the edge of the boat before hopping off. She squeezed Nancy's arm and looked her in the eye.

"Gran, a boat is always safe in the harbor."

Nancy looked at her curiously.

Charlotte continued, "But that's not what boats are for. A man named John Shedd said that. Just heard it in AP History. Good luck out there."

Nancy smiled. Charlotte gave her a big hug and jumped off the boat. She hopped on her bike and peddled off. The fading rays of the sunset illuminated the back of her beach cruiser, and Nancy realized the last remnants of her granddaughter's purple-dyed strands were fading. Her gorgeous honey-blond mane was coming back. And Charlotte was letting it.

As soon as she turned north toward home, Nancy called Ruthie, who picked up on the fourth ring.

"Hey," Ruthie said.

"Pray tell, where was our fourth tonight?" Nancy asked.

"Oh, shit, I'm sorry I missed the sail tonight. I had something I had to do."

"It's fine; it's just not like you to be a no-show. Is Otis okay?"

Ruthie paused before answering. "If you call a lump of fur that burps and farts all night okay, then yes, Otis is fine. Same old."

"Oh. Well, if it wasn't Otis, I don't understand . . ." Nancy didn't know where to go from there, upset at Ruthie's absence and then her purposely vague response. "We needed you—"

"I'm sure you did fine without me. I'm not exactly the strongest crew member."

"Ruthie, I needed you. Not because of your sailing expertise but for all the other reasons. I'm not strong enough. I can't go into this thing alone." Nancy could feel her emotions running loose like frightened horses in the dark.

"Nancy—" Ruthie interrupted sharply, but then softened. "Listen, I know. I'll be there. I'll always be there for you. I just had a thing. I'll tell you about it later."

Nancy got ahold of herself and finally said, "I'm sorry, I just . . . I need you."

"You don't actually. You don't need me. But I get why you think you do," Ruthie said.

Nancy stammered, and it all came out at once. "I can't catch my breath sometimes, Ruthie, and my heart races and I can't sleep. I scared of being alone. I'm scared of not being alone. I'm afraid I'm going to make some horrible mistake I can't undo."

"Too late."

"What's too late?" Nancy asked.

"You already made the horrible mistake."

"I did?"

"You married Roger. And look at you, undoing it all."

Nancy stopped and smiled. "True." She wiped her tears away and chuckled. "See? I need you. See you Friday morning?"

"Bright and early," Ruthie added. "Call me if you can't sleep."

"Okay. Oh, by the way, Pete wants you to call."

"Hmph," she responded, then ended the call.

Nancy poured another glass of wine and headed out to watch the moon. The call to Ruthie had quelled her jangling nerves.

CHAPTER FORTY

ALL HANDS, AND FURNITURE, ON DECK

On Thursday morning, the day before the Mermaids were to set sail for Newport, Santiago arrived on M dock bright and early armed with his tools, a crowbar, and a large dolly. To her surprise, some extra hands also showed up to help. Shep Wallace stood there gallantly, hands in the pockets of his camouflage overcoat. Peter Ellis was in attendance, armed with a rum and OJ in his Mount Gay tumbler, and even Mac and Tony showed up with warm smiles.

Tony said, "There's our favorite girl!"

"Mac! Tony!" Nancy happily greeted them with a hug. "I think its crap that Roger didn't invite you to crew the race."

"Ah, just as well. Roger's not himself these days," Mac said as he smoothed his moustache down.

"I know Roger. He's probably already celebrating," Nancy guessed.

"I don't know, Nance. We know Roger too," Tony said. "He's idling a little high."

Nancy looked at them both like they were nuts. "Impossible."

Mac confirmed it. “You just might be making him nervous.”

“As he well should be,” Santiago added.

“You guys are nutso. Roger is not afraid of me or my, as he put it, crappy tugboat.”

As Santiago predicted, marina gossip traveled faster than a sex scandal in Congress. Everyone had heard about Roger, the bet, and the fact that he was behind the Bayside Urban Renovation Project, or the Big BURP, and his devious plan to pave over King Harbor. People felt betrayed by one of their own. How could he, a fellow sailor, so easily agree to ruin their beloved marina for a huge concrete parking lot? It stank of unscrupulous greed, given the sheer scale of the project and blatant disregard for the locals.

Nancy stood there with a pirate’s crooked smile and looked around at the grizzled band of liveaboard rebels willing to fight against the Evil Empire of Roger and his BURP.

Santiago called the small crew to attention and said, “Our goal is to lighten up the *Gypsea*. But not so much to make her unlivable. The girls still have to rest and eat during the race. So, we are going to take out everything unnecessary unless it’s structural or indispensable. That should lighten her up enough to give her the advantage she needs.”

“Got it,” Peter Ellis said.

“Can I borrow that crowbar?” Mac asked Santiago, who handed it over.

“I’ll get the dolly,” Tony offered.

“I have in my possession one battle-tested beer cooler to replace the fridge,” Shep Wallace added.

The boys all got to work stripping the boat of its nonessentials. One by one, anything that didn’t make the *Gypsea* faster or keep her afloat came out of the boat and was set down on the dock. The boys removed three dollies' worth of boat-slowing ballast, including all of Nancy's candles, wineglasses, cat toys, dog beds, and other creature comforts that made the *Gypsea* her home.

At one point, Turk wandered over to see what was going on. "Smart," he said to Santiago. He took one look at Nancy and added, "My money's on you, kid. Keep the wet side down."

Nancy gave him a salute and a nod. "Aye, Cap'n. I'll do my best."

The whole of the work was complete by four that afternoon, at which point Nancy offered to take her demo crew to the Blue Water Grill for stiff drinks and cups of hot clam chowder.

After the second round of dark 'n stormies, the guys began to talk about the race. Each had his own piece of advice. Some of them had raced back in the 1970s when it was more of a free-for-all, while Mac and Tony had done it as recently as last year—and won. All their advice came as wise, time-tested stories and helpful hints.

"The Border Dash is famous for stalling winds just past the cliffs off San Elijo."

"The starting line is tricky because of the number of boats. Best to stay clear of the pack before heading for the inside line thirty seconds before the horn with a full head of steam."

"Squalls are common, so be prepared for them. They come up from the Southern Ocean and catch you unawares. One minute you're cruising at eight knots, the next you're drenched and reefing sails."

"Stay your course, unless the wind dies. Then get creative."

Nancy was taking mental notes when she noticed Santiago remained surprisingly quiet. She considered that perhaps the conversation of racing yachts was making the boat mechanic uncomfortable, beyond his knowledge.

At around six in the evening, the friendly gathering broke up with everyone wishing Nancy good luck in the race. They all ambled off in the directions of their boats, but Santiago offered to walk her back to hers.

As they wordlessly strolled, Nancy felt warm in the space between her and Santiago. His gentle energy made her relax. There was no need to ramble on about meaningless topics. Instead, there was an easy calm. It was a balmy night; a waning moon was rising from the east as the breeze rustled the palm trees overhead. Seals barked in the distance, and the dock creaked beneath their feet. The familiar sounds of seals barking in the marina, a light chain clanking against the dock master's flagpole, the gentle lapping of water against boats—now all of these sounds gave her comfort.

Santiago seemed to be studying the horizon in the twilit distance. Then he finally said, "Nancy, the wind has its own soul, just like each one of us. The Winds of Yamagaia are the bringer of both dawn and darkness. It is a ferocious spirit of change. It can whip itself into a warning and then a rage. You must be able to read it as it changes. If not, you are doomed to fight against it until exhausted and defeated. But, if you let the wind surround you and let it take you, embrace its energy . . ." Santiago grabbed both of her hands and cupped them in his, his eyes fixed on hers. "Listen to its song . . . it will change you and every direction you go."

She felt like she was floating off the dock, lost in his eyes and his poetry of the wind.

"Plus, I know something about that race." Santiago said this so matter-of-factly that it broke her dreamy spell.

"You do?"

Santiago gazed out over the horizon before answering. He took a deep breath and said, "I am a descendant of the great Portuguese navigators."

"Portugal. I knew it."

Santiago raised a skeptical eyebrow.

"Okay, I never guessed Portugal."

He grinned and continued. "I learned how to navigate by the stars, thanks to my grandfather, who taught me everything he knew when I was a boy. Sailing has always been in my blood."

Nancy was impressed, with both his history and his sudden desire to share.

"Also, I won the Newport to Ensenada race a time or two in the seventies."

Nancy stood awestruck. "You won it?"

"*Si*. Four times. So, I know something about it."

"Four times." Nancy stood agape at first, her surprise slowly turning into awe.

Santiago looked sheepish under her admiring gaze, then nodded. "I had a good crew," he said, trying to shift responsibility.

"You had a good crew . . ." She mulled that over for a second. Then she figured it out. "Wait a minute, you're saying it was *your* boat?"

"But of course."

"I thought you were a—and please don't take this the wrong way—a boat mechanic."

"I am," Santiago said. "But I also own a few boats."

"How many boats?"

"Well, I have three Hobie catamarans that I use to teach students in my sailing school, and then three fishing vessels. My sons run my commercial fishing business down in San Diego."

"You own six boats, a sailing school, and a commercial fishing business?" Nancy looked at him, incredulous.

Santiago smiled as if delighted at her reaction.

"Then why do you live so—" Nancy struggled to find an appropriate and not totally insulting way to say it. "Why do you live like this?"

"Like what?" he challenged her gently. "Surrounded by the pelicans and dolphins instead of men in suits? Teaching at-risk kids how to navigate the sea on a sailboat so that hopefully one day they can navigate their own destiny? Completely free to skinny-dip off the back of my boat rather than sit on a crowded freeway?"

"You skinny-dip?"

He nodded, "During the full moon, usually."

"Good to know," she said, and smiled. "When you put it like that, I see your point."

"We all build our own cages, and then we walk right in."

She sighed, thinking about the life she'd left behind, and said, "Even if gilded, they're still cages."

"Life is unpredictable and scary and wonderful all at once," Santiago added. "That is why I live like this."

She felt that warm, glorious breeze gently blow her silvery blond hair back. She felt the strength and the steadiness of it. She wrapped her arms around herself and then asked a question as much to the universe as to Santiago.

"What if I lose?"

"What if . . . such a short sentence, such a big question."

"This might all be over."

Santiago reached for her hand, held it in his, and then kissed it. "That's what the caterpillar thought—"

"—just before she became a butterfly." She finished the famous line and smiled.

Nancy looked into his eyes then, and the glint that she had always taken for friendliness shone in a different way. There was something behind it, something like a promise.

She reached for him but ended up losing her footing on a loose dock board. She almost tumbled when he reached for her so she wouldn't fall. They gripped each other tightly for a second, and then the grip loosened to a touch that brought them nose to nose.

As Santiago held her, the stars seemed to brighten just for them. That same warm wind drew them together. The closer he came, the more she could feel the warmth of his body next to hers. The scent of his Old Spice aftershave mixed with the salty air. He tucked a piece of her hair behind her ear and brought his soft lips to hers. His kiss was slow and intense. She surrendered to the joy of it, and it made her feel light-headed. She caressed his cheek and felt the roughness of his beard under her fingertips.

Later that night, Nancy Hadley realized she hadn't been kissed by a man in the way Santiago had kissed her in decades. Roger's rough, lipless pecks could barely be considered contact, let alone kisses. But this kiss, it left her giddy, warm, shaken. How she had missed indulging in this simplest and most luxurious of pleasures. But perhaps it wasn't the kiss but the man behind it. What a fool she had been for depriving herself of kisses and everything else that came with a man like him.

Santiago had shared a kiss and a secret with her.

As she had watched him stroll down the dock, hands in his pockets, she'd heard him whistling a slow, melancholy tune that reminded her of a siren song, and she couldn't stop smiling.

CHAPTER FORTY-ONE
ANCHORS AWEIGH

The early-morning sun had started to warm the decks of the *Gypsea* as Nancy readied the lines and stowed the sail covers. Suzanne supervised from the upper deck while giving herself a bath.

"Ahoy!" Pete Ellis called from the dock below.

Nancy had asked him to watch Suzanne while she was gone for the race, and he had happily obliged. She looked down and saw that he had a large bag of cat food in one arm and about a dozen cat toys dangling in his other hand.

"You think she'll like these?" Pete held up a handful of bright-pink mice-shaped toys.

"Pink is her favorite color." Nancy grabbed Suzanne off the upper deck and gently put her in her carrying case. She handed it over to Pete, who took it gently. "Thank you so much for looking out for her."

"I can't wait. It's been a while since I've had a copilot on my boat."

"She has her moments. The pelican might follow you. They've become fast friends."

Pete chuckled.

One by one, the girls showed up, bright-eyed and chatty, ready for the lazy sail down to Newport in time for the skippers' reception at four PM.

Ruthie, her auburn hair curled and perfect, was clad in bright-peach capri pants with little starfish all over them. She sashayed down the dock as her eyes came to rest on Pete.

Pete stood there with the cat case, a bag of cat food, and pink cat toys. He smiled in slight chagrin when he saw her. "Hi, Ruthie," he said softly.

Ruthie walked over without a moment of hesitation and drew him into an embrace. She kissed him and hugged him tightly again before letting him go. Pete couldn't quite return the hug with everything he was carrying, but he whispered, "I've missed you. What happened?"

Ruthie stood back and looked at him. Nancy thought she saw tears well up in her eyes.

"I'm sorry I haven't called."

"I thought I did something wrong."

"Never. You're my kind of cowboy. I will explain later."

"I'm just glad to grab you again, hot stuff."

Ruthie returned his hug and then whispered, "I'm all yours. As soon as we get back."

"I'll be waiting," Pete said as he cleared his throat and carefully carried Suzanne over to his boat.

"Thanks again," Nancy said to Pete. "We should be back on Tuesday."

Ruthie climbed aboard and gave her friend the reassuring hug she needed, a sign that all was okay between them after Nancy's emotional call the previous night. Lois followed with provisions from Boccato's Deli, including sandwiches and pasta salad. Judy fixed her sailing scarf and carried aboard the ice, wine, and water. Nancy had given the girls strict orders to pack as lightly as possible, and that included no heavy wine bottles.

Lois held up two canvas bags with nozzles at the end. "Gifts from Chris! Canvas wineskins! Super light! Each filled with an entire bottle of Chardonnay. He bought them on Amazon."

"Brilliant," Judy said, making a mental note that she eventually had to buy something on Amazon.

"I deem those acceptable," Nancy said with a wink.

"I deem those necessary," Ruthie added.

The sail from King Harbor to Newport Harbor was going to be a leisurely, all-day sail down the coastline. The weather was on their side, warm and sunny, with a gentle, steady wind that would carry them effortlessly all the way to Newport.

"I made a Jimmy Buffett playlist on Spotify," Ruthie said. She connected her phone to the stereo, and soon the famous barefoot songwriter was singing "Tin Cup Chalice" through the speakers. Nancy heard a familiar pop of a cork as she turned and saw Lois, who was sipping the bubbles from a newly opened bottle of champagne.

"Just a mini celebration," Lois said, returning Nancy's approving gaze.

Judy was ready with the plastic glasses. Lois poured, Ruthie cast off the lines from the dock, and they were off to the opulent harbors of Newport Marina.

Nancy noticed the difference in the *Gypsea*'s speed almost instantly. Without the heavier items on the boat and with her new sails, she moved much easier. She seemed to glide over the water instead of pushing through it. The balmy wind was blowing a steady twelve knots and the *Gypsea* was traveling at over seven, whereas typically she'd be doing only about five and a half. A noticeable improvement. The *Bucephalus* ran roughly seven and a half knots in this wind. The *Gypsea* might still be a tad slower than *Bucephalus*, but close enough. Nancy's technical skills could make up the difference.

What worried Nancy was what she didn't know. Roger had dominated this race for the last four years. He knew the way down the coast to Mexico, whereas she did not. While Nancy had always raced with him locally, she had never accompanied him on *Bucephalus* during the Border Dash. It was his last bastion of camaraderie with his male friends, and she'd let him have it.

Of course, thinking back now and considering all of his recent indecent behavior, it cast a pall over his happy stories of sailing glory. He had probably been hoisting up the skirts of half the cougars in Ensenada.

As Nancy quizzed the girls on all the necessary safety precautions and what to do in case of any conceivable emergency, she was impressed by their collective knowledge.

"A crewmate goes overboard. What do we do?" Nancy asked.

"Keep an eye on the man overboard at all times," Lois said.

"Throw the life preserver to the man overboard," Judy added.

"Bring down the sails, initiate the figure-eight maneuver to retrieve man overboard," Ruthie said, then looked heavenward. "And Sky Chief, if you're listening and I have any credit left with you, please don't let that be me."

"Well done, crew. We may not be swarthy or weather-beaten, but we are well prepared, and we smell much better."

"Aye, aye!" they cheered in unison.

They had marine-grade duct tape in case of a sail tear, an old-school nautical map in case the navigation system failed, emergency backup batteries for the walkie-talkies. And in the case of any other disaster, she reckoned they'd have to rely on their wits. Or the Coast Guard, God forbid.

For a large part of the day, the *Gypsea* stuck close to the coast as they sailed southward. They were accompanied by several dozen dolphins who raced under the bow of the boat. Seals poked their heads up as they passed by, heading toward fishing grounds, and pelicans flew like an armada overhead in search of lunch. When they came upon Surf City USA., also known as Huntington Beach, with its unmistakable pier, they knew they were closing in on Newport Harbor.

They were assigned to dock slip 143, a smaller part of the marina tucked behind the ostentatious yachts owned by ex-presidents, NFL stars, and the enterprising man who had invented Simple Green. The massive yachts dwarfed the humble *Gypsea*, and some even cast a shadow over their entire boat. They reached their assigned slip without a problem, plugged into shore power, and began to clean themselves up. The skippers' reception started in an hour. They had recently learned they were the only all-female crew to race in the Border Dash.

People had been talking.

The Mermaids had to represent.

CHAPTER FORTY-TWO
YOU GET WHAT YOU PAY FOR

Roger climbed on board *Bucephalus* armed with some last-minute provisions (bourbon, Fritos, cigars) just in time to see Claire showing off her cleavage and flirting with the young blond Swedes he'd hired as ringers. Magnus was smiling with his perfect Swedish teeth and flexing his tanned biceps for Claire while purportedly readying the lines. Linus was checking the winches, which presented the perfect opportunity for his crotch to be directly at Claire's eye level.

"So, how do you say *warm welcome* in Swedish?" Claire asked in a girlish voice as she fixed her cleavage and ogled the young studs.

"Oh, I'm sure they're picking that up," Roger said as he hoisted the bag of goodies onto the boat.

"Oh, Rog, there you are! Did you know Magnus and Linus are both from Gothenburg?"

Roger didn't know, nor did he care where the Swedish meatballs came from. Nor did he care that Claire was obviously hitting on them. What he did care about was how fast they could sail *Bucephalus* so as to ensure a win against Nancy and her merry band of silly hens. He'd heard about the Swedes from his billionaire New Zealand investor, who had watched the pair compete in the America's Cup in Bermuda the previous year. They spoke very little English, but they were strong as oxen and understood racing terminology. That was good enough.

Claire came up to Roger and put a hand on his shoulder. "I just came to wish you bon voyage, tiger." She bit his earlobe, and Roger winced. "Good job, by the way. You're more ruthless than I thought."

Roger gave her his shark grin. "I told you I knew what I was doing."

"Indeed. I'll meet you down at the skippers' reception. Can't wait for the fireworks." She leaned in for a kiss.

Roger grabbed her ass cheek and gave it a healthy squeeze, making sure the Swedes saw. The strapping towheads merely laughed and busied themselves with their deck chores.

He was the captain of this boat. And now everyone knew it.

* * *

From across the marina, Faye Woodhall waited on the dock for her driver and observed Roger Hadley crassly grab the buttocks of Claire Sanford, a backside she had had the misfortune of observing in all its naked glory. Good god, the man had no class. And curiously, no scruples either, as she had just learned from her last phone call. She was shocked to discover that the BURP, the very project that would spell certain ruin for the King Harbor Marina, was being piloted by the same man who was captaining the *Bucephalus*, none other than Roger Hadley himself. Curious, she thought, that he could hide his diabolical nature so well, for so long. It reminded her of her father, who had single-handedly destroyed their family, their legacy, and their reputation, to the point where she and her now-dead husband had needed to abscond to Southern California. An unforgivable chapter in her story. But Faye Woodhall had paid attention to the hard lessons of the past. Unlike love or loyalty, she knew greed had no boundaries.

She tapped her cell phone with her perfectly manicured nails as she pondered and watched *Bucephalus* set sail with two strapping blonds manning the lines and Roger at the helm. She surmised that Roger had gotten away with a lot of dirty exploits over the years, including his depraved debauchery with that low-class hussy, Claire Sanford, without punishment, or repercussions, or pain.

Perhaps he was due.

Faye dialed a number on her phone.

CHAPTER FORTY-THREE
THE SKIPPERS' RECEPTION

When the Mermaids arrived at the Corinthian Yacht Club for the skippers' reception, it was already a bustling hive of activity. The Border Dash had clearly gone all out this year, bringing in several ice sculptures in the forms of anchors, mermaids, and starfish. There was also a chocolate fountain and a full mariachi band to keep the crowd of roughly three hundred people entertained.

The main hall had crystal chandeliers hanging elegantly over marbled flooring, a huge buffet table with every type of seafood imaginable, and a prime rib table that flanked an entire wall. Large floor-to-ceiling glass windows looked down over the grounds, where sailing flags from all over the world were strung above the sprawling lawn that led down to the docks. Twinkle lights gave the scene a warm glow.

Nancy had her silvery blond hair pinned up and was wearing a classic navy silk shift dress with a low-cut back. In contrast, Ruthie's auburn hair was blown out like a lion's mane, and she wore a deep-purple A-line that showed off her shapely legs. Judy was wearing a conservative houndstooth jumper with two slips (just in case), and Lois wore white jeans with a bright-yellow linen top, her gold earrings glimmering from beneath her soft-permed blond locks. They hit the doors like an aging version of Charlie's Angels.

Nancy scanned the crowd to see if she could spot Roger so as to avoid him, with no luck. The last thing she needed was a surprise attack by him and his bimbo. She did, however, see Faye Woodhall, who was dressed handsomely in a black linen pantsuit, her hair up in a silver turban. She was looking over the raucous crowd like a disappointed queen who could no longer control her kingdom.

"I'm starved. Should I get the prime rib or some scallops?" Judy wondered.

"I'll help you decide. Go by the starfish sculpture. I saw champagne," Lois said.

"What a bunch of codgers." Ruthie looked over the room. Some of the older men had channeled Thurston Howell III as inspiration for their outfits that evening. The room was marked by navy-blue blazers and white patent-leather shoes.

She looked over at Nancy and saw her stressed expression. "A room with this many ascots cannot possibly make you nervous."

"No, not by ascots. Just by assholes."

"We need drinks," Ruthie mumbled, as she flagged down a server with a tray of martinis.

That's when Nancy saw Claire Sanford. Her dress was shiny, with silver petals pointing downward. Upon first glance, her unfortunate choice of dress gave the impression of fish scales, not helped by the fact that she stood near the smoked-salmon appetizer. Claire sauntered toward Nancy. Nancy felt herself become rigid.

"Well hello, Nancy," Claire said coolly. "Roger told me you were going through with this ridiculous wager anyway. Seriously, why waste the energy?"

Ruthie appeared with two cocktails and instantly said to Claire, "Tell your story walking, harpy."

Claire looked Ruthie up and down disdainfully and said, "Oh my, I've never seen a dress that purple. It's like coffin purple."

"Yeah, well, your ass has never seen a foot like mine, so move on."

Claire's jaw dropped.

Nancy snorted midsip with laughter.

Ruthie took a sip of her drink through the tiny straw, eyebrows raised, still staring at Claire, who finally slunk off to the other side of the room.

"What would I do without you, Ruthie?" Nancy said rhetorically.

Nancy scanned the room and saw something that made her stomach flip. Roger had entered the room with Glenda Hibbert on his arm. Her Glenda Hibbert. Her eco-warrior buddy from college. Nancy stood agape, trying to make sense of it.

Roger then let go of Glenda's arm, and she looked back at him with a gracious smile as she walked away to greet another set of people. He caught Nancy's eye and smiled triumphantly. He actually bowed. The bastard.

Ruthie, however, was still observing Claire, who was slinking around the room like a hungry cat. She had stopped to chat with a man who looked to be 110 years old. Ruthie shook her head in disgust. "Look at her. She'll chat up anyone who can still fog up a mirror."

"I'll be right back."

Nancy walked through the crowd to where Roger was, and then she motioned for him to meet her on the deck outside. He followed, a gin martini in hand. They met on the lush lawn and stood near a beautifully maintained boccie ball court that was set up for play. Nancy picked up one of the boccie balls, considered its heft, and then toyed with it as she figured out what she wanted to say.

Roger spoke first. "Well, well, if it isn't my competition. Hope you're up for it. The weather is supposed to turn."

"Did you come here with Glenda Hibbert?"

"No," Roger answered. "She and I just have a business deal, that's all."

Nancy squinted at him. "You cannot possibly mean that Glenda Hibbert is voting in favor of your BURP project?"

A low, rumbling chuckle bubbled out of Roger as he put a hand on Nancy's shoulder. "So you did work it out! The Bayside Urban Renovation Project is yours truly's. It is my biggest achievement to date."

"But that plan is a disaster. It'll ruin the beach community as we know it and turn it into a pretentious mall. A mall that could exist anywhere. It might as well be in Milwaukee."

"Oh, don't be so naïve. Someone needed to renovate that garbage heap we call a pier. You should be thanking me."

"Thanking you? Isn't part of your plan to backfill and pave over and destroy King Harbor to make way for parking?"

"We need parking."

Nancy shook her head in disbelief. "You've had a boat there for over thirty years. You've been a part of that yacht club; those people were invited to your daughter's wedding. Do you have no conscience?"

"To be honest, no. But don't give me that sentimental bullshit, Nancy. My company needed this big hit. You need it too. The

Redondo Beach pier needs some sort of renovation. Christ, it's a shithole."

"You're not making any friends, Roger."

"I have all the friends I need." He pointed over to Glenda Hibbert, who was chatting up a small group of well-dressed men.

"You do not have Glenda's vote," Nancy said sharply, more of a hopeful statement rather than a declaration of truth.

"Glenda was a tough one. Claire took a different tack on her, but it didn't pan out. It took a little more digging and some creativity, but I finally brought Glenda over to my point of view."

"You mean the dark side?" Nancy couldn't believe what she was hearing. "Not her."

"Oh yes, her." Roger took a sip of his martini. "I thought I'd need you to get her on my side, Nancy, but it turns out," he said as he relished his victory, "I don't need you at all."

Nancy's head was starting to spin. "So, why the bet?"

"Oh, I don't give a shit about the bet anymore, mostly because you don't have a snowball's chance in hell of winning. But I do love victory, and this one shall be my sweetest. You can count on a long, drawn-out, expensive divorce battle. I'll be damned if you get half of everything I earned. I told you I would win. I always win."

Now that Roger had Glenda's vote, the combination of the smug look on Roger's face, the knowledge that Glenda had somehow betrayed her, and the fate of her future with Roger caused a fissure in Nancy's being that churned like unreleased lava.

"Of course, if you're still in, I'm still in," Roger said on a parting note.

Nancy took the boccie ball that she was holding and launched it at Roger's head. He ducked, and it missed him, but it hit the octopus ice sculpture right behind him. It took the head clean off. The poor octopus now posed headless, its body melting and dripping onto the fruit plates below.

"Go fuck yourself, Roger."

Roger chuckled at her loss of control and let out a long, low whistle. The people who were milling about on the lawn stood shocked at what they had just witnessed. Nancy marched back toward the yacht club.

On her way up the stairs, Nancy looked over and saw Glenda Hibbert chatting up some asshole who was wearing epaulets on his shoulders. Glenda glanced her way, and Nancy glared at her. Glenda took a swig of her drink and came toward her.

Nancy had gotten to the top of the stairs when Glenda approached, coming up to her gingerly, guiltily. "I know what you must think, Nancy."

"Don't presume to know what I think."

"You think I'm a double-crossing, environment-betraying opportunist."

"I stand corrected. You know what I think."

Glenda hung her head for a moment before looking up at Nancy with an expression that conveyed both shame and inevitability. "I don't expect you to understand."

"How could I?"

"I know, but just hear me out." Glenda shrugged. "Roger came at me with this deal about the waterfront, told me that he knew the Monterey Bay sanctuary's status would be threatened next year with the new administration, that he had three other votes in his pocket that would help me keep the sanctuary if I helped pass his vote on the waterfront. He offered a deal that would keep the sanctuary safe for the next fifty years. This is how politics works."

Nancy sniffed but remained stern. She knew the otters were important to Glenda. The Monterey Bay sanctuary was her legacy.

"Nancy, someone is going to redevelop that waterfront. I didn't think it was so bad that Roger, and then by default you, would get to enjoy the benefits of that deal. Surely you can see my point on this. We're not kids anymore. We don't have the luxury of idealism."

Nancy looked at Glenda and saw the remorse on her face. "It feels personal."

"It's not, though."

"But it feels that way." Nancy shook her head.

"I hope you can forgive me one day, Nancy." Glenda walked away.

Nancy watched her wander off just as Judy and Lois ran up to her, frantic. "There you are!"

"Nancy, come, it's Ruthie," Lois said.

All three of them ran to the buffet table, where a small crowd had gathered in a circle. Nancy made her way through to see Ruthie collapsed on the marble floor. A small trickle of blood was coming from her nose and mouth. She wasn't conscious. A man was taking her pulse and checking her vital signs.

"Oh my god, oh my god, oh my god," Nancy mumbled, her heart racing as she knelt down and took her best friend's head in her hands. "Ruthie, can you hear me?"

Nancy looked up at the man attempting to help her. "She's alive," he said, "but her pulse is weak. We need to get her to the hospital. Are you aware of any drugs she's taking? Anything that would compromise her heart?"

"No, nothing I know of." Nancy looked at Lois and Judy.

Lois quickly said, "Nothing we know of. Ambulance is on its way."

A few seconds later, sirens could be heard arriving at the front door. Nancy had Ruthie's head in her lap, but she was still unconscious.

She watched as the paramedics gently placed her on a gurney and took her out to the waiting ambulance.

Nancy hopped in, and when the paramedics asked who she was, she answered, "I'm her family."

CHAPTER FORTY-FOUR
RED SKIES AT DAWN

Nancy sat in a hard plastic chair with her elbows resting on her knees and stared at the gleaming floors of the Newport Harbor Hospital. She had been waiting nearly ninety minutes before an exhausted-looking doctor came out to greet her.

"Are you Nancy? Ruth Davenport's family?" he said as he checked his chart.

"It's Ruthie," Nancy corrected him.

He looked up from his chart to meet her eyes. His lips grew into a thin line. "Right. Ruthie." He took the seat next to her and sighed heavily. "Well, she's fine at the moment. Her blood sugar was low, and she was dehydrated. But it's no wonder she's exhausted. I gave her a mild sedative so she can get some rest."

"Exhaustion? I don't understand."

"According to her attending physician in Redondo Beach, Ruthie is suffering from stage three lung cancer."

Nancy heard his words, and then she heard a white pop go off in her head, momentarily deafening everything else. It couldn't be. Not Ruthie. For a few moments, she gripped the tissue she had been holding, sat back in her chair, and stared up at the ceiling, not saying a word. She was reeling.

"I thought you knew . . ." the young doctor said.

Nancy finally came back to and said, "No. I didn't know."

He nodded. "There are certain immunotherapies that have proved very promising in some clinical trials, but I'm not sure if she's a candidate for them."

"Wait, are you telling me this can be treated?" Nancy became instantly alert.

The young doctor seemed to backtrack on the hope he had just offered and said, "In some cases it can be helpful, but . . ." He looked at his chart again. "You have to prepare yourself."

Those words . . . Nancy was instantly back in the hospital corridor with her mom's nurse Lorraine from so many years ago, her younger, naïve self filled with false hope for her mom's recovery. Lorraine had said those exact words. Then, in what had seemed like an instant, her mother was gone. A tremor started in Nancy as she sat frozen in her seat.

"Get in touch with her physician in Redondo Beach. They have an excellent oncology department at Torrance Memorial." He touched Nancy's shoulder as he excused himself.

Nancy sat there in that until she realized her legs had gone a little numb. Then she got up and headed into Ruthie's room.

CHAPTER FORTY-FIVE

AN UNEXPECTED TACK

The hospital room was dim when Ruthie woke up. Nancy was sitting in the chair in the corner texting when she heard Ruthie make a noise. She immediately moved her chair next to the bed.

"Hey, Ruthie, I'm right here." Nancy smiled and smoothed her friend's hair behind her ear. She felt cool to the touch.

"You should be on the boat."

"I'm here instead, you stubborn old hen."

Ruthie sat up, and the color slowly began to return to her cheeks. She looked down at the tray in front of her that was presumably food. She uncovered the plate. Underneath it lay a sad turkey loaf with a gravy-like substance and a heap of mashed potatoes that looked a little green. The staple of hospital cuisine. Ruthie grimaced.

"I came armed with bread and cheese," Nancy said as she brought over the plate of snacks.

"Ever a master of provisioning." Ruthie nibbled on cheese and then looked at Nancy.

Nancy stared at her best friend in the world, her chosen family. Her stomach flipped at the thought of losing her, and tears sprung to her eyes. She held Ruthie's hand urgently, as if to make sure of its warmth and her life force. Nancy felt shock, sudden desperation, and more than a little bit of anger.

As if she knew Nancy was angry with her, Ruthie trod lightly at first. "The docs tell you what's going on?"

"They had no choice; you named me as next of kin. How long have you known?"

Ruthie nodded. "Remember that back pain I had? Well, Advil didn't do the trick. I've only known for about a month. It's sounds like not much can be done."

"That's not true! There are some experimental drug trials that are on the verge of getting approved that have proven very promising with your type of lung cancer." There was an edge to Nancy's voice. Even if Ruthie was giving up on herself, Nancy sure as hell wasn't.

Ruthie ran her fingers through her hair and gave Nancy a straight face. "So I've heard."

"We will get you in at Cedars when we get home. Best in the city. Don't argue."

"Sounds good," Ruthie said dismissively. "What's going on with the race? Are the girls getting the boat ready?"

Nancy sat back. A line appeared between her brows as she grimaced. "What are you talking about?"

"The race, the race, what's going on with the race? Are you guys ready?"

"Ruth, we're not thinking about the race."

"Why the hell not?"

"Because you're in here. With stage three lung cancer."

Ruthie shrugged, frustrated. "So, you're not going to race?"

"Those are some strong drugs you're on. No, we are not."

Ruthie slammed down her crusty French bread and looked at Nancy, angry. "Did you already tell them that?" she asked.

"No. But I will as soon as I leave here. It's not easy for me to bow out, but . . ."

"I think it's what you want," Ruthie interrupted.

"You think I want to quit?"

"To be honest, yes."

"My best friend has stage three cancer, a small fact I wasn't even aware of until you starting bleeding all over the Italian marble at the skippers' reception, and you're lecturing me on being honest? The damn race is the last thing on my mind!"

Ruthie was quiet for a long moment as she gave Nancy a measured stare, as if considering her next words carefully.

"You have to race." Ruthie said flatly.

"No. The race is not important."

"What about the bet? You're just going to give in to Roger, that putz of all fucking putzes?"

"The bet is off, Ruthie. The whole thing is over."

"What do you mean?"

Nancy stalled, taking a sip of Ruthie's water. "Roger doesn't want me back."

"No shit. It was about something else."

"How did you know?"

"Because I know Roger. What was it?"

"It was about the BURP project. He needed Glenda's vote. Didn't think he could get it without me."

"Snake."

"Plus, it seems like he and Claire are still going strong."

"That won't last." Ruthie waved a dismissive hand. "She'll leave him for the next mortally vulnerable geezer. Nancy, more than ever, you have to race."

"I do not have to race. There's nothing on the line anymore."

"The hell there isn't. Your whole life comes down to this race." Ruthie shook her head. "Not in the way you think I mean."

"It's a sailboat race, for Christ's sake. You think I want revenge on Roger that badly? I'm not that selfish. No. I am going to be here for you!"

"I refuse to be the reason you bow out of this, Nancy. I'm not giving you the easy way out. You know why? Because you always take it."

Nancy sat back. "What the hell does that mean?"

"This whole thing is about you. Not me. Or the girls. Or Roger. Or a stupid bet. Or even revenge. That's all bullshit. It's about you. And it's about time. Your life was interrupted a long time ago by trauma you couldn't control, and something cracked in you. That tough little girl that I grew up with was hobbled by loss and sadness and choices made by other people. It weakened you. But she's there. I can see her in you. And that's the thing about life. It tries to break you, and it can—if you let it. Or you can choose to come back even stronger. And right now, my beautiful friend, you have that power. To choose. To be strong. To heal yourself. The only thing standing in your way now is you."

Nancy began to reel. Ruthie saw through her like no one else, but something she had said struck a chord. Excuses. She'd had some doozies. And somehow those excuses—her dad leaving, her mother dying, her faltering marriage to philandering Roger—had let her hide and fade into the background, as if she were part of the wallpaper on the set instead of being part of the play. That brave little girl inside of her had been silenced long ago in favor of a safe, stable life wherein nothing much happened. A life in which she was never the central character of her own story. Tears began to well up from a deep, long-forgotten place.

Ruthie took her hand when she saw the tears fall. "Forgive yourself, Nancy, for all that potential you think you wasted, for all of the times you felt small or insignificant, or for thinking you could have done better. Because it all adds up to right now. The past and the future are all twisted up together, don't you see? This moment, you are the skipper of your own life. And the wind is at your back. You are strong—you just need to believe it." Ruthie let the words hang there in the air, heavy like rain clouds plump with love and truth.

Nancy got up and went to look out the window. She wiped away her tears, but they stubbornly kept coming. "I can't do it alone."

"You're not alone."

"But you're sick."

"I'll get better." Ruthie hesitated. "Or maybe I won't. But Nance, I'm here right now. And now is all we've got. You can waste it sitting here watching me eat the world's worst mashed potatoes, or you can make it unforgettable."

"Why are you such a hard-ass?"

"It's my special gift." Ruthie smiled but didn't let up. "So, what's it going to be? Are you going to use my stupid cancer as your excuse to bow out? Because I will kill you if you do. Or are you going to use your God-given strength and find that tough girl who never took shit from anyone and win this goddamn race?"

CHAPTER FORTY-SIX

AND THEN, MUTINY

"She doesn't want us to quit." Nancy stood there in front of Judy and Lois, frustrated and tired, her eyes puffy from crying.

"We know."

"So, all of you are in on this together?"

"Kinda," they said in unison.

"Did you know about the cancer?"

They both hesitated. Lois finally answered, "We didn't know it was stage three. We only knew she was having some tests run."

"Why the hell did you not tell me?"

"Because we knew you wouldn't go through with the race if you knew. Plus, Ruthie threatened us."

Judy added, "Aggressively."

"And," Lois said, "she thought she'd be fine until after the race was over. So really, it's just a timing thing."

Nancy was flustered, and she took a moment to contemplate this turn of events. "So, I have a mutiny of love on my hands."

Lois and Judy both nodded.

Nancy sighed. "But the rules say we still need a fourth, and we don't have one. Who's going to be our fourth Mermaid?"

Just then, someone whistled.

Judy, Lois, and Nancy turned to see Charlotte bounding down the dock, backpack slung over her shoulder, an expression of glee and determination on her face.

"I think that's our fourth Mermaid, right on time," Lois said.

Nancy looked and saw Stella, fingers on her lips from the whistle she had just delivered, standing by the car in the distance. She walked toward the boat.

Nancy met her halfway. Charlotte raced toward her.

"Hi, Gran!"

Nancy held up her palm, and Charlotte high-fived her as she trotted toward the boat.

When Nancy reached her daughter, Stella, she brought her in for a hug.

Still in the embrace, Stella said, "I'm so sorry to hear about Ruthie, Mom."

She held on to her daughter in that life-affirming way that made her realize how precious it all was. Time, place, family. That her legacy was in fact in her arms right now. She whispered into her daughter's shoulder, "It's good to see you."

Stella let go. "Mom, I didn't know about Dad. You should have told me."

"I didn't want to damage your relationship with him."

"Always so noble, always the high road . . . but at a huge expense to yourself." Stella stared out into the distance and then added, "Mom, I need to understand you a little more. Can we do that when we get home? I think I've underestimated you all this time. You gave everything you had to me and Dad."

"I love you and wanted to see you happy, to see you succeed."

"Your job with us is done. It's your turn, Mom."

Nancy felt something stir inside her, something she had never felt before. She felt free.

She drew her daughter in for another hug and held back tears before she said, "Thank you."

Then she stood back, and they both looked to the *Gypsea*. Charlotte was already helping Judy and Lois ready the boat.

"Thanks for bringing Charlotte. I'm happy the girls called you."

"The girls didn't call me."

Nancy looked at her, confused.

"Dad did," Stella said as she squeezed her mom's shoulder. "I've got to run. Good luck, or what does one say to a sailor? Fair winds and following seas?" Stella kissed Nancy's cheek and walked off.

Nancy stood there processing what Stella had said as she watched her walk away. Then she turned toward her boat and her waiting crew.

"So . . ." Nancy wrung her hands and looked at Lois, Judy, and Charlotte. They looked expectant, as if they were soldiers yearning for orders. "Looks like we have a race ahead of us."

All three of them said in unison, "Aye, aye, Captain."

CHAPTER FORTY-SEVEN

READYING FOR BATTLE

Nancy awoke with a start at dawn on the morning of the race. She had been in the middle of a vivid, violent dream, in which she and her crew were just about to reach the finish line in Ensenada when a grotesque sea monster rose from the water, its eyes bulging and black, its menacing tentacles dragging her boat down, and its claws the same bright-red, lacquered color of Claire Sanford's nails.

She shook the vision from her head and rolled out of her berth. She splashed some water on her face, checked that everyone else was still sleeping, and quietly padded out to the cockpit to go over the nautical map and the weather forecast one last time.

As she studied the maps, she realized that the biggest decision was whether to go outside, inside, or along the rhumb line past the Coronado Islands off the coast of Tijuana. The rhumb line was the straightest shot to Ensenada. Usually the shortest distance between two points was a straight line, but that wasn't always the case in sailing when an ever-unpredictable factor like wind was involved. It was the rhumb line that Roger had historically taken, too. But many sailors were spooked by the rhumb line this year. Last season a boat had become disoriented in a fog that swept in after sunset, causing the boat to crash on the rocks at the Coronado Islands. Three of the four crew members on board had been killed. The tragedy was fresh in the memories of many in the race. Sailors were pragmatic and logical, but they were still a highly superstitious lot. Most sailors thought the rhumb line had been cursed since the crash, and this included Nancy. She wondered if Roger thought the same.

While the rhumb line was still the shortest way there, it was also the most boring. She remembered Roger bragging about his line after he won the trophy last year.

"You always keep your line. There's no need to get fancy. The rhumb line works. I'm proof of that theory," he said smugly as he drank champagne out of the big silver cup.

But that was exactly what made Roger a bad sailor. Nancy knew that in order to get the most out of the wind that was given to her, she had to read it and constantly adjust to changes. Roger had also been lucky when it came to the weather. For four years in a row, the weather had remained virtually the same. Light southwesterly winds, no squalls, no changes. When conditions were perfect, Roger, with his fast boat and his conservative line, had an advantage. But this year was different.

There was a small, squirrely storm rolling over the ocean, coming down from Seattle. It had been forecast to hit on the very day they were sailing down to Ensenada, but the reports kept changing as the storm kept shifting direction. The harbor master had warned everyone to stay alert and tuned in to VHF Channel 16 for up-to-the-minute reports on the weather. Until then, the same warm breeze that had been blowing up from Central America through Hermosa for the last six weeks, Santiago's Winds of the Yamagaia, were still with her in Newport, and Nancy felt fortified by its constancy.

Before long, the aroma of fresh-brewed coffee came from below. She looked and saw a hand rising from the galley, holding a steaming-hot cup for her. She gratefully took it.

Lois's head popped up next.

"Mind if I join you, Skipper?"

"By all means, I could use the company."

Lois climbed up, wearing her flannel pajama pants with little octopi all over them, her hair in a clip, her expression as excited as a kid's on Christmas morning. "What's up?" Lois asked as she inspected the nautical maps and sipped her coffee.

"Deciding on our line. There are two ways. The inside line and the rhumb line are the most direct routes, but they can have more feeble winds and more traffic."

"Okay, I follow."

"And then there's the outside line. It's not typical for a boat our size to take the outside line because it's more nautical miles, but if the wind is right, it's much faster. There's a chance the wind is going to change out there. There's a northwesterly wind that blows far offshore, wouldn't even touch the rhumb line. And if I'm right and this storm blows north to south, it could give us the extra speed we need to make up the distance."

"Does the storm put is in danger?" Lois asked.

"It shouldn't. In fact, given our timing, it should be right behind us."

Judy poked her head up. "Morning! Just making sure you two have coffee." She disappeared down below. They could hear the unmistakable sound of crinkly wax paper that held buttery croissants.

"I think you have to go with your instincts on this one, Nance. I can't give you an answer, but it seems like taking chances is your new thing, so . . ."

Nancy smiled and remembered the secret that Santiago told her about this race.

Judy came up on deck, armed with breakfast, as did a sleepy Charlotte, who was still wrapped in her blanket. She had a mouthful of croissant and nodded good-morning to the ladies.

"It looks like we're going to try the outside line for this race," Nancy said. Everyone looked down at the map as she traced the route with her finger on the map from Newport Harbor, past San Diego, outside the Coronado Islands off Tijuana, and finally into the harbor and the X that marked the finish line at Ensenada.

"So, this might be a wild and woolly ride," Nancy warned. "There's a storm coming from the north; it might hit us, or it might not. But one thing's for sure. It's going to bring wind and rougher seas with it. Especially if we go farther out to sea."

Judy clutched her napkin and nervously brought her hand to her throat. Lois looked sternly at the map. Charlotte finished her toast, stood up, and said, "Bring it. We can handle it." Then the teenager clomped off below.

Nancy looked at Judy and Lois. "Ah, the naïveté of youth."

"I'd give my right arm for her courage. And her skin," Judy said as she sipped her coffee.

"Well, you heard our youngest Mermaid. Let's get ready. The horn sounds in a few hours."

* * *

At three PM, they all took one last turn to run to the yacht club and use the facilities before taking off. As Nancy was coming out of the bathroom, she ran, full force, straight into Roger.

They stood there, not knowing how to handle the moment, and there was a long pause before Roger said gruffly, "I'm sorry to hear about Ruthie."

"Thank you, Roger."

"Please tell the old floozy I asked after her."

"I will. She said that if you asked after her, she had a message for you."

"Oh?"

"I think her exact words were, 'Don't get too comfortable with that trophy, bucko.' "

Roger chuckled. "I'm glad to see her particular brand of charm is still intact."

Nancy smiled. "It'll be the last thing to go."

"Our girl get on the boat yesterday?"

"Yes, Charlotte is officially our fourth."

"Good," he said as he looked down at her.

"Why did you do that?"

"I prefer a fair fight." Roger brushed some invisible thing off his shoulder.

Nancy nodded. But she knew there was more to it. It was his version of an act of kindness.

"Good luck," he said, rather stiffly.

"You too," Nancy said.

He turned and began to walk off. Then, turning once more, he took a long look at her, as if he wanted to say one more thing but just couldn't bring himself to do it.

Nancy watched him walk away, and when he got to the end of the dock, he met the Scandinavians, his America's Cup ringers. They were two strapping gents from some Nordic country, probably Sweden, who looked tall, strong, and determined. It gave Nancy a shiver.

"You see Roger's ringers?" Lois asked. "Brawny."

"Yeah. But Roger's still in charge, so at least we have that going for us."

Fifteen minutes later the Mermaids had finished their lunch, stowed away dishes, and secured everything that could possibly move, and then they motored out to the staging area. The first start time was two PM. They were in the sixth group to leave. Their start time was at four PM.

CHAPTER FORTY-EIGHT
CAST OFF YE BOW LINES

The starting line of the Border Dash was controlled chaos. The line went straight out from the NB10 buoy for a hundred meters to another marker. Every thirty minutes the horn would sound, letting loose another class of boats. All the boats in the class scheduled to take off would wildly maneuver for the perfect start.

The first to leave were the racing catamarans at two PM sharp. These were teams that used this race as a training ground for the Transpac Race from the coast of California to Hawaii. They ran fast and lean and finished the race in just over eleven hours. In contrast, *Gypsea*'s class would take anywhere from sixteen to twenty hours to finish. With any luck, Nancy was hoping to hit closer to seventeen hours. Last year, Roger had won his class in seventeen hours, forty-three minutes.

About five minutes before their allotted start time, all the boats in her class entered the staging area and began jockeying for position to cross the line first.

Given the wind speed and angle, Nancy mentally calculated exactly where she should be so that thirty seconds before the horn sounded, she could position the *Gypsea* to hit the start line at the perfect time and at full speed. Problem was, everyone else had that same idea. She was caught in a logjam of boats all vying for the same position, including Roger on *Bucephalus* and Turk on *Hot Rum*.

"Tighten the jib, Lois!" Nancy said.

Judy handed her the winch handle, and tightening commenced. Charlotte was on the bow, keeping a general eye on the surrounding boats. Nancy was at the helm surveying the chaos when her phone alert buzzed. Thirty seconds to go. She immediately yelled, "Prepare to tack!" and brought *Gypsea* about. The girls executed the tack flawlessly, and they were set to hit the line first and at full speed. But suddenly Nancy realized the other boats weren't following at the same pace.

She looked back and saw Roger in the distance. He gave her a sideways salute, with an absurd smile, as if saluting a soldier who was foolishly going up the wrong hill in battle. She looked down at her watch and the speed at which they were coming up on the line. They had timed it perfectly. They crossed the starting line at exactly four PM, but there was no horn. Where was the damn horn?

"Where's the horn?" Lois asked.

"Damn it. We're early. We have to cross again. Coming about again!"

They had to circle back around. The same dance of jib lines and winches happened while Charlotte kept her vigil on the front of the boat.

Ten seconds later, as Nancy and her crew were headed away from the starting line, the horn blew, and every single boat crossed over the line before they did. As of that moment, they were dead last.

"We're last, Gran," Charlotte called out flatly.

"Damn it," Nancy grumbled as she silently cursed herself for not remembering it in the race booklet. Even though their start time was at four PM sharp, the horn had been delayed for exactly thirty seconds to honor the crew that had died on the Coronado Islands last year. Nancy knew this, had forgotten, and was mad as hell at herself but said to the crew, "Oh well, it makes for a better underdog story."

There were about thirty other boats in their class, and they all were headed straight for the inside line to Ensenada. Judy looked back at their captain. "Well, there they all go. You sure about our strategy, Nance?"

Nancy nodded sternly, even though internally her stomach was in knots. Was she sure about this? She was barely sure she could keep everyone alive. But since no one liked to see a nervous captain, she followed up her nod with, "Aye, aye, let's take her out to sea."

The *Gypsea* tacked starboard and sailed out to sea, while all the other boats in her class headed for the inside line. They were on their own. She saw Roger, who looked back at her from the helm of *Bucephalus*, shake his head. She knew that particular gesture. It was his "Jesus, woman, you're wrong as usual" shake. *Up yours, Roger.* She sailed on.

For the next several hours, *Gypsea* and her crew sailed along unimpeded on her lone course. Once out well beyond the shore breezes, Nancy felt the wind shift as they caught a stiff north-westerly wind coming down from the North Pacific. Nancy felt a shiver as the temperature dropped. And then she realized, with an unexpected sadness, that the Winds of Yamagaia were gone. Those constant warm breezes that had blown her hair back, the wind that had woken her up, the gusts that had blown in the change that she so desperately needed, had left her. She briefly wondered if those winds were the magic in her sails. She'd felt stronger when they were with her. She thought of Santiago and what he might say. She was outside her comfort zone, but she also realized that it was these strong winds that she needed, indeed had wished and planned for, to win this race. She felt the whip of the cooler air from the north and shivered. She heard Ruthie's voice in her head, "Go get it, girl."

Charlotte had gone down into the salon to get sweat shirts and fleeces while Judy arranged the carnitas sandwiches from Boccato's, their favorite gourmet deli in Hermosa Beach. Franco, the store's lovable owner, had even included some Italian chocolates with a note of good luck for the girls. Judy passed out much-needed bottles of water. Lois applied her fourth coat of sunscreen and Nancy looked up at her wind vane.

The *Gypsea*'s new sails responded well to the stiff northerly winds and picked up speed until she was cruising between nine and ten knots, faster than Nancy had ever seen her skim over the water. They had already passed the first way point, and it was only seven PM. At this pace, they should be able to see the outer edges of the Coronado Islands right before it got too dark.

Sailing at night always gave Nancy the willies. The dangers were multiplied near the coastline, but out here, the only fear was running into a shipping lane unawares. Hearing a tanker horn could deafen you and scare you out of the way. Or, if your reflexes were slow, it could crush your boat into toothpicks. Tonight, however, the moon was full and bright, and Charlotte was an excellent lookout. She was camped out at the bow with a full bag of gummy bears and graham crackers.

True to Nancy's map and calculations, at around nine PM that night, in the fading light of the sunset, they could just make out the jagged rocks off the eastern tip of the Coronado Islands. They could also make out a fleet of boats. *Bucephalus* was leading them all.

"Grandpa Rog is in the lead," Charlotte said as she peered through the binoculars.

"I guess I expected it, but I didn't think they were getting the same wind as us."

"Binoculars do not lie," Charlotte said as she handed them over to Nancy.

She took a look and sighed. This was going to come down to the wire. And if she knew Roger, she knew that even without having anything on the line, he would do anything it took to win. She knew she had to outsmart him, but she also knew she needed a little bit of old-fashioned luck on her side.

Judy and Lois brought out cheese, crackers, and nuts as it grew darker. They sipped on tea and watched the waning light on the horizon. The running lights on the boat gave off a comforting glow as they skimmed over the water. They trimmed the sail so Nancy could stay on her line. Just before midnight, Lois put on a strong pot of coffee in the electric kettle for Nancy and the crew.

While Lois and Ruthie attempted to get a little rest, Charlotte stayed up with Nancy as they marveled at the night sky.

"Gran, is Ruthie going to be okay?"

Nancy took a long time to answer. The truth was hard for her to take. "I don't know. She's got stage three lung cancer. And the odds aren't good."

The news seemed to sadden Charlotte. She didn't say anything for a long time. "It's wild. I think she is so vibrant, so full of life. I can't imagine her being anything but the love warrior she is."

"Love warrior?"

"You know, someone who will do anything, even throw down against rage-y bikers or snarling zombies, for the people she loves."

"I love that you think of her that way."

Charlotte looked out at sea and said, "I think of you that way too, Gran. You're the love warrior supreme."

They heard it before they saw it. A great whoosh of an exhale and then a gentle splattering of water. A little seawater even splashed onto the boat.

Charlotte's eyes grew wide at the unfamiliar sound.

"Charlotte," Nancy exclaimed in a whisper. "Do you see it?"

Charlotte squinted into the night. The moon caught the silvery back coming out of the water, and then a slow, giant tail, almost as long as the *Gypsea* herself, rose from the water and sank below the surface again.

Nancy realized she was holding her breath, transfixed by the quiet majesty.

Charlotte reached for Nancy's arm. Together they sat there and stared down at the black water, marveling at what they had witnessed and hoping for the whale to come back up.

"What kind was it?"

"Out here, it was likely a Pacific Fin whale. Probably on her way down to Mexico to have her baby."

Charlotte smiled, and her eyes lit up. "Have a good journey, Mama Fin." She looked out over the water, and then she snuggled into her gran. Nancy put an arm around her. The moon shone bright, and for a glittering, peaceful moment, Nancy forgot all about the race.

* * *

The wind had dropped off some, but it was still chilly. They sailed through the night. A few more hours had passed, and soon the skies would turn pink with the dawn, and the wind would start to grow stronger before dying at midmorning. Nancy was obsessed with the weather reports like a new mother with a baby monitor. More than anything, she hoped Santiago was right. She hoped for the weather pattern to stay as they'd predicted. She hoped.

Charlotte finally grew tired and went below to try to take a short nap. Lois came up to join Nancy and to keep watch for ships or rocky outcroppings.

"Are you sure you don't need a break?" Lois asked.

"Nah. I'm running on gummy bears, coffee, and pure adrenaline."

Lois wrapped her black wool sweater around her and looked out over the sea.

"Your impending divorce might just be the best thing that ever happened to a bunch of old hens like us. Three months ago I was considering taking up scrapbooking. You know, where you buy tiny clothespins and decorative rolls of tape? Scrapbooking, for Christ's sake!" She let out a mystified laugh.

"Not that there's anything wrong with that," Nancy interjected.

"But instead I'm out here on a boat in the middle of the Pacific, risking life, limb, and possible drowning at sea. I've never felt more alive!"

"Slightly better than tiny clothespins . . ."

Lois studied the horizon and mused, "I know everyone has their own recipe for happiness. For some, its money. Or travel. Or Netflix bingeing. Maybe even scrapbooking. But the longer I'm around, the more I realize the thing that gets me going is to have a purpose. Doing nothing made me feel old for the first time. Might have even made me a little paranoid."

Nancy realized Lois's hypochondria might have been born of simple boredom.

"What's the point of trying to live forever if you're going to be dull about it, if you're not going to do anything special with all that time you have left?"

Lois's rhetorical question hung above the boat like an unanswered prayer. She continued, "As long as we're still breathing, we still have a chance to make it count, to make the most of it, to make it ours."

"These past few months have been the craziest, hardest, most painful, and yet the most exhilarating of my life," Nancy said. "And I don't know what's next."

"Silly girl." Lois let out another laugh and added, "That's the best part."

And just like that, the long-dormant dreams in Nancy's heart began to bloom again. She felt hope without doubt and knew that it led to a freedom of a totally different kind.

CHAPTER FORTY-NINE

THE SONG OF THE MERMAID

"All hands on deck!" Lois yelled below.

The girls scurried up to the cockpit. Judy was still adjusting her scarf and Charlotte was wiping sleep out of her eyes but desperately trying to wake up as Lois came up with another pot of coffee.

"What's going on?" Judy asked, concerned. Charlotte sat next to Judy, like a good soldier trying to stand at attention.

"Look," Nancy said, and pointed eastward.

The sun was about to break over the mountains of northern Baja. All the girls turned to watch the flicker of the sun's rays rise and beam across the sea, bathing the *Gypsea* in golden light as the clouds lit up like enormous pink cotton balls behind them.

Nancy gently interrupted the moment. "All right," she said softly. "We're heading into the last stretch of this race. Most of the other boats that took the more direct rhumb line are ahead of us. But they're going to be facing lighter winds when they turn toward Ensenada. They won't be as fast. We'll soon be far enough south, so when we make our final jibe and fly the spinnaker, we'll come into Ensenada like a song, on a straight and fast run that just might get us across the line first."

The girls looked at each other, expressions of doubt on their faces. They'd brought out the old spinnaker only twice during their training nights, and it had never gone well. The spinnaker was the largest sail, and when it filled with wind, it ballooned out in front of the boat, which was why it was called "flying." Problem is, it could collapse as fast as it could billow out. So, the wind and the direction had to be dead, solid perfect. In fact, a spinnaker fail, going as fast as they were, could make them keel over so far it might be disastrous. Nancy knew the boat could go over, with her best friends and granddaughter on board. And they were way the hell out in the middle of nowhere. She steeled her resolved, stopped conjuring up worst-case scenarios, and tried to tamp down her fear.

"I know we haven't had the best of luck with the spinnaker," Nancy said, sensing her crew's unease, "but I have a hunch we're due. We know what we need to accomplish. And there's no one in the world I trust more than you, my Mermaids. Are we ready?"

Judy adjusted her glasses and scarf and said, "That crowd better be ready for the Mermaids," and put out her hand in the middle of them. Lois quickly joined her with her hand. Then Charlotte nodded and added hers. Finally, Nancy joined. "Mermaids!"

"We're heading south on this outside line for about three more minutes, and then we make our move."

Everyone nodded.

The *Gypsea* was sailing fast and sure, and before long, the other racing boats came into view in the distance. Through the binoculars, Nancy could see Roger and *Bucephalus* in the lead, followed closely by Turk and *Hot Rum*. A long line of boats pursued the leaders.

Charlotte took another look through the binoculars. "Gran, Grandpa Rog looks pretty confident up there in the lead."

"Yeah, well, I've never met a man so confidently wrong as Roger," Lois said.

"He doesn't like surprises," Nancy said.

"Explains a lot," Judy added.

This was it. The final two miles to the finishing line. The sun glinted off the water as the sun rose high above the Northern Baja mountains that cradled Emerald Bay and the Port of Ensenada.

The *Gypsea* was traveling fast enough that seawater sprayed over the bow as they rode the rolling current. The wind was constant and steady. The crowds that gathered at the marina's edge were growing. Brightly colored umbrellas dotted the docks, and the sound of cowbells rang out from people cheering on the sailors. They could just make out the E72 buoy mark where the boats would make their final turn before sailing straight downwind to the finish line at the Ensenada Marina.

Nancy held the helm, staying on her line. A line that was taking her farther outside—away from the final buoy—and likely losing them further ground to Roger. Her mind was racing. It was now or never. Santiago's words came back to her.

There is a secret westerly wind. It's more powerful than the winds in Hurricane Gulch up in Cabrillo. It comes in way offshore, and it should happen just around the time the vessels are rounding the cliffs to come into Ensenada. Go out, way out. So far out that the other boats think you're abandoning the race. And she will greet you. When she does, be ready.

Santiago had told her of the famous wind that few sailors knew about off the coast. He had studied the weather, and this year conditions were perfect for this unpredictable zephyr to send them screaming back into Ensenada. But it was a huge risk.

Nancy was leading them directly to the spot that Santiago had pointed to on her nautical chart. Her plan was to jibe toward Ensenada the second Santiago's winds hit. The risk lay in the extra distance they'd have to travel. If Santiago's winds weren't there, they'd likely come in dead last. As she kept her line, she saw the look of worry on the girls' faces. "I know, I know. Trust me."

For the next ninety seconds, the *Gypsea* maintained her course at the point where the winds would come up.

But right then, the wind died.

The sails flapped and went slack. She looked up at her wind vane. It lazily rocked back and forth. They had entered a dead calm.

She looked at her watch and then looked up at the boats all sailing toward the finish line.

"Come on," Nancy said, more to herself than the others. Lois busied herself with organizing some line. Charlotte squinted into the sun, looking toward the shore. Judy sat there with her winch handles at the ready.

"Wait for it," Nancy muttered as doubt filled her. No wind. She couldn't wait any longer, they had to jibe directly to shore and the finish line. "Let's bring out the kite," Nancy said, referring to the spinnaker.

Judy and Charlotte headed up to the bow to unleash the spinnaker, but without wind, it almost hung limply in the water. They had to hold it up so it didn't spill into the sea. Another minute passed without a whisper of a breeze. Nancy shook her head and massaged her forehead. "Maybe I was wrong . . ." The boat sat there, barely moving. Doubt and dread crept in.

In that moment, Judy completely abandoned her indecisive nature and piped up, "No, it's coming. Be ready."

Nancy looked at her and had never loved her best friend more than in that moment when she needed it most. She beamed at Judy and then looked skyward and said a little prayer to her mom, Grace, who might have been watching. She whispered, "If you've got any pull up there with the Sky Chief, Mom . . ."

Nancy looked out to the vast, open sea and saw tiny ripples appear on the water all around them. A gust of wind whipped her hair back.

"Here it comes!" Charlotte yelled.

Nancy turned her back on the approaching wind and readied herself at the helm, hand steady on the tiller, sure of her direction, and waited for it to take her.

The wind began to fill the spinnaker slowly, and then all at once, it billowed out with a loud snap before them.

Known for their bright colors, spinnaker sails were a good way to tell one boat from another out at sea. Some more colorful sailors had them designed to more properly represent their personality. And that's just what Nancy had done. Her new spinnaker had arrived a week before the race, so the girls hadn't even seen it. She'd wanted to keep it a surprise. So, when the wind finally filled it and the girls could see it in all its glory, they beamed at Nancy. Charlotte and Lois even fist-bumped, which was saying something for a teen.

Nancy had the mainsail and the jib all the way out for a full downwind run, but it was their beautiful new spinnaker that made all the difference. They felt a jolt of speed as the boat went surging through the water so fast it created a wake. They smiled broadly as they felt their speed. Charlotte went up to the bow.

"We're closing in fast, Gran!"

It was true. The *Gypsea* was flying, and with every passing minute they were closing the gap on the other boats heading into Todos Santos Bay and the Port of Ensenada.

* * *

From the shore, onlookers witnessed twenty to thirty boats racing along the coastline, all coming south toward Todos Santos Bay on a glorious morning. The boats that had taken the inside line were under the cliffs, sailing in the light and variable winds.

"*Dios mio, qué pasa*?" An elderly onlooker shielded her eyes from the sun.

A small group standing at the marina's edge of the Emerald Hotel, who had been paying attention to the incoming boats along the coast, suddenly pointed out to sea, directly west.

"*La sirena*!" A man exclaimed, but the English speakers had no idea what he was talking about. "Gringos," he grumbled. Then he pointed excitedly and said in English, "The mermaid!"

This got the attention of Faye Woodhall, who stood with a morning brandy in her hand, watching the boats head toward the finish line. She, too, looked to the west. There she saw a massive spinnaker sail coming directly toward the marina at great speed. It had a beautiful giant mermaid on it, her golden hair flowing back over her turquoise scales. Faye smiled genuinely for the first time since the Reagan administration, moved to get a better vantage point, and murmured, "Come on, Mermaids."

* * *

Roger and his crew were still in the lead, despite the light winds that were affecting all the boats besides Nancy's on her outside line.

Roger saw Turk about two boat lengths behind him off *Bucephalus*'s port side. The other boats were far enough behind that Roger knew it was going to come down to him and Turk once again. All he and his crew had to do was make one last perfect jibe around the final buoy a half mile ahead, set their spinnaker, and pick up the trophy. Then Roger looked out to sea and saw it for himself.

A boat, with a mermaid spinnaker, was coming in at a crazy angle from the west on a straight run directly to the finish line. And it was coming in fast. They wouldn't need to jibe at the final buoy. He couldn't believe it. It couldn't be her.

He got his binoculars out as he cursed in broken Swedish to his ringer crew to do something, anything. He peered through the lens to see Nancy broadly smiling as she hurtled toward the finish line. Judy and Lois were on the lines; Charlotte was at the bow. He could not let this happen.

He bellowed at his crew to do something, which utterly confused them. They were on a perfect line to win the race.

Roger wildly pointed to Nancy's boat flying toward the final mark. The Swedes had obviously been thinking about all the beautiful senoritas they would be flirting with at the trophy presentation and hadn't noticed the interloper from the west.

Even the Swedes were a bit rattled, but then Magnus, being one of the best tacticians in the world, calmly informed Roger that he was certain they would beat the other boat to the mark and that, because they would be the leeward boat, they would have the right of way.

"Hold your course, Mr. Hadley. We've got them covered," Magnus said in broken English.

"It's Captain Hadley!" Roger hated that the smug Swede was telling him what to do, but he angrily held his course.

A key rule of racing was that as you approached a mark, for three boat lengths around it the leeward boat had the right of way and all other boats would have to give way.

Roger—well, actually Magnus—had made the same calculation, and a wide grin appeared on Roger's face when he realized he had Nancy snookered. Another win was literally right around the corner, and this one would be the sweetest of all. Maybe he'd even take Claire to Kauai to celebrate.

They were closing in on the final mark, and *Gypsea* and *Bucephalus* were on a collision course. Roger let out a wild laugh. Knowing Nancy's nature, she would have to luff off and watch him win it all again.

But Nancy did no such thing. She was within twenty meters of Roger and headed directly at his beam. Roger couldn't believe it. She was going to T-bone *Bucephalus* and put them all in real danger—

Just then, Nancy steered slightly behind Roger's stern and missed *Bucephalus* by less than three meters. She immediately spun the wheel hard to starboard, and the *Gypsea* followed and swept up underneath *Bucephalus.* This meant that Nancy was on the leeward tack and inside Roger as they approached the final mark. She had outsmarted him with a legendary sailing move—the same move Humphrey Bogart had used to win the inaugural Border Dash back in the forties. The move was called Humphrey's Hook.

The Swedes instantly realized that Nancy had outwitted them and that she now had the right of way. They were about to bear away when Roger maniacally bellowed, "Hold your line!" The strapping Swedes looked at their captain, who was now red in the face, and then looked at each other.

The boats were going to collide. Nancy had the right of way, but the most important rule of racing was to protect your crew. As Nancy held her line and the two boats were close enough to send a jolt of adrenaline down her spine, even the crowd on shore gave a collective gasp that carried across the water like a vocal tsunami. Then *Bucephalus* veered wildly to the right and miraculously cleared a path to the buoy before her.

Magnus, professional sailor that he was, had pushed Roger aside and grabbed the wheel to honor the rules of racing.

Mutiny was a serious offense. Historically, you could hang from the gallows for disobeying a captain's direct order. The Swedes knew this. But they also knew a crazy captain when they saw one. They weren't about to put themselves or another boat, with a child on it, no less, in danger for a recreational race. So, they disobeyed Roger and saved themselves from a collision, which allowed Nancy to round the mark in first, and with the best spinnaker reset in their short sailing history, the girls deftly had the boat back up to full speed within seconds.

Nancy briefly looked back and saw Turk and *Hot Rum* round the mark in second while Roger frantically tried to take back control of *Bucephalus* from the Swedes. He was raging and turning purple, two shades darker than eggplant, bellowing at his mutinous crew.

Nancy gave a quick wave and wink to Turk, who congenially waved back. It took Nancy and her crew of Mermaids a few seconds to realize what now was certain—they were going to win the race, and they had outsailed and outsmarted Roger to do it. Nancy bit her bottom lip and tried not to cry from sheer joy.

Ten seconds later the mermaids crossed the finish line, a full minute ahead of Turk on *Hot Rum*. They looked around at each other, making sure this was actually happening. The race master waved the victory flag and announced the *Gypsea* as the winner over the loudspeaker. They broke out into a laughter born of relief and joy. They had won the Border Dash. The Mermaids had won.

Lois had the champagne at the ready, and while Nancy, Charlotte, and Judy brought in the spinnaker, they heard the pop of the cork as she poured a glass for each of them. Even Charlotte was allowed a small sip with which to toast.

A sizable crowd had gathered at the shore, applauding the brilliant and brave moves the *Gypsea* had taken to win—a first-time entry and a first-time winner. Nancy drank it all in and tried like hell to hang on to the moment. Lois was waving to Chris, who was holding red roses for her on the shore. Nancy saw Stella and Sam there too, holding hands and smiling. And someone else . . . Santiago was there, his penetrating sea-green eyes twinkling, his smile broad and warm, his chest puffed out with pride as he tipped his hat to her.

Next to him she saw Ruthie, carrying Otis, and standing next to her was Peter Ellis, who was holding Suzanne the Cat. Ruthie saluted her and blew her a kiss, and Nancy began to cry.

* * *

A few hours later, Nancy and her crew were about to accept the Border Dash trophy cup for their win when Faye Woodhall approached Nancy in the bathroom. What was it with her and bathrooms?

"Nancy, I'm proud of you. It's a rare thing for a woman to be able to stake her claim and retake herself the way you have. You remind me of myself decades ago."

Nancy took that as a compliment. She knew Faye hadn't had the easiest life after the fiasco with her jailed Ponzi-scheme-running father. She was proof that all the money in the world couldn't make you happy. "Thank you, Faye."

"You know, I also heard a rumor that the BURP project had the votes to go through. Is that true?"

Nancy sighed heavily. That thought brought her temporary joy crashing down into reality. "Yes, so it seems. Looks like our marina will be gone soon."

"Not necessarily."

Nancy turned to look her squarely in the face.

"It looks like they will be just shy of votes in favor," Faye said coolly.

"Really? I thought it was a lock. With Glenda Hibbert voting yes, she was the swing vote. They have their five."

"There's Calvin Eldridge."

"The Reagan Republican? I'm pretty sure he's leaning toward a stern yes vote, him being notably pro-business."

"Yes, well, Calvin Eldridge is my lover," Faye said matter-of-factly.

Nancy was taken aback by her bald-faced honesty. Lover. Bold. She nodded her approval. *Go Faye.*

"You can count on a no vote from Calvin. He took another look at the plan and decided to nix it. I think we can rest assured that the future of our little marina is no longer in danger. Calvin will help put a more appropriate renovation plan in place of the BURP. After all, Old Tony's Crow's Nest is one of his favorite places in the world."

"Great mai tais," Nancy said as she nodded.

"And you get to keep the glass," Faye added with a wink.

Nancy found herself wanting to hug Faye Woodhall, but instead she saluted her as they shared a mischievous smile of victory.

* * *

The crew of the *Gypsea* stood inside the ballroom of the Emerald Hotel and Marina, where they had accepted their trophy in front of a crowd of landlubbers and sailors alike. From the corner of the room, Nancy noticed Roger and Claire arguing in whispers until Roger finally threw up his hands in frustration, slammed down his empty drink glass, and stormed out. Claire followed him like a flustered chicken, arms waving, frantic in her attempts to smooth things over, just like Nancy had done so many times before for so many forgotten reasons.

Roger was Claire's problem now.

Nancy held out a thin strand of hope that Roger would hand over the title of *Bucephalus* without an issue. But even if he didn't, she had the entire marina, Pete Ellis, Shep, Turk, Mac and Tony, Captain Horny, the recently reinstated Chuck Roverson, and Redondo Beach law enforcement on her side.

The last strand of Nancy's deep-rooted anxiety, her toxic copilot that had lurked by her side for so long, seemed silenced, its megaphone out of order. Her mind felt clear, bright, and calm.

On the far wall by the windows, Lois and Chris were trying to show Judy how easy it was to order new winch handles from an Amazon app on her phone. Judy, however, was unsure what kind of winch handle she wanted. There were so many choices.

Ruthie and Pete Ellis were sharing a bourbon as Nancy walked over. "Did you talk some sense into this old crone?" she asked Pete.

Ruthie hit Nancy on the shoulder. "Hey, I can come to my own senses."

"Does this mean treatment is in order?" Nancy asked hopefully.

Pete Ellis piped up. "I told her I'd roofie her bourbon and take her to treatment unconscious if she didn't agree."

"Fine, but if I lose all my hair, you're taking me wig shopping in West Hollywood to that fabulous drag queen place. I'm going full-on diva."

"You've got a deal." Nancy looked over and saw Santiago standing at the bar. He turned and walked toward her. "Um, excuse me," she said quietly.

Ruthie gave Nancy a little shove in Santiago's direction.

Her man of mystery removed his navy tam, a first, and came alongside her. A jolt of electricity shot through her when their eyes met. "Looks like the caterpillar became a butterfly after all," he said softly.

Nancy blushed and felt her eyes brighten. "Thank you for helping me. Part of this belongs to you."

"On the contrary, Nancy, this is all you." His eyes sparkled. He reached for her hand. She gave it. They stayed there for a moment, silent, saying things only the heart could hear. "Perhaps we can have a nightcap on *Gypsea* when this ceremony is over? I brought some rum," he said.

"A pirate never says no to rum." Nancy smiled. She let herself imagine more than rum in their future. Like more easy conversations. More kisses under the stars. More of whatever made her feel this excited, this at peace, this alive.

The chairman of the Border Dash race had asked Nancy, the captain of the only all-female crew in this year's race, to say a few words. She obliged and stepped up to the microphone.

"When I started this race, it was for all the wrong reasons. Life's funny that way. It's good at curve balls. But that's the point, I think. Nothing is guaranteed. Makes the time we have much more precious. I haven't always believed that the good guys win, that the poem always rhymes, that things always work out in the end. But what I have learned is that fear can defeat you, if you let it. It is so easy to do nothing. It costs nothing to stay the same. But where's the fun in that? If you take just one step in a different direction—lean into the shift in the breeze, take one tack at the right time—you can give yourself new ending."

Nancy caught Ruthie's broad smile. She finally added, "Thank you to everyone, especially my crew and to the youngest, bravest Mermaid of them all, my granddaughter Charlotte, who has taught me that happiness and courage go hand in hand. Fair warning . . . the Mermaids will be back next year."

Charlotte, who was standing next to Nancy, took her hand and held it up like she had just won a prize fight, and in a sense, she had. The room erupted in applause. The girls toasted to their win, and then a balmy, familiar breeze whipped around Nancy once, punctuating her moment with a private whirlwind that calmed as quickly as it started. A last kiss from the Yamagaia.

When it passed, the women held hands, beaming as they looked out over the crowd. Nancy had won in more ways than one.

She was her own victory.

RECIPE

SALTY MERMAID MARGARITAS

Ingredients

2 ½ oz Reposado Tequila (the good shit)
Squeeze ½ fresh orange
Squeeze ½ Meyer lemon
Squeeze ½ Lime
2 oz Guava juice
1 teaspoon Agave nectar

Shake well and pour over ice into glass rimmed with sea salt.

Plot your next move. Celebrate friendship. Love the moment.

ACKNOWLEDGMENTS

No one tells you how hard it is to go after a dream. And that most of the journey is filled with doubt, anxiety and frustration. It's easy to start. Hard to finish. But when you do get there, as with all labors of love, it ushers in a sheer, unfettered joy. My deepest thanks to the best agent ever, Ali Herring who saw the hidden gems in my manuscript, the merit of my older protagonist, and loved the story almost as much as I did. Thank you for being the Phoebe to my Rachel. Here's to many more, Ali.

To my wise and talented editor Tara Gavin who made my book instantly better and loved "that chapter about Roger." A huge thanks to the entire team at Alcove Press and Crooked Lane Books for bringing my Mermaids into the world.

A debt of gratitude to my wonderful book coach, Nicole Criona, who helped me get past a crippling roadblock with her wisdom, generosity, and gentle encouragement. Thank you to Philippa Donovan for her editorial skills in helping me whip my manuscript into shape. And to Diana Wilson for her excellent proofreading and kind, positive words along the way.

A huge heartfelt thank you to the incredible Kathy Hepinstall for her treasured friendship, spectacular writing advice, unending support, and impromptu tequila shots.

To the funniest novelist I know, Christopher Moore who actually wrote me back and said the right thing at the right time. Thank you. You are forever inspiring.

I'm lucky and blessed to have such a colorful cadre of strong and funny friends who have helped me along the way with everything from reading early drafts and offering an encouraging word to simply drinking wine with me when I got stuck. Thank you Jenny Pado, Amy Largent, Karin Couch, Christy Anderson, Kristy Ford, Jonathan Hum and Ivy Denneny Hum, Aaron and Katie Westfall, Eric Hampton, Stacy Orlandi, Brook Boley, Simone Pond, Gail 'Mama G' Talick, Michael Everard, Rick and Cynthia Reilly, Bob Rice, Stani Benesovsky, Kelsie Petersen, Andie Bedbrook, Kristen Carr, Gretchen Hahn Ayotte, Camille Sze, Shefali Valdez, Jean Bakewell, and Tena Dauler Carr and the Dynamite Girls for the original inspiration. And to my daughter Charlotte who helped me understand how funny, insightful, and beautiful a teen girl can be. I love being your bonus mom.

I could not have asked for a better 'Ride or Die' partner than my husband Mike 'Stein' Ayotte without whose short patience, strong pours, and unending love this novel would have never come to be. There's no one I'd rather sit next to when I type the words "The End" for this story in particular, or for life in general.

And finally, to my original mermaids, Judy Wikman, Lois Coffey, Maryann Makela, and of course, Nancy Niemi Talick.

Love you, Mom. Sail on.